Eve Ann

D.W. Belton

Acknowledgements

To the prayer warriors and those who truly believed in this project, I offer my most profound thanks. There is a piece of each of you on the pages of this book. Thanks to my lovely bride Tammy, my children, DJ, Danielle, Cady, Justice, Devin, and Maya. Thanks to Gayla, Nina, Courtney, and Cecil, my first readers who so graciously offered words of encouragement that kept me going. And a special thanks to my friend and brother, David Arndt, who believed in this project from its very beginning and refused to let me give up.

Prologue

Dallas
March 2010

W ith shaky, aged hands, she clutched the arms of her rocking chair. Her face contorted from arthritis, she pressed down hard. Ancient joints moved reluctantly at her command. She willed leg muscles too tired to do what they should. The elderly woman slowly made an ungraceful assent from her chair and shuffled across the room to an open window. Her grandson's letter clinched between two soft, wrinkled, fingers was light in her hand, but heavy on her heart.

Pointy spectacles suspended from a black nylon cord dangled at the end of her once elegant nose, allowing her to drink in the beauty of the unfolding spring day. The riotous scene of children playing in the park across the street reminded the woman of her daughter and grandson in years long gone. A warm breeze through the window told her this would be another sticky, sultry, Dallas summer. She wondered if she would live to see summer yield to fall once again. An ice cream cart appeared as if from nowhere. In an instant the cart succumbed to the onslaught of high pitched voices, dirty little hands, and henpecked mothers, struggling to find pocketbooks and coin purses. "*Some things never change,*" she thought, "*but thank God, some things do.*"

She removed the powder blue cardigan from her shoulders as a soft touch beckoned her back to the present. "Mrs. Beckwith," the reporter said in a soft voice. "Can you think of anything else about your grandson that might explain the phenomenal success of *Clay Pigeons*?" The reporter flipped the yellow sheet of paper he had been writing on to the underside of his legal pad.

In a cracked voice, Mrs. Beckwith responded without turning from the window. "No, I think I've told you just about everything that matters. I raised him the best I could after his mother died. And like I said, he never knew his father. I guess it just took a whole lot of prayer and the love of the Lord."

Looking at the piece of paper in her hand, he asked, "Is that a letter from him?"

"Yes." Mrs. Beckwith smiled as she spoke. She turned toward the young man. "It just came today."

"How is he?"

Mrs. Beckwith faced the young reporter. "He's doing just fine. He told me you'd be paying me a visit."

The reporter allowed a brief smile, then paused for a moment before asking the next question. "Has he written to you much since the Eve Ann incident?"

For a moment, the joyful expression on Mrs. Beckwith's face faded like the sun setting in the horizon. She contemplated the question. Then, like the dawn of a new day she smiled again with radiant beauty that offered the journalist a quick glimpse into the window of her past. Like a videotape in fast rewind, the years peeled away into a clarity of life one does not have to witness in order to believe and understand.

Mrs. Beckwith found her voice. "No, he wrote to me shortly after the whole thing happened, but until today, it had been years since I'd heard from him. I know he's a busy man. The fact that he hasn't written much doesn't mean he loves me any less." She looked at him over her glasses like a third grade teacher correcting a student, shaking her head condescendingly as she spoke.

The reporter looked as though he'd been slapped on the hands with a wooden ruler. "I know ma'am. I didn't mean anything by it. It's just that you're the last person I'll be talking to, and after interviewing dozens of people I still cannot account for how everything came together the way it did. This is by far the most intriguing investigation I have ever conducted. There are so many people that were not related by any cohesive element. Yet all of them had a part in your grandson's story."

Mrs. Beckwith chuckled at the reporter. She found his obsession over the facts amusing. "If you knew the One who put the whole story together you wouldn't be so confused. He does things like this in ways we cannot imagine." She turned back toward the window dismissing him.

The reporter paused pensively before closing his legal pad. "Well, I want to thank you for your time, Mrs. Beckwith. I'm glad I got a chance to meet with you."

With a twinkle in her dim eyes, Mrs. Beckwith looked over her shoulder and smiled at her young inquisitor, bidding him farewell.

The reporter walked down two flights of stairs and onto the sidewalk across from the park. He opened the trunk to his rented car and placed the legal pad in a box. It was one of four boxes full of yellow legal pads which contained much more than a simple article for his employer, the *New York Times*. Somewhere within the volumes of notes he had taken was a story that needed to be told.

Slowly, painfully, Mrs. Beckwith eased herself down, strategically repositioning her body in the rocking chair. She closed her eyes and drifted off with delicious memories of a life fully lived. The memories accompanied her to a deep and peaceful rest. Children's laughter penetrated the solemn lethargy of the room. The incessant but fading ring of the ice cream cart signaled its departure to the other end of the park. The smell of charbroiled burgers wafted in the air, and the atmosphere was charged with raucous energy, relentlessly invading the convalescence of a room where life had run its course. Like a metronome winding down, Mrs. Beckwith's rocking chair came to a halt in synchronous rhythm with her heart. She breathed a final breath, then left the room with a leap, headed home at last.

Chapter 1

The Fishbowl

Dallas
March 1, 2005

"Hey Mitch, do you think they're a couple?" Bart broke the silence between himself and the man relieving him as he chucked the last few books and papers into a large black shoulder bag.

Mitch was already staring out the window. He shook his head and sighed. A worn out toothpick protruded from his lips as he began to weigh in on Bart's question. Nestled between perfectly straight, perfectly white teeth, the toothpick danced up and down in Mitch's mouth.

"It's hard to say for sure. They've got something going, but I don't think it's like that."

Mitch placed both hands on his waist for a moment, then began to scratch his face with dry calloused fingers. The shift had just begun for Mitch but his mind was a million miles away. Stacy had promised him a surprise that evening and her surprises were usually worth waiting for. Mitch had only met Stacy a few months ago in a comedy of errors that should have scared her off for good, but she was now the light of his life. He had never met anyone like her. She seemed to make all the baggage in his life less important. Before, Mitch would have paid a lot more attention to the woman who was one-half of the couple Bart had just pointed out. But now all he could think of was Stacy, and he wondered what she had cooked up for his thirty-first birthday. She was supposed to be dropping by the fishbowl sometime toward the beginning of his shift.

With a massive six-foot-four-inch, two hundred forty pound frame, Mitch was an imposing figure in most settings. The product of a Cuban born mother and an Irish father, Mitch had an olive complexion, dark thick hair, and hazel eyes. Although he had never spent a day in the military, his square jaw and rugged appearance made him look like the poster boy for a United States Marine Corps recruitment ad. Since his days as high school football hero, Mitch rarely had trouble meeting women. He was known as someone who would do whatever it took to get what he wanted.

Until recently, marriage had not been an option for Mitch. He wanted to spread his wings and live it up. No one had trapped him yet, although once about five years ago Maggie had tried. Mitch had no problem accepting responsibility; he just didn't like being forced into anything. So, he paid the state-mandated support for the child he had helped bring into the world, and somewhere along the way, Mitch found that he really enjoyed being a father. Mitch saw his son, little Michael, as often as he could. He was amazed at how easy it had been to work out visitation with Maggie, who shortly after Michael was born moved to a small town called Ennis, about fifty miles south of the city.

Mitch was glad Maggie allowed Stacy to pick Michael up on those occasions when he had a long weekend off from work and he wanted to spend some extra time with his son. In fact, it seemed to Mitch that the two women got along quite well considering the circumstances. This didn't really surprise Mitch as he considered both Maggie and Stacy to be affable, reasonable, women. The thing Mitch had trouble understanding was Stacy's willingness to go out of her way just to please him. Mitch had known other women with a heart to please, but in most cases, they had wanted something in return for themselves. That was not the case with Stacy; for her, making Mitch happy was reward enough.

Mitch turned his attention to the couple in the waiting room in front of him. She was sweet summer cotton candy; he was the aftermath of a storm. Golden strands of sunlight framed a tapestry of facial symmetry. She wore beauty as though it were created to define and adorn her. Leaning back comfortably in the hard seat, she threw back her head when she laughed – her lips a parting precipice of joyful melodic noise that softly penetrated the room.

He was everything precious and dear scattered into places they ought not be. His face bore the marks of a hard life, lived without regret, remorse, or rancor. A gentle spirit surrounded him that transcended and defied his aesthetics. Knotted, uncombed hair and a patchwork beard circled his plump dark face. Poured into a seat designed for a frame one-third his size, he was comfortable as could be; careful not to move about too much for fear his double stitched pre-washed denim might give under the pressure.

"If they are a couple, they are the odd couple," thought Mitch.

She smiled at him often, gesturing. She gently stroked his hand. After a few moments, she handed him a ten dollar bill. He disappeared and returned a while later with a sack full of fast food from the hospital restaurant. As she ate, her long leg crossed – toes pointing toward him. Strappy white sandals dangled from a delicate pedicure. She chewed her food enthusiastically, periodically throwing her head back releasing riotous laughter as if his humor was infectious.

He leaned forward and dug around in his backpack for something. A chubby hand emerged clinching a thick, black, leather bound book with gold edged pages. He began to read, and she sat silently, fixated, her forehead wrinkled as she squinted, wanting to comprehend his every word. One hand held the book, and with the other he gestured large concentric circles, slapping on the arm of the chair next him, waving an arc before her brow. He gently laid the book down resting his chin between the palms of his hands. They sat quietly for a long moment. She broke the silence with a passionate battery of questions, rhythmically building to a crescendo as if the answers would unlock life's deepest mysteries. Now it was his turn to illuminate the room though not with a smile.

*

Bart and Mitch worked in a fishbowl, at least that's what they liked to call it. Fifteen feet of reflective glass made them voyeurs in the emergency room of an urban hospital. Theirs was a people watching profession. Police officers at St. Luke's Health Care Facility were more like security guards, but most of the officers believed their presence made a difference, even if it was just a matter of running a drunk off the hospital campus, or helping granny to her car late at night. When not assigned to the emergency room, they patrolled the streets surrounding and within the hospital campus, or walked the interior buildings making their presence known and providing a sense of security for patients, visitors, and hospital employees.

Established in a six-bedroom house in Dallas, Texas, by doctors Karl and William Schultz in 1915, St. Luke's had grown to a behemoth corporate, medical facility which sprawled over one square city mile, and had affiliate campuses throughout the Dallas/Fort Worth Metroplex. A combination of old and new, the campus buildings were composed of brick, steel and tinted glass construction, blended into a mosaic of architectural design.

The St. Luke's Medical Center Police Department was formed in 1983, out of their security force under a Texas Law which allows private corporations to establish their own police force. Most of those who worked as security officers prior to the Police Department being formed were sworn in as police officers as soon as the change became official. Bart was among the first to take an official oath of office following an eight month training academy.

The new recruit officers were trained in hand-to-hand combat, firing their service weapons, handcuffing techniques, report writing, and the Texas Penal Code. It was well understood by all that St. Luke's officers would probably never need to use their hand guns or need to do many other things that city cops did, but the training was still necessary just in case.

Still looking at the odd couple, Mitch decided to have a little fun with Bart.

"Do you think he'll take up a collection now?" Mitch mused.

He knew Bart was one of those Bible thumpers, and although Mitch felt a little guilty about poking fun at Bart since meeting

Stacy, sometimes a slight jab slipped out. He didn't mean anything by it and usually it didn't seem to bother Bart.

Bart shrugged his shoulders and chuckled nervously.

"Probably, looks like he's working up a sweat while he's at it. Look, I'm outta here; I gotta double back in the morning for some OT on the first shift."

Slinging the large black police bag over his shoulder, Bart stood up, walked out the door, and disappeared into the cool night air.

*

Bartholomew Bruce Gelical inhaled deeply then exhaled a long sigh. He didn't mind his job; in fact he often found certain satisfaction in what he did. High speed chases and adrenaline induced police excitement were not his reasons for joining the small corporate police department. For Bart, as he was called by friends, family, and coworkers, police work was a way to support the woman he adored and his three sons. He had many other interests that did not pay the bills, but policing was his paid profession. Living a double life had its share of perils, but the problem that consumed Bart most of the time was the game he played to fit in among peers that did not share his faith.

He didn't care too much for John Mitchell, whose lewd comments and cynical attitude were often insufferable. Bart learned the best way to keep Mitch from talking ad nauseam about his out of control life was to beat him to the punch with some off hand remark of his own and then head for the door as fast as possible. But each time Bart allowed himself to be sucked in he felt filthy. A deep abiding despair about Mitch's miserable existence filled Bart with a sense that he was not being true to his own faith. Bart said a silent prayer, *"God, use me as You please, and let my life make a difference!"*

Bart couldn't put his finger on it but something had been different about Mitch lately. Somehow Mitch seemed a little easier to take and his tone was a bit softer than usual. It seemed to Bart that Mitch talked less about his sexual conquests lately; in fact, he didn't talk much at all lately except when someone spoke to him.

Bart took long quick strides. His parking spot was a good four city blocks from the emergency room but he didn't mind the walk. Shift change took exactly thirty minutes, and he had to interact with his relief for the entire time whether he wanted to or not. Often, he did not. It was tough finding ways to relax around most of the guys on the department and thirty minutes often seemed like several hours. Bart would gladly have run out for fast food himself just to get out of the fishbowl for a while, but that was not possible. The long walk to his car was a time of purging and reflection, and Bart needed to clear his mind before focusing on things that mattered most to him.

The future was one of Bart's many pre-occupations and contemplating his personal future was always a rich source of pleasure. Tosha was pregnant with their fourth child and the pregnancy was going well. Against the doctor's advice, Bart and Tosha had decided not to abort this child. There was a substantial likelihood of complications due to Tosha's age, but the couple had faith that mother and child would survive. During the first trimester, Tosha turned forty-eight, which was well beyond her childbearing years.

Lost in deep thought, Bart ignored it at first. The unmistakable sound of a powerful V8 racing engine was moving toward him with deliberate speed. The impending situation didn't register until – looking up there was a tiny silhouette directly in front of the oncoming lights. Bart thought he recognized the woman. She was tall for a woman, about five feet nine inches with shoulder length straight black hair, slender and attractive. Bart could not recall where he had met her but she did look familiar. She was distracted, speaking to someone in a bright yellow SUV. She didn't see the little boy step off the curve and into the street.

A green hue coming from the traffic control device at the corner mingled with the bright lights of a dark red Corvette and produced a florescent glow against the dark evening canvass. If the scene were not so tragic it would have been beautiful. Bart had no time to think and only seconds to act. Twenty years of police work preceded by eight months of training would be put to the test for the first time. A voice screamed, breaks squealed, and the small child was pitched into the air like a soccer ball heading for the net. Bart felt nothing, knew nothing, saw nothing, and for the first time ever, wanted nothing. The night was suddenly cold and still.

Chapter 2

Personville

Texas
2001- 2005

A mere speck on the map, Personville, Texas, sits on State highways 164 and 39, twelve miles southeast of Groesbeck in southeastern Limestone County. It was founded in 1854 by B.D. Person, a native of North Carolina who moved in 1851 from Shelby County, Tennessee, to Shelby County, Texas. In 1854, he moved to what is now known as Personville, where there were already several families living at the time. The town; with an estimated population of thirty, most of whom lived in tents and other makeshift dwellings, had established a blacksmith shop and a dram shop. In 1855, the Personville post office was established with William Person as postmaster.

Originally some wanted to name the town Lost Prairie, and by 1857 it had grown to have six or eight permanent residences, three dry-goods stores, two mercantile stores, a bowling alley, and a cotton gin. In 1882, John Frank Boyd taught school and established the

Boyd Drug and General Merchandise Company. Over one hundred years later, in June 2001, Personville Texas became the birthplace of Rocky Jo-Bob Eubanks.

You wouldn't know it to look at him, but Rocky Jo-Bob Eubanks was almost four years old. At the young age of almost four, Rocky was a full-grown, in fact, over-grown man. He was five feet eleven inches tall and tipped the scales at three hundred pounds, three hundred and four after a good meal. Doctors estimated he was closer to forty years old judging by his body, scars, and other physical evidence, but as far as anyone in Personville or Groesbeck was concerned, it was nearly four years ago when Rocky came to life.

*

Having grown tired of the riff-raff from the bar which used to be in its place, the Groesbeck town council happily granted Bubba Lee Womack's request to open Bubba's Bee-Line Bar-B-Q in 1974. Bubba had come up with the idea for the Bar-B-Q when he was still a teenager. He saved every nickel he had made since then to open it. The Bee-Line was the first and only fast food Bar-B-Q in the area where you could grab and run or sit a spell. The house specialty was Bubba's famous recipe ribs with a side of grits, jojo fries, and lemonade, with peach cobbler for desert.

The building's brown brick exterior was painted an obnoxious shade of bright red, with yellow flames flowing up from the bottom. An orange neon sign depicting a fat smiling bumblebee holding a rib hung above the front entry. Customers stumbled across a warped wooden floor on their way to booths with red, ripped, vinyl covering and rickety tables that swayed from side to side. On the way to sitting down it wasn't at all uncommon for people to trip on a board that had come loose and sprung up from the floor, only to hear Bubba holler, "*Watch yer step, anything yeh break wit dem dare clumsy feet, yer gonna buy.*"

Bubba's Bee Line Bar-B-Q, or The Bee Line as the town folks called it was glassed in on the front side with a fire red wood shackle roof. White iron posts that resembled modern day hitching posts lined parking spots in the front. Located in the very center of Groesbeck on Yeagua Street and Ellis, folks would generally just pull up, grab a meal, and leave as suddenly as they came. But some liked to gather inside and discuss the pressing issues of life. There were many days when Bubba wished people in Groesbeck would learn to hang out and gossip at the barber shop like in any other respectable town, but Mario, the town barber had an annoying habit of chasing his customers out the front door with a sharp set of sheers if they choose to loiter after their hair cut was finished.

Bubba learned to deal with the commotion around his restaurant and every now and then he would remind his customers that loitering was against the law. When he was in a real bad mood, Bubba would threaten to call Luther Green, the local Police Chief, if they didn't either buy something or get out. In the end, no one listened to Bubba anyway; they just kept on talking as if he wasn't even there.

Pictures of Louis Armstrong, B.B. King, Duke Ellington, Count Basie, Ella Fitzgerald, Errol Garner, Benny Goodman, Bessie Smith, and a host of other blues and jazz greats lined the Bee-Line walls. Over the years, Bubba had won several local and regional awards for "Best Barbecue", which were also prominently displayed above the booths surrounding the interior.

It was a slow rainy night when Bubba stepped outside to empty the trash before heading home. He lifted the lid of the dumpster and almost didn't see John until a rat who had been licking blood from John's face ran down between his legs and under a pile of rotten cabbage near his feet. Bubba figured whoever it was in there was probably dead and that this would be bad for business. He fished the new cordless phone from his pocket and called Chief Green at home. Thin, dehydrated, and beaten to within an inch of his life, a town legend had his auspicious beginnings in a garbage dumpster behind Bubba's Bee line Bar-B-Q.

*

"You better get down to the Bar-B-Q Chief, one a dem drunks from da city done crawled up in my dumpster and kicked da bucket."

Chief Green was not accustomed to being awoken in the night. He had a deputy that usually patrolled the streets during the late hours. But the deputy had called in sick for his shift so Chief Green had contacted Sheriff Dempsey from Limestone County and asked him to cover the streets that night. However, Chief Green knew his arrangement with the County did not include nuisance calls like this one. It was for emergencies only. Chief Green rolled over and spoke into the phone in a calm voice.

"Bubba, is he dead for sure or is he just sleepin?"

"How am I sposed ta know fer sure if he's dead, dat's your job aint it?"

"I know Bubba, I know. Listen, if he aint breathin, he's probably dead, but yer gonna have ta do mouth ta mouth on em and try ta bring em back."

"Is you outta yo red neck mind, I ain't doin nuttin a da sort, you get down here and lay a kiss on this ole boy, cause I sure aint."

Chief Green had a feeling he wasn't going to get far with Bubba, but figured it was worth a try. Before hanging up the phone he came up with the brilliant idea of calling the Limestone County Paramedics first. Within a few minutes Limestone County ambulance 429 was en route to Bubba's Bee Line.

*

It had been years since Groesbeck had any real excitement, and this time Billy Conklin was called into service. Billy was a volunteer Fire Fighter for Limestone County and a certified EMT. After his pager went off, Billy called the Limestone County dispatch to see what the commotion was about. When he heard the details Billy sprung into action. Driving his red 1981 Toyota pickup down dusty Highway 14 he turned in front of Head Branch Missionary Baptist Church heading for the Limestone County Medical Center where he would pick up Medic Unit 429.

Billy knew he would have the attention of every Wal-Mart employee when he showed up for work later that day, but for now his mind was on what was in that dumpster outside the Bee-Line. When Billy arrived at Limestone County Medical Center, he met up with his partner Kevin.

"Did I hear dispatch right?" said Kevin who was already seated behind the wheel as Billy slid onto the passenger seat. Although he had been a volunteer firefighter for nearly four years, the most he'd seen was the occasional auto accident and routine cardiac arrests from the senior home or some private residence. It was rare that any of the volunteers were called to deal with a trauma that may involve foul play.

Billy was not in the mood to be quizzed. As senior man on the rig he would have to take a lot of responsibility for making sure everything went just right. A man's life hung in the balance, that is, of course if he wasn't dead already. Kevin's curious nature was the last thing Billy needed right now.

"Yep, you heard her right, and that means we gotta get there with our minds focused on our jobs. I dunno who this ole boy is, but he's countin on us knowin our jobs."

"I know all that Billy, but you gotta admit, it's kinda excitin'." Kevin's eyes were gleaming; this is what he joined the fire department for, this is what he felt called to do with his life. Kevin figured if he were in any of the big cities it would be like this every night, all night long.

After both men were seated in the rig they sped off with lights and sirens blazing toward Yeagua Street about three quarters of a mile from the Medical Center.

Kevin arrived at the Bee Line in record time and the two men jumped out of the rig and found Bubba still leaning over the dumpster shouting inside it with his voice echoing off the metal like he was hollering inside a large tin can.

"Is you dead or alive bouy? They'isa commin ta take ya now bouy so is you dead or not?"

Billy liked Bubba, but sometimes he figured Bubba must be a few bones shy of a full slab of ribs. Billy brushed Bubba aside, "If he was dead, do you really think he'd tell ya so, Bubba?"

"You ain't so smart, college bouy." Bubba staggered to the side as Billy pushed his way past and began his initial assessment of the patient inside the dumpster.

Billy looked into the dumpster and realized instantly that man's inhumanity to man didn't get any worse than this. The poor soul in that dumpster was no drunk who had fallen in trying to fish out wine bottles. He was fairly well dressed, had a recent hair cut, his teeth were not broken or decaying, and except for the severe beating he had received, he looked to be in relatively good health. Without a doubt, this man was the victim of a terrible crime. Kevin checked for vital signs and realized the corpse had a faint pulse and shallow breathing. Billy and Kevin wasted no time carefully lifting the man out of the dumpster.

"Kevin, get that nasal canula, hook up a line to the co2 tank and start it up slow, we need to get a cervical color on him right away too."

"Okay boss, I got it."

"I'll start the IV and when you get that o2 going, get on the horn and let Doc Evans know this guy has a slow pulse and shallow breathing and that we've started an IV drip and established an airway." Billy turned to Bubba. "Bubba, put on these plastic gloves and hold this towel firmly against that big gash on his head."

Bubba screwed up his face as though he were about to say something stupid and began to push the gloves back toward Billy before Billy retorted decisively. "Look, I don't need any of your usual attitude right now Bubba this is a matter of life or death and this guy needs our help. Now put on these gloves and apply light pressure to this wound before I give you one just like it."

Billy and Kevin worked feverishly on their patient as a well-synchronized machine, gently laying him on a stretcher, inserting a nasal canula, and connecting IV lines.

Within a few minutes they were ready do go. Billy and Kevin retraced their route back to the Limestone County Medical Center and came to a screeching halt in front of the tiny ER entrance, greeted by the entire ER Staff and Dr. James Evans, Chief of Staff.

*

Contrary to Bubba's prediction, Dumpster Man was great for business. People from all across town poured into the restaurant to ask about the strange man he had found in his dumpster. At first Bubba just enjoyed the attention, but soon his entrepreneurial senses kicked in and he set down a strict written policy which dangled from the ceiling just above the register.

"Ifin' ya wanna to hear the story, ya gotta order something whilest the story's bein' told."

Bubba could hardly keep them away. Folks filled their faces with ribs and brisket while Bubba told the tale which grew and grew until it took on a life of its own. After a while, Bubba put a new Dumpster burger on the menu which sold like crazy. A few months after the strange man in the dumpster arrived, business was still booming at the Bee-Line.

*

Over the next four days the new patient, John Doe, slipped in and out of consciousness – in and out of death's grasp. He had lost a tremendous amount of blood and his skull had been caved in by a blunt object. After two successful surgeries to stop the internal cranial bleeding, it was still too soon to tell if there would be permanent brain damage to either the frontal or temporal lobes of John Doe's brain. In fact it was too soon to tell if John would live at all. A decision had been made to wait until the swelling had gone down in the patient's brain before inserting a prosthetic skull under his scalp to replace the portion which had to be surgically removed. Whoever this man was, he had an incredible will to live. It was clear that whatever had caved in his skull had missed the hippocampus; therefore while he may someday resume normal brain function, retrograde amnesia was a high probability.

Dr. James Evans monitored John Doe's vital signs and prescribed various treatments, but the prognosis did not look good. The human brain is a fragile organ, and that is exactly why God had given human beings a thick skull to protect it. Doc Evans would never understand why people did some of the hideous things they did to one another. He found it incredibly tragic how hard people worked to inhibited the body's natural defenses through senseless acts of violence. John Doe finally lapsed into a coma on the fifth day.

It would be twenty-four long weeks before John finally woke up, disoriented, and having no idea who he was or how he had gotten there. He had no wallet, driver's license, or any other means of identification. Doc Evans said he might never regain his memory completely, but that time alone would tell.

Upon regaining consciousness, John Doe began to build strength at a remarkable rate. If he hadn't been in such good physical condition, he never would have survived the first four days after his surgery. Unfortunately, John's status with the hospital was tenuous at best. He had found a special place in Doc Evans' heart, and the good Doctor had decided to waive all his personal fees for John's treatment. However, even as hospital administrator, there was little

Dr. Evans could do about the ever increasing hospital costs for John's medicine, lab work, and other treatments. In addition to the financial concerns, recovery for John Doe would be slow and painful.

Because he was unable to move around much, John lay on his back and stared into the air as if he were looking for someone or something. At first, speaking was painful for John. His jaw had been wired shut to repair a compound fracture. Even though the wire had been removed while he was still in a coma, his jaw was sore. Therefore the nurses would ask him questions, and he would blink once for yes, and twice for no.

About three weeks after coming out of the coma the stiffness in his jaw began to wear off and John was able to speak slowly. It was clear that he had no idea where he was, or who he was, but he somehow seemed grateful to be alive. Six weeks into John's new life he smiled for the first time when a random visitor named Jo Bob opened the shades on the hospital window one starry night. Jo Bob Jackson came to the hospital each day with his cousin Willie Eubanks. He and Willie were curious about the ill-fated stranger found in the Bee-Line dumpster and the nurses let the two men into John's hospital room reasoning that it was probably good for their patient. Jo Bob and Willie spent hours in the room talking to John even though John was incapable of responding at first. Sometimes they would just sit and read to him.

Jo Bob and Willie read all kinds of books to John and when his jaw felt better they listened to him talk about the books they had read to him. When he was well enough to sit up by himself, Jo Bob and Willie played checkers with John, who was a shrewd and cunning checker player. Most of the time, the boys sustained several severe losses whenever they played checkers with John. Most of all,

John enjoyed having someone read to him. In particular, he enjoyed having Willie read to him from the New Testament Bible he brought from home. When he was well enough to read for himself, John sat for hours devouring everything he could get his hands on just to acquaint himself with his new world.

As soon as John was able to eat regular food, he immediately took to the thick ice cream with nuts and chocolate the nurses brought him. After each meal, John would request a second helping of Rocky Road Ice Cream, and the nurses always gave in to John because he was such a good and sweet patient. So, John Doe became Rocky Road Doe.

The week after Rocky came out of the coma, the sister board of Head Branch Missionary Baptist Church, which was only about two blocks away from the hospital, came to pay their respects. They held a "come to Jesus meeting" with Rocky that the Limestone County Medical Center will not soon forget. They piled into the small hospital room and stacked their hats one on top of the other. Those ladies rolled up their sleeves, took out the KJV Bible, and began to let Rocky know he was alive and in Groesbeck by divine appointment.

"Good evening, Mr. Doe," said Sister Jackson, a slender woman in her mid-sixties. "We heard about your unfortunate circumstances and wanted to let you know that you are not alone, but that the good Lord has a plan for your life."

Rocky, still unable to talk well at the time, listened intently and his eyes began to grow large with excitement.

"We don't mean to intrude, but we thought it would be a good idea to pay our respects and let you know that there is a place for you in the Kingdom of God," said Sister Shepherd.

Rocky slowly nodded his head as if giving his permission for the Sisters to proceed.

The ladies preached and sang, read the Bible, and shook their tambourines. Sister Clarence passed out twice, having been slain in the Spirit, but then, she always did have to over do things a bit. Those ladies put on one heck of a show, more than once being threatened with eviction if they didn't keep the noise down. But most of all, they loved on Rocky like no five ladies loved on a broken man since Christ was brought down from the cross. And in the end, Rocky gave his heart to the Lord.

"When you get outta here, you come by the church, you hear?" Sister Mary Smith, a plump woman in her late forties, laid a fleshy hand on John Doe's head and smiled warmly. John nodded his head in agreement.

Three months after Rocky came out of the coma Doc Evans said he was healthy enough to leave the hospital. The problem was that Rocky had nowhere to go. He had become somewhat of a celebrity in town when he was first found in the dumpster because nothing like Rocky had ever happened in Groesbeck or Personville before. But after a few months, most of the regular visitors had stopped coming to see the mystery man at the Limestone County Medical Center except Jo-Bob Jackson and Willie Eubanks. So, when the time came for Rocky to be released, Jo-Bob and Willie adopted him.

Jo-Bob and Willie shared a small two bedroom abandoned farm-house in Personville, Texas on the edge of town. The deed to the farm was in Jo-Bob's daddy's name, and he promised them they could stay there so long as they tried to make a go of farming. Jo-Bob and Willie were in their early thirties and knew near nothing about farming, yet they managed to stumble into good fortune more often then one would expect. Since Jo Bob and Willie had the heart to adopt Rocky, they felt it was only right that he carry their names out of respect. So, Rocky Road Doe officially became Rocky Jo-Bob Eubanks.

*

From the time he set foot in the farmhouse, there were two things Rocky showed a deep passion for, eating and reading. Each day Willie would stop at the library and bring Rocky more books on history and theology. Rocky devoured anything having to do with Christianity and history, he just couldn't get enough. Jo-Bob wondered how Rocky ever got as skinny as he was when he came to the hospital because he was packing on the pounds now at an alarming rate. Jo-Bob's job was to keep the food coming and to help Rocky with his therapy. The cousins figured with Rocky healing the way he was, it wouldn't be long before he could help out on the farm.

The cousins figured right. Three months after Rocky Jo-Bob arrived on the farm, he was making a substantial contribution. In the course of one day, Rocky Jo-Bob would feed chickens, hogs, cows, and weed the back forty. Rocky continued to grow in stature, packing on weight faster than anyone expected. The cousins didn't mind how much Rocky Jo-Bob ate because he never asked a wage for his labor, Rocky Jo-Bob worked for food and nothing else. The cousins paid $100.00 per month on Rocky's astronomical hospital bill, knowing it wasn't enough to make a dent, but feeling they should try to do something.

When he wasn't out in the fields working with the cousins, Rocky was at the church with the sister board or in the library reading everything he could get his hands on that had to do with theology and church history. One year after Rocky Jo-Bob came out of the coma, he was Personville's leading theologian and church historian. So much so that Pastor Jesse Meeker often left the pulpit for weeks at a time in the capable hands of Rocky Jo-Bob. Soon, he became known by most of the town's people as Pastor Rocky Jo-Bob Eubanks.

After eighteen months, Rocky had devoured everything in the church library, the county library, and the community college library that interested him. Rocky began to feel the time was coming when he would have to move on. He had an unquenchable desire to learn more about the Lord and he could not get what he needed in Personville. Rocky Jo-Bob decided to take his GED exam and head north to Dallas to complete his education. The Dallas/Fort Worth Metroplex was well known for its seminaries and Bible colleges, that is where Rocky felt he had been called.

*

He arrived in Dallas in September of 2003 to attend old man Criswell's Bible College. Rocky made friends fast among all the students, and was known to hold huge Bible studies in the student lounge where even the faculty would come and listen. On occasion, if one looked closely, a faculty member could be seen taking notes at one of Rocky Jo-Bob's studies. Not that any of them would admit it, but so goes the legend.

Melissa and Robbie McCree had attended several of Rocky Jo-Bob's Bible studies and quickly became close friends with him. His teachings on Ephesians, Colossians, and Corinthians had helped the couple navigate through many rough spots in their new marriage.

When Robbie was rushed to the hospital with a 104 temperature during a nasty bout with pneumonia, Rocky Jo-Bob was the first person Melissa called to be with her in the emergency room of St. Luke's. For the cost of fast food, Melissa knew Rocky Jo-Bob would bring her closer to the Lord, which is exactly where she needed to be.

Chapter 3

Stacy

Dallas
March 1, 2005

S he was a mess from head to toe – a sobbing, blubbering mess. Her face, a kaleidoscope of colors as mascara mingled with blood, watered down by salty tears dripping first on her black leather jacket and resting finally on the denim that stretched over her long shapely legs. She couldn't believe she was actually crying. As a newly hired nurse she had been assigned to the Emergency Room. Blood and guts were common in any level one-trauma center, and that's where she had cut her teeth in the nursing profession, St. Luke's Hospital Emergency Room. But this time it was somehow too personal; cops don't fall everyday, and cops held a special place in this nurse's heart. A man she had only seen once before was lying lifeless in front of her. She had taken the old plastic pocket mask from the large shoulder bag she carried and began mouth-to-mouth resuscitation - she desperately wanted the CPR to work.

She had seen patients die before, and believed death should be faced with dignity. The man in front of her was heading for the next world and it seemed there was little that could be done about it. The blood flowing from his lacerated femoral artery was dark red, which was not a good sign, and he had begun to make that gurgling sound deep in his throat that usually precedes death. He had several deep lacerations to his head as well, and after removing his jacket, shirt, and flack vest so she could begin chest compressions, she could see dark spots forming just beneath the skin indicating there was probably some internal bleeding.

A large crowd had gathered and fortunately one of her co-workers from St. Luke's ER appeared out of nowhere to help with chest compressions. The persistent scream of an ambulance could be heard in the distance. Stacy kept saying between breaths, "Hang in there partner, you're not going to die on me." The March air was cold, her tears were salty, and even she wasn't encouraged by the incantations she whispered over the dying man.

*

Two hulking medics pulled nurse Stacy Bernard to the side and took over. The lead medic produced a large purple ambu bag, applied the plastic mask to the patient's mouth, and began squeezing the bag. The ambu bag was designed to perform the mouth-to-mouth resuscitation in lieu of a human being, and it sent enough oxygen into the patient's lungs to make his chest rise and fall with each squeeze. The other medic attached sensors from the new Automated Electronic Defibrillator (AED) machine. Immediately the machine jumped to life and an electronic voice came from the AED.

"Stand clear," and then, "Shock Advised."

The lifeless body lurched in an upward arch, his back contorting with the electric current which sent shockwaves to his fibrillating heart.

"No pulse Dan" said the lead medic.

"Clear," said his partner.

"Still no pulse, continue CPR."

"Shock Advised" said the AED."

"Clear."

"I got a pulse."

"Let's load and go."

"Call it in, and let St. Luke's know we got one of their cops in the box. Set up an IV line as soon as you get in." The lead medic rushed toward the driver's door then looked down to see a small child standing alone by the side of the road. He had minor scratches but no serious injuries.

"Is anybody here with this little boy?"

"I think he's with Bernard, let's load n go." The junior partner swung the rear ambulance doors closed as he jumped into the back. Stacy Bernard gathered her tiny companion and held him close as her mind drifted back to a far away place and the people whose lives were so very dear to her. Rocking too and fro with the little boy huddled in her arms; she remembered simpler times before much of the tragedy in her life had defined the woman she became.

Chapter 4

The Bernard's

Minneapolis
June 2, 2001

R eclining under the stars on a hot, sticky night, father and daughter sat in the front seat of a yellow 1968 Mustang convertible. It was summer 2001 and Alethea Bernard was only twelve-years old, but someday the sporty compact would be hers. It was a hobby car and little by little, Dad was putting it back together. Nick Bernard loved his baby girl with all his heart. He cherished every moment with her. In another four years she would be old enough to drive and Nick had promised the car would be ready when she got her driver's license.

They looked up at the stars smacking on the plums Nick plucked from a plastic farmer's market bag. The two of them fantasized about life on other planets as Nick spit seeds from his mouth with jet-like propulsion in an attempt to hit the coffee can laying on the ground next to the car. Every so often, with pinpoint precision, one of the seeds would shoot into the can. Ting-ting-ting. Each time one of the seeds went into the can; high fives were exchanged in midair. Father and daughter relished the nothingness of the moment.

Nick was a science fiction buff who loved Star Trek, Star Wars, and anything having to do with the future. Morgan, Nick's wife, often scolded him about filling their only daughter's head with such nonsense, but it didn't slow him down for one minute. Those quiet nights and mindless babble about space creatures made a twelve-year-old daughter look into the eyes of her father and believe anything was possible. She loved him intensely – she loved everything about him. Morgan only wished she could get her husband to talk to their daughter about something other than stargazing. It wasn't that Nick didn't have knowledge to share with his daughter. Nick poured his life into children that were not his own, but when it came to Alethea, it seemed he just couldn't get beyond basic silliness. Morgan simply could not find wisdom in the way Nick spoke to his only daughter.

"It's getting late you two and we've got church in the morning." Morgan stretched her stubby neck out the porch door beckoning her family inside.

"Just another half hour mom, I still haven't found Cassiopeia yet."

"Mind your mama child, Cassiopeia's gonna be there tomorrow. Besides these mosquitos are eatin' you alive."

Nick had grown bored with the plums, they weren't exactly what he considered a fun snack food, but spittin seeds was a lot of fun. Given a choice, he'd much rather be munching on some corn chips, or fresh baked cookies, but Morgan had him on a strict diet. After nearly a year of working out and eating rabbit food, Nick had trimmed off over one hundred pounds. Now the trick was to keep the weight it off in order to please the woman who loved him and wanted to keep him around for a few more years.

"Are you glad you lost all that weight, Daddy? You sure look a lot better, but how do you feel?"

"I feel fine; just miss all that good stuff we used to eat. Course it doesn't make you big as a house like it does me." Nick chuckled to think of his tiny daughter putting on weight; she was as thin as a rail. "Yeah, I guess I'd have to say, your mama knew what was best for me, and I ain't complainin."

"So then, you wouldn't be interested in those peanut butter cookies me and Mama baked for choir rehearsal tomorrow then would you? I mean, that wouldn't be the reason you're trying to stay up later than me would it?"

"You think you're so smart don't you? I was planning to spend some quality time with my true love tonight if you have to know."

"I thought I was your true love, Daddy."

"Well, yeah, but then, well, you know, there is that gorgeous hunk of woman inside who's about to holla at you again."

"Oh yeah, her. Well, I guess I can share you with her. After all, she is my mother, and your wife."

She buried her head in Daddy's muscular chest and clung to him for a few extra moments before......

"Girl, don't make me come out there after you. And you have business inside too, Mr."

"Ooohh, you have business huh? You guys kill me; you act like I'm still a little girl and don't know what you're talking about."

"You better mind your own business and get in that house, *little girl.*"

She giggled and skipped into the house. Nick couldn't help letting out a little laugh himself.

"Daddy's got business, Daddy's got business," Alethea taunted while skipping into the house with two bushy pig tails bobbing up and down all the way.

Nick shook his head and smiled as he snatched a black vinyl cover off the ground and stretched it out over the Mustang. The paint on the car was worn out and it would need to be restored, but Nick knew the cover would protect the car from interior damage while the convertible top was being refurbished. He'd bought the cover because the harsh Minnesota winters were hard on cars. This particular classic sports car had been hauled by trailer all the way from California and had never been driven in the Minnesota snow and slush. Nick had purchased the car from his next door neighbor's mother, who had bought it new, had rarely driven it, and had now grown too old to drive it. The neighbor knew Nick was looking for something to fix up for his baby girl, so he made the arrangements for the sale with his aging mother. The wind kicked up and blew dust and dirt around Nick's ankles all the way up to his head. He was grateful for the cool breeze - it felt good. The clear dark sky wrapped elegantly in a galaxy like jewels presiding over a city that feigned quiet and assumed an almost small town ambiance.

Nick had learned the art of marriage through several trials and errors. He and Morgan were married shortly before he graduated from college, but their marriage ran into serious trouble early on. Fortunately they were smart enough to wait until they were in their late twenties before having their one and only child. Young marriages were tough, and Nick and Morgan's marriage was no exception. From the beginning they argued about everything from money to careers and domestic responsibilities. After years of hard work, they had learned to make their peace with one another. They learned to compromise on the things that didn't matter much and to work through the things that did. Nick and Morgan had discovered the dance of marriage. Now they found intense joy in pleasing each other whatever the cost.

Nick loved Morgan dearly and because he knew she could have married better he was often astounded that she still loved him. Sometimes he felt like he was Morgan's pet project as much as the Mustang was his. She loved him, and tonight was their night for quality time. Nick knew from experience not to take her love for granted, so he headed for the door.

There were many things Nick and Morgan enjoyed about the house they shared in south Minneapolis. It had a large fenced in yard with two old oak trees which provided shade during the hot summer months. The French Tutor style house was a beige stucco construction with a burgundy red roof. Although there were only three living in the home now, its three floors, four bedrooms, and two baths provided more than enough space for everyone. The screened in rear porch with a suspended swing had been a favorite feature and key selling point when they purchased the home back in 1985.

As Nick walked up the three steps that led to the porch door, he saw the Dawson's brand new Cadillac pull into the driveway next door. Nick knew Sam Dawson hadn't left the car for his teenage daughter, Daisy, to drive while the rest of the family was out of town for the weekend, so he decided to take a look. Just as Nick grabbed the porch door handle, he saw three young men open the car doors. He watched for a while then realized something was terribly wrong.

Nick had never seen these men before, and they didn't belong there.

A tall slender white man who looked about twenty-five or thirty years old got out on the drivers side and looked both ways before sliding the keys down into his pants pocket. A short Hispanic man got out of the passenger side and took a long look in both directions before gently closing the door behind him. Another white male, probably the oldest of the three, stumbled out of the back seat and immediately ran to the side of the Dawson's garage.

"Quiet down man, we don't need nobody checkin' us out."

"Chill Poncho, I gotta pee, ain't no body looking at you anyway."

"Both of you need to shut up, I ain't tryin' to do no time behind dumb stuff."

Nick walked up to the edge of his yard and started toward the car. He waited until he was only a few feet from the driver's side door before making his presence known.

"Can I help you guys?"

"Uh, no," said the startled Hispanic, "We, uh, we were looking for Daisy."

"She let you drive her parent's car?"

"Yeah," said the tall one, "is there a problem?"

"No, I was just checkin' to see if everything was okay." Nick looked down into the car and noticed what looked like a black revolver on the rear seat where the older man had been sitting. There were two open 40-ounce bottles of beer on the leather seat, and the rest of the car looked a mess. Nick's eyes darted from the gun to the Hispanic man on the other side of the car, whose eyes also shifted between the gun and the man talking to Nick.

The Hispanic man broke the silence, "Do something man, this is your part of the deal."

Nick turned around.

Smack!

Nick dropped to the ground with the first blow to the middle of his forehead from the 4X4 piece of wood fence post Sam Dawson had laying in the yard. The blows kept coming until Nick lay unconscious with a thick pool of blood oozing from his head.

Alethea Bernard didn't know it at the time, but before returning to the house with thoughts of convertible Mustangs and constellations on her mind, she had seen her father for the last time that hot sticky night.

Chapter 5

The Joint

Oak Park Heights, Minnesota
June 1, 2001

G erry North closed the file on his desk and breathed a heavy sigh. It was out of his control; there was nothing more he could do. The inmate whose criminal history was chronicled in this file would soon be released back into society, and Gerry knew better than most that this man was not rehabilitated. Countless times over the past eight years, Gerry had called Derrick "Ellum" Havelock to his office for a case review. Nothing in Ellum's demeanor or tone suggested any sign of contrition, remorse, or a desire to change. In fact, Gerry was certain the man would return to his ways as soon as he was released.

In the early 1980s, The Minnesota Department of Corrections made a departure from the rehabilitation model to a concept of providing an atmosphere conducive to an inmate rehabilitating himself. Despite an atmosphere rich with opportunity to rehabilitate, Ellum, like so many inmates, seemed to prefer his life of crime.

Gerry North was the Case Manager in Complex Two of Minnesota's maximum-security correctional facility at Oak Park Heights. Construction for the prison was completed in June of 1982. The first prisoners arrived from the Federal System in December that same year. Built in a circular design into the side of a hill in Oak Park Heights, Minnesota, the prison was created to house the worst of the worst. Inmates that had committed extremely violent crimes in other correctional facilities, or those whose street crimes mandated a life sentence, were sent to Oak Park Heights where the chances of escape were not good at all. In the twenty-three years since OPH opened its doors, no one had successfully escaped custody.

The State of Minnesota abolished its parole board and established sentencing guidelines which gave a specific sentence for each crime committed given the offenders criminal history. A departure from the guidelines is rare but can occur if a judge is willing to write a detailed explanation for the departure. On the first day of incarceration, each inmate is given a set number of years for the crime they commit, and beginning that first day they receive "Good Time," or time off from their sentence. Therefore, an inmate sentenced to an eleven year prison term might only have to serve eight years with good time, but only if they are never subject to discipline. However, for each day the inmate spends in segregation for a violation of institution rules, they loose three days of good time. Ellum was a model inmate who was determined to get out early. As such, he never spent a day in segregation. Therefore, after an eight-year stint for aggravated robbery, Derrick "Ellum" Havelock was set to go home.

*

Just north of downtown Dallas there is a half-mile stretch of bars and restaurants known as Deep Ellum. The area runs from Malcolm X to Texas Street, and from Elm to Main Street. The strip became known as Deep Ellum because Elm was more often pronounced Ellum by the local night club clientele. The Mad Dog, a hang out for young adults who are barely of drinking age, and some who are underage, was one of the bars in Deep Ellum. The Dallas Police Department had conducted several raids on the place and made several arrests. In spite of both raids and arrests, the owner continued to pay the fines, and nothing changed. In 1993, three deaths changed what raids and fines could not.

Twenty-one year-old bouncer, Derrick Havelock spent his time at the front door of the Mad Dog looking for just the right kind of action. Derrick refused to take any mess off anyone. His ability to quickly end a fight or disturbance is what landed him the job. He quickly sent anyone causing the least bit of trouble hurling into a brick wall, or if they were lucky, out the door. In August of 1993, Derrick was escorting one underage drunk out the back door of the bar when he met up with two of the drunk's friend's, ages eighteen and nineteen. The three youths jumped Derrick thinking it would be an easy fight, but they did not count on the loaded gun Derrick kept in his waistband. Before anyone knew what had happened, Derrick fired three shots and had taken the lives of all three.

Derrick never did time for killing the three youths because he had a Texas hand gun license, and was legally employed to provide security for the bar. However, under pressure from the Dallas Police Department and the Dallas City Council, the owners fired Derrick and initiated tougher rules on dealing with underage drinking. After the trial, Derrick moved north to live with friends in Minneapolis.

He resided in the Twin Cities only three weeks before being arrested by Minneapolis police for the aggravated robbery of a convenience store. Derrick had hog tied the clerk and beat her unconscious for taking too long to get the money out of the till. News of Derrick's Wyatt Earp style shoot out in Deep Ellum followed him to prison, so his prison nickname became "Ellum."

*

Gerry shoved the file in his drawer and looked up to see Denny Hagel standing in front of him. Denny, the correctional facility's chaplain, was once a correctional officer supervisor who had worked closely with Gerry over the years. Denny considered Gerry among his best friends.

"What are you anguishing over now?"

Gerry looked down at his desk, removed his glasses, and began to rub his forehead using his thumb and forefinger until it was red. He looked up at his old friend. "Just closed the Havelock file, he's not gonna make it Denny, he's gonna recidivate".

"And here I thought the gifts of prophecy were no more. Man, you really can read the future."

"You're not funny, and if you weren't a member of the clergy I might."

"Oh hush, that tough guy routine doesn't work on the inmates and it ain't gonna work on me."

Gerry allowed a brief smile, "How do you do it friend? How do you look at this mess day in and day out and not let it drag you down?"

"Gerry, if I tried to manage the lives of these prisoners in my own strength, I would look a whole lot worse than you do now. My ability to hear what these guys confess, and still sleep at night knowing what some will surely do when they get out comes from a source outside myself. You're trying to handle this on your own and its tearing you up inside."

"I know, its just that society expects us to make a difference in the lives of these guys when they come here and each time one goes out that door and I know he is up to his old tricks, I feel like I have failed the people that pay our salaries."

"Gerry, if you're gonna do this work you have to either not care, like several of your coworkers, or you have to cast your burdens on the Lord, because your shoulders were not made for that kind of load." "*Come unto me, all ye that labor and are heavy laden, and I will give you rest.*" Denny quoted the scripture from heart.

"I know, Matthew 11:28. Look –Denny - I love ya - but you have got to stop trying to save me, I've heard all this before and I'm just not ready yet."

Denny snapped his wrist around in front of his face and pretended to look at his watch, "Tick tock Tick tock, you think you have all the time in the world my friend, but you don't. The day of the Lord is at hand." Denny walked out of the office and began talking with some of the inmates near Gerry's door.

Gerry's office in Complex two was glassed in on all sides so that everything going on in the office could be seen by the correctional officers assigned to the complex. OPH had seven complexes, or cell blocks simply named complexes one through seven. Each unit housed fifty-two inmates in a computer-controlled steel environment that was designed for maximum security. Each of the complexes had a TV Room, a small weight room, four janitor closets and four defendable living units, each consisting of a row of thirteen inmate cells. Correctional Staff were allowed access to each complex via computer-controlled doors that were several inches thick. Each unit was staffed with three Correctional Officers who rotated in and out of working the security bubble, a computer operated, control center for the unit. A case manager and a correctional lieutenant shared an office in each complex.

Gerry rubbed his forehead a while longer then picked up the phone and dialed a number.

"This is Gerry North from OPH, just confirming with you that we will be sending Derrick Havelock, Department of Corrections number 787645 to you tomorrow?"

"Yep, we got him in the system, he's a Texas boy right?"

"Yeah, but he cannot leave Minnesota until expiration."

"Any detainers outta the Lone Star State that you know of?"

"Nope, he did a three-way killing back in 93, but was never indicted. Anyway, he's a bad boy and I don't think anything we did here changed that much."

"Gotcha, we'll keep an eye on him, you take care Gerry"

Gerry hung up the phone and prepared for his exit interview with Havelock, who would be there any second. Expiration, which is the date Ellum's sentence officially expired was not until March of 2004. Until then, he would remain under Minnesota Department of Corrections supervision.

*

"Wazup North?"

Derrick Havelock swaggered into the office as though he owned the place. He slunk down in the chair across the desk and hung one leg over the chair's side rail.

"Have a seat Derrick," Gerry said sarcastically.

"You just ain't about to call me Ellum, are ya?"

"Nope, it just reminds me of how our system fails more often then I want to think."

"Have it your way, I think you're just bent outta shape because you can't keep me here any longer."

"Well, you're right. I do wish we could keep you locked up a while longer."

Derrick put both feet on the floor in front of him and leaned forward intensely toward Gerry. "Why do you care? I mean what difference does it make to you if I rehabilitate or recidivate? At least when Chaplin Denny preaches to me I know where he's comin from and why he does what he does. It may be a bunch of bunk, but at least he believes in something. What about you North? What do you believe in? And why does any of this stuff matter to you?"

"I guess I would like to believe I did something to earn my money here. You make me feel like I have failed the people of this state."

Derrick smiled and ran his fingers through his hair, slouching again in the chair. "Well, sir, fear not. I believe you have done a valuable service for the citizens of this great state. You see, I have no plans of stickin around this frozen hell hole any longer than I absolutely have to, thanks to the pious, sanctimonious attitude of you and everyone like you I've met here. But if it means anything to you, at least the stuff Denny says has given me something to think about." Derrick let out a sinister laugh. "Your act however, needs a bit of polish, sir."

Gerry decided not to respond to Derrick's speech, but rather stood and gestured toward the door. "You're all set for 180 Havelock, good luck."

The two men stared at each other for an uncomfortable moment. Gerry let the silence be. After a moment, Derrick stood up and walked out the door of the glass office for the last time. Gerry watched him leave and wondered if it were possible for a killer and a thief to speak any truth into his life. He didn't like the implication of it, but somehow Gerry felt he had just been rebuked by the Devil himself. It didn't matter anymore; tomorrow Derrick Havelock would be in the custody of 180 Degrees, a half way house in Minneapolis for felons released from state prison.

Derrick passed several inmates on his way out of Gerry's office.

"Yo, Ellum. When you see Razor, tell him I'll be looking him up when I get out."

"I'll tell em you sent out a holla." Derrick walked into his cell which was already packed up, stretched out on the bed, and began to think about what tomorrow would bring.

*

Tall and lanky, and with a ruddy pockmarked complexion, Razor was not particularly attractive. Yet he never ceased looking for ways to improve, or rather increase, the female company he kept. Razor also kept his eyes open for new opportunities to make a fast buck. The young girls that patronized the "First Avenue Bar," a dance club made famous by Minneapolis' own Prince back in the early 80's, would pay good money to get into the bar if their credentials were not in order. If money was in short supply, but they had intangible aesthetic, qualities, other arrangements could always be made. It never failed to amaze Razor how far these young suburbanite girls would go to rebel against their parents and society, but so much the better for him.

Razor had been in and out of correctional facilities since doing two years in Red Wing, a Juvenile Correctional Facility. He was incarcerated at Red Wing from ages fourteen through fifteen. Razor was one of those children virtually raised in custody. Most of his convictions were for petty thefts and other property crimes. Considering his predilection for nefarious means of supporting himself, Razor had recently decided to recruit a small band of thugs to perpetrate crimes with him. Nothing was beyond Razor, but so far the only thing he had going for him was that he had not yet committed a violent crime. Therefore, Razor needed some muscle. So, when Razor heard that his old prison buddy Derrick Havelock soon be released from Oak Park Heights, he began to recruit Ellum for the gang.

The plan was fairly simple; Razor would use the connections he had made through the club to find some decent homes to burglarize. Ellum would provide any enforcement services needed. The newest recruit to the little band was Ricardo Garcia, who would do whatever grunt work was needed.

Chapter 6

Daisy

Minneapolis
June 2, 2001

D aisy Dawson was a middle child, fourth born out of eight and the only daughter of Sam and Kristen Dawson. For nearly three decades, Sam Dawson earned his living as a mail carrier for the US Postal Service. On a civil service salary, Sam had raised three adult children, paid off his home, and saved a nice nest egg while keeping his family intact. Daisy loved and respected her parents, but like most teenagers, she believed her parents were seriously out of touch and clueless about how the world really works. They meant well, but simply did not understand kids today. Daisy argued with her parents about the way she dressed, her choices in music, and most of all she argued with them about spiritual things. She felt they were trying to shove their spiritual beliefs down her throat. Daisy reasoned that she was a good person who treated others well, so there was no point to all their religious humbug.

The Dawson's attended True Vine Community Church, a non-denominational evangelical church on Fifty-Fourth Street and Chicago Avenue in South Minneapolis. The congregation was well integrated with people from several racial and socio-economic backgrounds. Daisy liked church well enough, especially the youth group activities. Her youth pastor and next door neighbor, Mr. Nick Bernard, was a kind man who really seemed to care about the kids in the church. Nick spent a great deal of his spare time with the kids, taking them on canoe and camping trips, cookouts, and bowling. The highlight of Nick's youth ministry was the sci-fi club he had created which took science fiction books and movies and made Christian applications from them. Nick held candid conversations with the kids about all kinds of things that were important to them. Once in a while, he would share the gospel with them, and many of the kids would make a commitment to follow Jesus Christ as Lord and Savior of their lives. Daisy knew Nick meant well, but she simply did not share his beliefs.

As far as the church and community were concerned, Daisy was a typical, popular, all-American teenager. She sang in the youth choir, was kind and loving toward her brothers, and had held down a job at Rainbow Foods Grocery Store for the past three years. When Daisy turned sixteen, she took her driver's test and passed on the first attempt. She had tried to talk her father into buying her a car of her own but he had said she was not ready for the responsibility yet. Sam Dawson had driven old raggedy cars for years because he believed it was important to pay cash if one wished to own a new car. So he drove older cars that were barely held together for over ten years before he was able to pay cash for a brand new 2001 Cadillac Seville STS. Daisy begged Sam to give her the broken down 1977

Ford he had been driving, but Sam was convinced the last thing his seventeen-year-old daughter needed was a car to take care of. Daisy thought it was awesome that Nick had bought her grandmother's car for his daughter, Alethea, when she was still only twelve. She wished her father could be more like Nick.

On a hot sticky June weekend in 2001, Sam Dawson planned to fly his wife Kristen and four youngest sons to California to visit his aging mother. It would have been a long drive, even in the luxury and comfort of his new car, so he purchased airplane tickets for the family. Daisy, who would soon be eighteen, didn't want to go, so Sam and Kristen decided to leave her home alone. Nick and Morgan Bernard agreed to keep an eye on the house and Daisy while they were gone. Sam made it perfectly clear to Nick that Daisy was not to drive his car while he was away.

Leaning over the fence between the two yards, Daisy saw Alethea Bernard sitting on the rear porch steps. "Did your dad get any more work done on the car this week?"

Alethea set down the book she was reading. "Yeah, he just changed out the carburetor. He said the old one was bad and that's why it wouldn't stay running after we started it up."

"Did it work?"

"I think so. We had it running for about an hour a little while ago."

Daisy looked toward the ground, gave a sarcastic grin, and shook her head from side to side, "Crazy world, huh? Looks like you'll be driving your own car before I will."

"I doubt it. You're probably gonna buy your own car before I get to drive this one."

Young Benny snuck up behind his big sister. He was ten years-old and loved to hang out with Daisy whenever he could. Nuzzling his head impishly under her arm, he looked up at his big sister, "Why don't you get your boyfriend to buy you one?"

"Benny," began Daisy. "I love you with all my heart, but sometimes I really wish you would watch your mouth. You don't know anything about a boyfriend, so you really shouldn't be saying stuff like that"

"Is he someone from school?" asked Alethea.

"He's someone in my adorable little brother's imagination." With that, Daisy grabbed Benny in a headlock and gave him a knuckle noogie. She then wrapped her arms around Benny's neck and smothered him with kisses.

"Eeewww, that-is-dee-scus-ting," said Benny.

Alethea laughed hard and almost fell off the steps. She turned to Benny, "What time are you guys leavin?"

"My dad says we have to leave for the airport in ten minutes, Daisy's drivin us."

"Your dad's letting you drive the Caddy?"

"Yeah, to the airport. Then I have to bring it right back and put it in the garage. Fun, fun."

"What'cha gonna do while they're gone?"

"Just hang out, catch up on some reading, spend some time with friends."

"You wanna ride to church with us on Sunday?"

"Yeah, that'd be cool. What's your dad got planned for us older kids this week?"

"I dunno, he's been really busy lately and we haven't had much time to talk. We're supposed to spend some time workin on the car tomorrow night, but we may just sit around and catch up on things."

"Have you heard anything from Stacy lately?"

"Yeah, she called a couple weeks ago. My dad finally talked her outta that cop stuff. Now, she wants to go into nursing. They've got some good nursing programs down there in Texas and she thinks that's what she wants to do now."

Daisy became silent and melancholy for a moment. "I sure do miss her, how about you?"

"Lots!"

"Tell your dad I'll come over about eight o'clock Sunday morning. I better get goin."

Alethea stopped Daisy before she had gotten very far from the fence. She got up off the steps and began to walk toward the fence.

"Hey, Daisy." Alethea paused for a moment. "I know this is kind of a sore subject with you, but have you given any more thought to what my dad and your parents have said to you about getting saved?"

Daisy let out a long sigh. "Go get inside Benny, Mom and Dad are gonna be waiting for you." Daisy turned to Alethea as Benny scampered into the house. "I think about that stuff all the time Alethea, but I just don't agree with it all the way. I mean, I try to do the right thing, and I don't hurt anyone. I just can't believe I have to make some promise to Jesus in order to keep from going to hell."

"Daisy, you are a nice person, in fact you are one of the kindest people I ever met, but that is not good enough. Sin is not what we do, sin is who we are. God loves you so much and doesn't want you to go to hell, but if you choose not to call upon the name of Jesus, and trust Him for your salvation, hell is exactly where you are going."

Daisy looked down at her feet then back up at Alethea, "You're a sweet girl Alethea, and I know you mean well, but I just cannot buy that right now – it just does not seem right to me. I don't see myself as a sinner, I am a good person."

"Do you believe in oxygen?"

"What kind of stupid question is that?"

"Well do you?" Alethea persisted.

"Of course I do, why do you ask?"

"I was just wondering, do you really think it matters whether or not you believe in oxygen? I mean if you don't have it, you will stop breathing whether you believe in it or not. Right?"

Daisy shrugged her shoulders and looked quizzically at Alethea before responding. "Yeah, I guess so."

Alethea continued. "So what makes you think God and His plan for saving humankind is any different? It's not about you and what you believe, Daisy, it's about God. And if you do not accept the free gift of life He has given you, you will spend eternity regretting it. I'm only saying all this because I care, Daisy."

Daisy hung her head and thought about what Alethea had just said. Alethea had a knack for asking penetrating questions, and putting things in a way that made it difficult to argue with her. "I know you care, Alethea." She began to smile slightly. "How did you get so smart for such a pipsqueak anyway?"

"I've got a smart dad."

Daisy leaned over the fence and beckoned Alethea to come closer. When she got close enough, Daisy wrapped her arms tightly around Alethea and held on for a long moment. "I'll give what you said some more thought, okay?"

"Okay, see you Sunday."

Daisy walked slowly back to the house thinking about what Alethea had said. She really was smart, but Daisy had her own view of life and eternity. Daisy couldn't understand why her salvation was so important to everyone else. She had listened to her parents and her older brothers talk about Jesus for years and she knew they all felt strongly about their faith, but that did not mean Daisy had to believe the same thing. Daisy wanted to taste life to its fullest. She wanted to try new things, meet new and interesting people, and maybe even check out different religions. Daisy believed that if a person had a good heart, they had just as much right to heaven as anyone else, even if they had done bad things or belonged to a different religion. Daisy turned her thoughts to the weekend. She had plans to start living this weekend, and with the family out of town the time was right. When Daisy got back to the house everyone was ready to go.

*

The Hubert H. Humphrey Terminal at Minneapolis - St. Paul Airport was not very busy. The family was flying out on Sun Country Airlines, which made it easy for Daisy to drop everyone off and keep moving. She hugged her family and told them to say hello to Grandma for her, then slid back behind the wheel and drove off. As Daisy passed the Mall of America she considered stopping for a movie and a bite to eat at the food court, but decided to play it cool for her first night alone. Tomorrow would be exciting enough and there was no need running unnecessary risks today. She got on 494 heading west, then 35W heading north, then got off on the 46th street exit. Daisy backed the Caddy into the garage when she got

home and walked in the back door of the house just in time to hear
the phone ring.

*

"Hello"

"How's my little angel?"

"Where are you?"

"180"

"I can't believe you're really here, I mean what time did you get
there?"

"A few hours ago, I figured I'd give you time to get the family
on the plane before callin' you. Is everything set for tomorrow?"

"Yep, seven o'clock at Rudolph's, do you know where that is?"

"Let's see, Franklin and Lyndale."

"Yeah, what are we gonna do after dinner?"

"Got a friend I want you to meet downtown. You ever heard of
a club called First Avenue?"

"Who hasn't? Is that where were goin?"

"Yeah, I gotta take care of some business, and then we'll see
what happens next."

"Please tell me you're not up to no good, Ellum."

"Don't start playin mommy to me, little girl, I can take care of
my own business."

"I know, I know, don't get your undies in a bundle."

"Look, someone else wants to use the phone and my turn is up.
Don't forget what you were supposed to bring?"

"I don't see why you can't just believe me. Why would I lie?"

"I believe you, I have just never heard of anything like it, and I know I've never seen proof of it before."

"Whatever."

"I'll see you then."

"Okay, I'll see you tomorrow."

*

Daisy hung up the phone, kicked her shoes high into the air, spun around once on the ball of her right foot and fell flat on the bed right on her back. She smiled a sly smile as she looked up at the ceiling. This was the start of something great, she could just feel it. A wrong number had been the beginning of a telephone relationship with Ellum. They had spoken regularly on the phone for the past six months, and when she found out he was being released to a half way house in Minneapolis, they began to plan their big night out. No one could have guessed that her father would plan a weekend getaway for the family the same weekend Ellum was due to be released, but Daisy felt she was the luckiest girl alive right then.

Daisy wasn't foolish enough to think she was in love with Ellum. He was an exciting man who seemed to have a good disposition. She wanted to get to know him, but she wasn't seriously pursuing a romance. Daisy rebelled against her parents, but not everything they said was nonsense. She agreed with them that she should remain pure until she was married, and Ellum was not going to talk her out of that. But if he could show her a little of the life she had been sheltered from, it would be well worth the cloak and dagger routine she had played for the past six months just to keep this relationship secret. She began to pick out what she would wear tomorrow.

Daisy never considered herself attractive, but she got a lot of attention from the boys at Roosevelt High School. In the fall, she would begin her first semester at the Minneapolis Community College and no doubt she would get plenty of attention there as well. She was 5'7' tall and although not heavy at 135 pounds, she was not petite either. Daisy had her father's fair complexion, and her mother's naturally curly blond hair and blue eyes. Most of her life Daisy dressed very conservatively, but at around sixteen years old, her taste in clothes became more contemporary. Daisy picked out a floral colored sundress with white sandals and set them aside for tomorrow. If she was going to go out on a limb, she would at least dress like a lady.

*

There were some great memories in that old house, thought Daisy as she began to awake the next morning from a restful night's sleep. It was hard to believe, but at one time there were ten people living under that roof in four average sized bedrooms. Kristen Dawson made use of every inch of the house's three thousand square feet. As was typical for Minnesota construction, the Dawson home had both a basement and an attic. In 1983, the year Daisy was born; Sam realized the family was running out of space. So he made the wise choice to have the basement renovated from a damp and gloomy storage space into a living space that could be used as a bedroom. Four years later, Sam spent all his overtime earnings to have the attic renovated in the same way.

Daisy had inhabited the same bedroom her entire seventeen years. As the only girl in the family, she was the only one who qualified for the privilege of having her own room. The two oldest boys, Sam Jr. and Ron, were serving in the Marines; and Patrick was in his sophomore year at Hamline University, a small private college in St. Paul. Patrick was an above average student who someday planned to study law. The twins, Carl and Corey had just finished their junior year at Roosevelt High School, while Dustin was looking forward to his freshmen year at Roosevelt. Then there was little Benny, perhaps Daisy's favorite, who had turned ten in May.

Benny was Daisy's baby. She cared for him and loved him up just like he was hers. It was Daisy who rocked Benny to sleep at night when he cried. Daisy changed his diaper, bathed him, and when he was ready, it was Daisy who taught Benny how to ride a bike. When Benny got off the bus after school, it was Daisy who made him a snack and did his homework with him. It often seemed like Daisy was the second mom in the house to everyone, but to Benny she was especially important.

Daisy had some incredible memories in the Dawson home, learning to ride her bike in the drive way, birthday parties in the back yard, and those ridiculous all night camp outs in front of the garage. Each Sunday after church, Mom and Dad would invite friends over who brought more casseroles than most people knew existed. They ate, laughed, and talked about the Bible. Usually, the Bernard's would stop over, and in the early years; Stacy would be there every week. It was Stacy who usually called off the evangelists that started in on Daisy immediately after dessert. Stacy was a Christian herself, but for some reason Daisy couldn't figure, Stacy seemed to understand that Daisy was not going to be pressured into conversion. Stacy had been gone for two years, and it felt to Daisy as though she had lost her best friend in the world. Daisy got dressed and did next to nothing most of the day in anticipation of the evening with Ellum.

*

Sitting down on soft leather seats behind the wheel of her father's Cadillac STS the following morning, Daisy felt in control. She turned the key in the ignition and heard the powerful Northstar V8 engine come to life. The Cadillac eased out the garage and onto the driveway turning west onto 46th street. Daisy merged onto 35W heading north and drove the five mile stretch to the Lyndale exit which led her around to Franklin Avenue right in front of Rudolph's Barbeque.

Daisy knew who she was looking for; Ellum had sent her several pictures of himself, but no matter how many he sent, they always looked the same. A background done up in pastels, with wide brush stroke images of fancy cars and men and women out on the town. In each picture Ellum stood center stage holding a cigarette – profile pose – wearing a sleeveless undershirt called a "Wife Beater." Ellum was muscular but not a body-builder type. He had a thick build and one could tell he liked to work out, but he didn't bulge, and he lacked the usual prison tattoo's one would expect to see. Daisy hoped he wouldn't be wearing the Wife Beater. She offered to pick him up at 180, which was only a few blocks from the restaurant, but Ellum insisted that she meet him at Rudolph's.

The two immediately recognized each other as soon as Daisy walked through the door.

Ellum smiled broadly, "Well, you look better than your pictures."

"Thanks," she smiled warmly, "did you have any trouble finding the place?"

"Nope, couldn't have been any easier."

"Why didn't you just let me pick you up at 180? It wouldn't have been a problem."

"I know, but it's nice outside, and I need to learn the neighborhood, don't I?"

"I guess so, did you already order?"

"No angel, I waited for you."

Daisy wished he would not call her angel. She did not feel at all like an angel right then. She had lied to her parents, and was taking advantage of their trust. She was anything but an angel. If there was any doubt as to whether or not romance was an option, Daisy put it to rest right away. Romance was out of the question. This was one of those times when Daisy felt a strange tugging at her heart – a certain longing to consider the things Nick, Stacy, Alethea, and her parents had tried to share with her. She felt an unusually strong desire to withdraw from her present situation and to draw close to God. In light of her current circumstances, Daisy decided it was best to keep her feelings in check until she could think without having to be polite.

Ellum held Daisy's chair as she sat, "I suppose you know this menu by heart."

"No, not by heart, but I usually order the same thing when I come here. In fact, it's a lot of food, so if you like ribs we could split it."

"Sure, what is it?"

"The John Wayne, it has beef ribs, fries, slaw, and Texas Toast, just for you."

"Okay, let's do it."

Ellum waved the waitress over and the two ordered their meal. Rudolph's was a tribute to Rudolph Valentino the legendary romantic film actor. The walls were lined on all sides with stills from famous films like "Gone with the Wind," and "The Great Train Robbery." There were also pictures of famous faces of yesteryear, like Barbara Streisand, Jane Fonda, Marilyn Monroe, John Wayne, Ronald Reagan, and Clint Eastwood. Many of the booths had been autographed by famous people who came to dine in the restaurant in its heyday. The lighting was dim, and the crowd was obviously made up of middle class people with an excess of time and money. "Did you bring it?" Ellum asked.

Daisy slipped an envelope containing a thick piece of paper out of her purse and handed it to Ellum. "See." She took the piece of paper out of the envelope and held it up for Ellum to see the title to her father's Cadillac.

"You weren't kiddin. He actually paid cash for a brand new Cadillac."

"I told you, my dad is a world class penny pincher. If there were a penny pinching event in the Olympics, my dad would win the gold!"

"Well now, that is commendable."

The two made small talk as they ate. Daisy wondered often during the meal what she was getting herself into; this was not at all like her. Meeting a strange man who just got out of prison was the stuff other girls did, not Daisy. Why was she there, and what did she think she was going to prove by spending a night out on the town with this man she had only just met.

"That was pretty good," said Ellum trying to make polite conversation as a segue to leaving.

"High praise indeed from the proud man of Texas, the barbeque capital of the known world."

Ellum laughed, "You ready to get outta here?"

"Whenever you are." Daisy put the car title back into her purse while Ellum paid the bill. The two slid off the booth, stood up, and walked out into the night, making more small talk on the way downtown in Sam Dawson's brand new car. Ellum pointed out an open parking spot on Seventh Street just outside the front door to the First Avenue Bar. Daisy parallel parked the Caddy, then dropped the keys into her purse.

"Let's go meet Razor," said Ellum grabbing Daisy's hand.

"Great," thought Daisy, *"I'm with a guy named Ellum, going to meet a guy named Razor."* They walked to the front door, where a tall, lanky guy with medium length hair and a bad complexion stood eyeing up women as they walked into the club.

"My man, wazup?"

Razor stood up straight when he saw Ellum and grabbed Ellums' hand tight. Ellum pulled Razor into his chest hard, and slapped him loudly on the back."

"My man, wazup wit you? Hey meet a special lady, this is Daisy Dawson."

Elevator eyes, Razor looked Daisy up and down like he was looking at a steak dinner he was about to devour. "Hey girl, lookin good."

"Get your tongue back in your mouth, Razor. Show some respect."

71

"Whatever, man. Your boy the Mexican is already here; he's got a booth in the back near the dance floor."

"I'll holla at you in a minute."

As Ellum led Daisy toward the back of the bar, a short Mexican nodded at Ellum then turned away. The two passed the dance floor and headed toward what appeared to be a back door. "Where you takin me, Ellum?"

"I need to show you something, but not here."

Daisy had an uneasy feeling about this, but she followed Ellum anyway. The door led to an alley behind the bar, Ellum closed the door behind them and pulled something from the back of his waistband. Daisy's eyes were as big as dinner plates, "What's that for?"

"Hand me your purse with the car keys, Daisy. Who have you told that you were meeting me tonight?"

Daisy didn't answer at first.

"Who did you tell?" Ellum's voice grew to a cruel roar.

"Nobody. Do you think I wanted to advertise what I was planning to do? I didn't tell anyone, what do you want from me?" Daisy was terrified – she could hardly breathe – there was no way out of this one.

"I want you to give me your purse, the car keys, and I want you to die."

"What"

The last word barely escaped her lips as a large red flame flew out the end of the muzzled automatic. A hole the size of a quarter appeared in the middle of Daisy's forehead. She was dead before she hit the ground. *What was that pungent smell?*

-Sulfur-

Chapter 7

Tosha Gelical

Dallas
March 1, 2005

Navigating the Highway 75 corridor that runs north-south through Dallas without losing all pretence of decency requires equal parts patience and grace on a good day, but today was not a good day and this had not been a good night. March 1, 2005 was a date Tosha Gelical would never forget; it was a day to test her faith. As she darted in and out of the late night traffic between Richardson and downtown Dallas with tears running down her cheeks, she dug around in her purse trying desperately to find her cell phone. *"If people in Dallas could ever figure out that the left lane is for passing, it would truly be a miracle."* Tosha found her phone and made a harrowing attempt to dial a number before the phone wound up on the floor near her feet when she dropped it during a shaking fit. She bent down long enough to grab the phone only to find herself closing in fast on a beer truck that had slammed on its breaks just before the LBJ Freeway interchange. Tosha slammed on her brakes just in the nick of time. After composing herself, Tosha tried the number again.

"Mom, try to calm down. Are you driving?" Anthony, Bart and Tosha's twenty-two year-old son, was studying law at Ann Arbor School of Law in Michigan. He was the first person Tosha thought to call after hearing from St. Luke's that Bart had been in an accident.

"Yes, I'm driving – look son, I have a feeling this is bad, I mean real bad. I wouldn't alarm you, but I think you better get on a plane and get back here."

"Okay, if that's what you want I will catch the first flight out, but I really need you to calm down, Mom. It won't help Dad or the baby any if you get into an accident on the way to the hospital."

Anthony was getting worried, but he didn't want it to show. It suddenly occurred to him that for the first time in his life, he needed to be strong for his mother because apparently his father, the rock of the family was in trouble. "Mom, just drive. Slow down and drive. Don't try to call Nate or Joseph; I can call them from here on my way to the airport. I'll call you as soon as I know when my flight is coming in. Can you tell me exactly what the hospital said?"

"Oh baby, they said your daddy was on his way to the car after work when he saw some little boy run out into the street. People that were there said he ran in front of the car and tossed the kid to the side, but the car ran right into your daddy."

Tosha's voice became shaky and she had to stop several times to compose herself. "They say he probably saved the kid's life, but it doesn't look good for your daddy. It just doesn't look good at all. Please hurry, son."

"Mama, I want you to know that as soon as I lay down this phone I'm gonna do two things. I'm gonna book a flight, then immediately without packing a thing, leave this apartment and head for the airport. Are you still listening to me, Mama?"

Tosha sobbed, then managed a yes.

"Okay, where exactly are you, and how fast are you driving?" Anthony reached for his Bible which was in the top drawer of his desk.

Tosha's voice came over the line, still shaky but stronger. "I just passed 635 and I'm approaching Walnut Hill Lane, I'm going seventy-five."

"Okay, I want you to slow down to sixty-five, can you do that for me mama?"

"Okay son, I'm slowing down to sixty-five."

"Good. Now you have a few minutes before you reach the hospital, I want you to listen to me, I'm going to read to you from Psalm 142."

"Okay," Tosha was beginning to feel a little better.

Anthony began to read, *'I cry aloud with my voice to the Lord; I make supplication with my voice to the Lord. I pour out my complaint before Him; I declare my trouble before Him. When my spirit was overwhelmed within me, You knew my path. In the way where I walk they have hidden a trap for me. Look to the right and see; For there is no one who regards me; There is no escape for me; No one cares for my soul. I cried out to you, O Lord; I said, You are my refuge, My portion in the land of the living, Come heed my cry, For I am brought very low; Deliver me from my persecutors, For they are too strong for me. Bring my soul out of prison, so that I may give thanks to Your name; thy righteous will surround me, for You will deal bountifully with me.'*

"Mama, Dad is in God's merciful hands now, and God loves him more than any of us ever could. Get to the hospital quickly and safely, but know that your husband is in the loving care of his heavenly Father. I'm on my way mom. Please try to calm down."

"I will, baby." Tosha was still crying but regaining her composure. "I'll calm down. Get here soon."

*

Tosha turned her cell phone off and turned on the car radio to one of the Christian music stations. She decided to take her son's wise advice and calm herself. Tosha continued south on Highway Seventy-five and got off on the Live Oak exit. She drove east on Gaston Avenue until she arrived at St. Luke's, which was a madhouse of activity. Tosha struggled to get out of her car. Eight months pregnant, she waddled immediately into the emergency room holding her lower back as she walked. Bart spent so much of his time at work in the ER, and Tosha had heard a lifetime of stories from the "fish bowl" perspective. Lt. Marie Jackson from the St. Luke's Police Department greeted Tosha as she walked into the ER and assured Tosha that everything possible was being done for Bart. Tosha had met Marie several Christmas parties earlier, and had seen her there with her husband every year since.

"Is there anything we can do, Mrs. Gelical? Are your sons on the way?"

"Yes, Anthony is on his way from Michigan, and the other two should be here any minute."

"Do you need someone to pick Anthony up at the airport?"

"I'm sure he's made some arrangements, but I'll let you know. Thanks Lieutenant, right now I just want to see my husband."

Dr. James Roberts, Tosha's physician was also in the ER; he took her aside and held onto her for a moment. Lt. Jackson quietly walked away looking as though she were useless.

"I need to see him Jim, I want to see my husband."

"I know you do, but right now you need to give the Doctors a chance to do their job, and they cannot do it with you in there."

"Jim, that's not good enough, I need to see him."

"Tosha, you have to give them a chance. I just came out of the operating room and trust me he is getting the very best of care right now, I am concerned about you and the baby. You're doing well but you're only at thirty seven weeks, I don't want that baby coming early Tosha, I think we have enough to worry about with Bart."

"I've carried and delivered three strong boys, Jim, and I think I know when I'm okay." Tosha spoke firmly, she was regaining her control.

"I know, Tosha, let's not forget, I was there all three times." Dr. Roberts allowed a reassuring smile. "I've reserved the family room; I assume Nathaniel and Joseph will be here shortly. Let's step inside where you can sit down, and I'll get you something to drink. When I get back I'll explain what I know so far."

"Thanks Jim." Tosha squeezed his hand before letting go.

The family room was set aside by the hospital's social service team for families that needed a place to deal with grief or a bad report from the doctor. The hospital recognized that it was often best to sequester the emotional response of a family dealing with such things and allow the family a safe environment to care for each other. Therefore, a small room off to the side near both ER waiting and surgery was set-up for this purpose. The room had two long couches, one of which pulled out into a bed, and four high back chairs. Two smaller over stuffed chairs also pulled out into beds, and there was a long coffee table in the center of the room. A private restroom was on one side of the room, and on the other was a long counter space with a few Bibles, a telephone, and several boxes of tissues. The room was dimly lit and decorated in soft earth tones, with a large print of DaVinci's "Last Supper" on the longest wall. Dr. Roberts disappeared into the hallway – Tosha eased herself down into a chair and began to pray. When she looked up, a woman covered with dried blood walked into the waiting room with Dr. Roberts.

"Tosha, I want you to meet Stacy Bernard. She was there when it happened. Stacy, this is Mrs. Tosha Gelical, Bart's wife."

Stacy tried to hold it together, but the tears just streaked down her face when she saw Tosha, who fell apart as well. The two women who had never met melted into each other's arms and wept uncontrollably as Dr. Roberts set two cups of coffee on the small table next to the couch in the family room where they stood.

Stacy found her voice first, "I picked up my friend Mitch's son and was on my way to the ER to visit him; it was supposed to be a birthday surprise. Then Meredith saw me standing at the light and she pulled up just to tell me her husband is in recovery and going home this weekend, then Michael stepped off the curb – I didn't see him."

Stacy began to sob again – her breaths came in short staccato bursts, she stopped long enough to get herself under control.

"When I looked back down he was in the street and this car was coming – I saw Bart come out of nowhere and then Michael was flying through the air, I thought he was hit but then Bart went flying over the top of the car – there was so much blood, and he was just trying to save Michael."

Stacy could not stop crying, and now it was Tosha who comforted. As Stacy let loose, Tosha held her hand and reassured her.

Dr. Roberts cut in, "They're working to repair a severed femoral artery now. He lost a lot of blood but fortunately he has a common blood type. They have inflated one of his lungs which was punctured by a broken rib, and we're fairly certain his kidney was also ruptured. I spoke with, the primary surgeon, and he feels that if Bart makes it through the first few hours post op, the worst may be over. Their only other concern is whether or not he will loose his right leg. The car that hit Bart was extremely low, so instead of the bumper hitting him above the knee, he was hit below the knee where the bone is less dense, and it simply shattered. The fact is, Bart's in for a long night, and all we can do is wait it out."

"That's not all we can do," said Tosha with a look of determination. The two women, who seemed to have instantly become kindred spirits read each other's minds, and immediately bowed their heads.

After a short prayer, Tosha looked at Stacy, "Did I hear you say your friend is Mitch who works in the ER?"

"Yeah, he works with Bart. This is his little boy, Michael." Michael, who had been standing next to one of the high back chairs in the family room, took a step forward. The little boy had curly black hair and puffy red cheeks which had been bandaged. His clothes were torn and his pants were ripped open, exposing skinned knees. Michael looked about four years-old, and right then he looked particularly sad. He climbed onto the couch and onto Stacy's lap, then rested his head on her breasts. "Can you say hello, Michael?"

Michael looked at Tosha and turned away – then, turning away from Stacy he looked Tosha right in the eye and said, "I'm sowwy Mizter Bawt got hurt." Tosha teared up for a moment, then stroked Michael's chubby cheek with the back of her hand.

"Do you know Mitch?" asked Stacy.

"No, I mean I've met him, but I can't say I really know him."

"I met your husband once, Mrs. Gelical. In fact it was the day I met Mitch. He seemed like a real gentleman to me, and a real sweet man."

"He is. He's the best." Stacy and Tosha sat and talked while Michael fell asleep in Stacy's arms. Dr. Roberts excused himself and went back out on his rounds, promising to check in on Bart and report back to Tosha shortly.

*

Anthony, true to his promise, hurriedly made flight arrangements online, grabbed his keys and rushed out the door. His drive to the airport was brief, and he thanked God there was a flight leaving in two hours with a connection in Houston allowing him to fly into Love Field at six o'clock in the morning. On the way, Anthony called Nate and Joseph. Joseph, a junior at Dallas Baptist University was sound asleep when Anthony called at eleven o'clock in the evening.

"What? Who? Wait, just a minute, what are you talking about, I just talked to Dad about an hour ago before he left work. He was just fine."

"I know, Joseph. This just happened about a half hour ago. Mom's on her way to St. Luke's right now, and I think she's gonna need you there."

"You comin in to town?"

"I'm on my way to the airport now; my flight gets in to Love Field at six in the morning. I'm gonna need a ride bro, can you come get me?"

"Of course, I'll be there. Hey, Anthony," Joseph paused for a long moment.

Anthony spoke up. "He's gonna be alright Joseph, but pray like you've never prayed before. Dad is being taken care of, but right now Mom really needs us, so pray then get over there."

"I'm on it."

Anthony arrived at the terminal with a good half hour to spare, so he sat down and began to reflect on life with his father. Bart Gelical led his family as a loving but often distant father. Anthony could not remember a Christmas, birthday, first day of school, sporting event, or any other special occasion where his father failed to make an appearance. However, it sometimes seemed a cruel irony that Bart Gelical had three sons because he rarely availed himself of wrestling with them on the floor or throwing them a football on a fall evening in the back yard. He was a gentle man who always seemed to be in deep thought. During his sporadic attempts at humor, Bart Gelical became the life of the party. His sometimes childish antics were absolutely hysterical. As Anthony grew into manhood, it occurred to him that far too often he missed out on seeing his father's warm magnetic smile. Bart was a man who never really grasped his endearing gift of personality and the way people were attracted to him.

A man of average attractiveness, Bart's red hair and freckles made him look years younger than his forty-nine years. Recently, he had begun running up to three miles, three times per week, and he tried to make it to the gym at least four times per week. Bart believed his overall fitness would be an asset with the new baby coming.

Anthony felt fortunate. He had only warm feelings about his childhood and home life. He knew other kids with fathers that were more typical in the way they interacted with their sons, but Anthony saw his father's distinctiveness as an advantage. In the Gelical family, Bart took on the role of insisting that the family attend church on a regular basis and have weekly family devotions. Bart also labored hard each day to make sure Mom could stay home with the children. And when it came time for Anthony to prepare for college, Bart insisted upon working extra shifts just to make sure Anthony didn't have to work a job and let his grades suffer. Despite what sometimes appeared as indifference, Anthony felt assured that his father loved and cared for his children.

Anthony had many conversations with his father since leaving Texas A&M for Ann Arbor Law School. Bart's mood had seemed to darken over the past year and nothing drew him out of his funk. Even the news that he would soon be a father again didn't lift his spirits. During their many conversations, Bart had confessed that his courage left something to be desired, as he more often than not failed to take a stand on spiritual things around the work place. Bart also lamented that he had failed to embrace the spirit of the Great Commission by not getting involved in street evangelism.

*

By six o'clock the morning of March 21, 2005, the slumbering masse gathered in the St. Luke's ER family room began to stir. Stacy had spent the entire night with Tosha and two of her sons, Joseph and Nathaniel. Bart had survived four hours of surgery and was in recovery, but it was still too soon to tell if he would make it. Dr. Roberts came in and out of the family room with a report about every hour and a half. Joseph had left to pick up his older brother Anthony at the airport. At six fifteen in the morning Mitch poked his head in the family room. "I thought everyone would be asleep. Any word on Bart?"

Tosha looked at Mitch with red puffy eyes and said, "He's in recovery now. It'll be a while before we know anything for sure. How are you, Mitch?" She shifted her weight on the rollout bed and sat up to speak to Mitch.

"I'm fine, Tosha. The question is, how are you?"

"God is good Mitch, I feel comforted by His grace."

"You have a wonderful son, Mitch. He looks just like you." Tosha managed a smile as she addressed Mitch.

"Thanks. He's a handful." Looking at Stacy, he continued. "Stacy, I can drop you off at home so you can clean up and get some rest. If you want to come back, I'll bring you."

Stacy smiled at Mitch. She was well aware of the Bible's teaching on pursuing romantic relationships with people outside her faith, and her relationship with Mitch was a source of constant inner turmoil, but there was something more than romance between them. She felt an unnatural pull toward him. Stacy knew their relationship could only go so far if he continued to reject Christ. She had been clear about that with Mitch. There was something beyond her personal feelings that drew her into a relationship with Mitch, a relationship that was far more of a friendship than a romance. She spent much of her time witnessing to Mitch, and to her surprise, Mitch actually listened to her. She turned toward Mitch and gathered the sleeping Michael in her arms and began to get up.

"Sure, Mitch, that would be nice. I think I'm still a little too shaken to drive right now. Happy Birthday."

"Hold on a minute." Tosha placed a hand on Stacy's arm, coaxing her to stay seated. "I want to have a word with this handsome young man for a moment."

Tosha led Mitch into the hallway by the hand. Mitch began to speak. "Tosha, I can't tell you how sorry I am, and how grateful I am for what Bart did. I feel terrible about the whole thing. I…"

"Mitch," Tosha took her time, choosing her words carefully. "I'm sure you're aware of our faith, our beliefs." Mitch nodded his head. "Did you know that Bart prayed for you on a regular basis?"

"No ma'am, I…"

Tosha interrupted again. "Bart kept a prayer journal, and as a couple we shared each other's prayer concerns and we talked about what we see God doing in our lives and in the lives of others. Bart has a heavy heart for you, Mitch. It was his hope and prayer that someday you would come to know the Lord."

"Ma'am, I – I don't know how to respond to that. Like I said, I appreciate what Bart did. That took…"

"Nothing less than the will of God and the example of Christ for Bart to sacrifice his own life for the life of your son." Tosha completed Mitch's sentence. "Bart had given himself to God completely, and he decided long ago that God could use him in whatever way He saw fit. I don't know why that car hit my husband, or what will happen to him now, but I do know that God is still in charge of this universe, and that He works all things for His good purpose. I know you don't share my faith, but in light of what has happened and the potential cost in human life, I would consider it a personal favor if you would think long and hard on what I just said to you. You have a wonderful son, and I think that little lady in there is rather taken by you too. The Lord has been good to you, Mitch. You think about what I have said."

Tosha let go of Mitch's hand and walked back into the family room. Stacy and Michael came out the same door as Tosha went in, and the three made their way toward the ER waiting room.

*

As Stacy, Mitch, and Michael walked through the ER waiting room, Melissa McCree slept peacefully with her head leaning on Rocky Jo Bob's shoulder. She moved slightly – nudging Rocky Jo Bob in the ribs just enough to bring him to consciousness for a brief second. Melissa stirred and saw Rocky Jo Bob with the strangest look on his face, "Everything okay, Rocky?"

"Yeah, jes fine. For a second, I thought I recognized dat woman who jes walked out."

"What woman?"

"Neva mind, go back ta sleep."

*

Stacy looked at Mitch as they approached the automatic door leading out of the ER, "Do you know that man sittin' with the attractive white woman over there?"

"Nope, they've been here all night. I think her husband is being treated back in ER. The big guy sat there preachin' up a storm when I first got to work last night. Bart asked about 'em too just before he left. He thought they might be a couple, but I told him they probably were not. Why do you ask?"

"Oh, nothing. For a moment, he looked familiar, but it couldn't be. Never mind." They walked out of the hospital and into the cool morning light.

Chapter 8

Melissa McCree

Dallas
August 2003

B orn in Eldorodo, Oklahoma in 1909, Wallie Amos Criswell placed his faith in Christ at a revival meeting when he was ten years old. At age twelve, he publicly committed his life to ministry after preaching a fiery sermon at his pet dog's funeral. Criswell earned his Master of Theology and Doctor of Philosophy degrees from Southern Baptist Theological Seminary in Louisville, Kentucky, and shortly thereafter married his sweetheart, Betty Harris, the pianist of the Mount Washington Baptist Church where Criswell served as pastor.

In 1944, the Criswell's moved to Dallas, Texas, accepting a call to the First Baptist Church of Dallas. The previous pastor had been none other than George W. Truett, who had led the congregation for forty-seven years and helped to found a Dallas Medical Facility which is now a part of the Baylor Health Care System. In 1969, Criswell, led by his love for the inner city, founded "The Criswell

College" to train young people for ministry. Criswell's dream was to pastor a small inner city church on a corner, but instead, the Lord used him to build a huge ministry with two prongs that endured over five decades. W.A. Criswell served as pastor of First Baptist Church and as president of the college he founded until 1995.

Criswell's love and concern for the inner city led to the support of more than fifteen missions and chapels staffed with pastors. He also helped to sponsor The Dallas Life Foundation, Dallas' largest shelter for the homeless. On January 10, 2002, at the ripe old age of ninety-two, Wallie Amos Criswell was laid to rest. Almost three thousand mourners packed into the First Baptist Church of Dallas where Criswell once stood in the pulpit. They came to say goodbye. Clinched in Criswell's right hand, as he lay in his casket, was a Bible. This was the tearful request he had made during a sermon he preached several years before his death. On a hot Dallas morning in August 2003, Melissa Moore stepped across the threshold of W.A Criswell's pedagogical legacy – the citadel of spiritual empowerment he had left behind for generations into the eschaton.

Melissa Moore's arrival at Criswell was as much an escape from her point of origin as it was a gateway to her destination. She had always wanted a Christian education, but perhaps as important as the content of her education was the place where she was to receive it. Melissa had all she could take of her small town roots, and the narrow mentality of the family and community in which she grew up. Raised in a fine Baptist home in rural East Texas, Melissa understood and accepted the tenants of her faith and of her denomination, but she was convinced there was more.

If her parents had had their way Melissa would never leave home; she would meet and marry a local boy. However, this was an unacceptable option for her. Melissa wanted to learn about urban mission, and experience life from something other than a small town perspective. She reasoned, if the gospel was big enough to reach across the globe, it was surely big enough to reach across Texas. Stirred by a sermon series on grace she heard on the radio by a prominent evangelical preacher from Dallas, Melissa became enamored with the idea that her continued sheltered existence was contrary to the Great Commission. She concluded that it was nothing more than the grace of God which saved her, and that if she could be saved, so could sinners in an urban environment. With that notion, Melissa set forth to experience life in "the real world."

Nineteen year-old Melissa Moore parked her black 1986 Chrysler Lebaron in the Criswell parking lot. The car was a reluctant going away present from her parents and it had 160,000 miles on it, but Melissa was grateful to have it. She locked the doors and walked across Bird Street and into the main entrance of the school. A short flight of stairs led up to the main floor of the school where faculty and students had assembled to assist the new arrivals.

Dressed in powder blue capri's, a white button down blouse, and white tennis shoes, Melissa was almost more than Criswell College could handle. Her blonde hair was cut just below the ear, parted on the right side, it was stylishly curly and just a bit country. Wearing only a touch of lipstick, a tasteful amount of eye shadow, and no rouge, she was simply stunning without trying in the least.

Melissa grew up knowing her looks gained her an inordinate amount of attention from both men and women. It wasn't that everyone was necessarily attracted to her, though surely many were. The fact is that most people were not accustomed to seeing someone so very attractive. Melissa had grown used to the attention, and usually tried to play down her looks. Walking toward the counter at the top of the steps, Melissa could see a cheerful female student helping another student find her way. Melissa waited patiently in line, and when the student in front of her moved away, she was face to face with the student helper who stared for a brief moment before speaking.

"Hey there, may I help you?"

Melissa smiled and held out her hand, "Hi, my name's Melissa Moore, and I'm a new student looking for the registration area."

The student grabbed Melissa's hand and gave it a friendly, firm shake. "You local or new in town?"

"I just rolled off the freeway and into town, I haven't even found a place to live yet. Right now I'm staying at the LaQuinta over on..." Melissa dug around in her purse for the piece of paper she had written the motel address on.

"It's on Central Expressway, not far from here," the girl interjected. "My name's Karen Underwood. I'm a junior here, and if you need anything let me know. Registration is in the gym. It's through these double doors and around to your left. You'll find tables set up along the four walls of the gym with large letters. Go to the table with the first letter of your last name and they will have a name tag and registration packet for you."

"Thanks." Melissa was surprised by the friendliness of the students so far. Karen beckoned the next lost freshmen to her counter while Melissa moved toward the gym to register for classes.

The lines for registration were long, but the process was smooth and quick. Melissa registered for Systematic Theology, Hermeneutics, English Grammar & Composition, and Personal Evangelism. She stopped at the Security Desk and registered her car for a parking sticker before leaving the gym. Melissa walked out of the gym and around the long information table at the top of the stairs. On her way down the stairs and toward the door, Melissa heard someone calling her name.

"Melissa, hey wait up a second." It was Karen Underwood; she was running down the stairs toward Melissa. "How'd it go in there? Did you get all the classes you needed? It's usually pretty slim pickins for newbies but hopefully you got something worth while."

Melissa rolled her eyes then looked down, "Yeah, I got all my classes, but now I have to go to some place called DTS just to get my books, and I have no idea where that is. I'm, shall we say, directionally challenged."

Karen laughed a sincere laugh, then spoke with a calm reassuring voice. "DTS is the seminary just a couple blocks from here. Our bookstore was losing money by selling textbooks, so they made some sort of deal with the seminary. It's within walking distance, but if you have a car I recommend you drive. This isn't exactly a nice neighborhood, ya know? But it's just down Gaston, take a right on St. Joseph, then go two blocks till you reach Swiss and take another right. You'll see the seminary bookstore right on the corner. They'll hook you up with everything you need for your classes."

Melissa's countenance lifted. "Thanks, that was very helpful, but I think I'll walk."

Karen studied Melissa for a moment, "Look, my roommate graduated at the end of the summer and is moving back home to Tennessee in about a week. To be honest, I could probably find a roommate without too much trouble, but I'm looking for someone who's a real genuine, sold-out-for-Christ, Christian, and you look like the real deal to me. I'm usually a good judge of character, and

I don't think I'm wrong about this. I'm not judgmental, but I just don't have time for people who talk the talk, but don't want to walk in His sandals, if you know what I mean. It's just, well you'll find there are a lot of phonies out there and I don't have time for people that want to say they're Christians but want to live like the world lives."

Melissa smiled one of her famous smiles and lit up the room. She could not believe what she was hearing; this was someone she could learn from, someone who could help her in the pursuit of a real Christian experience. "What's the catch?"

"My goodness," Karen began, "You have got to be trouble with that smile and those looks. How'd you get so ugly anyway? Is your whole family ugly or is it just you?"

Melissa laughed at herself. It was the first good laugh she'd had since telling her parents she was moving to the big city. "I think we're gonna get along real well," said Melissa.

"I think so too," Karen said with a smile of her own, "Stop back here about four o'clock this evening and you can give me a ride home. If you don't mind bunking on the couch for a few days, then helping me and Jessie move a bunch of boxes, that's really the only catch. Rent is $250 per month and you'll need $200 up front to cover your share of the damage deposit."

Melissa looked at Karen quizzically, "Jessie?"

"Jessica Miller is my current roommate, you'll love her." Karen was encouraged by the look on Melissa's face; it meant she was not okay with her having a male roommate. Perhaps she had made a good call with this newbe.

"Oh, right, sorry." Melissa's smile returned. "Thanks, Karen. You don't know how much this means to me, and I won't let you down. I'll be back at 4:00 sharp. I'll pick you up right here." Melissa took the steps down two at a time and burst out the doors to the main entrance. *"It was going to be all right, it was really going to be okay here in Dallas."* She thought.

*

The walk to Dallas Theological Seminary was an education in itself. Melissa thought, this is the stuff she'd come to the big city for. Wallie Criswell's dream was to have an inner city ministry, and that is exactly what he got. The Criswell College was located near downtown Dallas in an area populated by lower income black and Hispanic people. For the most part, Melissa was ignored as she walked along Gaston Avenue. People went about their business, whatever that might be, without paying much attention to a new girl in town here to learn about the Lord. Melissa saw run down apartment buildings, as well as broken bicycles and cars that no longer worked. Men and women drank beer out of forty ounce bottles, while loud hip hop music boomed from car trunks, hand held radios, and out of windows. The hip-hop blended with the Latino stylings of mariachi bands and created an avant-garde fugue which sort of defined the surroundings.

Local shops catered to the urban clientele, selling ethnic foods and offering automotive service and lawn care. The smell of barbeque from the local hickory joint mingled with the thick greasy aroma of Church's Fried Chicken and Whataburger restaurants. Melissa took it all in and loved every moment of it. A convalescent home was located on the corner of Gaston and St. Josephs, where Melissa took a right, heading toward Swiss Avenue. There, the elderly got around as best they could in motorized wheelchairs and walkers that went too slow. This was the urban experience Melissa had signed up for, but as she reached Swiss Avenue everything changed.

The sight of a lush, green, well-manicured lawn and expensive sculptures which surrounded the carefully maintained buildings of the Dallas Theological Seminary was surreal in this almost war-torn environment. As Melissa stepped onto Swiss, she thought she'd walked into another world. The DTS Bookstore was on the corner of Swiss and Apple just as Karen said it would be, but what Karen had not explained was the campus' out of place beauty in the midst of despair. Seminarians carrying heavy book bags walked between the buildings with a serene look of contentment and fulfillment on their faces. Professors moved about at a hurried pace discussing deep theological issues in button down shirts and ties. Just across from the seminary on Live Oak Street was the Deluxe Inn, a place where one could live for a day, week, or month, so long as the bill was paid. On all four corners of the seminary, the urban decay was obvious, but within the campus boundaries there may have been indifference, but certainly not ignorance. To Melissa, this was an odd place indeed.

Inside the bookstore, Melissa was reminded of the name behind the voice which opened her mind to God's grace. Books written by the prolific favorite son of Dallas Theological Seminary, Chuck Swindoll, lined the bookshelves in a shrine. Melissa took a moment to browse the selection before purchasing her textbooks for school. She read the cover and the first few pages of Chuck Swindoll's, *The Grace Awakening* before deciding she would purchase it. As she turned away from the bookshelf, she knocked a thick commentary from the hands of a student who was also fixated on the Swindoll collection.

Apologizing, Melissa bent down to pick up the book. "I'm sorry, I wasn't paying attention, I was just looking at this book and I.... Look I'm sorry, I'm usually more graceful than this."

"Apology accepted. Thanks. Excuse me." The student turned and walked away. He was tall, about six feet, two inches tall, athletically built with short cropped hair and a goatee. Melissa guessed him to be in his mid twenties, and probably a DTS student.

Melissa found all the books on her list and left the bookstore at about one o'clock. Still too early to pick up Karen, she decided to walk back to Criswell and have a look around the school. She walked the five blocks back to Criswell and went through the east entrance instead of the west entrance she had originally gone through. Melissa walked up another short flight of stairs and turned left at the long hallway before her. She walked through a set of double doors and down the hall. The college had once been the Gaston Avenue Church and still looked much like a church on the inside. The auditorium to her right was once the church's main sanctuary; in the basement there was a large banquet room with a stage and smaller rooms surrounding the banquet hall with a fully functional kitchen. Farther down the long corridor, Melissa saw a gathering of people outside what used to be the college bookstore. The bookstore, which no longer sold textbooks, was converted into a coffee house where students could buy snacks, sandwiches, coffee, and either study or visit with one another.

There appeared to be some sort of commotion as Melissa approached the entry. Inside, a heavyset black man with a salt and pepper beard stood at the front of the bookstore speaking in a strong, deep voice. He was preaching a sermon and held the room in wrapped fascination as he spoke. Melissa decided to listen in while she waited for Karen to get off work.

"The life of a believer is marked by service to God and service to one another. Works do not save, but the grace of God saves us from the penalty of death. But for the grace of God, we all would perish, and who among us has anything that was not given to them? If you want to know the truth, we may all be surprised at who will be in the Kingdom. Salvation is a thing only Christ understands or can judge. But sanctification is marked by service born of love. Love your neighbors as yourselves."

Melissa wondered out loud which professor this was in the bookstore.

"He's not a prof. He's a student just like us." It was the guy from the DTS bookstore, and he was talking to Melissa.

Melissa looked at him for a moment before she spoke. "I see you can be social and polite. I'm surprised you allowed yourself to speak to me."

"I'm sorry about my behavior back there. I'm just trying to be careful, not rude."

"Careful about what? I don't bite."

"I know, like I said – I'm sorry – I suppose I was less than friendly back there. I'm new in town and I guess I don't know how to act in this environment yet. Hey, my name is Robbie McCree. Pleased to meet you."

"Melissa Moore, and you still didn't answer my question. What are you trying to be careful of."

Robbie ran his fingers through his hair, front to back, puffed out his cheeks then blew hard, and dropped his head. "Listen ma'am, I'm a new Christian – real new. I love the Lord now, but I came from a pretty unholy past – and well – you're a very attractive woman, and I just didn't want to give you the wrong impression."

Melissa had to admit; she enjoyed watching "Mr. Stud Muffin" squirm. "Okay," she said with a sly smile, "What exactly would the wrong impression be?"

Robbie began to blush. He turned his head away from Melissa refusing to look into her deep blue eyes. He jammed his hands into his pockets and began to speak. "I guess I didn't want you to think I was hittin' on you or something like that, cause I wasn't. I was standing there, and you're the one who bumped into me. I was just mindin' my own…"

"Relax, I was just messin' with you, and I don't think I would've assumed you were hittin' on me if you had just made some quick polite conversation. Look, none of us have this Christianity thing completely figured out. When you get right down to it, we're all just people fightin' our natural instinct to do wrong. So hey, don't sweat the small stuff."

Robbie smiled and began to loosen up. He had a wonderful smile, and although Melissa hadn't originally thought he was handsome, his smile was beautiful. "Thanks for putting me at ease about that. Like I said I'm new to this. A friend of mine dragged me to one of those Promise Keepers events this past spring and I gave myself to Christ on the second day."

"Whatchu mean dragged you. Didn't nobody drag yo' sorry butt."

Melissa and Robbie realized for the first time that the preaching had stopped, and the preacher was standing beside them.

"What up ma' brotha? Who's the lady?"

"Rocky, this is Melissa, my new friend. Melissa this is Rocky Jo Bob Eubanks from Personville Texas."

"Pleased ta' meetcha' ma'am. You better watch who ya keep company wit around here though, I hear there's a few heathens amongst us." Rocky winked at Robbie.

"I liked your sermon Rocky, how long have you been at Criswell?" Melissa looked at Rocky and waited for a response. He had some nasty scars on his face, but gentleness pervaded his presence and his inner being was simply dominant.

"Well, I started here when I was two, and I'm goin' on four now, so I guess bout two years now." Melissa had a confused look on her face. Robbie jumped in.

"Rocky suffers from what is known as retrograde amnesia. He was found in a garbage dumpster in Grosebeck a couple years ago, and nobody knows how he got there or who he is, only that he was beaten and left for dead."

Rocky jumped in, "Yeah, but da good Lawd wasn't done wit me yet, so here I am learnin the Word of Truth, and hangin out wit sinners and tax collectors like yo new friend here."

"Well, Mr. Eubanks, it's a real pleasure to meet you."

Karen snuck up behind the trio, "Hey, I see you met Rocky."

"Yeah, she met me, what of it?" Rocky winked at Melissa.

"You gonna help me move Jessie next week Rocky?"

"What's on da menu?"

"Pizza?"

"Well, so long as deres pizza, and God's people fo cumpney, I guess I'll be dere."

"Cool, by the way, Melissa's movin in to Jessie's room."

Robbie looked at Karen and Melissa, "You two are roommates?"

"Yeah, I'm just meetin' all kinds of nice people today. I can hardly believe it." said Melissa.

"God is good, idn't He?" said Rocky.

"Amen." Said Melissa, who locked arms with Karen and walked away looking over her shoulder at Robbie. Robbie smiled tenderly at Melissa.

Rocky shook his head, "Oh man, you got it bad. You betta watch yo self."

"I don't know what you're talkin about, Rocky."

"Now ya know, God don't like ugly, and He don't like liars either." Both men laughed, then parted company.

*

The next six months were a blur for Melissa. She and Karen became best friends who did just about everything together. Usually, Robbie tagged along, finding any excuse to be around Melissa, which wasn't all bad because despite Robbie's short time as a Christian, he was a brilliant theologian and always willing to help Melissa with her coursework. Rocky joined the trio as often as possible, especially when there was a meal involved. Melissa loved listening to Rocky talk about theology, church history, and just life. For someone who couldn't remember anything prior to four years ago, Rocky had an incredible mind.

Melissa was aware that Robbie was attracted to her, but she felt a certain comfort in their relationship as it was. The two spent time together, but it was usually with Rocky or some other students present. Both Rocky and Karen were aware there was some chemistry between Robbie and Melissa, but they had learned to keep their mouths shut about it after a few harsh words from both of them. Rocky and Robbie were Melissa and Karen's guests for Thanksgiving and Christmas, and as the New Year drew near, Robbie and Melissa found they were spending more time together without Rocky and Karen than they did with them. By spring of 2004, Robbie and Melissa had fallen deeply in love which worried Melissa to no end.

During finals week that May, Melissa sat on the back porch of the duplex she shared with Karen. Rocky was inside using Karen's computer for a paper that was due. He stepped out on the porch with a sack of plums that Karen had picked up at the farmers market and looked up at the stars, which was exactly what Melissa was doing.

"Didn't figya you fo a stargazer little girl."

Melissa was startled, having been lost in thought. "Oh hey, Rocky, what's up?"

"Jus finished wit dat paper for Soteriology we had due."

"Yeah." Melissa said half-heartedly, "I just finished mine yesterday. What'd you mean about stargazing?"

"Oh, jus something I like doin' maself, I think it come from ma before life. I jus' like ta sit under da stars and look up at em', think about what it mus be like not bein bound to dis body on dis here earth. Sometime I look at those sci-fi shows dae got on TV an I realize even lost people can tell da story bout Jesus wit out even knowin' it." Matrix, Star Trek, Star Wars, all of em jus tell da story bout how Jesus come ta save dis world, but lost people jus cain't find it within demselves ta call it what it is. It's da savin' power of our Lord. You can call em' Luke Skywalker, or Neo Anderson, or Captain Kirk, but dae jus talking bout Jesus, dats all."

Melissa had never thought about it like that, but it made sense to her, and rather than fill the moment with an impertinent response, the two of them leaned back on the porch and gazed into the stratosphere. Ting, ting, ting, Rocky managed to spit several of the plum seeds into a coffee can near the porch. "Rocky, do you think I should marry Robbie?"

"Well, I spec somebody's gotta marry the pathetic thing, might jus as well be you."

Melissa slapped Rocky on the shoulder, then leaned into him, wrapping her arms around his thick neck, "I love you, Rocky Jo Bob."

"Yep, I spec you do, little girl, I spec you do."

*

Fall weddings can be fantastic and naturally beautiful as the leaves begin to change colors and the air becomes cooler. Robbie and Melissa were married on a cool Saturday in October, with Karen as the maid of honor and Rocky Jo Bob Eubanks as Robbie's best man. The ceremony was long but the guest list was short. The couple possessed limited resources and it was mostly family and a few close friends in attendance. A small chapel in McKinney, Texas, served the couple's needs well. The white building with green trim had a pulpit which faced ten rows of pews on each side of the building. Recorded music piped through the room as Robbie and Melissa exchanged the vows they wrote for each other. The wedding was picture perfect, set in a small town that made one think of everything nostalgic in the new hope of a new love.

What the wedding lacked in excitement, the first year of marriage had in spades, but it wasn't the kind of excitement newlyweds would have hoped for. They had love in abundance, but neither Robbie nor Melissa had fully understood what they had signed up for. Delusions about happily ever after dissolved into the real complicity of two lives merging violently into one. Having set themselves up for disappointment with expectations of marital bliss, anger and resentment settled in as Robbie began to realize he had not married a princess and Melissa realized she had not married a knight in shining armor.

Melissa struggled in school because Bible College required a type of analytical thinking she was not accustomed to. She often needed clarification about assignments that many other students understood intuitively. Melissa looked at the world very literally and it was not uncommon for her professors to become impatient with her wooden interpretation of matters that were meant to be understood figuratively. Robbie struggled to understand the fundamentals of Christian marriage. He loved Melissa dearly, but he did not understand how to support her through difficulties in school. Robbie was a natural academically, and with an exquisite analytical mind, he fit right in at Criswell. At home, he always managed to say or do the wrong thing, which sent Melissa over the top with anger.

There were also misunderstandings about their roles within the marriage, so they argued almost constantly. After one such argument, Melissa stormed out of their one bedroom apartment stating she'd had enough. She returned at two o'clock in the morning after spending several hours with Karen, who refused to accept Melissa's decision to bail. When she returned, she found Rocky laying a blanket over Robbie, who had fallen asleep on the couch. Melissa paged through Robbie's Bible, which was lying on his chest and found that it was highlighted in several sections of Ephesians, Genesis, and Corinthians. Each of the highlighted sections dealt with the marriage covenant. Melissa knew Robbie was trying, but she was simply ill equipped to handle the marriage.

Robbie and Melissa knew they were in over their heads in marriage and that they needed some help. Melissa approached her Christian Counseling professor to see if he could counsel them through their marriage difficulties. The Professor was not available but advised her to consider Rocky Jo Bob as a counselor. In a pervious semester, Rocky had written a term paper on marriage and family based upon the Book of Ephesians that he described as nothing short of brilliant. He said that although Rocky had no formal training in family counseling, he could at the very least give them some guidance from a scriptural basis that would surely be helpful.

Rocky began to counsel the two on marriage weekly. His lack of counseling credentials was not a problem because the newlyweds couldn't afford a credentialed counselor anyway. Therefore, the arrangement was perfect. Melissa brought home an extra Chick-Fil-A meal from work on Tuesdays and Wednesdays, and Rocky would open up the Bible and talk to them about the marriage covenant designed by God in Heaven for man and wife. Slowly over the next several months the marriage got on the right track.

On March 1, 2005, Robbie came down with a nasty strain of flu that was going around, and Melissa was terrified. Robbie came home from class with a headache and feeling hot. Melissa took his temperature and it was up to 101. She gave him some Tylenol and sent him to bed without studying - Robbie did not protest. He tossed and turned for a few hours, and when Melissa took his temperature again it was up to 103. She got Robbie into the car and started off to

St. Luke's Emergency Room, which was a few blocks away. She'd called Rocky before leaving, and by the time she arrived, he was there with his book bag, ready to stick it out for the night. As Robbie was being treated, Rocky read his Bible, and preached to Melissa about divine healing, faith, and prayer. Melissa responded with a battery of questions, which Rocky answered as best he could. In fact, he answered in a way that she understood better than when she questioned her professors at school.

She fell asleep with her head on Rocky's shoulder and awoke to see him stare at a woman in a way she had never seen him look at anyone before. Rocky didn't know why he responded to the strange woman the way he did, but Melissa was certain it had something to do with Rocky's mysterious past. Melissa decided right then that with all Rocky had done for her and Robbie; she was going to learn Rocky's true identity.

Chapter 9

Boy Meets Girl

Dallas
November 2004

As a child, Stacy often resented the wise counsel of her older brother Nick. Then there were days like today when she thanked God Nick had been there for her. Just four and a half years ago she had been determined to pursue police work like her father. However, Nick really did know what was best. Ray and Susan Bernard had borne only two children, spaced fourteen years apart. They thought they would only have one, but on February 14th, 1980, Stacy came charging into the world. By the time she was five years old, Nick was in his first year at Bethel College studying for ministry. By the time she was seven he was married. Her mother, Susan Bernard, died of heart failure when Stacy was nine. By the time she was twelve, her fathers tragic and sudden death left her orphaned. Nick and Morgan took Stacy in and raised her through the teen years and into adulthood. For all practical purposes, Nick and Morgan had been her parents.

Nick had talked Stacy out of pursuing police work, but Stacy discovered nursing on her own. She did a ride-along with the Dallas Police Department shortly after arriving in Dallas. After several trips to the hospital with the police officers she rode with, she fell in love with trauma room nursing. It became easier to accept the fact that she didn't have the right temperament for police work once Stacy found her true calling. Stacy poured herself into studying nursing at El-Centro College in Dallas's West End and was a prize student. During her first year of nursing school, Nick died a violent death, which only made Stacy more determined to succeed. She made it through with flying colors. Morgan had flown out to Dallas with Stacy's then teenaged niece, Alethea, the previous spring for the graduation.

*

Stacy finished a grueling sixty-minute cardio vascular workout at the St. Luke's fitness center and reached for the towel she had laid on top of the treadmill. From somewhere behind her came a baritone voice, "Hold up lady, that's mine."

Stacy turned to see a giant of a man stepping toward her at warp speed, sweating profusely with not a hair out of place. His dark olive complexion and perfectly straight teeth were a bit overwhelming at first. It's not that Stacy found him attractive. In fact, she thought he looked absolutely ridiculous, almost like he had a "pretty boy" make-over done on one of those TV reality shows. Stacy often found it interesting to see how white men in Texas reacted to her. Back home, where interracial dating was fairly common, white men hit on her regularly, but here they would take long lingering looks, but shy away from making a first move. "I'm afraid you must be mistaken, this is my towel, I just set it here a moment ago when I got off this treadmill."

"No, I'm afraid it is you who is mistaken, I set mine down right here on my way to the weight room a moment ago and this is it."

"Look, if you want it, it's yours. I'll get another one."

"I'm not trying to be a jerk, it's just that I know where I put my towel, that's all."

"Okay. Like I said, take it. I will get another one."

Another man who looked like one of those really in shape older guys approached the two. "Hey, Mitch, you left your towel over there on the Stairmaster and someone wanted to use that machine, so I thought I'd bring it to you."

"Hey, Bart. I didn't know you were here," said Mitch.

"I was on the leg press doing an undercover sting. Someone's been mixing up the dumbbells and the Chief assigned me to investigate." Bart poked fun at Mitch.

"Cute, Bart, very cute," Mitch fired back.

"Who's your friend?"

"I dunno, but she's not my friend, and after the way I just stuck my foot in my mouth she may never be."

"I'm Stacy Bernard, and you are?" Stacy turned toward Bart, but Mitch interrupted.

"John Mitchell, pleased to meet you."

"I was talking to the gentleman, but it's nice to meet you too."

"Oh, sorry."

Bart couldn't hold back a chuckle. "I'm Bart Gelical, pleased to meet you ma'am."

After four years, Stacy was still tickled by southern charm. Bart turned and walked away, leaving Stacy and Mitch standing in front of one another feeling a bit awkward.

"Look, I'm really sorry, that was stupid. I really am a nice guy, and that was just not like me."

"No harm done," said Stacy. "How do you two know each other?"

"We're both cops here at the hospital."

"St. Luke's employees huh, I'm surprised I haven't seen you around the emergency room. What shift do you work?"

"I work deep nights, Bart works middle shift."

"Oh, that would explain it, I work days. Well, I better get going, I'll see you around."

"Yeah, see you around Stacy."

Mitch shook his head as he walked away. Stacy walked in the other direction. *"What an idiot"* she thought, *"and so arrogant."* For the most part, Stacy loved her job and her new adopted city. There were some distinct cultural differences between Minneapolis and Dallas, and the contrast in weather was really easy to take. More than anything, Stacy enjoyed being in such a rich environment for Christianity. There were several Christian radio stations, it seemed there were three churches on every block, there were Christian book stores, and in general, people were much more inclined to express their Christianity in Dallas than in Minneapolis.

Although she had met a few interesting men at Oak Cliff Bible Church where she attended regularly, Stacy was not particularly interested in dating. She was young and had time to figure out what she wanted in a mate. There just didn't seem to be any hurry. Rather than pursue romance, Stacy had decided to master nursing and learn as much as she could on the job before considering either a Masters Degree in nursing, or medical school. When the time came to settle down she knew the man of her life would have to posses the unique qualities of gentleness, godliness, and leadership she saw modeled in her brother and in her father. Stacy had no delusions and knew it would be difficult to build a marriage as solid as Nick and Morgan's. Those two simply knew how to make a marriage work, and Stacy was not going to settle for anything less than what she saw in that marriage.

Oh, how Stacy missed her brother, his wise council, and the confident way he lived his life. It wasn't fair that the Lord took him at such a young age, with a little girl who was still dependent upon him. In a few months, Alethea would turn sixteen, and Stacy promised to be there for her sweet sixteen-birthday party. Stacy recalled Daisy's sweet sixteen and how disappointed Daisy had been that she didn't get a car for her birthday. There was so much tragedy there, with both Nick and Daisy dead, it was sometimes too difficult to go home and visit because of the thick aura of sadness that just kind of lingered in the air.

*

At six o'clock the following morning, Mitch gathered his belongings from the patrol car anticipating the end of a long shift. He had worked the deep night shift for five years and was very comfortable with the hours. But when the shift was over, it was time to head out. In the early days of Mitch's career with St. Luke's PD, he was aware that police officers were inclined to supplement their income with either part-time work or overtime. However, Mitch had his own philosophy about such things. He believed if a person could not make ends meet working forty hours per week, what they needed was a better paying job. Michael had changed all that. Although Mitch had no problem supporting himself and his wild night life on his police salary, child support added a monthly payment that sometimes necessitated overtime. As much as Mitch disliked working overtime, his responsibility to Michael trumped all such animosities. Therefore, Mitch occasionally volunteered for an extra shift if it came available.

Usually Mitch signed up for extra middle shift hours so he could start early and get done at his usual time, but today he filled in on the day shift. Mitch was assigned to patrol duties this morning which meant driving the squad car. The overtime shift would have been far more manageable if he had been assigned to the fishbowl where the duties were minimal.

Yesterday kept creeping into his thoughts. He'd made a complete idiot of himself at the gym and that woman no doubt thought he was some sort of racist. *"A racist, I'm half Cuban myself, why would I be a racist? And what was Bart of all people doing at the gym? The incident was embarrassing enough without Ned Flanders charging to the rescue."* As Mitch got behind the wheel of his police cruiser he decided to put the whole stupid incident out of his mind. It wasn't worth thinking about any longer.

Mitch did his initial checks of the cruiser, making sure the lights, siren, and police radio were in working order. Then he took inventory of the trunk and made sure all the necessary equipment was in place. Leg restraints, AED machine, Shotgun, Slim Jim, glass breaker, medical bag, it was all there. He put himself in service over the two-way radio and called out his initial mileage to dispatch, "1104 starting in vehicle number 89, mileage is 23277."

"Ten Four" the radio cracked, "Can you check a possible signal twenty in lot two? A visitor reported seeing a black female wearing dark blue sweats on the ground with a white woman near a Yellow Hummer. The caller says the black female looks homeless and may be trying to rob the other woman."

"Ten four, en route." Mitch replied.

*

Stacy stepped out of the shower and heard the radio she had left playing in her living room. Generally, Stacy kept the radio on all day tuned to either 100.7 the Word, or 94.9, one of Dallas' Christian music station. Rebecca St. James was singing; *"Wait for me, Wait for me darling, and I'll wait for you."* It was Stacy's theme song; she hummed along with the tune as she got dressed. She had learned not to put on her uniform until she got to work. Whenever she walked from the parking lot to the Emergency Room with her uniform on, she was stopped by about one hundred people on the way questioning her about where this or that was located on the hospital campus. It wasn't that Stacy didn't want to be helpful; she just knew that if she stopped every few feet to answer people's questions it would take forever to get to work, so she followed the advice of her coworkers and wore something else to work and kept a clean uniform in her locker.

Stepping out of her bathroom and into her bedroom with a towel around her midsection and another wrapped around her head, Stacy hummed and sang along with Rebecca St. James. Stacy had been twenty-one years old before she ever used makeup. It's not that she was a tomboy; she just never thought she needed it. Morgan and

Nick told her all the time that she had such natural beauty; there was no need to spoil it with a bunch of makeup. A lot of her friends in junior and senior high school used makeup, but after seeing what a hassle it was for them, Stacy decided it was convenient to believe her brother and sister-in-law.

Nick and Morgan were not just boosting Stacy's ego; she truly was a natural beauty. She was 5'9" tall, she never suffered from teen acne, and she had a deep brown complexion. Her almond shaped eyes were a soft brown, with long lashes and petite eyebrows. She kept her hair permed, not so much for aesthetic reasons, but because it was so much easier to manage when it was straight, neat, and no longer than shoulder length. Stacy never struggled with her weight; it didn't seem fair because her brother Nick had to work hard to keep the weight off. Stacy was never a big eater, and she loved physical activity, so the weight was easy to manage. As she grew into adulthood, she filled out nicely and her figure was almost perfectly symmetric. During high school, the boys simply would not leave her alone. Stacy was asked out for every dance and every prom the school held, but she turned down each invitation. She simply had no time and no interest in boys. Dressing up was fun, but she did so only for church and special occasions. For the most part, Stacy was a blue jeans and sweat clothes kind of girl.

Stacy left her apartment on Carroll Avenue and headed for the Hospital at around 6:15 so she would have time to get to work, change and be on duty by 7:00 AM. She parked in lot 44 and started the short walk to the Emergency Room. As Stacy crossed through lot 2 she heard the faint sound of someone crying. Stacy looked around and at first didn't see anyone. Then, as she passed one of those obnoxious looking new SUV's that were originally used for the army, she saw a woman sitting on the ground crying.

"Ma'am, are you okay? That always seemed like a stupid question to ask someone who was sitting on the ground crying, but Stacy didn't know what else to say.

"No, I don't think so." The woman said between sobs. "My husband is dying, and I don't think I'm handling it very well."

The woman was middle aged, about fifty or fifty-five years old. She was over weight, but meticulously well kept, her makeup and nails were flawless, and her hair had recently been done. Her head was lowered toward the ground, but she looked up long enough to see the attractive black woman standing over her. "I don't suppose this is a very dignified way to behave now is it?" The woman forced a smile and wiped the tears from her face, causing her makeup to run a little.

"Is there anything I can do?"

"No, I need to face this and be strong for my husband. I'm all he has and it doesn't help if I'm falling to pieces. He's taken such good care of me all my life and I think it's time I took care of him during these final weeks."

Working at a hospital was an excellent place to learn how people deal with death of all kinds. There were the sudden tragedies that often defined the deaths she saw in the emergency room. There, the suddenness of death was often the most dramatic. On the other hand, the slow anticipatory death of a cancer victim and the way the family dealt with their grief was also an interestingly sad study. Having suffered loss herself so many times, Stacy's heart went out to anyone going through what this woman was going through. A desire to help these very people is what drew her into nursing in the first place.

"Ma'am, do you have any family here with you? Is there a pastor or someone you can call? We have a chaplain here at the hospital. I can call him if you'd like."

"Thank you, that's very kind of you. It's just that I thought this would be easier, you know? No, I don't have a pastor or any family here. My husband and I are from Houston, we came here so he could receive a bone marrow transplant, but his body is rejecting the marrow, and it doesn't look like he will survive."

Stacy studied the woman for a moment, then said, "What's your name, sister, and what is your husband's name?"

"My name is Meredith, my husband is Calvin"

"May I pray with you?"

The woman's shoulders sank, her bottom lip began to quiver, and a flood of tears began to roll down her plump face, she was shaking uncontrollably. "Yes, yes, would you please pray with me?"

Stacy knelt down next to her new friend, "Father, You are the divine healer, the redeemer of souls, the one who makes all things work for His good. Lord take Meredith into Your loving hands and comfort her as only You can. This life holds many mysteries for us, but Father, You know all things. We pray that You would heal Calvin, we do not rely on the wisdom of men, doctors, and others who practice medicine, we rely upon You for strength and healing, that You may glorify Yourself in this situation. We offer this prayer up to You in the sweet name of Your son, Jesus the Christ, Lord of Lords, and King of Kings."

Meredith laid her head on Stacy's bosom and cried uncontrollably for a few more moments, then began to wipe away her tears. "Thank you. What's your name?"

"Stand up and keep your hands where I can see them." A familiar baritone voice came from behind them.

"What?" said both women in unison.

"Keep your hands where I can see them and stand up slowly."

Stacy said between clenched teeth, "Are you speaking to both of us, or one of us?"

"Don't get cute. Just stand up and keep your hands where I can see them."

Stacy stood up slowly and turned around facing the officer. She immediately recognized Mitch from their encounter at the gym, even though at that time he was not in uniform and was not pointing a gun at her head. "Oh great, you again. Just when I thought this day couldn't get any better." Stacy had gone from fear to rage within seconds.

"You know this man?" said Meredith. "What is his problem?"

"Ask him. It looks like I'm about to be arrested by St. Luke's finest."

"What are you doing here? What's going on?" Mitch took a step backwards fumbling to place his service weapon back in the holster.

"Those would have been excellent questions to ask before you decided to draw down on a couple of damsels in distress."

"Look, I'm sorry, I got a report…"

"And you saw a black woman on the ground with a white woman and…"

"Don't make this about race, I was just doing…"

"May I go now, or did you need to frisk me?"

Mitch did an about face, got in the cruiser, slammed the door, and sped off. "1104 to dispatch, everything is fine here, there was no problem, show me clear, false alarm." Mitch spat the words into the microphone.

Meredith was shaken and a bit angry. "I am so sorry about this ma'am. I never even got your name."

Stacy smiled at Meredith, "There's nothing for you to be sorry about. This was not your fault. My name is Stacy Bernard; I'm a nurse here in the ER. Look I gotta go."

"Stacy, I just want to thank you again, it's not often that you find someone who truly cares."

The two women hugged, then Stacy continued walking through lot two, while Meredith got in her truck and drove away.

Buffoon, thought Stacy.

Prude, thought Mitch.

*

Several days later when Mitch checked his department mailbox, he saw the usual annual company Christmas party invitation. He'd never gone to one of those parties and doubted he ever would. Although there would surely be a large number of single women there for him to meet, Mitch had a strict policy about not dating women from work. The Dallas social scene was booming for a young single adult, so there was no need to go sniffing around the worksite for action. Mitch took the invite and tossed it into the garbage can on his way out the door just in time for the cleaning crew to empty the can and wheel it away. It had been a miserable shift, and Mitch wanted to get home quickly, change out of his uniform, and go pick up Michael for the long weekend.

The phone rang shortly after Mitch walked through the door; it was Diane, a fitness instructor from the St. Luke's Health Care Facility Gym. Mitch and Diane had met a few weeks before when he took a yoga class that she instructed.

"I thought I would have to leave a message, don't you work nights?" Diane sounded surprised that Mitch picked up the phone.

"Usually, but I worked a little OT today on the day shift, so I just got home. I thought you'd never call. Have you been playin it cool with me?" Mitch softened his tone as he spoke to Diane.

"No, just been busy, by the way, how did you know it was me?"

"Welcome to the year 2004, caller ID."

"Oh, yeah. I was just calling to see if you were going to the St. Luke's Christmas party."

"I wasn't planning on it. I never do."

"Well, I was invited by a friend and was hoping you might be there."

"You have a friend that's a St. Luke's employee?"

"Yep, her name is…"

"I don't need to know, you can tell me all about it at the party next Saturday. It'll give us something to talk about."

"You don't strike me as someone who has trouble finding ways to make conversation, Mitch."

"Actually, I don't. But I find it more interesting to leave as many mysteries out there to discover as possible, even small details like the names of your friends."

"Okay, have it your way. I'll see you next Saturday."

"I'll see you then."

*

The holiday party was held on the seventeenth floor of St. Luke's main tower. The party was jam packed with St. Luke's employees and their guests. Mitch was not used to rubbing shoulders with people he worked with, and to be honest, it made him a bit uncomfortable, but he wanted to spend some time with Diane. He could see Bart and his wife Tosha in a quiet corner talking. It amazed Mitch that after being married some twenty years, they still seemed to be in love with one another. Bart got up and brought Tosha a glass of punch. When she stood up to use the ladies room, Bart got up, and held her chair as though it was a first date. When they talked they held one another's gaze with a tenderness Mitch didn't understand. *"What did people who had been married for over 20 years find to talk about, and how could they still be interested in one another?"* Thought Mitch.

Distracted by watching Bart and Tosha, Mitch almost forgot about Diane. He turned away from Bart and Tosha and then sauntered over to the bar to order a drink.

As Mitch backed away from the crowded bar, he bumped into someone.

"Whoa big guy, I'm right behind you." A familiar female voice addressed Mitch.

It was too late; Mitch had backed right into Stacy Bernard and spilled her virgin strawberry margarita all over her beautiful, festive green, formal gown. It was ruined.

"Oh man, I am so sorry, I didn't…"

"I should have known. You again."

"This is great. Look I'm sorry about your dress. I'll take care of the cleaning."

"You bet you will, Joe Friday."

Diane appeared out of nowhere, "Stacy, what happened to your dress?"

"Twinkle toes here just plowed into me. He seems to have a knack for making a complete fool of me whenever he can."

"You two know each other?" Mitch and Diane spoke at the same time.

Stacy's icy gaze bore into Mitch. "Let's just say, we've bumped into each other a time or two."

Stacy was absolutely stunning in her teal green evening gown. Her hair, piled high on her elegant head, dangled down in curly spirals from a cone-shaped design drawn together with thin braids. Her complexion was a deep luscious caramel; her almond shaped eyes were the deepest brown, with only a touch of eyeliner. Her lips were full, luscious red, and perfectly shaped. Had it not been for the huge stain Mitch had just deposited on her midsection, she would have looked like a runway model. Stacy took a napkin and gave the stain angry strokes, flicking margarita in several directions. She was madder than a hornet, and the more she tried to get the stain out, the angrier she became. The angrier she became, the more ridiculous she looked trying to salvage the dress and the evening. Mitch knew it was wrong, but he couldn't keep the laugh that was building in his belly under control.

Stacy's eyes narrowed as she stared at Mitch with complete contempt, "Now I know you are not about to stand here and laugh," she said, eyes boring into Mitch's forehead.

Mitch tried hard to suppress the laugh, but it was no use. "I'm sorry, but if you could just see yourself standing there wearing that margarita."

Diane began to laugh as well. "You do look kinda funny, girl." Stacy stood with her hands on her hips and her mouth wide open for a moment looking from Mitch to Diane. Suddenly, Stacy gave in and the three of them burst into hysterical laughter. When the laughter calmed down, Mitch grabbed another napkin from the bartender and offered it to Stacy who, smiling, accepted it.

"Mitch, this is my friend Stacy; Stacy, this is my date for the evening, John Mitchell." Stacy and Mitch shook hands and began to talk as Diane went to find a towel. The two talked for several minutes and when Diane returned, neither of them even noticed she was there. Diane, knowing how to take a hint, left the two alone and found someone else to dance the night away with while Mitch and Stacy continued talking. It was two o'clock in the morning, and the party was breaking up, but neither Mitch nor Stacy realized how much time had passed. They found each other completely engaging as though they would never run out of things to talk about. Over the next four weeks, they were rarely apart, leaving each other only to work and go to their separate residences to sleep. Whether it was in their plans or not, a new romance had begun.

Chapter 10

Ray Bernard

Minneapolis
May 25, 1992

ew things carry a more somber, sober mood than a police officer's funeral. On May 25, 1992, The Minneapolis Police Department mourned the loss of one of its own. A senseless act of cowardly violence in a neighborhood school had claimed the life a decorated officer, well respected by the department and the community he served. Raymond Nicolas Bernard's life came to an end in the city's most notorious school shooting. The heroic actions of Officer Bernard surely saved lives, but in the end, he lost his own.

An angry seventeen year-old with a chip on his shoulders arrived at Henry High School early in the morning of the shooting; he was on a mission and would not be deterred. Marching into the school through the doors that faced east toward Newton Avenue North, Alonzo Mason had murder on his mind. The school maintained an office for the Police Liaison on the first floor near the west entrance. It was a small office, but it was in the main hallway where the officer was accessible if needed. Alonzo attended North High School some four miles south of Henry, but his sweetheart Margarita Sarai attended Henry, and word got back to Alonzo that she had been dishonored by Troy Westin, one of Henry High School's varsity basketball stars.

It was lunchtime, and Alonzo walked through the main hallway and downstairs to the school cafeteria. Under the baggy shirt Alonzo wore, he carried a fully loaded Beretta nine millimeter handgun with four extra magazines. Alonzo had no plan to survive his assault, and he did not intend to allow Troy to survive either. The cafeteria was jam packed with students, teachers, and aids. The atmosphere was charged with the energy of youngsters taking a break from cerebral exercise. The volume rivaled that of a rowdy pep rally. It was difficult to see where his victim was, and Alonzo was running out of patience. He removed the Berretta from his waistband and raised it in the air which got the attention of everyone standing near him. Alonzo figured that if he fired a few shots in the air he could clear the room enough to spot Troy.

Students began to spread out like cockroaches. One of the students, Tyra Erickson, managed to flee upstairs in the commotion to the Police Liaison Office just as Alonzo's first shots rang out. Ray was not in uniform. He only wore his uniform on the first and last day of school; today being neither, Ray wore a sport coat, button down shirt with tie, and slacks, and no bullet resistant vest. Ray ignored Tyra's plea to come right away long enough to grab his two-way radio and call in to central dispatch for backup.

"This is 2104 Henry High School Liaison Officer Bernard, I need back up Code Three to the Henry High Cafeteria, shots have been fired. I repeat, shots have been fired."

"Copy that 2104, officers responding, come to channel four."

Ray heard the Alert Tone Oscillator, a piercing sound designed to get the attention of all officers monitoring a police radio. The dispatcher repeated the request for backup on all channels and the responses started pouring in on channel four. Ray shoved the two-way radio in his pocket and ran out the door and down the stairs to the school cafeteria.

*

Ray Bernard began his career with the Minneapolis Police Department June 11, 1962, with high hopes of changing the world. Two years later he married his high school sweetheart Susan Austin. On January 10, 1966, their first child, Nick, was born and fourteen years later on February 14, 1980, Stacy was born. Ray and Susan hadn't planned on Stacy. They had tried to conceive again shortly after Nick was born, but their prayers went unanswered. After a few years of trying, they assumed it just was not meant to be. When Stacy did finally come along, she was the most wanted baby girl in the world.

Ray, Susan, and four other families in south Minneapolis formed True Vine Church in the spring of 1970, with Pastor Terrell Jenkins. As an extra bonus, Pastor Jenkins agreed to work as a volunteer with the Police Chaplin Corps. Years later, Pastor Jenkins and Ray spent hours talking over Ray's plans for retirement. Ray considered Terrell Jenkins to be his closest friend, but when the Pastor advised Ray to take a desk job during his last few years with the department, Ray would have no part of it.

"I'm a cop, Terrell. That's who I am, and that's what I do. I can't be tied to no desk. It just won't do for me, that's all."

*

Ray rushed down the stairs and eased his way toward the cafeteria with his thirty eight snub nose revolver drawn and his back to the wall. Ray could hear the raised voice of a teenaged boy demanding to know where Troy Westin was hiding. Ray inched his way along the wall and poked his head around the doorway of the cafeteria to get a look inside. He could see the boy holding the gun was young, and he looked scared. The boy's voice quivered when he spoke and his hands were visibly shaking. Ray inched his way inside the cafeteria at a ninety degree angle and was able to see the boy's face for the first time. Ray knew this child, and he didn't believe Alonzo Mason was a killer.

"Alonzo, it's me, Elder Bernard from True Vine."

Alonzo snapped around and faced Ray, "I got no problem with you or anyone here, Mr. Bernard, but I intend to kill Troy and I will take out anyone who gets in my way."

"Alonzo, listen to that sound, do you hear that?" The distant wail of several police sirens bearing down on the school nearer by the second was impossible to miss, even in the basement.

"Yeah, I hear it, and I don't care about dying, and I don't care about killing. This is a bad place for you to be, Mr. Bernard."

"There's nowhere else for me to be right now, son. This is it. How about both you and I walkin' outta here today in one piece?"

For the time it appeared as though Alonzo was considering Ray's proposal, but it was only a matter of minutes before most of the Minneapolis Police Department would file into the room. Ray Bernard's thirty years of police work confirmed in him that Alonzo's resolve was weakening.

"Alonzo, you've always been a reasonable person. Don't you think we can talk about this?"

Alonzo was beginning to sweat profusely. His hands shook violently, and he started to cry.

"Look, Alonzo, I'm putting my gun back in my holster. I just want us to talk this through."

"I don't wanna go to jail, but Troy deserves to die for what he did." Alonzo said.

Just then Alonzo spotted Troy Westin under a table near Raymond. Alonzo stopped shaking and a look of determination came over him once again. Alonzo found his target and raised the Berretta.

Raymond realized his window of opportunity had just closed. He stepped toward Troy, but spoke to Alonzo.

"It doesn't have to go down like this Alonzo, if you don't drop that gun the officers coming will shoot you."

Alonzo didn't lower the gun. Troy froze right where he was. Raymond suddenly realized he had made a bad decision. Alonzo was no longer listening to Raymond, and Raymond had put his weapon away as a gesture of good faith in the negotiation. Raymond began to remove the revolver from his holster. Alonzo realized what Ray was doing and pointed the gun in his direction. As Ray's hand found the revolver, Alonzo fired two shots into Ray Bernard's chest. In a moment of confusion, Alonzo lowered the weapon as dozens of kids, faculty, and school aids tackled him and took the Berretta out of his hand. Just three weeks from retirement, Raymond Bernard was dead. Officers arrived on the scene as Alonzo was being restrained; one of the responding officers was rookie Mel Sanders.

*

Officer Mel Sanders had never seen so many cops in one place at one time in his life. There were literally hundreds of police officers from every department in Minnesota, and several from around the region. The Minnesota State Troopers wore their dress uniforms, a rich burgundy color with shinny black paten-leather belts and boots. The St. Paul Police Department had sent over half their force, some three hundred in all. There were even Canadian Mounted Police. The procession, which led from the Fourth Precinct in North Minneapolis to True Vine Church on 54th Street and Chicago Avenue in South Minneapolis, included six hundred thirty police vehicles with light bars going in full rotation. Mournful citizens lined the streets along the fifteen mile stretch with signs which read, *"We will never forget you Ray"*, and *"Thanks for thirty years of service to our community."* Mel Sanders never felt so proud in his life.

After a tear-jerking sermon preached by Pastor Terrell Jenkins, the procession began to make its way to the gravesite with Ray's coffin leading the way. At the gravesite, Mel saw Raymond's two children, twenty six-year-old youth pastor Nick Bernard, and his younger sister, twelve year old Stacy Bernard. The Bernard family found a special place in Mel Sanders life that day, and he determined he would never forget the sacrifice they had made. Nothing compares to beginning a police career by watching another officer die and attending their funeral. The only thing that thing that makes such a situation more dramatic is when the slain officer was your Field Training Officer, as Ray was to Mel.

Ray taught Mel Sanders the ropes before he went to work in the School Liaison Unit. Each Minneapolis Police Officer works with five field-training officers over a period of five months. Ray Bernard was Mel's final field training officer. It was Ray who taught Mel the finer points of street survival, but more than that, Ray taught Mel to have a heart for people and not to forget why he put the badge on in the first place.

"Kid, don't let anyone convince you the people you deal with every day don't matter. It's not a question of how much money they have or even if they have a job; they are all people for whom the good Lord died. Our job is not to judge them, but to serve and to protect. Whatever you do on this job, remember, if it doesn't lead to serving and protecting the citizens of Minneapolis, then you have no business doing it. Treat people with dignity and respect regardless of where they come from, and you'll do fine in this business."

Mel respected the fact that Ray was bold with his beliefs. It could be that he was so bold because he was so close to retirement, but Mel respected him just the same. The day Ray Bernard died; Mel made a promise to himself to look after Ray's family as best he could.

*

In the spring of 2001 Mel Sanders had been promoted to Sergeant Investigator in the homicide unit. On June 5, 2001, Mel was to assigned squad 1110, the homicide car, when he received a call on his two way radio to check out the skeletal remains of two people found in a burned out car in the alley behind the First Avenue Bar in Downtown Minneapolis. Mel was particularly interested in this call because Morgan Bernard had reported her husband Nick missing four days before. In an odd coincidence their neighbor's seventeen year old daughter, Daisy Dawson, had gone missing with the family car at about the same time. Mel made his way downtown as quickly as possible; he decided not to call Morgan until he had something to report. Mel hoped Ray Bernard's son was not one of the two bodies in that car, but he had a bad feeling, and those bad feelings of his were rarely wrong.

As Mel pulled into the alley, one thing was perfectly clear. The burnt out car was not a 2001 Cadillac which the Dawson's had reported missing along with their daughter. The car was an older model Ford that had been burned hot. Mel was no arson investigator, but it was obvious someone had used an accelerant to torch this car in order to make it burn faster and hotter. The bodies inside the car were badly burned and it would take a while before anyone would be able to make a positive ID, even then it would take dental records to be certain. The stench in the alley was thick and pungent. The car continued to smolder as officers gathered evidence. A preliminary search of the area indicated there were spent shell casings on the ground, and blood splatters on the wall behind the bar.

The next day, Mel got a call from the Bureau of Criminal Apprehension saying serology results, which would reveal blood type and some DNA information, were not in yet, but that they were certain it was a male and a female in the car. They also determined the two were more than likely dead from gun shot wounds before the fire started; both took point blank hits to the head. So far, it was beginning to look more and more like this was the Dawson girl and Nick Bernard in the car, but Mel could not figure out how the two found themselves in an alley behind a downtown bar.

The serology results came back in two weeks and concluded there was blood and DNA at the scene from both Nick Bernard and

Daisy Dawson, but the actual DNA tests on the bodies, which was a much more expensive set of tests, had not been completed. Lt. Mackland, head of the Minneapolis Police Homicide Unit, closed the case and determined the additional tests were unnecessary. The bodies matched the gender, height, weight, and ethnicity of two persons reported missing during the same weekend, and blood and other body fluids from both victims were found at the scene.

After going over the statements taken from Morgan and Alethea Bernard, and the Dawson's, Mel determined that Nick must have interrupted the killers in the process of abducting the girl and was shot in the Dawson's driveway. The killers must have taken both Nick's and the girl's bodies to the alley in order to dispose of them by torching the car. Traces of Nick's blood were found in the Dawson's driveway, and the house had been ransacked and burglarized. Sam Dawson had reported a large cache of government bearer bonds were taken from the home in the burglary and the car was never seen again.

Mel closed the case, but in his heart, he was never comfortable with it. Mel felt the department had done Ray Bernard, a man who had given his life for the city, a disservice in the investigation of his son's death.

Chapter 11

Digger

Minneapolis
June 2, 2001

Roger "Digger" Jones was having a great day. His grocery cart was full and overflowing with cans, he'd eaten a good meal at the Salvation Army Harbor Lights shelter, and he had plans to spend the night in Elliot Park with some friends. Life was good. After picking through the dumpsters behind the City Center Shopping Mall, Digger headed over to the warehouse district where most of the downtown bars were located. Homeless life in Minnesota was not bad in the summer, and this was a particularly nice summer in Minneapolis, but Digger had plans to move on soon. He'd been in Minneapolis this time for one and a half years and was getting restless.

Digger, as he was known by the local cops and shopkeepers, would breeze into town every two to three years, then leave as suddenly as he had appeared. No one knew for sure where he came from or where he went when he left Minneapolis. No one even knew for sure what his real name was. Digger was a transient homeless person who didn't drink, do drugs, or commit any serious crime. The worst thing Digger was guilty of was irritating the downtown nightlife with his loud and bold preaching. Digger preached till his voice went out or until one of the beat cops told him to move on and stop bothering folks. But in truth, Digger was never really a bother to anyone. For the most part, if someone was not in the mood to hear Digger preach, he just moved on by himself.

It was Saturday night and Digger walked south on Hennepin Avenue toward Ninth Street. Having saved nearly three hundred dollars, which he kept in a rented locker at the bus depot, Digger wanted to purchase a one-way ticket out west to visit friends he hadn't seen in a very long time. Digger turned the corner at Ninth Street and Hennepin and headed west toward the Greyhound Bus Depot. He moved faster than most people would have expected. In fact Digger was in excellent shape for a homeless man. Staying in good shape had kept him alive on the streets for years. Digger was just shy of six feet tall, and was a muscular 195 pounds. He had a dark completion and his short nappy hair that looked like it had never been combed. Although he was dirty most of the time, when offered a shower at the shelters, he always accepted. Another key to Digger's survival was that he had learned to get along with other homeless people on the street; he never kept anything on him that someone else would want to take. And he kept his mouth shut unless he was preaching to the masses.

Skillman and Strong, the two Minneapolis Police Beat Officers who patrolled the area spotted Digger as he made his way onto Hawthorne Avenue.

"Hot Diggity Dog, what's the word Digger?" Strong smiled as he made his greeting.

"What's goin on preacher man?" said Skillman."

Digger knew the two cops well. They were nice guys so long as you played it straight with them and didn't break the law on their beat. When he had rolled into town for the first time back in 1985, it was Skillman and Strong who told Digger where the homeless shelters were and explained to him how to stay on their good side. Digger listened well and was always glad he did. Whenever there was something going down on the streets, Digger would give the two cops whatever information he had.

"Just praisin' my God. How bout you two brothas, you doin okay?"

"Same ole same ole," said Strong, "I see you're headin' for the depot. You pullin' up stakes again?"

"Gotta keep movin. Cain't stay in one place too long. You know me."

Skillman smiled and leaned close as he spoke, "Tell me somthin' good before you leave Digger."

Digger thought for a moment. He rubbed his chin, then looked at the two cops. "Look, rumor has it Razor's puttin together some muscle to start pullin' some jobs on the Southside. That's all I know. He may have some bad dude getting outta OPH that's hookin' up with em. That's all I know."

"When you think you're comin' back again, Digger? Next year maybe?" Skillman asked.

"Dunno, Lord willin', I jus might."

"When you plan on leavin' this time, Digger?" said Strong.

"If they got a bus leaving tomorrow for where I'm headin', I guess I'll leave then. You fellas take care now."

"Later, Digger." The two cops went on their way, and Digger walked into the bus depot to purchase his ticket.

It was getting late, but when Digger left the depot and headed toward Seventh Street, he decided to check out the First Avenue's dumpster for more cans. Because of the teenybopper clientele they catered to, the First Avenue was one of the bars in the area that still used aluminum beer cans, so Digger knew he could make one last good score there before leaving town the next day.

The huge dumpsters outside the First Avenue were wide and deep. If they were full, one had to dig around through a lot of trash to find the precious aluminum cans that brought in a price of thirty cents per pound; but if the dumpster was only partially full, one would have to do more climbing in order to get to the bottom without injuring themselves. Many of the homeless people who were alcoholics would fall in due to their state of intoxication, or they would crawl in sober, find some unconsumed beverages inside, then fall asleep inside the dumpster drunk. Staying too long in a dumpster could be deadly. If the trash collector picked up the dumpster while someone was inside, they could be dumped into a rolling compactor and killed.

Digger smiled as he passed the old broken down Ford parked in the alley. The Minnesota winters had gotten to the body and it was rusted through on the bottom. Digger had once owned one of those cars back when he was a teenager. He used the rear bumper of the car to climb up to the edge of the dumpster, then he eased himself down inside. The sun had gone down so it must have been after nine o'clock at night. It was difficult to see inside the dumpster but Digger felt a few cans toward the bottom. He had decided to start pushing some of the trash around the bottom to look for more cans when he hard the rear door to the bar open and close. Digger wasn't particularly worried about anyone finding him in the dumpster. Most of the time, if he encountered an ornery janitor they would just holler at him and tell him to get outta there. But rather than deal with the hassle, Digger figured he would just wait it out and see if it was just someone out to have a smoke or something. Digger listened as the two people who came out the back door began to talk.

"What's that for?"

"Hand me your purse with the car keys, Daisy. Who have you told that you were meeting me tonight?"

"Who did you tell?"

"Nobody, do you think I wanted to advertise what I was planning to do? I didn't tell anyone, what do you want from me?"

"I want you to give me your purse, the car keys, and I want you to die"

"What?"

Digger heard the unmistakable sound of a muzzled pistol and a body falling, followed by the sound of the door opening and closing again.

"Man, you are one cold blooded dude." Ricardo Garcia had just walked out the back door to the bar. "I heard the whole thing."

"Yeah, whatever, gimmie the keys and help me get her into the trunk, the more she bleeds out here, the more we may have to clean up. If she only bleeds out a little, I aint gonna worry about it so long as it doesn't draw attention." While Ricardo was impressed with what had happened, Ellum showed no signs that killing was anything more than a part of doing business.

Eve Ann

In a panic, Digger scrambled to his feet, knocking several glass bottles against the wall of the dumpster. He kicked his way to the top of the dumpster and over the side.

"What was that?" asked Ricardo. "Look, that bum. He's running over there."

Ellum lifted the automatic and took careful aim at the back of Digger's head, he squeezed the trigger and Digger dropped onto the concrete alley floor.

Digger experienced unusual warmth like nothing before. It wasn't like feeling warm, it was more like being warm. He had a sensation of comfort and relaxation as he had never imagined. He heard, no, he felt, a soft voice beckon him, drawing him within the source of the voice. He saw nothing, heard nothing, was confused by nothing, and yet was aware of everything. The voice beckoned, "Come Roger, you who were weary and heavy laden, come enter into my perfect rest. Come, thy good and faithful servant."

-And he was gone-

*

Ellum lowered the gun. "Help me get 'em over here, we better put 'em in the trunk with the girl. Come on, stop staring. We've got work to do."

The two men dragged both bodies to the trunk of the Granada. One of Daisy's sandals slipped off her foot as they dragged her body head first toward the Granada. The sandal landed in the streak of blood that oozed out the gaping exit wound in the back of her head. When they reached the trunk of the car, Ricardo opened it and the two men dropped her inside. They repeated the process with

136

Digger's body. In the back seat of the Granada were three full five gallon cans of gas, Ricardo opened the back door and reached for the gas cans.

Ellum grabbed his arm, "Not yet. Just close the trunk. I wanna be on the highway before anyone starts poking around this bonfire. Get her purse, and check his pockets for anything that looks like an ID. Don't worry about that shoe or the blood; it's not enough to draw attention. They'll probably find the burning car before they find that stuff anyway. Ricardo searched Diggers pockets, grabbed the bus ticket, closed the trunk lid, then joined Ellum in front of the Ford.

Ellum and Ricardo walked to the front of the bar where Razor was waiting. Ellum spoke first, "You ready for a brief vacation to a warmer climate?"

Razor smiled, "Yup. Is the deed done?"

Ellum gave Razor a look bewildered look, "I can't believe you feel the need to ask."

"Just checkin'. Let's roll."

The three men got into the Cadillac with Razor behind the wheel, Ricardo riding shotgun, and Ellum in the rear. Ellum removed a black revolver which he carried as a back-up weapon from his front pocket and laid it on the back seat. He poked his head into the front compartment of the Cadillac, "Did you get my travel package like I asked?"

Razor returned Ellum's look of bewilderment, "I can't believe you feel the need to ask." He handed Ellum a brown paper sack with two ice-cold forty ounce bottles of beer inside. Ellum smiled with delight, and tore the bag open.

*

It was no random chance that led Ellum to Daisy Dawson, it was sheer persistence. For the price of admission into the First Avenue and a cheap cocktail, Razor had gathered valuable information about a middle-aged mail carrier who kept a huge stash of government bearer bonds in the den of his south Minneapolis home. One of Daisy's classmates had proofread a Civics report Daisy had done on government bonds and thought it was interesting that her father invested so much in them and that he didn't keep them in a bank safe deposit box. Daisy explained that her father simply felt more in control if he kept his valuables at home where he could keep an eye on them. Later Razor allowed the teen entrance into the First Avenue, then quizzed her in a conversational way about her neighbor's habits. The teen offered the information she had learned from Daisy, thinking she was just making enough conversation with the ugly bouncer to get rid of him, never realizing she was leading the lamb to the slaughter. For a few more cheap drinks, Razor managed to get Daisy's phone number, which he passed on to Ellum, who was in prison at the time.

Ellum dialed the number almost a dozen times, reaching Sam and Kristen Dawson, and nearly all the Dawson children, before finally getting Daisy to answer the phone. When she did, Ellum laid on the charm, claiming to have accidentally dialed the wrong number. Over the months that followed, Ellum couldn't believe his luck as Daisy told him that her father had just paid cash for a brand new Cadillac. Ellum needed cash to get started once he was released from prison, and this little girl had just opened the door to cash and a car that would bring even more cash. Clear title on a brand new Cadillac was rare but in the southern states, Ellum knew he could sign off on the title as Sam Dawson and sell the car at a good price. If he managed to keep the girl's death a secret for a few days, he could make it out of town without being stopped in the car, so torching Ricardo's beat up Ford with the girl inside was the smartest option. Ellum planned to be long gone before anyone missed the Dawson girl.

Over six months Ellum developed a relationship with Daisy and managed to gain her trust. He knew her parents were very religious and would not approve of her talking to him; he used that to his advantage. The more he told her how wrong it was for her to spend time talking to a sinner like him, the more she seemed to relish the idea. Daisy Dawson was putty in his hands. He would have those bonds and the car even though it would cost Daisy her life.

*

By the time the threesome arrived at the Dawson home, Ellum had consumed both forty ounce bottles of beer and his bladder was full. As soon as Razor had stopped the car, Ellum ran behind the Dawson's garage to relieve himself. When Ellum finished his business behind the garage, he found Razor and Ricardo speaking with a nosy neighbor. For Ellum, situations like this did not call for a plan or a discussion. Situations such as this required an immediate response. Ellum found some landscaping timbers on the ground next to the garage. He still had the automatic pistol in his waistband, but he didn't want to take the chance of drawing attention before he had found and removed the bonds from the house. Ellum walked up behind Nick Bernard as quietly as he could. When Nick turned around, Ellum stuck him in the head hard. He did not want this man to wake up in the back of an ambulance giving a description of his attackers before he had made his getaway. The last thing Ellum wanted was to blow his chances of selling the Cadillac. The nosy neighbor had to go, and he had to go now.

"That was pretty smooth," said Razor after the bludgeoning. "It looks like you just made our cool car pretty hot."

"Watch your mouth, Razor, and help Poncho here get him in the trunk. We'll bring him back to the old Ford, and just have a three for one barbeque."

"My name is Ricardo, not Poncho, okay?"

"Whatever, Poncho, just load up the body."

"You're starting to pile up the bodies, Ellum," said Razor. "We need to cut this out or we may never make it outta here."

"Shut your trap and do as I say. This doesn't have to be a problem."

Razor and Ricardo lifted Nick's body into the trunk as they were told. Ellum went into the house to Sam Dawson's den, right where Daisy had said the bonds were kept. Figuring out where the bonds were kept in the den was easier than Ellum had expected. He tapped the butt of his gun on the floor, and when he heard the hollow sound in a section of the floorboards. He pulled them up and removed a metal case which contained the bonds. Ellum walked out the back door to the house and saw Razor and Ricardo looking very anxious. He raised the metal case in the air in a gesture of triumph and his partners in crime were suddenly relieved. They got back into the Cadillac just as they filed out, and headed back downtown on 35W Northbound.

Razor popped the trunk on the Cadillac after backing into the alley right in front of the beat up Ford. Ricardo got out, opened the trunk, and began to pull on Nick's blood soaked T-Shirt to get him out headfirst while Ellum and Razor stayed behind talking. Ricardo leaned his entire weight into pulling on the T-Shirt, tearing it off Nick's bloody torso. When the T-Shirt tore Ricardo went flying backwards with the shirt still in his hands. He stumbled into the garbage dumpster knocking over several cases of beer and wine bottles outside the dumpster, then dropped the shirt near Daisy's sandal. Just then, someone opened the rear door to the First Avenue. Ricardo hid behind the dumpster. A janitor wearing a dirty gray uniform walked out the door partway, not able to see the trunk of the Cadillac from his angle, then, with the door open, he began to speak to someone inside.

"Do you want me to take out this garbage or not?"

"Yeah, just come back here a second, I need you to go back downstairs and help the guys down there move the inventory that just came in. It'll take about fifteen minutes of your precious time,"

"Alright, you're the boss."

The janitor slipped back inside, closing the door behind him. Ricardo ran from behind the dumpster and back to the Cadillac.

Ellum stuck his head up first and yelled at Ricardo, "Close the trunk and grab the gas. Hurry! We'll dump this guy when we get on the road. Let's get this barbeque started now and get outta here."

Ellum and Ricardo began to pour gas all over the Ford. They used two cans of gas just to soak down the inside of the trunk where the bodies were left. Ellum laid wood which was lying near the dumpsters on top of the bodies and soaked the wood as well. When all three cans were empty, Ricardo got back inside the Cadillac, and Ellum lit the fire with a single match. The car went up in flames immediately and produced a massive heat that was overwhelming. Ellum ran back to the Cadillac and Razor punched the accelerator.

Ellum spoke to Ricardo, "Did you fill up the tank on the Ford like I told you?"

"Of course. It's full."

"Good, then we should be hearing a loud…"

BOOM! The Ford blew up rear end first as the gang rounded the corner onto Hennepin. Ellum knew the heat and flames would consume the bodies and keep anyone from trying to put out the fire themselves. By the time the fire department responded, the heat in that trunk would have burned the bodies to the point wherein recognition would take quite a long time. The plan was working fine, but they had to get rid of the body in the trunk of the Cadillac. Ellum had already decided, the body would need to be dumped several states away in order to buy him the time he needed to stay cool.

Chapter 12

The Road to Groesbeck

Highway 35W
June 3, 2001

The Cadillac glided down the highway smoothly, and the gang was feeling good. They rode in silence through the first and second ring southern suburbs of Richfield, Bloomington, Burnsville and Lakeville before Razor spoke up, looking for approval from Ellum. "Did you notice Ricardo and I found some plastic in that garage to lay down under the neighbor's body?"

Ellum responded, "No, but that was good thinking, blood in the trunk draws more questions when we try to sell and it lowers the price. Now keep it within the speed limit, I don't need you getting stopped along the way. Let me see the ID"

Razor dug into his back pocket and handed the ID to Ellum. Inside was a well-done fake Minnesota Drivers license with Ellum's picture and Sam Dawson's name and address. "Well Mr. Dawson," started Razor, "You have one fine automobile here, oh and, I'm so sorry to hear about your lovely daughter." All three men laughed heartily.

Ricardo asked, "How much do ya think we can get for the Caddy, Ellum?"

Ellum sat back in the seat and thought for a moment, "We can mess up just as easily by asking too little as by asking too much. We need to look at the blue book and see what its worth, because if we don't ask enough there will be suspicion. Right now, I'd guess it's worth at least thirty-five to forty grand, but we'll check it a little more carefully when we get to Texas." The three men continued to ride in silence, stopping for fuel in Des Moines, Iowa, about five hours into their journey. Ellum took out Daisy's purse, removed two one hundred dollar bills and her identification, wiped the purse clean with his shirt, and discarded the purse in the gas station trashcan. He paid for the gas and some food for all three before they returned to the highway. They didn't stop again until reaching Kansas City, Missouri, where they once again refueled the Cadillac.

Eight hours into their sixteen hour trip south, Ellum told Razor to wake him before they reach Dallas because he needed to get some sleep. It was about seven o'clock in the morning, and Ellum figured they would reach Dallas by one or two o'clock in the afternoon. He needed to shut down for a while and plot out their next move. Ellum found his best ideas came when he was sleeping.

*

Ellum awoke quickly when Ricardo rubbed his shoulders. "Hey Ellum, get up man, we're here."

Ellum was groggy from the beer, but he sprung to life dismissing the fog in his head, "Where are we?"

"Denton," answered Razor.

"I told you to wake me up before we got to Dallas."

"This is before Dallas. I said we're in Denton,"

"Idiot, that's like sayin' we're in Bloomington, not Minneapolis. It's all the same thing, you moron. I wanted to dump this body before we got to the big city. Look, forget about it. Just keep drivin' south. When you get into Dallas, look for highway 45 heading north back outta Dallas."

"Alright," said Razor, "But I ain't gonna be too many more idiots and morons, man. You need to save that crazy talk for someone else."

"Just drive the car."

They continued to drive out of Dallas looking for a discrete spot to dump the body some distance from the city where they planned to sell the car and the bonds. It was Ricardo who saw the sign for Personville along Highway 164, "Hey that looks like a nice sleepy town."

"It's as good as any. I'm tired of wandering around this rural dump, pull over wherever you find a good place to dump him." Ellum was not in a good mood at all. Razor continued to drive until they came to the small town of Groesbeck. It was four o'clock in the afternoon, and people went about their business in the tiny town. Razor chuckled at the names of various businesses while Ellum kept his eyes open for a park or landfill.

"That's a good one, Bubba's Bee Line Bar-B-Q, what kind of hick joint is that?"

"I bet you can't get a decent burrito in this place," offered Ricardo.

"Pull into that alley," said Ellum. Razor turned into the alley behind Bubba's, it was quiet and deserted. Ellum ordered Ricardo to pop the trunk and the three men got out and hoisted Nick's body into the dumpster. After disposing of Nick's body, the gang closed the trunk and drove out of town and back toward Dallas.

They found a small neighborhood auto dealer in south Dallas where they sold the car for thirty-four thousand dollars. Ellum looked up a few of his old buddies, who directed him to a fence where they sold the bonds for fifty percent of face value which brought them another sixty thousand dollars in cash. Ellum did not want to risk questions by trying to cash the bonds legitimately, and he knew the fence would not cash them locally. As long as Ellum was on the run from the Minnesota Department of Corrections' supervised release, a suspicious transaction of bonds purchased in Minnesota and cashed in Texas could draw the authorities to look for him. Sam Dawson selling his Cadillac in Dallas would raise enough red flags.

The three men split the proceeds from the car and the bonds evenly and parted ways. Razor planned to get back to Minneapolis before his disappearance from the First Avenue Bar began to look suspicious, while Ricardo had family in Texas that he planned to look up. Ellum had plans of his own which he did not feel the need to discuss with the other two. He took his share of the money, and headed to that part of the city which bore his name.

Chapter 13

Stacy and Mitch

Dallas
March 2, 2005

Stacy was full of anger; she was full of righteous anger with Mitch. She had gotten in deeper with him than she knew better to, and it was beginning to backfire badly. She loved Michael with all her heart and sensed a strong presence of God within the child, even though she knew he was not of an age to make an informed decision. She also had very strong feelings toward Mitch and was frustrated that he did not see a reason to accept Christ himself. She never pushed, but she consistently kept her faith in front of Mitch – discussing Biblical passages or making relevant application from the Bible to everyday situations. Shortly after they met, Stacy brought Mitch to church with her. He seemed to enjoy himself. But Mitch refused to accept any further invitations. After witnessing the accident which nearly took the lives of Bart and Michael, and spending the night with Tosha, Joseph, Nate and Michael, Stacy felt the need to talk to Mitch with direct boldness.

The conversation had started as they left the hospital the hour before. Stacy had asked Mitch if he knew the man sitting with the cute white woman in the waiting room, but Mitch's response seemed to offend Stacy.

"What exactly do you mean when you say he was preachin' up a storm, Mitch?"

"Nothing. I just mean he had his Bible out and was raisin his voice and goin on about this and that – you know – slammin his hands on the chairs and all that stuff that preachers do."

"You say that like it's some sort of freakish thing, or like the man was somehow disingenuous."

"I am not implying anything, Stacy. Why are you so sensitive about this? Who is he to you?"

"He's my brother, Mitch. If he believes in and worships the same God that I do, he is my brother, and it just seems like you cannot understand what my faith means to me."

*

Mitch paused for a moment. It was one of those awkward moments between he and Stacy where Mitch knew he was on the outside looking in. There was something about Stacy's religion that was not satisfied with going to church on Sunday, dropping her money into the plate, and living her life. For Stacy, everything had spiritual overtones; everything could somehow be drawn back to her faith in Christ. Sometimes Mitch found Stacy's religion overbearing and unreasonable. He had learned to live with the fact that their relationship would not be a sexual one. Mitch was okay with waiting until they were married because for the first time in his life, he was beginning to feel that marriage was a possibility. What Mitch found difficult to live with was the pressure he felt to assimilate to her faith. Even though she did not directly pressure him, the way she talked and lived her life simply put him on the spot. Stacy's entire life was wrapped up in what she believed about God.

Mitch attempted a rebuttal, "I do understand what your faith means to you, Stacy. Your faith is what makes you the woman you are and what allows you to see beyond the man that I am. Your faith enables you to see the man that I could be. Your faith is what drives you to take such good care of Michael and me when you owe us nothing at all. Your faith is what I love about you. I understand what your faith means to you because I understand what your faith does for me. I just don't share your faith."

"Mitch, that was the sweetest and most tragic thing you have ever said to me." Stacy held Michael in a tight, tearful embrace as they rode in silence the rest of the way to Stacy's apartment.

When they arrived at Stacy's apartment she stormed into the shower while Mitch poured a bowl of cereal for Michael. Mitch didn't get it, why was she so upset? Michael was unusually quiet, and in his own little way he seemed to be upset with the way his father had treated Stacy. Michael wasn't very interested in his cereal.

"What's the matter buddy, don't you like the cereal?"

"If you weally love her, don't make her cwy." Michael pushed the cereal bowl away, got down from the table, and sat on the couch by himself.

Mitch was about to correct his son when he realized Michael may have been right. He also realized he had just told Stacy he loved her. Mitch had never done that before. Stacy was the first woman he had confessed love for. She was the first one he had considered marrying.

*

Stacy stood in the shower angry and frustrated; she didn't know what to do. Mitch was being a bonehead and there didn't seem to be anyway to resolve the situation. Suddenly, Stacy realized Mitch had said, "I love you." Stacy stopped scrubbing. This was a whole new game now and she was in over her head. She had never intended things to go this far. She had been using her relationship with Mitch as an opportunity to share the love of Jesus, not to pursue a relationship with an unbeliever. How did this happen – how did she let things get to this point, and what made him think that she would….. *"I love him, too. I have fallen in love with Mitch. It's not just about Jesus, and it's not just about Michael, I've fallen in love and started to yoke myself unequally with an unbeliever. No wonder I'm so mad. I am personally involved in the outcome. If Mitch doesn't choose Christ, then I have to choose to move on."*

Stacy spent another ten minutes on the floor of the shower crying because she had gotten too far involved with Mitch and because she had lied to herself. She had to do something and she knew she needed to be honest with Mitch – completely honest. She turned off the shower and wrapped a towel around herself. Stacy dressed and went out to the living room where Mitch and Michael sat. Without saying a word Stacy took Mitch by the hand and led him to her breakfast table where Michael's cereal bowl remained. She took a moment to gather her thoughts and to say a silent prayer. She looked Mitch in the eye, then found her voice.

"Mitch, what do you think is going on here? Why have I been so upset?"

Mitch could not hold her gaze. He looked down at the floor. "I guess I insulted you by the way I spoke of the preacher. I usually try to watch what I say about Christians because I know how you feel. Out of respect for you, I even try to watch what I say to Bart because I feel like I am betraying you if I make snide remarks about Christianity."

"So you think the issue is my sensitivity about Christianity or Christians?"

"Yes, I think I just say the wrong thing and stick my foot in my mouth sometimes."

Stacy was silent for a moment, "If I understood you correctly, you said you love me."

Mitch exhaled and scratched his head. "You heard me correctly Stacy, I do love you."

"Mitch, I would never marginalize your feelings as I know they are real, but I honestly don't think you and I understand love the same way. You see, I love you too Mitch, but for me love is not what I feel; love is about sacrifice and about seeking the higher good of the object of my love. Mitch, I love you enough to pray for you every day. I pray that someday you will know the love of Christ and that you will know how to love another human being with the sacrificial love that Jesus Christ demonstrated – not just felt – but demonstrated for humankind. I pray that God will give you eyes to see how he has sought you, loved you, and pursued you. Mitch, I pray that if death parts us this very moment, it will not be the last time I see you, but that we would enjoy eternity together with the creator of the universe. Do you understand what I am saying to you?"

"I think so."

"What do you think happened last night? What do you think Tosha was trying to say to you? Do you really believe all this is just a bunch of random occurrences?"

"I guess I'm not sure what's happening."

Stacy was crying again – gesturing with her arms – pleading with Mitch to hear her. "Mitch, four years ago on the same night, two people who were very important to me left this world. One was a seventeen year-old girl named Daisy. Someone put a gun to her head, and blew her brains out. She is dead now, and I loved her very much. She was one of the sweetest people I have ever known, but she waited too long to make a decision for Christ, and now I believe she is in the pit of hell suffering until the end of time and beyond. My brother Nick was the other person killed in the same incident. I know someday I will be with him again because he trusted in the Lord Jesus Christ and loved him with all his heart.

"Mitch, the events of the last twenty four hours are not random occurrences. God is trying to use these events to open your eyes. You say you love me and I believe you, but love is giving part of your hard earned money to bring real salvation to people in a land thousands of miles away. Love is mowing a neighbor's lawn when that same neighbor cursed you the day before. Love is praying for a co-worker who mocks your faith every chance he gets. Love is jumping in front of a speeding Corvette to save a child you have never seen. Love is hanging on a cross for those who hung you there. Love is not what you feel, it is what you do. Mitch if you love me, then love the God who created both me and you."

"In the end it doesn't matter how good you think you are. Mitch, just like my friend Daisy, if you haven't called upon the name of

Jesus, you will spend eternity breathing sulfer in never ending torment, regretting every chance you had to make things right between you and God. I'm not trying to scare you. I'm trying to get you to open your eyes – open your heart and let Jesus come in. The things I have said, I said because I love you too, Mitch."

He slumped back in his chair and fell silent for a moment before speaking. "You think God is trying to get me to open my eyes?

"Yes, Mitch, I do. I think God loves you much more than you can possibly know, and he does not want you to spend your eternity in hell."

"If God loves me so much, why doesn't He just make it so I go to heaven and not hell?"

"Because He loved you enough to give you free will to choose Him, or not to choose Him."

Mitch was silent for a while. He rubbed his face then turned his gaze back on Stacy. "If what you say is true, I just wish He would give me a sign."

Mitch and Stacy had forgotten about Michael, who jumped off the couch and crawled into his daddy's lap. Michael cupped Mitch's face with his two pudgy little hands and spoke directly into Mitch's face, looking him in the eyes, "He will show you, Daddy. Eve will show you."

Mitch and Stacy looked at each other curiously, "What does that mean, buddy?"

"I don't know." Michael shrugged his shoulders and slid down from Mitch's lap. He went back to the couch and continued watching TV.

"What was that all about?" asked Mitch.

"I have no idea, Mitch. Children's minds are much more open than ours and they often understand the things of the Lord with better clarity than we do. On the other hand, it could just be some sort of four year-old nonsense. Regardless, you ought to think about what we have talked about."

"I will, Stacy."

Stacy turned off the TV and scooped Michael up in her arms. Mitch followed and the three of them headed for the door. Stacy turned and spoke to Mitch before they got to the door. "Do you ever wonder why Maggie has been so easy going with you about Michael?"

"Kinda. Do you know why?"

"The first time I went to pick up Michael, she was downright hateful toward me. At first I thought it was because of my color. Then I realized it was only because she had all of her self esteem tied up in her attachment to you. We sat and talked that night. She had been visiting a Baptist church there in Ennis and was trying to understand what it meant to be a Christian. She saw the cross on my necklace and asked if I was a Christian. I told her I was and she asked if she had to forgive you in order to become a Christian. I told her that becoming a Christian would give her the power to forgive, and the power to let go, but that doing so would not make her a Christian. We prayed together that day and she accepted Christ. Maggie is so loving toward you because of her love for Christ, Mitch."

*

The drive back to St. Luke's was as silent as their drive to Stacy's apartment. This time the silence was not due to tension between

Stacy and Mitch, it was the result of Mitch wrestling with all of what Stacy told him. Mitch wasn't sure what he believed anymore. He knew it was strange to find that Bart of all people had prayed for him, and although he had a suspicion Stacy prayed for him, it hadn't occurred to him that she prayed for him the way she described. Mitch had never considered the possibility of a real God, but the one thing he was certain of is that the Christians he had dealt with in the past day or so were serious about their faith.

Stacy had admitted she also loved Mitch, yet rather than creating a celebratory mood between them, love had introduced an insurmountable problem into their relationship. Mitch knew nothing of the love Stacy talked about. In Mitch's world, people took care of themselves and those who they had some obligation to. Mitch had learned not to put himself in a position where he would be obligated to anyone, but according to Stacy obligation meant nothing.

The whole idea was foolishness to Mitch. If there was a creator of the universe, He wouldn't want anything to do with the likes of Mitch, let alone pursue Mitch as Stacy suggested. Cops are capable of some heroic stuff, but it didn't make sense that Bart, a man with three sons, a wife, and a child on the way, would sacrifice his life for the life of a child he didn't know. It also didn't make sense that a good and just God would allow an innocent seventeen year-old girl to spend eternity in hell if someone like Mitch could go to heaven just by saying some prayer to Jesus. Mitch had a lot to sort out.

*

"Nick would know what to do now," thought Stacy. Nick always knew what to do or say at a time like this. As long as Stacy could

remember her big brother had been leading people to Christ. Nick talked to everyone he met about Jesus. It didn't matter where he was or what the circumstances were, Nick found a way to talk about Jesus. He had such a loving way with people that they first responded to Nick, then – and most importantly – to Jesus. Stacy remembered attending her older brother's youth group and watching as the other kids responded to the message of Christ and the way Nick interacted with them. Her father was so proud when Nick decided to take over as youth pastor of the church, but Nick felt ill-prepared and thought people would see nepotism in the appointment. Ray Bernard tried to assure his son that it was his heart for the lost, and in particular his heart for children that earned him the position on the True Vine Staff, and not the fact that his father was an Elder.

Nick was ordained by the church at the young age of twenty-two, but he never received the formal training he felt was necessary to do the job well. Nick received his Bachelors Degree from Bethel College and planned to attended seminary, but life kept getting in the way. He was a brilliant student with a particular love for historical theology. Although Nick was never comfortable in the pulpit, the few times Pastor Jenkins let him preach, the sermon was well received by the congregation.

After some of the rough spots in Nick and Morgan's marriage were smoothed out, Nick devoted a portion of his time to marriage counseling, and he was very good at it. He was especially gifted with taking unsaved couples that came to the church for either pre-marital or marital counseling, and leading them to Christ. Stacy felt certain that if Nick were there now, he would know how to talk to Mitch. Nick would help Mitch understand the importance of the decision to reject Christ.

Stacy missed her brother, and although she didn't think about him every day, today she wished he were near. It had been a long time since Stacy had thought about Daisy. After speaking with Alethea, following the funeral, Stacy felt certain Daisy never made a decision for Christ. Alethea had taken her father's death hard. The added burden of believing she was probably the last person to talk to Daisy about Christ and that Daisy did not become a Christian devastated her. Alethea spent the next three years feeling a deep guilt about Daisy until Sam Dawson sat her down for a heart to heart talk. Sam had explained that Daisy had every chance to accept Christ, and that no one was more hurt by her rejections than he was, with the exception of Christ Himself. However, in the end, we each have to make our own decision. After several such conversations, Alethea slowly learned to forgive herself.

*

Stacy and Mitch arrived at St. Luke's and said an awkward goodbye. Michael wrapped his little arms around Stacy and kissed her on both cheeks. Stacy buckled him back into his car seat and turned to Mitch.

"We've said a lot in the last hour Mitch. It will probably take a while for both of us to sort it all out. But in the meantime, I want you to try to understand something. The thing that makes all this so urgent for me and thing that makes me so passionate, is that I have learned from experience how fleeting this life is. We only get one chance at this life, and if we don't make our decision during this lifetime, it's over. Daisy waited too long Mitch, but you don't have to. After Nick and Daisy died, I began to see things very differently.

Now I know that when I say goodbye to someone I care about who doesn't know Christ, I may truly be saying goodbye to them for the last time. But when I say goodbye to a believer, one who has accepted the free gift of salvation, what I am really saying is, until we meet again. I want to see you again Mitch, here in this life, and in the next. I want to know that goodbye really isn't goodbye."

Mitch had no idea how to respond to what Stacy had said. He looked at her silently for a moment seeing beyond her incredible beauty. He was beginning to realize that although he had always been attracted to her outward beauty, at this moment he was discovering a dimension of Stacy's being that was beyond description.

"I'll call you later, Stacy." With that, Stacy closed the car door and walked away.

*

Mitch spent the remainder of the morning and into the afternoon at the Stonebriar Mall. He owned a small condominium in the northern suburb of Frisco near the mall. Michael loved to go shopping there. Mitch assumed he did a lot of shopping with his mother and had simply gotten used to it. Unlike many men, Mitch didn't mind shopping; in fact he rather enjoyed it. Lately, he was particularly fond of shopping to buy little gifts for Stacy. Mitch had always been careful about buying things for Stacy because he knew she was a woman of integrity and would be turned off by anything appearing to be too generous or too expensive. Therefore, Mitch spent a lot of time shopping at Christian bookstores, and a few other shops where he found t-shirts with a Christian message, or places that sold religious knick knacks like crosses, Bible cases, and such. Mitch also had enough sense to occasionally feed Stacy's fitness cravings by purchasing work-out gear for her. One time he even bought her a rather feminine looking workout bag.

While wondering through the mall, Mitch stopped at one of Stacy's favorite Christian bookstores and approached the counter.

"I'd like to purchase a Bible, sir." Mitch said to the sales clerk at the counter.

"Yes sir, our Bibles are in section "D," aisle four. They're arranged according to version, and hard and soft covering. If you're a King James person, we have a fantastic deal on a large print hard cover which comes with an excellent concordance."

Mitch was immediately aware that he had been more at ease the time he bought Stacy a spandex jogging suit and had to explain to the female sales clerk at the sporting goods store what size top Stacy wore. Mitch had no idea there were options for a Bible. He had always thought a Bible was a Bible. "Um...well...I'm not...that is. I don't think I'm...what are those choices again?"

The sales clerk smiled warmly at Mitch then looked down at Michael, who seemed to be enjoying his father's predicament. "New Christian or checking it out?"

Mitch loosened up a bit, "I want to understand, and I thought reading the Bible would be a good place to start. I have no idea what I'm doing, so a little help would be great."

"No problem, sir. I tell you what; King James can be a bit intimidating for a new reader. Let's see, what do you do for a living?"

"I'm a police officer."

"Okay, my guess is that the amplified version would not be a good fit for you. You look like a pretty intelligent guy who likes to solve his own mysteries, and you would probably out-grow a student version pretty quickly. I'm going to suggest this NASB, which has a hard cover with wide margins and a concordance, you're gonna want to write lots of notes in those margins. I also have a Nelson commentary that I think will work very well for you. The commentary is not as detailed as the ones that only cover one book of the Bible at a time, but it is great for answering some of the general questions you will have as you read your new Bible. Would you like a case to go with that?"

Mitch knew the Bible case was a good idea, not just for carrying the Bible to church but also for keeping markers and pens in the side pockets. "Yes, do you have any leather ones?"

"Sure, we have burgundy and black left, but we should have some others coming in next week if you want to wait."

"Burgundy will be fine, thanks"

The sales clerk rang up Mitch's purchase and placed them in a bag. "Sir, if I can make one more suggestion?"

"Certainly, you've been a big help so far."

"Start with the gospel of John – the version you have is clearly translated and you need to start by understanding who God is and what He has done for you. John is the best place to start if you are seeking truth that is easy to understand."

Mitch paid for his purchases and left the store feeling better. He was confused, but at least now he had some sort of plan to make sense of it all, and he could live with that. He and Michael had lunch at the food court; Michael seemed to regain his appetite. They caught a quick children's matinee at the theater, then headed back home to settle down for the night. Mitch would need to get Michael back home to Ennis the next morning so he figured an early bedtime was in order. Besides, Mitch decided he would crack open his new Bible as soon as Michael went to sleep.

*

One of the things that often dumbfounded Mitch was Stacy's insatiable desire to please. Her specialty was surprises. Last month, shortly after Mitch moved into his new condo, Michael turned four. Stacy called Mitch at work on Michael's birthday and told him she had already picked up Michael and that she had a surprise for him. Mitch wasn't surprised that Stacy had picked up Michael; she had gotten into the habit of doing that the day before Mitch's days off just to save him the drive to Ennis. Stacy never spent the night at Mitch's old apartment or at the condo, but Mitch found it convenient to give her a key when she started picking Michael up on a somewhat regular basis. When Mitch arrived home the morning of Michael's birthday, Stacy had completely remodeled the spare room in Mitch's condo and made it into a bedroom for Michael.

The walls were painted a powder blue with a "Finding Nemo" border stretched along the high corners. There was a plastic desk full of paper and color crayons for Michael to draw pictures on, and a small dresser in the corner. Mitch had purchased a bed shaped like a race car for Michael before he moved in, but had been too busy to put it together. Stacy had assembled the bed and had bought a Luke Skywalker bedspread to put on it. When Mitch asked Stacy why she had chosen Luke Skywalker, Michael interrupted saying, "Stacy says Luke is like Jesus." Mitch never did quite understand that one, but he thought the room was magnificent.

*

Mitch finished reading Michael a story and he fell fast asleep. It was time for Mitch to dig into the Bible and see what he could learn. He was dog-tired, having been up for over twenty-four hours, but he felt strangely energized as he began his study. Lacking any better place to start, Mitch opened the Bible and looked at the table of contents, finding the gospel of John on page 938. Mitch began to read. *"In the beginning was the Word, and the Word was with God."*

Mitch continued reading into the night, and by morning he had read through all John's gospel, Acts, and into Romans. Stacy walked into the condo early Monday morning after spending another night at the hospital with Tosha and the boys. She walked into the living room expecting to find Mitch and Michael ready to leave for Ennis but the living room was empty. She made her way around to Michael's bedroom but it too was empty. Stacy figured if she didn't find them in the kitchen she would retreat and call Mitch on the phone. She was not inclined to check Mitch's bedroom, but she was concerned because she had seen his car parked in the lot out back. Stacy walked into the kitchen and found Michael sitting on a kitchen chair looking at his father, whose head was lying on the table with the Bible opened to Romans chapter three. With a yellow highlighter Mitch had outlined verse twenty-three.

"Mitch, are you okay?"

Chapter 14

The NCIC

Clarksburg, West Virginia
September 11, 2001

Human history is checkered with atrocious acts of mass violence perpetrated by mankind, events so horrific they will never be forgotten and perhaps from which certain societies may never fully heal. Germany and all of Eastern Europe is forever stained by the holocaust which claimed the lives of six and one half million Jews over a period of three and one half years; Japan by America's bombing of Hiroshima which claimed the lives of one hundred-twenty thousand people immediately, and an additional hundred-twenty thousand, people over the next several weeks and months, Rwanda by the annihilation of almost eight hundred thousand Tutsi's and Hutu's in one hundred and twenty days, and America by the deaths of over three thousand people in a matter of seconds on the morning of September 11, 2001.

The effects of September 11, 2001 are pandemic, pervasive, and periphrastic, effecting thousands of systems, and dozens of governments around the globe, inciting war, and consuming economic and human resources beyond our ability to calculate. The events which took place on that date touched lives in ways we will spend generations trying to comprehend, and shook our confidence in the nation's security which, Americans had taken for granted far too long. One of the smaller, perhaps least significant, effects of 9/11 occurred in the Clarksburg, West Virginia offices of the National Crime Information Center (NCIC) where Barry Kensington labored to enter information into the NCIC super database.

Formed under the Department of Justice Act of 1973, the NCIC was designed to assist local law enforcement agencies with tracing crime trends and solving crimes. The massive database contained files on stolen property, missing or lost persons, crime statistics and other useful information. Barry was one of many data entry personnel responsible for entering information on stolen automobiles and automobiles used in the commission of a crime. His assigned geographic zone was the Great Lakes area including Michigan, Illinois, Iowa, Wisconsin, and Minnesota.

As law enforcement agencies sent information into NCIC, data entry personnel would grab the ticket produced via computer printout, codify it, and enter it into the appropriate database so it could be merged with other information and made available to agencies that needed it. Law enforcement agencies requested information from the computer database about automobiles that had been stolen or used in a crime, and regardless of where the vehicles turned up in the country, the NCIC computers gather the information and send a report back to the requesting agency.

After Lt. Mackland closed the Bernard File, Sgt. Mel Sanders sent the vehicle identification number of Sam Dawson's Cadillac to the NCIC and listed it as a vehicle stolen in connection with an unsolved homicide. Mel worked every witness he could dig up on the case, checked with the local beat cops, and brought in everyone he could find that might have any information about Nicolas Bernard and Daisy Dawson's murder but had come up empty handed. The only thing he knew for certain was that the car and bearer bonds were missing from the Dawson home, and that DNA from both victims was found at the scene of the burned out Ford behind the First Avenue Bar. Mel had filed the stolen auto report with NCIC because it was standard procedure. He knew the title had been taken from Dawson's home, and whoever committed the murders would try to sell that car.

*

At eight-fifteen on the morning of September 11, 2001, Barry Kensington sat at his desk munching on a blueberry bagel smothered with blueberry cream cheese. Barry kept his eye on the full glass of orange juice at his workstation because the vibrations from the rapid conveyer belt which delivered tickets to his workstation sometimes overturned a full cup and Barry was set on drinking every last drop. Barry had just finished talking to his fiancée Ruth Bellcourt who worked as a transcriptionist for a small law firm in lower Manhattan. The couple planned to marry in spring of 2002.

By eight forty-five that same morning, Barry still had Ruth and their future on his mind. In Barry's right hand was a new computer generated ticket from a hit out of Corsicana, Texas. The hit was produced as a result of the sale of a 2001 Cadillac STS with an original Minnesota title. The VIN number on the Cadillac came back to a stolen vehicle from Minnesota connected to a double homicide. Without warning, Barry's boss Vince charged into the room.

"Does anyone have the news on their radio?"

Everyone looked at him with astonishment. No one was allowed to have radios in the data room, so the question seemed odd. Vince continued, "A jet airplane just crashed into one of the twin towers of the World Trade Center. I need a radio or TV in here right away."

A young intern ran out of the office and reappeared with a small twelve inch TV he found in the conference room storage closet. Barry was on his cell phone hitting the redial button for Ruth's office over and over again; her law office was barely two blocks from the twin towers. The TV blinked to life, and all thirty people in the tiny data room sat fixated on the sights and sounds which followed. The ticket in Barry's hand fell between his desk and the desk next to him which were less than a quarter inch apart. As Barry watched the small television, a look of stark terror appeared on his face.

Barry had never really prayed before. He wasn't sure he believed in God, but as he redialed Ruth's number over and over again without making contact he felt helpless. He attended church with family and friends on the major holidays like Christmas and Easter, but for the most part, these were things Barry did because he thought it was the right thing to do, not because of any spiritual conviction. God was fairly irrelevant in Barry's life, but at that moment he would have said or done anything if he thought it would bring Ruth back from the unknown. In the commotion, Barry dropped to his knees and cried out to God in a quiet but audible voice, asking Him to spare his beloved Ruth from this certain death. Barry continued to hit the redial switch for the next four hours.

By one o'clock in the afternoon Barry heard the sobbing tearful voice of his beloved Ruth across the line of his cell phone. She was unharmed but absolutely terrified by what she had witnessed. His desk a complete shambles with spilled, dried, and crusted orange juice mingled with the remains of a once coveted blueberry bagel with blueberry cream cheese, and a dozen broken pencils lay in a disjointed mass, Barry sat on the floor clutching his knees to his chest. For the first time in hours Barry breathed a sigh of relief, then knelt where he was to praise God and thank Him for sparing the life of his true love. While a nightmare had ended for Barry, the grieving and healing of a nation had begun. Perhaps the most insignificant casualty of the terrorist attack on America lay in a crumpled heap on the floor between two desks where it would remain for another four long years.

*

Four years and two children after the September 11th attacks, Barry Kensington was promoted. Vincent Cromwell retired from his position as Data Room Supervisor and Barry was named as his replacement. In the process of moving his personal effects, Barry dropped an anniversary card from Ruth between his desk and the one next to it. Barry moved the desks apart and found what everyone finds when they move furniture after four years. There were pencils, erasers, wrappers from lunches years gone by, and a crumpled piece of data paper printed by an out dated and long ago replaced dot matrix printer. Barry read the paper, dated 9-11-01 and spoke to Tamika, his new replacement.

"This is an old one, I don't know how it got here, but you better enter the info just in case it was missed. If it was already entered and someone just forgot to discard the hard copy, it'll notify you that it's a duplication error and kick out the new entry. But I think its better safe than sorry."

Tamika smiled at her new boss, "Boy, I wonder how that could have gotten there? It almost looks like it could have been sloppy work."

"Hey," Barry started in, "You're not paid to be a smarty pants." Barry smiled back at Tamika, "On a serious note, that was one crazy day around here, and I might have dropped it, but I gotta tell you, under the circumstances I have no regrets about where my mind and my loyalties were at the time."

"I hear Ruth was in Manhattan during the attacks."

"Yeah, she was working at a law firm right in Manhattan. For four hours I really thought I had lost her. The world could have stopped spinning and I wouldn't have known."

Tamika looked at Barry and asked softly, "She really means a lot to you doesn't she?"

Barry paused for a moment and reflected on those four hours back in 2001. "I love my kids dearly. They mean the world to me, and there is nothing I wouldn't do for them, but if it weren't for Ruth they wouldn't even be here. I love Ruth with all my heart, and at that time there was nothing more important to me in the world then her. But I learned something that day that I will never forget. Ruth is God's child, and if it were not for God, there would be no Ruth. Right here in this spot on September 11th, 2001, I gave my heart to Jesus and I gained a love I never could have imagined. Yeah, she means a lot to me, but it took Jesus to show me how to love her as

God's child. As much as I love Ruth, I have learned to love my God even more. So, that's my sermon for the day at no extra charge. Now get that slip entered, someone may be counting on that information. After all, that's what we do here, right?"

*

Tamika presented a toothy smile. She liked Barry as a coworker, and she was certain she would like him as a boss. She thought it interesting that after working in the data room for two years, it wasn't until now that she knew Barry Kensington was a Christian. Then she realized, Barry probably still didn't know she was believer. Tamika thought, *"What is wrong with this picture?"*

Chapter 15

Lt. Sanders

Minneapolis/Dallas
March 6, 2005

The Minneapolis Police Department divided the city into five precincts numbered one through five, with the downtown precinct called the First Precinct. The two precincts with the highest crime rate were the Fourth and Third Precincts respectively and there was an interesting bit of irony surrounding the Fourth. The precinct building was built on the very site where much of the city's crime was generated during the years between 1970 and 1980. In 1972, under funding from a national charity, a community center called "The New Direction" was constructed at 1920 Plymouth Avenue North in Minneapolis. The grant allowed for construction of the physical plant and for the hiring of staff to run youth and other community based programs designed to combat the civil unrest and racial tension that was endemic to the area. During the late 1960s the area had been the site of several race riots, homicides, and even the shooting death of a Minneapolis police officer. The New Direction was supposed to offer alternatives to the violent trends that had begun during this era.

Over time, the center became a hang out for ex-cons and active felons in the area who took advantage of government created jobs. The center did little more than generate an unjustified payroll for unskilled, unmotivated, and unruly thugs. After a series of violent incidents on the site the city closed down the center and demolished it. In its place, a new police precinct was erected to establish order out of the chaos. Construction for the new, state-of-the-art facility was completed in spring of 1990.

Set within its urban environment sat the shining new Police Precinct dedicated by Mayor Donald Frazier and the Minneapolis City Council. The dark granite structure resembled an urban fortress in the midst of urban assault. The small thick glass windows and brick walls which surrounded the grounds reassured the community that order had been restored. The architecture starkly contrasted the dated and run down shopping center next door and to the west. The shopping center was had been reduced to a liquor store with an attached grocery store, both of which sold second rate goods at inflated prices.

Mel Sanders sat at his desk in the Fourth Precinct opening his departmental mail, grinding his teeth, and loathing the meeting he had to attend within the hour. The department had initiated a crime fighting model based upon a New York Police Department tactic developed by Chief William Bratton. Bratton and his right-hand man Jack Maple referred to their program as COMSTAT, or Computer Statistics for law enforcement. Minneapolis dubbed their program, CODEFOR. By bringing up to date computer generated data to officers working the streets, Minneapolis hoped to enjoy some of the success that New York had enjoyed. Commanders from each precinct and division of the department were responsible for crime in their area. The fall out for any increase in crime flowed downhill quickly and with a loud thud at the bottom. Crime in the Fourth Precinct had spiked recently, and this was Mel's week to place his head on the chopping block at the CODEFOR meeting.

In his pile of mail, Mel found the usual garbage from the upper echelon of the department and the occasional thank you letter from a community group he had helped out of one mess or another. He shuffled the papers on his desk to prepare for the CODEFOR meeting which was due to start in the next few minutes when he found a letter from the NCIC. Mel tossed the envelop onto a pile of other papers realizing it had been years since he had any pending cases with info out to the NCIC. Mel pulled his sport coat on just as the phone rang. He yanked the phone off the receiver.

"Hello, is this Sgt. Sanders?" A sweet voice with a slight southern drawl came over the line.

"Yes, this is *Lieutenant* Sanders. What can I do for you?" Mel placed an emphasis on the word lieutenant as he spoke.

"I'm sorry to disturb you, sir, but I was told that you were assigned to the Homicide Unit back in 2001, and I'm a student in Dallas, Texas looking for information from police departments in your area about a possible assault I…"

"Listen, ma'am, I was just on my way out the door to an important meeting. Can I ask you to leave your information with our desk officer? I will call you back as soon as possible."

"Um, yeah, sure that's fine. I have a lot of other calls to make, and I really didn't mean to bother you."

Mel felt bad. He hadn't meant to be brash, and he was usually better with the public. He was having a bad day, and the last thing he wanted was to give an interview to some wide-eyed student half way across the country who was no doubt looking for some grisly details to add to her school paper. "Listen, I didn't mean to be rude. Why don't you give me your name, and if I get some extra time, I'll call you back okay?"

Melissa gave Lt. Sanders her phone number.

"Okay, ma'am, like I said, if I get a minute, I'll call you back."

Mel hung up the phone and rushed out the door to his meeting. There were many days he wished he were still working homicide cases and not running the Investigations unit at the Fourth Precinct. He liked his job most of the time and felt he was able to pass something important on to the younger officers in the department. What Mel really missed was feeling like he was directly involved in fighting crime. Today he just hoped he could get through this meeting without saying something that would get him in trouble with the department brass. He wasn't sure what they expected from the police officers that worked so hard for the department. Springtime always brought out the worst in criminals.

*

Melissa was feeling discouraged. She knew she was no detective but she had expected some kind of break. There were about a dozen or more large police agencies in the Midwest area and she had contacted each of them with no luck at all. She started with the Chicago Police department mostly because they were the largest, but that turned out to be more of a problem than an opportunity.

The City of Chicago was so large and they had so many cold homicide cases they didn't have the manpower to work cold assault cases which no one kept track anyway. Madison, Wisconsin was just as swamped trying to keep on top of missing persons cases, and in the end, she got nowhere with them. She had also contacted Milwaukee Police, Des Moines, St. Paul Police and the Minneapolis Police before trying several smaller agencies, all with no luck.

Her quest began after a series of questions she had asked Rocky Jo Bob about his "before life" as he liked to call it, and an afternoon she had spent with Jo Bob Jackson and Willie Eubanks in Personville.

"Rocky," Melissa began, "What do you remember about your before life?"

"Nuttin' really, jus know I usta like stargazin' like I told you b'fore. I know I was loved bah someone, an I know I loved others, but dat's really all I knows. Doc Evans thinks I was an educated man cuz when I started talking I had a pretty good cabulary. He also said mah weight's gone up an down a few times too."

"Does it bother you to think about who you were? I mean, don't you wanna know for sure?"

"I done tried tah' figure it out but I cain't remember nuttin'. I jus' figure when da' Good Lawd wants me ta know, He'll let me know."

*

Jo Bob and Willie were likable characters and Melissa immediately understood where Rocky got his charm. The cousins provided the most useful piece of information in the puzzle, but they weren't exactly the type of people who were used to thinking analytically about anything. Most of all they just missed their adopted son and asked Melissa to tell Rocky to get back home more often if he could. During her conversation with the cousins they told Melissa they always thought Rocky came from somewhere up north for two reasons.

First, during the winter months when the temperature in Northern Texas dropped down to a cool thirty or forty degrees, Rocky would go outside with nothing more than a sweatshirt on and just keep doing his chores. The second thing the cousins told Melissa is that when Rocky started talking he did have a big vocabulary. He understood words they had never heard of and whizzed through volumes of books at an incredible rate. But the thing Melissa found most interesting is that Willie and Jo Bob said when Rocky started to talk, at first he sounded like a Yankee, and that it took months before he started sounding like a proper Southerner.

*

Mel Sanders returned to his office after the CODEFOR meeting. It had not been as bad as he thought it would be. Crime was up in the Fourth Precinct, but the Chief seemed pleased with the tactics they had deployed to combat burglaries and street robberies. Mel settled into his chair and began to open the mail on his desk. He couldn't imagine what the NCIC wanted with him, but he figured he might as well take a look since he had the time. After reading the letter, Mel dialed the number listed for Barry Kensington. The two men had a long talk before Mel decided it was going to be a long day indeed.

Mel got on the phone with the First precinct desk. The First precinct covered the downtown business and entertainment district as well as three residential neighborhoods. There were a couple of downtown beat officers Mel needed to talk to right away.

Dave Strong and Jim Skillman walked into Mel's office about an hour after he had placed the call to their commanding officer. He knew they would be confused as to why they had been summoned, so he decided to try to ease their minds right away with a little small talk.

"Jim, Dave, how you guys doin'?"

"Doin' okay L T,"

"Dave, how's your old man, I hear he got a place up on Milacs Lake last year. He getting any fishin' done up there or just drivin' your mom crazy."

Strong laughed a little, "I imagine he's doing a little of both sir. He loves retirement though. He misses the department, but he loves not having to be here."

"He taught me a lot when I came on. He was a great cop."

Never much for small talk, Jim Skillman spoke up, "do you mind telling us why the heck we're sitting' down here in the Fourth Precinct talking to an Investigative Lieutenant sir?"

Mel shifted in his seat nervously before speaking. "I got a new lead on an old case guys, and I thought you might be able to help me out a little. You guys remember Ray Bernard don't you?"

"Of course," said Dave, "He and my dad were partners for a while."

"That's right," said Mel. "And you may recall his son Nick was killed a few years back."

"Don't think we'll be forgettin' that one, sir. That happened on our beat," offered Jim.

"I know, that's why I've asked to see you guys. I was wondering if you could tell me anything you remember about that time frame."

Dave spoke up. "I think everything we remember is in the report. We came in and gave a statement, but that was a while ago. I don't know that we could offer anything new. What was your new lead?"

"Well, I got a hit back from NCIC on an old auto V.I.N. I sent in just before Mackland closed the case. Apparently a car connected with the case wound up down in Dallas, Texas, of all places, and nothing in my files points there. So I was just hoping you guys could help out."

Skillman and Strong sat for a while and tried to think of anything that might help, but neither of them could think of a thing.

"Sorry," said Strong, "it looks like we're both drawing a blank here."

"Well, if you guys think of anything please let me know. I didn't get to know Nick Bernard real well, but his daddy was something special, and if for no other reason than out of respect for him I'd like to dig into this a little further."

"Well sir, if we can help, we'll give you a call, but in the meantime I guess you'll have to see what you can dig up on your own," offered Jim Skillman.

Both beat cops got up and headed for the door, and in unison, both men turned and snapped their fingers. "Digger," they both said at once.

Dave continued, "I haven't seen Digger since that big car fire out back of the First Avenue where Bernard's body and that girl's body were found in the trunk."

"Who is Digger?" asked Mel.

"One of our snitches," said Dave. "He used to breeze into town about every year or so, but we haven't seen him in several years. He told us the day of that fire he was leavin' town so we didn't think anything of it, but come to mention it, he hasn't been back."

"Did he give you any information before he left town?"

"Said Razor was putting together a gang to pull off some Southside jobs, but we didn't follow up on any of it because Razor got sent up to Oak Park Heights a few months later and was found dead in his cell."

"Thanks, guys. That may be helpful."

*

Melissa started by checking the major newspapers in the midwest region of the country during the period when Rocky was found at Bubba's Bee Line Bar B Q. She found that Chicago, Minneapolis, St. Paul, Des Moines, and a few other cities reported unsolved or mysterious assaults during that period. She then began to systematically contact each of the police departments in those cities to see if they could shed any light on the matter or share any information with her. So far, she had run into a brick wall. A handfull of the cases involved women or people of a different race than Rocky, and with others she just didn't get any cooperation. After calling Lt. Mel Sanders, Melissa decided to call in quits until she could gather some more information.

Four hours after her call to the Minneapolis Police Department Melissa sat by the side of Robbie's bed giving him another dose of the powerful antibiotic the hospital had sent home with them. Robbie was getting better, and that made Melissa happy. He had missed a huge chunk of school, but under the circumstances, his professors agreed to give him extensions on his deadlines. If he continued to improve, he was expected to return to school after the weekend. As Melissa kissed the top of her husband's head, the phone rang.

"Hello, McCree residence."

"Yes, may I speak with Melissa McCree?"

"This is her."

"Melissa, this is Lt. Sanders from the Minneapolis Police Department. Is this a good time?"

Chapter 16

Alethea's Birthday present

Minneapolis
March 6, 2005

For a time, the passing of life from this world to the next ceases precious relationships until loved ones are reunited in eternity. In the meantime, the ones left behind are consoled or in some cases tortured by reminders of the past. Bitter sweet memories of a person, place, or time once held dear – now departed. Sometimes a wedding ring or a watch become the connection between what was and what will be, sometimes it's an old sports car that collects layers of dust and debris from years of neglect. Alethea's Mustang remained a constant reminder that daddy wasn't coming home, and that his promise to present her with the car for her sixteenth birthday would not happen. A completely refurbished convertible top lay in it's packaging on the back seat, and the tattered car cover was still in place. Now, only weeks from her birthday, Alethea Bernard sat on the back porch of her south Minneapolis home looking at a car that once held so much meaning.

Morgan looked out the kitchen window at her daughter and wondered what must be going through her mind. Soon they would go through another anniversary of her husband's death. Morgan suspected that fact couldn't be far from her daughter's thoughts at that moment.

It would be difficult to find any physical resemblance between Alethea and her Aunt. As Alethea grew into womanhood, she took on a different kind of attractiveness which was not nearly as obvious. There were times when Morgan thought it unfair that Alethea's genetic make-up was closer to her own, then at other times, she was grateful, realizing how difficult it would be to see her husband's face each time she looked at her daughter.

At almost sixteen years-old Alethea was only 5'5" and it was unlikely she would get much taller. Morgan only stood 5'2" tall herself. Alethea had her father's dark complexion, but that was about all. Her hair, which she refused to have relaxed, remained in braids most of the time and she had a muscular build. She was a fiercely competitive athlete who combined her physical attributes with pent up anger and frustration to punish most of the boys that dared step onto the soccer field with her. Alethea was just as competitive academically as she was athletically, earning an impressive 4.0 GPA all three years of junior high school and the first two years of high school.

When she wasn't studying for an exam or writing a paper for school, Alethea was involved in some sport, but her weekends were reserved for the church activities she so dearly loved. Alethea taught the younger children's Sunday school lessons with a passion unrivaled since her father was the youth pastor.

*

Caught up in the ethereal realm of day dreams Alethea fell into a sort of trance with her eyes wide open. In her mind she heard the sweet angelic voice of a little boy calling her as though he were right next to her, whispering in her ear. "Go meet Eve, and say hello to her."

The voice came from somewhere Alethea could not discern, but she responded, "Yes, that's it. I'll go to meet Eve."

Another more familiar voice interrupted Alethea's trance. It came from across the fence.

"What are you talking about Alethea, are you okay?" Benny leaned on the fence much like he usually did before hopping over and joining her.

Alethea realized suddenly she had been daydreaming; she looked up to see fourteen year-old Benny begin to climb over the fence. "I'm sorry… I… were you saying something about Eve?"

"You should know," Benny shrugged his shoulders, "you were answering me kinda like in a trance."

Alethea looked surprised, "I was?"

"Yeah, remember you asked me last Sunday to come up with a line for God to say to Adam when he is about to see Eve for the first time?"

Alethea realized Benny was talking about the children's play she and Benny were trying to produce for the children's ministry at the church. Benny must have been standing there for a while talking to her without Alethea knowing he was there. "Yeah, I'm sorry. What was it?"

"Okay, God puts Adam into a deep sleep, and when he wakes up he's real groggy and doesn't know what God has done. So God gets Adam up, leads him to the middle of the garden and points in the direction of where Eve is. Then God say's in a deep booming voice, "GO ADAM, GO MEET EVE AND SAY HELLO TO HER." I realize it's kinda corny, but hey, it's a children's production right?"

Alethea didn't answer at first but continued to look in the direction of the old Mustang. After a few moments of silence she looked at Benny with a bewildered expression. "Were you saying that line to me right now, I mean, was that your voice I heard?"

"You're thinking about him aren't you?" asked Benny in a concerned voice.

Alethea slowly lifted her head and offered a partial smile, "Yeah, I guess it's just the time of the year when I get like this."

"I know what you mean. I think about Daisy a lot at this time too. Alethea, there's something I've been meaning to ask you." Benny paused for a moment as he jumped down off the fence and walked toward Alethea. "You know how I was kind of attached to Daisy when she was alive?"

"Yeah, you two were practically inseparable."

Benny continued, "Well since the funeral, I feel like I kinda latched on to you the same way. I mean – I clung to you the first two years like a magnet and used you like you were replacing Daisy. Anyway, I was just wondering – well was it ever like a burden to you?"

Alethea looked up at Benny. Tall and handsome, his voice changing, he was beginning to grow a blond mustache and that awkward teenage scraggly beard boys his age tend to grow – to skimpy to shave – too much to ignore. She stood up and wrapped her arms around Benny tightly – Morgan watched and listened as the two teens talked.

"Benny," said Alethea, releasing her embrace, yet holding Benny by the shoulders at arms length, "all of us in these two houses lost so much that day, and most people cannot begin to imagine the pain that filled two homes and the hearts of each one of us. But God never gives us more than we can bear, He sends his emissaries to minister to the wounded heart. You were as much a gift from God to me as I was to you Benny. It was never a moment's inconvenience, and as we bore each other's burdens, standing shoulder to shoulder for those years, I leaned on you just as much as you leaned on me. I don't ever want you to forget that – ever."

Now it was Benny's turn to hold Alethea, "Your parents sure do know how to pack a lot into a name."

*

Benny smiled and started for the fence he had climbed so often over the years to visit with Alethea. He remembered a conversation so long ago between himself, Daisy, and Alethea.

"Alethea," began six year-old Benny, "What kind of name is Alethea? It sounds so funny." Benny sounded out each syllable of the name, "Ahh-Lee-Thee-Ahh."

Daisy smacked her brother on the head causing Benny to flinch, "You are so embarrassing. Never mind what her name means, it's a pretty name even if it doesn't mean anything at all."

Alethea smiled at the two of them having a secret treasure she wanted to share. "My mom and dad told me Alethea is a Greek word."

"Well, tell us, what does it mean?" asked Benny.

Alethea sat up straight, puffed out her chest, and with the proudest smile on her face she answered, "Alethea means truth."

*

Benny looked over his shoulder after climbing the fence back to his yard, "Are you gonna let my dad help you get the Mustang going as a birthday present?"

"I dunno, I'm still thinking about that. I do appreciate his offer though."

"Well think about this; oh speaker of truth, my dad always regretted he didn't give in and get Daisy a car when she was sixteen. Personally I think he makes a bigger deal about it than Daisy ever did. The other day the insurance company called and said his old caddy was found down in Texas. Dad bought it back from the insurance company thinking it will bring him some peace but I got a feeling it's only gonna make him feel worse. But putting the old Mustang back together is different. I hate to speak for my dad, but I really think this would be a good opportunity for you to help him sort of deal with Daisy's death. If that makes any sense. I guess this would kind of help him find closure. Is that the right word?"

Alethea thought for a moment before responding to her neighbor and friend. "Yeah, I think that's a perfect word, closure. And before I forget, that's a good idea for the play, 'GO MEET EVE.' I don't know why, but I like it."

"I'll talk to ya later, Alethea," Benny hopped over the fence, "I've got football practice in the morning so I better get goin'."

Alethea waved at Benny and headed back into the house where Morgan was standing. "Hey I was thinking about doing something different this year for your birthday. What would you think of heading down to Dallas and spending some time with Stacy?" said Morgan when Alethea walked in the door.

Alethea's eyes grew with excitement. "Mom, are you serious? I mean, please tell me you're not joking."

Morgan shook her head looking almost disgusted, "No dear, I'm not kidding. Why would I joke about something like that?"

"I'm sorry, Mom. It's just that you don't make suggestions like that very often."

"Well, I have to be honest; I'm a little concerned about your aunt. I thought it would be a good time to go visit her and check things out a bit."

"Oh, are you concerned about the "Mitch" factor?"

"Well – yes – I am concerned about the," Morgan held up two fingers on each hand and bent them at the joint making quotation marks, "Mitch' factor. I think she may be getting in over her head with this guy, and she needs some help. I'm also concerned about that awful accident she witnessed."

"Yeah, where that cop was almost killed?"

"You are too young to have remembered your grandfather's death, but it was every bit as hard on Stacy as your father's death was on you. It wasn't so bad that Stacy witnessed the accident, but the guy was in his police uniform, and the child he was trying to save was Mitch's son. I just worry about what must be going on in her head as she gets more and more mixed up with this guy. I also wonder what she must be feeling after watching a police officer almost die in her arms."

Alethea would have remembered her grandfather's funeral with perfect detail even without the hundreds of pictures her mother kept in a dingy water stained box in the basement. She was convinced she would have remembered even though she was only three years old at the time. Alethea recalled the long endless line of police cars with their lights going. She remembered seeing hundreds and hundreds of police officers in full uniform walking down Chicago Avenue leading up to the church. She also remembered the signs that lined the streets as they drove the route from the church to the graveyard where her grandfather was interned. She asked her father what the signs said. One of the homemade ones held up by a little girl along the procession read, "Thanks for sharing your grandfather with us, Alethea. We love you and we're praying for you; 'Lyndale Elementary School Kindergarten Classroom 102.'" That sign was burned into Alethea's mind, and the memory of it alone would never allow her to forget her grandfather's funeral.

"I agree with you, Mom. I think we should go see Stacy. The fact is, I really miss her, and I bet she misses us too."

"I was also thinking," Morgan hesitated for a moment, "that we might let Mr. Dawson work on the Mustang a little while we're away."

Alethea didn't want to look in her mother's eyes at that moment. Instead, she looked out the kitchen window toward the Mustang which sat on four flat tires.

"Alethea, I just want you to think about something for a moment. We may never know for sure how your daddy died, or why, but the best police can determine he died trying to protect Daisy. Sam Dawson is a good man, but any man in his position would have wished he could have been there to protect his daughter. He will spend the rest of his life wondering if his baby girl would still be alive had he been there. He can't change that Alethea, and he can't thank your daddy for trying to do what he was not there to do himself. Give this good man a chance to do something that says thank you to the daddy you lost. Let Mr. Dawson try to make up for the fact that your daddy cannot be here to do what he promised you he would do. If you let him, this could also give Mr. Dawson a chance to show his love for Daisy in the only way he can right now. On the other hand, if you don't let him do this, you may be denying him the only opportunity he may ever get to bring something positive out of all the pain this has caused us all."

Alethea thought for a few moments longer before speaking again. "Okay, I'm going to let Mr. Dawson work on the Mustang. I hope it helps him deal with what happened, and who knows, seeing that car restored may in some way be a blessing to me too. I have to be honest, Mom, the reason I was hesitant to let him work on the car is because it just seems like if I let him do that, I'm finally giving up on Dad, and I didn't want to. But now I think its time I let go for good."

*

That evening Morgan thought about her conversation with Alethea. It took a long time after Nick's death for Morgan to truly appreciate the relationship between he and Alethea. For so long, Morgan had wrongly assumed it was a shallow relationship built on silly and superficial things that didn't matter. Watching Alethea grieve and attending countless counseling sessions with her revealed the rich and deep nature of their relationship which had many icons of significance, the car being only one. As father and daughter had built a car, they had built up their relationship. The car became a catalyst for bringing father and daughter together around a shared goal. Eventually this planning and working on the car would come to a climax with Alethea arriving at maturity and taking an allegoric flight of independence. Independence would be signified by Alethea earning her drivers license and the freedom of having her own car.

Understanding the relationship between Nick and Alethea was an important factor in understanding Nick's ministry at the church and the legacy of hope he left to the many kids to whom he ministered. While he was alive, Nick had tried to explain to Morgan what he was doing, but she was far too literal in her thinking to grasp the intangible nature of Nick's pedagogy. To Morgan, a car was just a car, and the science fiction he went on about was just silliness that held no real meaning. As she spent time with the kids who were part of Nick's youth ministry, Morgan became increasingly aware of how he managed to take the truth of the Bible and apply it to things the kids could easily relate to. In the end, Morgan concluded that far from being an enchanting and lovable flake as she had thought he was, her husband sat on the precipice of sheer brilliance as a father and as a youth pastor. This revelation drew her into a deeper love and appreciation for the husband God had blessed her with. Then, for reasons she would not comprehend this side of heaven, God had taken him away from her.

*

That evening after Alethea had gone to bed Morgan dialed Stacy in Dallas to relay their new plans. Stacy answered after a single ring.

"Hey sis, what's up?"

It was obvious Stacy had been crying. Morgan rolled her eyes, laid her left hand heavily on the counter next to her, and placed her right hand on her right hip. "Girl, what's goin' on now? What did he say? What did he do? Is Michael okay? Why aren't you sayin' anything, girl? Speak up."

Stacy, who had been trying to interject a response after each question gathered her thoughts for a moment, "I can't believe the nerve of him, Morgan. You'll never guess what he said to me."

"Look Stacy, me and Alethea were planning to come out there for her birthday in a few weeks but forget that, we're comin' now. Look, he ain't worth it Stacy – I know you love that little boy, but there is only so much you can do. Look we can talk some more when I get there – Girl, if I wasn't a Christian I would…"

"Morgan would you shut up for a minute? What are you talking about?"

"Well he's got someone else right? He's dumpin' you right?"

"No Morgan, he didn't dump me – we're not even going out like that – I mean, okay – well maybe it is a little like that – But we don't…. Look, what I'm trying to say is that he told me he loves me."

Morgan's hand slipped off the counter and she nearly lost her balance for a moment. "Oh Lord, it's worse than I though, girl. What did you say?"

"I gave him a long speech about agape love, and I even told him about Daisy and Nick – I dunno', I probably didn't make any sense at all. He's probably more confused now then ever."

"What makes you think that?"

"He went out and bought a Bible the same day I made my speech and he's been real quiet with me. He just doesn't seem to want to talk to me or anything. Morgan, I think I may have driven him away. He hasn't called me in three days and all he does is read the Bible, I don't think he's even called Michael since I took him back home the day after he bought that Bible. Morgan, I'm really getting scared."

Morgan relaxed for the first time since their conversation began. She smiled and had a melancholy look on her face as she spoke. "You haven't messed up anything, Stacy, but I think it's time to spend some time on your knees."

"What do you think is going on with him?"

"The same thing that went on with me when I found the Lord. It sounds like Mitch is a lot like me. He needs to make sense of Christianity, and that is not an easy thing to do. He needs to understand what the Word of God is saying, and more importantly what the Word of God is saying to him. He's a smart man, and he's strong willed enough not to just accept what others tell him. Look sweetheart, you did the right thing by pointing him toward the Word of God."

"But I didn't tell him to pick up the Bible."

"Did you talk to him about spiritual things you had learned from the Bible?"

"Yeah but...."

"Have you honored your covenant before God and tried to keep His commandments?"

"Yes but...."

"Have you insisted that if he wants to have a relationship with you, then he has to have a relationship with God?"

Stacy was beginning to understand what her wise sister-in-law was getting at. She stopped crying and began to smile for the first time. "Yes, Morgan, yes, I did do all of that."

"Then what you did was lifestyle evangelism. You planted seeds and it's time to let the Holy Spirit cause the growth. It's also time for you to get on your knees. I'll share something with you that a wise person whom I respect more and more each day once shared with me from a book by Lewis Sperry Chafer called *True Evangelism*. Mr. Chafer said, it's important that Christians spend less time talking to men about God, and more time talking to God about men. So take your concerns to the Lord, and watch him produce a miracle in the life of your Mitch. Be certain your motives are right and that you want this conversion for the sake of God and not for your own. And then let God do what God does."

Stacy felt a sense of hope and joy which lit her up inside. She loved Morgan so much and wondered how she ever would have made it through life since her father died without Morgan's wise counsel. She realized how much she had missed Nick and wished he were there to talk to. Then she was aware of how God, in His infinite grace, had led Morgan to call, and to stand in place of Nick when Stacy needed him. In fact, Stacy realized this was only one of many times Morgan had been to her what Nick used to be. She spoke into the phone again, this time with a voice of triumph and encouragement.

"Thanks Morgan, I can wait a couple more weeks to see you and Alethea so don't bother rushing out here now, I'm fine. Besides, it's been pretty hectic around here lately with Tosha and the boys. I've been spending a lot of time with them, and I know you will just love her when the two of you meet. I was wondering though. Lewis Sperry Chafer is the man who founded Dallas Theological Seminary near where I work. So who was the wise person who shared his words with you?"

Morgan smiled a broad smile before answering. "Nicholas Bernard, your brother."

"I should have known. I'll see you soon."

Chapter 17

Working the Case

Minneapolis
March 6, 2005

M elissa poured herself another cup of coffee and set it down next to her legal pad. A stack of articles photocopied from newspapers in the Midwest area lay in a heap on the kitchen table. She was frustrated with her lack of progress, yet she felt certain the answer to Rocky Jo-Bob's identity was somewhere before her. She had been over every detail in the articles, and cross referenced the information with what she had discovered in her interviews with a few police agencies. So far it had all been a dead end. Melissa had decided to go over all of it once more before giving up for the day. The phone rang as she sat down at the table.

"Hello, this is Lt. Sanders with the Minneapolis Police. I spoke with you a couple hours ago. Is this a good time to talk?"

"Yes sir, this is a good time, thanks for calling me back so soon," said Melissa.

"Yes, Ms...."

"Misses. I'm Mrs. Melissa McCree my husband is Robbie McCree."

Mel proceeded cautiously. "I'm sorry ma'am, I meant no offense."

"None taken. I'm afraid I'm just one of those women who enjoys letting the world know she's married. Don't mind me." Melissa hoped she hadn't offended the police officer.

"Okay, if I may continue."

"Please do, I'm rambling."

"Yes, when we spoke last it sounded like you may have some information for me regarding an old case, is that correct?"

"Actually I was hoping you could help me with one of your old cases." Again, Melissa felt herself getting off to a bad start. She began an apology. "I'm sorry, it's just that I've talked to so many police departments lately I have no idea how far I got with anyone so I probably seem a bit disorganized."

"Okay, well let's see if we can't get onto some common ground. Why don't I start by asking you which of my old cases you were interested in." Mel grabbed three aspirin out of his desk drawer and swallowed them with some cold coffee left in his mug from the day before. He winced from the cold bitter taste of the coffee.

Melissa's voice came back over the line. "Could you hang on for just a moment, sir?" Melissa shuffled some papers on her desk before finding her notes on the Minneapolis case.

"Okay, you're with Minneapolis police, right?"

"Yes, that's correct ma'am."

"Well, it says here in the June 8, 2001 edition of the Minneapolis Star Tribune that two bodies later identified as Nicholas Bernard and Daisy Dawson were found burned beyond recognition in the trunk of a car behind the First Avenue Bar in Downtown Minneapolis. In a September editorial section of the same paper you were quoted as saying the DNA evidence used to confirm the identities of the two bodies was inconclusive."

"Yes ma'am, I believe I did say that. Can you tell me what your interest in all this is?"

"Well, on June 4th, of 2001 a good friend of mine turned up in Groesbeck, Texas, which is about forty five minutes from Dallas. He was badly beaten and suffers from retrograde amnesia as a result of what happened to him. Anyway, I'm trying to find out who he is, and I guess it may be desperate, but I'm checking with police departments in your area to see if you have had any unusual disappearances or other unsolved cases that might help me figure out my friend's true identity. So, I was thinkin', if the person who was burned up in that car was not Nicholas Bernard, then maybe my friend is Nicholas Bernard."

"Yeah, that is kind of a wild theory. To tell you the truth I might not have called you back but I just got the strangest letter from an agency in West Virginia that helps cops like me out with our investigations. Anyway, in the case you were just talking about, a 2001 Cadillac disappeared from the scene of one of our victim's homes and that car just turned up in your neck of the woods. It's been in Texas since June, 2001, but a glitch in the system kept us from knowing about it until now."

"That must have been some kind of glitch, mister."

"It was. Apparently the glitch was somehow related to 9/11. Ma'am, the man who was killed in this case was the son of someone who meant a lot to me. So I'm really interested in any information that would shed some light on what actually happened."

"I hope I can help, and again I apologize for my rambling. I guess it's just the way I am. Sometimes my way of communicating can be a bit irritating. I think I irritate my professors all the time. And, Lord knows I have a way of raisin' the hairs on the back of my husband's neck. Well sir, I don't know about any Cadillac but I think my friend Rocky Jo Bob might have come from your neck of the woods."

"Can you describe your friend to me?"

"Well, he's a large black man, weighs about three hundred pounds, near six feet tall. I guess he's probably between forty and fifty-years-old."

"Listen, Mrs. McCree, I'm going to be in Dallas in a few weeks for a convention and until I get there, I think it would be best for you not to mention the name Nick Bernard or anything else we've discussed with your friend. Do you think you could meet with me when I get in town?"

"Sure!"

"Thanks Melissa, I look forward to seeing you when I get there."

*

Mel hung up the phone after talking to Melissa McCree and held his face in his hands. The phone on his desk rang and jarred him back to reality.

"Lt. Sanders?" A deep voice with a thick southern drawl came over the line.

"Yes, this is he"

"Hi, this is Bob Buetler from Big Bob's Auto Ranch down in Corsicana, Texas. My sales associate told me you called while I was out. I assume it has something to do with that bad penny I got out back."

"I'm afraid so. I was wondering if you have time to answer a few questions Mr. Buetler."

"Call me Bob."

"Yes Bob, can you tell me anything about the person you got the car from?"

"Sure, the first time or the second time."

Mel was confused and wondered if there was something in the water down there that made everyone talk double talk.

"I don't understand Bob, what do you mean the first time or the second time?"

"Well, I got the car on a straight buy back in June of 2001. Then I sold it around the first part of September that same year. It was a brand new Caddy. I don't do a whole lot of new car business. See, I just run a small lot in the country and most of my customers are just looking for something to get 'em around town real good. But every now and again, someone's lookin' for somethin' special, so I figured I'd take it off his hands real cheap and sell it at a profit. Thing is, the guy had a clear title on the car and said he was just tryin' to get out from under it cause he's come on some bad times and needed the cash. So I bought it outright. It sat the whole summer til' Milt Daniels decided it was time to put some class in his act, and he took it off mah' hands. Then Milt sold it back ta' me when his wife Harriet run out on em' an he needed cash justa' make his house note. So, I bought it back from em' bout a month ago an didn't think nuttin' of it til' the next guy I sold it to tried ta' register the title and got it back sayin' the car was stolen outta' Minn-an-en-apliss."

Mel listened to every word Bob said and took notes. "Can you describe the man who sold you the car the first time?"

'Sure, there ain't no fergettin' him. He was bout 6 feet tall, blond hair, medium build. He had a short Mexican and a skinny fella' with em'. The skinny white guy had stringy hair, crooked teeth, and the nastiest skin u'ed' ever seen. I tell ya' dat' boy's face looked like a dog ad been chewin' on it. Oh, an one other thing, no offense, but the skinny fella' tawked' jus like a Yankee, kinda', like you."

"Can you think of anything else, Bob."

"Nope, but do ya' know how I'm sposed' ta' get mah' money back on dis' deal partner?

"No, I'm afraid I don't. The insurance company already paid out on the stolen vehicle claim so they're the rightful owners of the car now. I'm sure you know they plan on pickin' it up soon, and as soon as we've had a chance to take a quick peek at it for any evidence that might be in it after four years, we will release it right back to them. I would guess you have a fair claim against the NCIC since they're the ones that should have caught the snafu before it got to this point. I do appreciate your help though, sir, and I hope it all works out for you."

"Well, me too. I hear there was some real tragedy ba'hind' dis' here car an I hope all this'll help da' famlee' put things behind em'."

"Me too Bob, you take care."

*

Mel knew the description of one of the men who sold the car to Bob sounded familiar but he couldn't figure out why. It wasn't the original case files that had Mel thinking about the description; it was something much more recent. He wasn't even sure it was the description itself that was familiar, it could have been anything. It was getting late and Mel wanted to get home early. He didn't have anything or anyone special to go home to, he just wanted to get out of the office for a while and think about something other than police work. He was beginning to get the itch. When an investigator started really working a case, he got the itch. The itch is that nagging feeling that keeps you up for days working the angles, checking leads, and shaking down every snitch you can get your hands on. Mel was developing that itch again, and it felt good.

Mel was a single guy, and always had been. It wasn't that he didn't want to be with anyone, he just hadn't made it a priority. Mel liked his privacy. He liked doing things his own way. He liked knowing that when he got home at the end of the day; everything would be exactly as he left it that morning. Over the years, Mel had seen many marriages come and go. Cops came on the department married to one person, and within a year, they were divorced and married to someone else. Most of the marriages he had seen in his years were not good ones, so Mel figured the smartest thing to do was to stay single.

He pulled his car out of the Fourth Precinct parking lot and turned east on Plymouth toward downtown. At Seventh Street he headed across the Highway 94 Bridge then took 19th Street toward 35W southbound. Mel lived in the south suburb of Bloomington, not far from the Mall of America. He liked the quiet neighborhood he lived in and the drive to and from work was often therapeutic.

Driving east on cross-town highway 62 Mel exited at highway 77 south turning off at the Old Cedar exit which led to the two bedroom condo where he had lived for the past fourteen years. Mel parked in front, grabbed his briefcase out of the back seat, and walked the narrow path which led to the first floor entrance of his home.

If ever there was a bachelor's pad, it was Mel Sanders' humble abode. The hanging artwork looked like someone had walked into his house and started throwing cheap prints off a Wal-Mart truck at all four walls. The furniture was functional and durable, but followed no known pattern of coordinated design. Positioned directly in front of a twenty-five inch TV screen was an overstuffed recliner with the remote control velcroed to the right arm. The place was neat, clean, and capable of sheltering one from the elements, but had no frills other than the coveted entertainment center which was the focal point of Mel's living space.

Once inside, Mel turned on the six o'clock news just as the newscast began. Robyn Robinson led the news with a story about gangs in Stillwater Prison using knifes to cut and stab their enemies.

"Razor!" Mel stood up and shouted the name. That was it; Digger said Razor was putting together a bunch of his cronies from the joint to pull off some jobs on the Southside. Mel had arrested Razor on several petty charges over the years and the beat cops said he was getting active again about the time Nick Bernard was killed. Mel didn't pay much attention to the information at the time but in a strange way it all made sense to him now. However, as far as Mel knew, Razor had never been to Texas. No matter, Mel could not dismiss the description Bob gave of one of the men who sold the Cadillac to him; it was far too much for coincidence.

The next morning Mel got to the office early and fingered through the Rolodex on his desk. After finding what he was looking for, he dialed the number and waited for an answer.

*

"Complex Two, Gerry North."

"Hey Gerry, this is Mel Sanders with Minneapolis Police, do you remember me?"

Gerry was not thrilled to acknowledge his recollection of Mel Sanders. Years ago, he and a bunch of other corrections staff decided it would be a good idea to head into Minneapolis and sample some of the nightlife. They wore out their welcome at two or three bars before agreeing it was time to visit the strip clubs in the warehouse district. Gerry quickly became bored with the entertainment at the strip club, and full of too many Jack and Coke's he wandered out to the parking lot where he found an absolutely gorgeous black Mercedes Benz 500 convertible with the top down. After swerving from side to side and from front to back for several minutes admiring the fine piece of automotive engineering, Gerry leaned forward.

When the proud owner of the car emerged from the rear exit of the club with an exotic dancer under each arm, Gerry let a stomach full of mixed beverages and Buffalo wings flow right onto the car's leather seats. The owner of the Benz was not amused. Mel Sanders and his partner at the time witnessed the entire incident from their squad car parked nearby, and after getting their hysterical laughter under control; they managed to intervene in time to save Gerry from what would surely have been a terrible beating.

Mel helped Gerry into a cab, and before the cab pulled away, Gerry offered Mel his business card. It never occurred to Gerry that he would get a call from the man who saved his hide years later.

"Yes, I remember you. I hate to admit it but I do."

"Hey don't sweat it; I wasn't calling to rub your nose in anything. No pun intended."

"What can I do for you, sir?" asked Gerry, not really wanting an answer to the question.

"I'm working a cold case right now. I was wondering if you know or remember an inmate with a street name, Razor, who spent some time at your joint?"

Gerry brightened up realizing the call had nothing to do with his reprehensible behavior so long ago. "Yeah, I know of him, but I'm afraid that won't do you much good. He's dead. He has been for a few years now."

"Yeah, I know about that. I was wondering if you know of anyone in particular he hung out with while he was there."

"I'm sorry, that really isn't much to go on. These guys have lots of people they hang with depending on the situation. Can you be any more specific?"

"Well, we think he may have been involved in some nasty business here in Minneapolis back in 2001. I know he was out most of 2001, but didn't he come back to you guys around December of that year on another one of his typical petty charges?"

"Yeah, that sounds about right. I'm not looking at his file right now, but when he came in, he came straight here to Complex Two. Somehow, he came into a little money the summer before, bought a bunch of dope and got the bright idea to go into the crack business. He wasn't much good at it though, a couple of your boys popped him selling to teenagers right out of the First Avenue Bar. A few months after he got here, he was found down in our segregation unit with a T-shirt wrapped around his neck. That's really all I know."

"Do you know if Razor had any connection to Dallas, Texas, Gerry?"

Gerry North was silent for a long moment before speaking. The wheels were spinning in his head, and a few things were beginning to add up.

"Well, this really isn't much, and it doesn't necessarily have anything to do with Razor, but there was another inmate back in 2001 that Razor was in contact with while still on the streets. And the guy I'm thinking of was from the Dallas area."

"What's his name?"

"His street name is Ellum, but his real name is Derrick Havelock. What kind of crime are you looking into if I can ask?"

"It's a double murder, someone killed a young girl and a man that may have been trying to help her, then stuffed the bodies in the trunk of a car and torched it."

"Well, that sounds like Ellum. That's pretty grisly stuff."

"Any idea where we can find this Ellum now?"

"No, but I'd like to know about it if you find him. His sentence expired in 2004, but he ran from One-Eighty the day after he was released, so technically we still get him for another three years, if we ever find him."

"When exactly was this guy let out?"

"Hold on a second, and I can tell you for sure." The line was silent for a few moments while Gerry checked his files. "Looks like he was released June 1, 2001."

"Thanks Gerry, I'll keep in touch if I find out anything."

"Look Mel, I owe you one, and I gotta' tell you, if you find this guy Ellum, you be careful. He is real bad news."

Chapter 18

It is well with my soul

Dallas
March 9, 2005

A little over a week after the accident Tosha was learning to sort out what had happened and what was about to happen. Bart continued to recover slowly from two successful surgeries; the first to stop internal bleeding and repair a severed artery in his leg, the second surgery was to repair a ruptured spleen which was not discovered initially. Now Tosha prepared herself for the next surgery which would claim Bart's right leg just below the knee. Tosha was grateful for Bart's favorable prognosis, but she was concerned about how they would survive and how Bart would adapt to life as an amputee. The surgery itself did not present any immediate risk and the doctors said Bart was physically up to it. But, Tosha worried about Bart's mental and spiritual health because he had become increasingly withdrawn and angry about his condition.

Anthony spent the entire week he was in town at the hospital refusing to return to the house for so much as a single night's sleep in his old comfortable bed. The most he would accept was a brief visit to the house for a shower and change of clothes before returning immediately to the hospital. Nathaniel and Joseph spent most every day at the hospital as well. Joseph slept at his college dorm room, Nathaniel shuttled the family minivan to and from the house with clothes and other supplies the family needed. In the evening, Tosha and her three sons congregated in the hospital chapel for prayer after Bart's pain medication had lulled him to sleep. Tosha found a great deal of strength in the company of her sons, and realized she and Bart had done a good job of raising three fine men.

In her private devotional time Tosha prayed for John Mitchell. Tosha had become very attached to Stacy over the past week and through their conversations Mitch found a place in Tosha's heart as well. Tosha reasoned that the Lord had placed Mitch on Bart's heart as well as hers for a purpose she did not yet understand. Stacy brought delicious meals she had prepared at home which kept the family going. By Tosha's request Stacy brought Little Michael to the hospital twice. She found herself strongly drawn to Michael, who had taken to Tosha as well. It seemed to everyone that Michael had a strong spiritual connection to God that none of them compre-hended. When Tosha brought Michael in the room to see Bart, the embattled patient brightened up for the first and only time. After Michael had gone, Bart sunk back into a depression that concerned his family. Tosha finished reading to Bart from Ecclesiastes 5 then laid the Bible on her lap.

"Why did you want me to read that scripture to you, baby?" Tosha was happy to read to her husband but was confused about what he saw in what she read.

"It comforts me, and helps me ask questions of God."

"Bart, I'm concerned about you. I have to ask you something, and I know you'll answer me honestly."

Tosha paused and thought about how to ask the question. She knew her husband was a man of faith. She didn't want to upset him by implying anything to the contrary. After a moment, Tosha leaned over Bart and addressed him directly, but gently.

"Have you given up on God? Do you feel like He has forsaken you?"

Bart, who had been looking out the window on the side of the room opposite Tosha turned his head and looked his wife in the eyes. "I haven't given up on God. I have failed God, and I wonder if he hasn't given up on me."

A tear rolled down Bart's face – no crying – no expression – just a tear.

"Baby, why would you think that? Why would God ever give up on you? Do you think that because He has allowed calamity in your life that He's given up on you?"

Bart remained expressionless and spoke in an even tone.

"The good Lord chastens those whom He loves, and not a one of the patriarchs went without some time of testing, I know all of that Tosh, but I have not been a faithful servant. I have failed time and again to share His love with others. I prayed for Mitch, but I despised him at the same time. Like Jonah, I did what I thought I was supposed to do begrudgingly, and I never thought someone like Mitch was good enough for the kingdom."

"I remember the day after he met Maggie, you know, little Michael's mama. You should have heard the rancorous garbage that came out of Mitch's mouth about how he had maneuvered his way into her bed. Moreover, she was just one of many I have had to listen to that man talk about over the years. I prayed out of a sense of duty, but I never opened my mouth to witness to him. When I saw him at the health club with Stacy that day, all I wanted was to let her or whomever he may have been talking to know what a buffoon he was and to warn her to stay away. But I didn't care enough to share God's love with him. Now I think God has had about as much as He can take of my hypocrisy."

"There is no higher calling for the Christian than evangelism Tosha, I dropped the ball – he remains unsaved – and now Stacy, Michael, and Maggie are at risk because of it."

Tosha smiled warmly at her husband knowing he needed time to heal, not just from his physical injuries, but from the emotional injuries he began to inflict upon himself long before the accident.

"Bart," she patted his hand softly, "let God be God."

They held each other tightly in the hospital bed while Bart wept from the depths of his despair.

*

Shortly past noon Stacy poked her head into the hospital room and found Bart and Tosha locked in a sweet embrace. Neither saw her, so she paused for a moment at the door and beheld true love as she hadn't seen it since Nick had died. Bart's head was all but lost in the bosom of his wife; she gently stroked his red wavy hair and softly – sweetly – began to sing to her beloved in a beautiful soprano voice.

When peace, like a river, attendeth my way
When sorrows like sea billows roll

Whatever my lot, Thou hast taught me to say
It is well, it is well with my soul
It is well (it is well)
With my soul (with my soul)
It is well, it is well with my soul
Though Satan should buffet, though trials should come
Let this blessed assurance control
That Christ hath regarded my helpless estate
And hath shed His own blood for my soul
My sin, 0 the bliss of this glorious thought
My sin, not in part but in whole
Is nailed to the cross, and I bear it no more
Praise the Lord, praise the Lord, 0 my soul!
And Lord, haste the day when my faith shall be sight
The clouds be rolled back as a scroll
The trump shall resound and the Lord shall descend
Even so, it is well with my soul

Stacy quietly listened as Tosha sang and was soon lost in a child-hood memory. It was her father's funeral; Stacy sat in the front pew of the church with Nick, Morgan, and little Alethea as Pastor Terrell Jenkins delivered one of his finest sermons.

*

"Joy and pain are two sides of the same coin we call the Christian experience. You see, it is impossible to truly under-stand the blessings of the Father, without experiencing the sufferings of the Son. Oh, I know you've heard that before but knowing it and experiencing it can be two different things. You see today is not just a day where we put to rest a beloved public servant, or an elder – father – husband – or saint. Today we will lay to rest a man who I personally called friend."

Pastor Jenkins began to tear up and one of the ushers rushed up to the platform to offer him a tissue, which he accepted, then continued.

"Raymond Bernard was a man well acquainted with the two sides of this coin. He was a man who loved deeply and grieved deeply himself. You see, Brother Bernard suffered loss just like we suffer today. But Brother Bernard also knew about the other dimension of Christ's passion, and that is the dimension of self-sacrifice. We will never truly understand what Christ did for us on the cross, but we are charged with the responsibility to try. And our fallen brother here went far beyond what any of us would do to demonstrate sacrificial love when he walked into the valley of the shadow of death, fearing no evil, with the presence of God surrounding him from all sides. Our dear Brother Bernard could do this because he had confidence that whatever happened, God was by his side."

"There are many whose lives fill books and documentaries and cry out from the grave just to tap us on the shoulder and tell us that we can be confident as Brother Bernard was confident. We have just cause to know that whatever may come, it is well with my soul. The great hymnist Horatio

Spafford understood this well. Having departed from his wife and four daughters, delayed by a business trip, he had intended to join them on a trans Atlantic voyage from New York to France in November 1873. He received a telegram nine days later informing him that the ship had vanished in the oceanic depths of the Atlantic, and that while his wife Anna had survived, all four daughters had perished. On a voyage back to New York, Spafford's ship crossed the very spot where just twelve days prior his precious daughters had perished, and rather than curse the God of heaven for his plight, this humble man wrote the famous hymn, "It is well with my soul." And so I ask you to join me in singing this favorite song of Elder, Officer, Friend, Husband, and Father, Raymond Bernard and to let its meaning resonate within you as you plums the depths of the song's meaning, and let the love of God wash over all of us this moment in our time of grief."

*

The singing stopped and Stacy stood in the doorway.

"Come on in, Stacy. Why are you just standing there like that?" Tosha sat at Bart's bedside waving her arm and beckoning Stacy into the room.

"I'm sorry, I didn't mean to intrude. I was enjoying your singing, and I guess I just got lost in thought."

Bart wiped the tear from his eye.

Tosha spoke again. "Well I'm not much of a singer, so what were you thinking about so quietly?"

"First of all," Stacy began with a somewhat firm tone, "you have a wonderful voice… and… well, I was just thinking about my father's funeral."

"I'm sorry about your father," Bart said flatly.

"Its okay," said Stacy. "He died several years ago when I was just a girl, but when Tosha was singing, it just reminded me that they sang that song at his funeral."

"How did your father die, Stacy?" asked Tosha.

"He died the same way you almost lost your life, Bart."

Stacy now had Bart's full attention, his blue eyes pierced and bored into Stacy like jagged icicles. Bart didn't need to prompt Stacy to clarify herself. His look said it all.

"I guess with all the commotion around here over the past week I never got around to telling either of you that my father was a police officer. He served the Minneapolis Police Department just a few weeks short of thirty years. I dunno, maybe that's why it was so hard for me to see what happened to you Bart. I saw your uniform as soon as you were hit, but it wasn't until I started working on you that I realized you were the same man I met in the health club that day Mitch and I met for the first time. Then I saw you two at the Christmas party last year when Mitch and I kinda got to know each other better. Before he and I started talking that night, I sat and watched him watching the two of you over in a quiet little corner of the room."

"I'm not sure what Mitch saw when he looked at the two of you, but you reminded me of my brother Nick and his wife Morgan. Mitch just stood there staring for a long time. I was going over to the bar to give him a hard time. Before I could say anything to him he bumped into me and spilled the strawberry margarita I was holding all over my new gown. To be honest, I didn't even realize it was Mitch staring at you, I thought it w as just some lovesick puppy that I was gonna harass. Anyway, once we got to talking Mitch told me the two of you had three sons. When I saw you lying on the ground that night, I just couldn't help thinking that if you didn't make it your sons would go through the same thing I went through when my father died."

"So your dad was a Minneapolis cop?" Bart's look had softened considerably.

"Like I said, almost thirty years," said Stacy.

Tosha looked a little confused. "You said we reminded you of your brother and sister-in-law. Is either your brother or your sister-in-law also a police officer?"

Stacy cupped her face in her hands for a brief moment. She sat down on an empty chair for the first time since walking into the room, then raised her head smiling.

"You'll get to meet my sister-in-law Morgan in a couple weeks. She and my teenage niece will be in town visiting for a while. I think you'll absolutely love them both. My brother Nick is another tragic story; he was killed about four years ago. We think he was trying to defend our young neighbor Daisy at the time. The neighbor's home was being robbed and police think Nick saw what was happening and tried to protect Daisy. Anyway, both Daisy and Nick were killed in the incident."

"Oh my goodness," said Tosha, "what you have been through."

"It's okay. He was a great man. No, he wasn't a cop." She looked at Bart, who smiled for the first time. "He was a youth pastor at my father's church. And right now if I know my brother Nick, he's stating the finer points of engine mechanics to St. Paul and using the lesson to correct the great Apostle on his use of grammar and syntax in the koine Greek sentence structure."

*

Stacy, Bart, and Tosha had a good laugh which helped to ease some of the tension in the room. Bart was intrigued by what Stacy had said and for the first time since the accident, he began to feel a little closer to God. The laugh did him good. Bart had forgotten what it was like to laugh or to enjoy the company of fellow believers. It wasn't that he didn't have people around that cared for him and loved the Lord; Bart had just gotten into the rut of pushing people away. He began to feel guilty for the way he failed to engage Anthony in conversation while he was there. Bart decided he needed to call Anthony and at the very least, thank him for being there with the rest of the family.

Stacy stopped laughing and cleared her throat. "Okay, enough of the long faces, anyone for fried chicken? I just happen to have a twelve piece box in my bag here with mashed potatoes and macaroni and cheese." Bart, Tosha, and Stacy enjoyed one another's company and were soon joined by Nathaniel and Joseph.

Chapter 19

God's perfect work

Dallas/Minneapolis
March 12, 2005

The room fell dark and silent. The sound of soft, cautious, footsteps began faintly in the back of the room, growing only slightly louder as a lone man walked up the center aisle toward the platform. A single light appeared and illuminated a rugged wooden structure on the platform next to a work bench. The man, wearing black boots and coveralls, mounted the platform and lifted a shinning hammer from the workbench. He began to hammer a nail into the wooden structure. Ping. Ping. Ping. The structure resembled something like a shoe shine stand – unfinished – and unattractive. The hammering stopped. The man lifted the hammer high into the air and began to speak in a strong, booming, amplified voice that filled the room.

"This is the hammer of God. It is a marvelous hammer, the best in all the world – and I wield it and exalt it in the name of the Lord Almighty God for His perfect good." From the workbench the man retrieved a large Bible and held it high in the air with his other hand at equal height with the hammer. "This is the Word of God. I read it, speak it, teach it, and exalt it in the name of the Lord Almighty God."

Pastor Terrell Jenkins had begun his sermon and all eyes and ears were tuned to him. No one stirred. No one whispered. Like Moses on Mount Carmel, he had the undivided attention of his audience.

"This is a peculiar way to begin a sermon, and a peculiar way for your pastor to dress." Pastor Jenkins slid his thumbs up and down the inner seam of his overall's straps, then he stretched the straps outward before releasing them with a loud slap against his chest. The tension in the room was released as chuckles echoed throughout the congregation.

"But you see, I have begun my sermon in a peculiar way, and dressed in this peculiar way because we are living in some rather peculiar times which sometimes require a peculiar message delivered in a peculiar way." Practically unseen, two figures whisked away the old rugged shoe shine stand then replaced it with something else. Jenkins continued his homily. "I present you with three questions, a riddle if you will. Is this hammer in my hand worthy of exaltation? Is this Bible worthy of exaltation? Is there any tool used by man for God's higher good worthy of exaltation?"

"Saints, my heart is heavy today, and I fear for the Body of Christ. Turn with me please to the book of Ephesians, chapter two, where Paul labors to describe the unity of the church and the glory of God."

Alethea leaned close to her mother and whispered in her ear. "Mama, when we get to Dallas, can we shop for an outfit for my birthday?"

Leaning close, Morgan whispered a terse response. "I suppose so. I'm sure your aunt will want to take you for a girl's day out. Now quiet down, I want to hear this."

Alethea liked Pastor Jenkins sermons but she could not concentrate on it today. She had only been to Dallas a few times to visit her aunt, and nothing could have made for a happier birthday than this trip. Stacy and Alethea talked over the phone as often as possible, but lately, it seemed both of them were too busy to connect. During former trips to Dallas, Stacy had taken Alethea to The Galleria, an indoor mall in North Dallas. This time, Alethea hoped they could visit the Stonebriar Mall in Frisco which was larger and had many of the shops the Mall of America had.

Pastor Jenkins continued his sermon and held everyone's attention with the notable exception of one teenage girl anxious to see her beloved aunt.

"In the hands of a skilled craftsman a hammer is a powerful tool and can be used to create wonderful works of art, strong houses to live in, and fine furniture for our enjoyment. In the hands of a malevolent man, a hammer can cause great destruction to property and even lives. And so it is with the word of God. In the hands of a righteous man or woman the Bible is a powerful tool for bringing the Word of God to a world that desperately needs it. But in the hands of men with dark hearts, it has been used to justify war, slavery, genocide, and all other manner of evil. The Word of God is not this book in my hands." Pastor Jenkins held the Bible high in the air. "The Word of God is alive and although represented by, and found within the pages of this book, it cannot be confined to these pages. The fact is that a hammer and a Bible are only tools that can be used for good, or for evil, depending on the heart and intentions of the one who wields them. A hammer is not worthy of our love or respect, but the craftsman that uses it to create good things is. This Bible is not worthy of our love, but oh saints, let me tell you about the Savior who is the Word of God."

The congregation began to erupt in applause and amen's.

"Preach, Pastor!" said a man near the front row.

"Take your time now!" came the shout of a woman in the middle of the room.

Pastor Jenkins continued, "And now saints let me ask you about something else. What of our beloved country America?

"Come on, Pastor."

"Alright now!"

*

Mitch turned down the FM radio in his cruiser long enough to advise dispatch of his location. He keyed the cruiser's base radio, "1303."

The radio chirped and a female voice spoke in short staccato bursts, "Go ahead with your traffic 1303."

Mitch responded, "I'll be signal 66 headed for a signal 43 at the senior center."

The dispatcher chirped in again, "10-4, 1303, advise when you're back on campus."

"10-4"

Signal 66 or, "Off campus business," and signal 43 meaning, "Building Check" were two of the many codes St. Luke's police officers were required to use. Mitch thought most of the codes were pretty silly, but not wanting to be written up for insubordination, he complied with department policies and used the codes. Mitch thought it would have been considerably easier to just say in plain English that he would be off campus checking on the senior center.

Mitch turned the radio back up and continued listening to an interesting sermon by Terrell Jenkins who was becoming his favorite preacher. He tried to picture himself in the church Stacy grew up in listening to the congregation encourage the preacher with spontaneous shouts and praises. Mitch wondered if he were a Christian, would he be one of the loud ones whose praises were heard even over the radio broadcast. He laughed to himself and headed north on Malcolm X Street which was extremely dark as usual. In front of an old abandoned storefront, dozens of men and women lay sound asleep on dirty blankets and flattened cardboard boxes. A few walked to and fro as though they had important business to tend to with heavy plastic garbage bags slung over their shoulders containing everything they owned in this world.

Over the years, Mitch had made this trip hundreds of times without much thought of the homeless people who camped out in all kinds of weather. March nights in Dallas were fairly mild, and on this particular night it was only down to the mid sixties with no rain. Hard as he tried, Mitch could not imagine what it must be like to live day by day in the street and have no place to call your home. Why hadn't he noticed these people before, or had he? In a way he had noticed them, but it had never occurred to Mitch to give them any real consideration. If these people wanted to get off the streets, they probably could, so why should anyone worry about the plight of a bunch of people who were homeless by choice when they seemed to care so little about themselves? Mitch realized that it was not their physical well being that mattered, but the fact they had given up on life that was so sad. Right or wrong, Mitch had people in his life that cared about his spiritual well being, and now Mitch wondered who cared about the souls of these people.

Pastor Jenkins was working his way into a passionate plea to his congregation and Mitch listened closely.

"Hammers, Bibles, money, and, yes, even an entire nation are nothing more than tools that can be used to bless someone or condemn them. What will you do with what you have? Somebody out there has a skill and can use that skill to build someone up. Somebody out there has a word from God that needs to be spoken to someone willing to hear. Somebody out there has a pocket full of money and food they can use to feed a person in need. What are you waiting for? Do you want to be used by the Master Craftsman, or are you going to keep what you have, and be used by the enemy of light?"

The congregation was beginning to roar with excitement, and Mitch felt a tugging at his heart but was not sure why. He knew the broadcasts were taped and that this particular sermon had been delivered a week ago, but somehow he felt Pastor Jenkins was talking to him. Just then, as Mitch drove north on Malcolm X, he looked to his right and saw a frail figure sitting in front of the gas pumps of an old dilapidated gas station. She was bent over at the waist and sitting by herself, bare foot, filthy from head to toe, and rocking back and forth. Mitch spun the cruiser around and pulled up next to her. "You okay, ma'am?" asked Mitch.

The women looked up, saw the police cruiser, and began to shake her head from side to side. "I ain't botherin' no one. I'm homeless and just sittin' here mindin' my own business."

When she spoke, Mitch could tell she was missing several front teeth, and those she had left were rotting and about to fall out. He had seen enough crack users to know one when he saw one, and this woman was a heavy user.

"I'm not here to bother you I just wanted to make sure you were okay. You looked like maybe you needed some help or something." Mitch began to put the cruiser back in gear.

"Well," she got up and began to walk toward Mitch. "Could you spare a dollar or a drink of water?"

Mitch pulled the water bottle from his lunch box. She grabbed it and sucked it dry within seconds.

"Do ya have anything to eat in there?" She said peering through the window just inches from Mitch's face. Her foul breath and body odor were almost more than Mitch could stand. She smelled of urine, cigarette smoke, and unwashed flesh; and she had several small open sores around her mouth that oozed pus. Mitch managed to grab onto a power bar that was near the top of his lunch box. There was a frozen dinner in there as well, but Mitch figured a frozen meal wouldn't do her much good.

"Here, it's a power…"

"I know what it is. I can read ya' know." She snatched it out of Mitch's hand and tore into it ravenously.

Rather than taking offense to what the woman had said, Mitch understood she had probably grown accustomed to being very defensive with people. For reasons he could not explain, Mitch took an enormous amount of pity on this woman who devoured the power bar as though she fully expected him to change his mind any moment and grab it back.

Mitch spoke cautiously, and quietly, "I'm sorry. I didn't mean to condescend, I'm sure you are fully capable of reading the wrapper."

"A person in my station in life," she said between smacks on the power bar, "gets used to condescension, and trust me it would take a lot more than that to offend me." She continued chewing the last of the power bar.

Mitch realized he was staring and decided to leave her in peace. "Look, I'm gonna take off. I gotta get back on the job. I hope the food and water helped."

She gave Mitch a peculiar look. "Thanks. What do I owe you?"

The implication gave Mitch a queasy feeling, so he put the cruiser in gear and pulled away from the gas station, continuing north toward the senior center. On the way back, he passed by the same spot, but the woman was gone. Mitch figured she had found someone to sell herself to so she could earn enough money for another rock of crack cocaine. He pulled into a space in the police headquarters parking lot.

Once inside, Mitch pulled out his frozen dinner and popped it in the microwave, still thinking about the pitiful women he had encountered. Mitch reflected on Pastor Jenkins's message and wondered if he had done the right thing. Here he was thinking like a Christian, but he was not a Christian at all. Mitch wondered what was coming over him when he heard a shrill "ding" from the microwave. He pulled the frozen dinner out of the microwave and had an idea. With a smile and a look of elated determination on his face, Mitch walked back outside to the lot where his cruiser was parked. He jumped behind the wheel with the hot dinner in his hand and drove back to the abandoned gas station.

*

Morgan and Alethea were silent as Pastor Jenkins brought the sermon to a close. The tiny light began to grow brighter in the spot where the rugged Shoe Shine Stand stood at the beginning of the service. As the light grew brighter a glistening and beautiful Shoe Shine Stand appeared. It was smooth on all surfaces and reflected the light which trickled down from above the stage. The delicate curves, with masterfully crafted tongue and groove patterns inscribed the corners of the box with detailed precision. With a decorative lathe, hand carved figurines of a shoe shine boy on each end of the box served as handles.

Pastor Jenkins stood tall over the Shoe Shine Box then took it in his hands and raised it over his heard. With a loud resounding voice he challenged his congregation. "This wooden box is the work of a master craftsman, but we do not give honor to the hammer or the work of the master, we honor the Master Himself. I will not exalt the hammer, or the Bible, or the finished work of the Master. I will praise and exalt the Master alone. What about you my brothers and sisters? Are you a hammer? Then let the Master take hold of you and make something wonderful while you give God the glory. Are you a rough piece of wood in need of a craftsman to bring out the beauty that lies within? Then let your God shape you into a magnificent work of art. Let God have His perfect way with you, and exalt Him for who He is, but take no credit for yourself. Give God the glory." Pastor Jenkins set the Shoe Shine Box down and the lights faded on stage as he began to pray with the congregation.

While the congregation filed out of the church Morgan and Alethea stopped to tell Pastor Jenkins how much they enjoyed the sermon.

"Wonderful sermon, pastor." said Morgan.

"Thank you, Sister Bernard. And how are you young lady?" Pastor Jenkins looked at Alethea and smiled.

"It looks like I'll be in Stacy's adopted homeland next week. Can I bring her anything from you two?"

Morgan looked shocked. "Next week? What are you doin' in Dallas next week? We're planning to be there next week too."

Now it was the Pastor's turn to look shocked. He smiled, "Praise the Lord, I guess we'll be there at the same time." You remember Mel Sanders, I'm sure."

Morgan, still a bit shocked nodded. "Yeah, I remember the detective."

Pastor Jenkins continued, "Well, he is goin' out there for some conference, and asked me to tag along with him. At first I said no, but then a friend of mine who used to pastor a church down in Fort Worth – where I attended seminary – told me about a little get together several of our classmates are having at the same time, and that was pretty much all it took to twist my arm. Why are you two goin'?"

For my birthday, Alethea spoke up cheerfully.

"Well that sounds wonderful," said Pastor Jenkins, "maybe we can all get together for a meal while we're there. I'll call the house before I leave and let you know where I'll be staying."

"That would be fine," said Morgan. "We'd love to get together with you while we're there."

*

Terrell Jenkins grabbed the phone on the first ring.

"Hey Pastor, this is Mel Sanders. Are we all set for Texas?"

"Absolutely, and you won't believe who else is traveling that way."

Mel didn't like the sound of this. "Who?" he asked.

"Morgan and Alethea Bernard are planning to be in Dallas at the same time we're gonna be there."

Mel was not pleased with this news at all. "Did you ask them to come, Pastor?"

"No, but I wish I had thought of it. You know Stacy is living down there now."

"Yeah, I know, Pastor, and I was hoping we could keep this between the two of us. The reason I asked you to meet me down there concerns them. I know you don't like all this secrecy, but trust me, I meant well. I just think it would be better if they didn't get involved in this right now."

"Mel, I have to tell you, this makes me a bit nervous. That family has been through a lot, and I don't know what you're up to but you have always been a good man so I'm willing to hear you out on this. But I warn you, this had better be good, this family means a lot to me. I would hate to put them through any more than they have already suffered."

Mel paused for a moment to think. This was getting out of hand fast and he had to control the situation.

"Look Pastor, I didn't want to tell you about this til' we got down there, but do you remember that I was never really satisfied with the investigation into Nick's death?"

"Of course, and I appreciate that you never led the Bernard's on with any false hope either."

"Well, I think there is a possibility, a slight possibility I should say, that Nick may be alive and in Dallas, Texas, not far from where Stacy is living."

Terrell was silent for a long moment before speaking. "I know you're not a foolish man, Mel, so I'm willing to listen to what you have to say. But I have to tell you, this family is extremely important to me and I cannot imagine what you think you have found that would justify dragging these people through more pain then they have already experienced."

"They're very important to me as well, Pastor, and I wouldn't dream of doing anything that would hurt them. That's why I wanted you there. If this is Nick and he is living right in Dallas, how long do you think it will take before he and Stacy see each other? My sources tell me this guy who may be Nick has some sort of amnesia and doesn't know for sure who he is, but he turned up at almost the exact same time as Nick was presumed dead."

"Mel, if it were anyone other than you I would have hung up the phone some time ago, but I have listened to what you had to say even though I'm having trouble believing what I just heard."

Sanders continued, "There's more, Pastor, much more. You remember the Dawson's Cadillac?"

Jenkins shifted the receiver into his other hand and slowly eased himself down into a soft chair in his study. "Yeah, I remember that car. It was Sam Dawson's pride and joy. He spent months after Daisy was killed guilting himself over caring more about the car than his daughter. Yeah, I remember that car well."

"Well the car also turned up in Dallas at about the same time as the guy who might be Nick. I got a call from a woman down there who say's she's best friends with this guy. He matched Nick's description, but with a few somewhat significant differences that can be explained. Look, all I'm saying is that this is worth checking out, and if it turns out to be Nick, he is going to need you there to help him make sense of all this."

Terrell Jenkins was silent for a long moment before speaking again. "I'll go along with you on this Mel, but I'm warning you again, we have to be careful. There are a lot of tender feelings here."

"Thanks, Pastor. Do you think you can keep this between us for now?"

"I do not condone lying, and if it comes down to it, I will be honest with Morgan, but I will try to avoid the subject until we have had an opportunity to check things out down there."

"That's all I can ask, Pastor. And, I appreciate your willingness to help."

"I would do anything if I thought it might somehow bring some light to these good people. I'll see you in Dallas, Mel."

Terrell Jenkins hung up the phone and immediately sank to his knees in prayer.

*

Mitch drove back to the abandoned gas station in a hurry. He didn't want to take the chance that the woman had left the area completely. Something about bringing a hot meal to this homeless woman made Mitch feel more alive than he had felt in a long time. He drove south on Hall Street past the railroad tracks and turned east again on Malcolm X. It was dark outside but several homeless people wandered up and down the street aimlessly. The garbage that lined the streets carried a sickening smell. The stench of beer and rotting food was heavy. It looked like a refugee camp, but people in cars simply drove by without taking notice of the tragic scene before them. When Mitch arrived at the gas station there was no one in sight. He drove around to the rear of the building and saw two men passing a paper bag between them with what was obviously a forty ounce bottle of beer inside, but the woman was nowhere to be seen. Mitch drove up and down the street then down the alleys on both sides but could not find her. He was ready to give up when he spotted her sitting on what was left of a brick wall on the west side of the street. Mitch's mood brightened as he pulled the cruiser along side her and beckoned her to step up to the side window.

She looked sad and afraid as she approached.

"I'll go get your water bottle," she said.

Mitch smiled at her.

"That's not why I came back. What's your name, ma'am?"

She paused for a moment before responding.

"Wendy. My name is Wendy."

"No Wendy. I'm not gonna run you for warrants. Here, I thought you could use something hot to eat."

Mitch handed Wendy the hot dinner which she took sheepishly.

"Is this for me?" Her eyes widened.

"Yes, Wendy, it's for you."

Wendy looked as though she would cry for a moment, then she smiled a toothless smile that lit up the night. Mitch could see for the first time that this woman, although she looked forty or fifty years old, was probably no more than thirty. Mitch could also see that Wendy was once very a very attractive woman. At some time, someone surely must have loved Wendy. But it was hard to tell from looking at her now.

She held the meal like a newborn baby, and stroked the top of the package as though she were loving a precious something that was all hers.

"Thank you, officer. Thank you so much for this."

"You're welcome, Wendy. Enjoy your meal."

Mitch began to drive away when Wendy called out to him.

"Officer, Officer."

Mitch stopped the cruiser as Wendy began to speak. Her voice was shaky, and she brushed the hair from her eyes. Wendy cleared her throat and cautiously peeked into the car on the driver's side.

"Are you an angel?" she asked in a sweet resonating voice.

Mitch hung his head – speechless for several long seconds.

"No ma'am, but I have met a few lately. May God bless you."

He drove away into the night with God heavy on his mind.

Chapter 20

Too Close for Discomfort

Dallas
March 16, 2005

Mitch set the Bible down on an end table next to the couch. He was dog tired, confused, and a bit frustrated. He had never been so intrigued by an endeavor in his life. His study of the Bible had completely enraptured him. He couldn't stop thinking about what he had read. It had started the day he left the hospital with Stacy and Michael. Since purchasing the new Bible at the mall Mitch read it as often as he could. He was reluctant to ask Stacy for clarification on Biblical issues because he wanted to discover as much as he could for himself. His reading left him with several unanswered questions. Mitch felt as much as he now enjoyed being a better person; he was a long way from becoming a Christian.

Stacy had stopped over to make dinner for Mitch and Michael. Their relationship had taken a strange turn since the day after Bart's accident. It seemed as though things had suddenly become very serious – their conversations were not as playful or optimistic as they had once been. There were times when Mitch wished he had never told Stacy he loved her. It was true, but that revelation had put a spin on their relationship he had neither anticipated nor desired. Although he continued to read the scriptures for understanding, the last thing Mitch wanted was for Stacy to get the impression he was doing it to hang on to her. A discussion about that very subject took place over dinner. They didn't argue. Rather, they acquiesced to a mutual understanding without specificity. Mitch was seeking truth for his own good reasons. Stacy was allowed to feel good about it so long as she understood Mitch's intentions.

Stacy set a cup of coffee down next to Mitch's Bible. "Well now Mr. Melancthon, how's the systematic theology coming along?"

"Who is Mr. Melancthon?"

Stacy smiled. "Sorry, he was a sixteenth century theologian. A protégé of Martin Luther who developed the first protestant systematic theology. It just seems that with the tenacity you're tearing into those scriptures..."

"I'm no theologian, nor do I want to be." Mitch lowered his head and rubbed his temples as he spoke through clinched teeth.

"I know Mitch. I was just trying to lighten the mood around here. It just seems like the only thing either of us has to smile about lately is Michael. I guess I'm concerned about where our relationship is going."

Stacy sighed heavily, stretching her hands toward her knees as she sat down slowly. Michael sat on the couch next to Stacy, imitating her moves as though he were ready to weigh in on the conversation.

"Hey buddy, why don't you go see what's in the toy box to play with," said Mitch.

Michael contorted his face and slid off the couch reluctantly.

"Are you two gonna tawk gwown up tawk again?"

"Yes." They said in unison.

Michael pouted into his room and began to play quietly with a toy.

"I'm sorry Stacy, you're right. In fact I was just thinking the same thing. It seems like things have gotten too serious between us. I wonder if either of us knows where to go from here."

Stacy changed the subject. "What book of the Bible are you reading now?"

"Job."

"Did you read through the entire New Testament?"

"Yup."

"Finding any answers?"

"Nope, just more questions."

Stacy paused for a moment before continuing. "Mitch, do you remember reading 2 Corinthians 6:14-15?"

"I remember reading Corinthians, but I don't specifically remember that passage. Why do you ask?"

"I've been stuck on that passage since the day after Bart's accident, and we had that little talk. You know the one where we both proclaimed love for one another."

"I've thought a lot about that talk myself." Mitch looked down at his shoes, lost in thought.

"Mitch, we're on dangerous ground here. And, I have to admit I'm playing with fire."

"Why would you say that? If you're talking about our spending time together, I have understood and respected your vow of celibacy until marriage, and I'm okay with that Stacy. I still enjoy spending time with you, and I cannot imagine that's all bad."

Stacy smiled and looked directly into Mitch's eyes. "It's not all bad Mitch, but it is dangerous. We hang out together as though we were a family and we're not. There is no covenant which commits me to you or you to me. We spend time together here in your place alone. And, I would be lying if I said I didn't desire intimacy with you. That feeling is only amplified by the time we spend together. I would never think of pressuring you to do anything, but we both know that our relationship either has to go forward or end."

Mitch knew what Stacy said was true, and her words burned into him. He wanted to marry Stacy, but he wanted to be sure it would work. She was right, they had moved too fast into a cozy relationship and allowed feelings to grow before either of them had a chance to determine how they wanted to proceed. Mitch gathered his thoughts.

"What are you suggesting? Do you think we should stop seeing each other? I won't lie to you either. I think about being intimate with you when we're together, but I respect you enough to hold back. We both know there will never be intimacy without the commitment of marriage, so do we just stop now before it goes any further?"

"Mitch, the problem is deeper than just you or I making a decision to marry. I must do what my Lord has commanded me to do regarding marriage. That's why I asked you if you had read 2 Corinthians 6:14-15. Open your Bible and read what it says there Mitch."

Mitch continued looking at Stacy while he reached for his Bible on the end table and turned to the New Testament.

"Do not be bound together with unbelievers; for what partner-ship have righteousness and lawlessness, or what fellowship has light with darkness? Or what harmony has Christ with Belial, or what has a believer in common with an unbeliever."

Mitch sat the Bible back down and stared at the floor, he couldn't bring himself to look at Stacy. He didn't understand all of what he had just read, but he understood enough to know that he had just read Stacy's marching orders, and the end was near. He knew he would never make a false profession of faith just to keep Stacy, and he knew he was not convinced that Christianity was right for him. Mitch was torn. Stacy had begun to tear up. Her voice quivered when she spoke.

"Do you know why God prohibits intermarriage between believers and unbelievers?"

"Because God is the ultimate bigot?"

Mitch immediately regretted making the remark. He was hurt, and he knew he was losing the only woman he had ever loved. His only response was anger at the God who would cost him happiness. "I'm sorry, that was an unfair attack."

"Mitch, I tried to tell you before, and I'll tell you again. If you think this is about my feelings, you have missed the point. You should be sorry about what you said because by saying it you blaspheme the only True God, and because it simply is not true. I hope you continue to read the Bible, Mitch, and I hope you get the answers you're looking for, but you have got to understand this is not a game, and it is not a matter of study for the sake of knowledge. It doesn't matter how much I believe you know, what matters is how much of what you know, you believe."

"Read Deuteronomy 7:3 and Ezra 10:2-4. Then read the book of Joshua and see what God told the children of Israel about mixing with people outside the faith and how it would ultimately destroy them. God is no bigot, he simply knows that oil and water do not mix, and that you cannot make a happy marriage when one person understands and lives by the truth of God while the other one is destined for hell simply because he refuses to accept the truth. That kind of mixed marriage makes for the worst kind of chaos and misery any two people can imagine."

"Mitch open your eyes, you have an even bigger problem than just whether or not you lose me. If you never accept the truth in that Bible you're reading, right here, this side of death, you will go to hell. And in this life, you are about to experience the incredible power of losing someone who has come to love the Lord. And I'm not talking about me."

Mitch jerked his head up and looked at Stacy.

"Then who are you talking about?"

"Me," came the tiny voice from inside his playroom. Neither Stacy nor Mitch realized he had been listening.

"Yes, Michael." Stacy said through tears. "He is growing in the Lord each day, Mitch. Right now he prays for you nightly and daily. He prays for you with his mother, and with me, but the day will come when his belief and your lack of belief will drive a wedge between the two of you. It's a certainty. Look at Matthew 10:34-39."

Mitch looked up the scriptures then let the Bible fall on his lap as he leaned back, clasping his face tightly between two hands.

"Are you telling me that my son will begin to hate me if I don't become a Christian?"

"I don't know if he will hate you, Mitch. What I do know is that he will learn to hate your sin. The true believer learns to love God above all earthly relationships. The day will come when the simple fact that you have turned your back on God will make it just as difficult for Michael to tolerate a relationship with you, as it will me. I know this is tough stuff Mitch, but for the Christian, nothing compels us like the love of Jesus."

Mitch was stunned. He knew Michael was infatuated with his mother's new religious beliefs and it was obvious he enjoyed spending time with Stacy as she shared her faith with him. But Mitch had never considered the possibility that this might come between them. He figured Michael might choose a different path in life than him, and Mitch was okay with that, but it didn't make since to him that his only son would someday turn his back on his own father. This made about as much sense to Mitch as everything else he had read in the Bible.

It seemed to Mitch that the Bible was full of unexplainable situations like the book of Job he had just finished. He decided to take a chance and ask Stacy a question.

"Stacy, why did God allow Satan to torment Job? And why was He so hard on Job's friends in the end?"

"Some things God chooses to answer, and some things he decides not to answer. We don't know exactly why God allowed Satan to torment Job any more than we know why God allowed Bart to be hit by a car and to lose his leg. Job's friends tried to explain God to Job in ways that do not match His true Character, and God felt the need to speak out against them. Regardless of why God allowed Job to be tormented, we know that God loved Job, and we know that through the experience, Job was able to draw closer to God and to understand the power, grace, and love of God better. Why did you ask?"

"I guess I feel a bit like Job right now, I feel like I'm about to lose everything that is important to me."

"Well, Mitch I know this is difficult, but I think you're beginning to understand. You may lose me. In fact, we may lose each other, Mitch. But my hope and prayer is that somehow, as the Lord wills it, you will find God in all of this. As for me, I have to be careful because the closer I get to you, the farther I walk from Christ."

Stacy stood to leave and turned around to grab her purse. When she turned back toward Mitch something unprecedented happened. Mitch was right in front of her, closer than he had ever been before. The two had established clear physical boundaries in their relationship from the beginning. No kissing, hand holding or other physical contact. Mitch stood before Stacy with tears in his eyes and his arms outstretched toward her. They came together in an embrace and held on tightly for what seemed like hours, so entwined it was difficult to tell where one person ended and the other began. Suddenly Mitch understood the danger Stacy had tried to describe in a way he had never expected.

Stacy's scent was intoxicating. From any distance, Mitch had enjoyed the fragrant perfume and the body sprays she wore, but this was different. The perfume mingled with the soft smell of springtime which came from her hair. This along with the natural pheromone of her body created a symphony of sensation that sent electric pulses up and down his spine in spastic rhythms. His pulse quickened as his fingers interlocked around Stacy's tiny waist. Her taunt skin expanded and contracted with each of her rapid breaths that came in controlled staccato bursts from a mouth doused in mint, and lips full and sumptuous. The chemical reaction was too intense, causing sensory overload. Their hearts beat like tandem snare drums of a marching band. Mitch pulled away out of fear and desperation. A line had been drawn in the sand, then breached. He retreated to the safety of his own personal space.

*

They parted without a word. Stacy walked out the door and closed it behind her. Stopping on the other side and praising God for intervention that surely saved her from the weakest moment of her life. As Stacy walked to her car on weakened knees, she realized it was over between her and Mitch. She could no longer control herself, and it was wrong to play with fire any longer. She ached from head to toe and wished there was another way out. In her heart, Stacy knew there was no other way and that this relationship had gone on longer than it should have. Now it was time to walk away. It would be tough, but it was so necessary.

*

As the door closed behind Stacy, Mitch eased himself down into the chair he had been sitting in. He too knew it was over, and there was nothing he could do. It made no sense to hug Stacy. He couldn't figure out why he had done it. Now, because of his carelessness, she was surely gone forever. With his face in his hands, Mitch shook his head from side to side wondering what to do next. Michael played quietly in the next room. Soon Mitch would have to drop him off at home. He got up and began to clear the dinner dishes from the table and to pack up Michael's things. It made no sense to Mitch that God would create love in his heart for the first time just to take it away. It all sounded like some sort of sick game to Mitch. The more he thought about it, the sadder he became. He was going to miss her. There was no doubt about that.

*

Michael fell asleep almost as soon as Mitch fastened him into his car seat. Earlier that day, when Mitch arrived home from work, he had parked his car behind Stacy's in the driveway. Later, when Stacy needed to run to the corner store to pick up a few items she needed for dinner, she drove Mitch's car. As Mitch pulled out of the driveway to bring Michael home he turned on the radio expecting to hear the smooth jazz station he usually listened to. But Stacy had tuned the radio to FM 100.7, The Word. Mitch was just about to turn the channel when something the radio preacher said caught his attention. The program was another taped broadcast from True Vine Ministries and Pastor Terrell Jenkins was just getting warmed up on a sermon using Mathew 10:32 as his text.

During the trip to Ennis, Mitch listened to the entire message and thought he understood Matthew 10:32 better by the time he arrived at Maggie's door, but he still had questions. Maggie answered the door with a pleasant smile which always made Mitch wonder if she wasn't seeing someone new.

"Hey, Mitch, did you two have a good visit?"

"Yeah, I guess we always do. Stacy just left a little while ago. She made roast beef and potatoes for dinner."

"How is Stacy? I haven't seen her in a couple weeks."

"She's fine." Mitch was still holding Michael, who had begun to wake up.

"Hey, little guy. Did you have fun with daddy?"

Michael nodded his head.

"I better get him to bed, Mitch." She took Michael from Mitch's hands.

Mitch looked uncomfortable, and Maggie could tell he had something on his mind.

"Mitch, would you like to come in for a minute; you look like you need to talk about something."

"Thanks – there is something – a question I wanted to ask you."

"Come in, Mitch. Make yourself at home."

They walked into Maggie's living-room and Mitch took a seat in an empty chair while Maggie brought Michael to his room. The first room beyond Maggie's front door was the living room, and Mitch had never gone beyond it. It was nicely decorated in earth tones with a large black leather couch and two grey cloth overstuffed chairs gathered around a rectangular coffee table. The walls were tastefully adorned with Picasso prints and a few metallic art designs that were somehow soft and surprisingly feminine. On the mantle were pictures of Maggie's family and an old boyfriend who Maggie had once told Mitch was locked up in a Minnesota prison. He was the great love of her life, and she kept the picture for sentimental reasons. Whereas the picture used to be in a drawer at her old place in Dallas, for some reason it had taken on significant meaning in Maggie's life since becoming a Christian. Maggie returned from putting Michael down to sleep.

"So, what's on your mind?"

Mitch remained uncomfortable, but thought Maggie might be able to help out. So he decided to overcome his discomfort and plunge in. "Stacy and I had another long talk about religion. She showed me the Bible passage that said she could not marry me if I was not a believer, or a Christian."

"Yep, that's 2 Corinthians 6:14"

"Right – anyway – she went on to tell me that eventually the love of God would turn not only her away from me, but also Michael. I was listening to this preacher – I think he's from up north where you came from – his name is Jenkins."

"Oh yeah, that's my old pastor, Terrell Jenkins from True Vine. I haven't heard that name in years. When I was a kid I used to go there for a while, but I didn't pay too much attention to him at the time. Anyway, let me stop talking. Go ahead. What was your question?"

"Well, Pastor Jenkins was saying that when Jesus said he did not come to bring peace but a sword, he was just explaining that non believers like me will not live in harmony with believers, and that even though you may be related to someone by blood, if you really love Jesus the way you're supposed to, you'll grow apart from people that don't love what Jesus loves."

Maggie looked truly concerned with what Mitch was saying. "Are you worried about your relationship with Michael?"

"Of course I am." Mitch said standing up, and gesturing wildly while he paced in front of the coffee table. "I'm pretty sure I've lost Stacy, and now it looks like I'll lose my son too if I don't become a Christian. It just doesn't seem fair that I should have to lose so much. I love Michael, and you know it. I don't think I should have to prove my love for Michael or for Stacy by following a religion I don't believe."

Maggie paused for a brief moment before speaking. "If you love Michael, and if you love Stacy, love the God who created them."

It was the second time Mitch had heard that line. It was beginning to define his reality. He didn't like the implication, but more and more he could not escape the truth that whoever this God was, He had made a profound impact on the lives of people Mitch cared very deeply for, and while that was reason enough to learn more, it was not compelling enough to change his heart.

Mitch stopped pacing and knelt down. He held Maggie's hands, but not her gaze.

"Is there any good news in all this?"

"Sure," said Maggie, "Malachi 4:5-6."

She let go of Mitch's hands and got up as if to say, it's time for you to leave. Mitch caught the hint and stood also. Before turning to leave, Mitch smiled back at Maggie with genuine affection.

"You really are a changed woman aren't you? I mean, you are sure about all this."

"I've never been so sure of anything in my life, Mitch, and my daily prayer is that you will know the joy of the Lord as I do."

Mitch gave Maggie a quick hug. Not like the embrace he and Stacy had experienced a short time ago, but more like a brother hugging a sister. He appreciated Maggie taking the time to listen to him and he marveled at the change in her personality. For the first time, he began to regret the way he had dishonored and mistreated her.

"Maggie, I'm sorry for – I mean I wish I hadn't – well I just…"

"I know, Mitch. Give it to God."

Mitch walked out the door and down the short concrete path to his car. He got behind the wheel of his car and sat for several long contemplative minutes. After sitting in silence, Mitch turned to the small Bible he now carried in his car and looked up Malachi 4:5-6.

"Behold, I am going to send you Elijah the prophet before the coming of the great and terrible day of the Lord. He will restore the hearts of the fathers to their children and the hearts of the children to their fathers, so that I will not come and smite the land with a curse."

Chapter 21

Ellum Interrupted

Dallas
March 18, 2005

Ellum was a happy man. Everything was going just as he had planned. Free for four years, he was, by his own definition a success with all loose ends effectively tied. Ellum had more than enough money, thriving businesses, a nice place to live, and his future looked bright. He had proven that with proper planning and the will to do whatever was necessary, there was nothing he could not accomplish.

His investments had paid off well. After splitting ninety-four thousand dollars three ways, Ellum took thirty-two thousand dollars and became silent partner to a cash strapped crack cocaine dealer in South Dallas. After turning a quick profit of fifty thousand dollars in six months, Ellum began buying used cars as fast as he could. He found an empty car lot at a good price on Ross Avenue near Carroll and paid a year in advance on the lease. Starting with only fifteen cars, Ellum's car lot was instantly profitable, mostly because of his unethical business practices.

Ellum left the car lot, driving south on Ross to Peak, where he went east to Commerce Street and headed toward Downtown. He drove through downtown Dallas toward I-30, and he passed the Texas Book Depository where Lee Harvey Oswald had stood with a high-powered rifle in a fourth floor room some forty years earlier. It occurred to Ellum as he drove by that Oswald had truly made an indelible mark on history. Oswald was a crook of monumental proportions, but he was also a classic screw up. Ellum realized that like JFK, he too was riding in a drop top Ford. The ghoulish irony made him laugh out loud. Ellum passed the depository and headed west on I-30 toward Oak Cliff where he now owned a dozen rental properties which brought him a substantial amount of passive income.

His short-cropped hair blew in the wind as the brand new convertible Thunderbird gathered speed and leveled off at sixty miles per hour. One of the things Ellum had learned to do well was avoid drawing attention from law enforcement. Therefore, while he enjoyed the power of the sports car, he knew it was in his best interest to obey traffic laws as much as possible. The CD player was turned down low – saxophonist Dave Coz blew a catchy jazz melody and Ellum contemplated his good fortune before his cell phone chirped and brought him back down to earth.

"What is it?" Ellum's tone was sharp.

A raspy male voice came on the line. "I'm not gonna use names but listen carefully. You took care of one in the joint up north, but I found the one that got away. If you still want em you'll meet me at the West Transfer Station at four o'clock sharp."

"Who is this, and how did you get this number?"

"You'll find out at four o'clock and no sooner. Like I said, if you want em, be there."

"Do you know who you're messin' with here? I asked you a question. Who are you?"

"No names, player, but I suggest you watch your speed. You're movin' kinda fast, and there's cops all over this highway. You wouldn't wanna get a speedin' ticket. By the way, that's a nice looking T-Bird, but you look kinda stupid laughin' to yourself when you drive."

Just then Ellum saw a dark colored GMC Tahoe with its windows completely tinted pull out in front of him on the left then swerve right to the other side exiting the freeway before he could follow.

This was not good. Ellum had maintained a low profile since arriving in Dallas but somehow he must have gotten sloppy. Someone knew who he was, and what he had been up to. To make matters worse, he had allowed himself to be followed. It was two o'clock in the afternoon so Ellum had plenty of time to take care of his business in Oak Cliff before heading back to the West End.

*

The property he owned was in a low-income part of town where Ellum knew he could demand rent that was twice what the property was worth, and the tenants wouldn't complain about the lack of upkeep. The apartments were in bad shape and worth about three hundred dollars per month in rent if the plumbing and electrical had been up to code and working, which they were not. Ellum's tenants had been evicted from so many places for drug trafficking, prostitution, and other offenses they couldn't find anyone else to rent to them. Ellum also knew that by keeping women on the lease who received government assistance he could charge up to eight hundred dollars for rent and the check would come directly to him each month. He not only didn't care what his tenants did on the property, in some cases, it was his dope they sold. With this arrangement, Ellum was able to make double and triple money on his investments.

On occasion the city would threaten to issue him a citation for debris that had accumulated around one of the rentals, or for some other nuisance. In such cases Ellum knew a few people he could pay cash to take care of these minor clean ups. Today he needed to meet with one such crew, inspect the work they had done, and pay them so they could go and do whatever they did to amuse themselves. Today's crew was a group of illegal Mexican immigrants who worked extremely cheap. Ellum had found the lead worker hanging out behind one of his buildings. The man was looking for work, and Ellum had just plucked an order of condemnation from the front door of his rental property. Apparently the city had become impatient waiting for him to clean up the mess one of his tenants had left on the property.

One of Ellum's tenants called him early that day to tell him about the city's notice so he drove out to the property to check it out. Upon arrival, Ellum found a man hanging out looking for work, so he explained the job he needed done as best he could and made an agreement with him for one hundred dollars cash to get the manual labor done.

Ellum turned off the freeway at Camp Wisdom Road and made a right turn. He drove this road regularly and was always fascinated by how people chose to live in squalor. In this land of opportunity, there was self-induced poverty that Ellum just could not understand.

Making money was no secret; it was a simple matter of creativity, motivation, and a willingness to take advantage of every opportunity for cash that came one's way. He always thought it strange that the only thing these people seemed to do consistently well was build churches and increase their membership. Right there on Camp Wisdom Road were three of the largest black churches in Dallas; Concord, Oak Cliff Bible Church, and International Body of Christ. It seemed to Ellum that if these people would put their church planting skills to work in a business context, they could really make some money. But instead, they would rather find ways to praise a God that couldn't even put fifty cents in their pockets.

Ellum rolled into the driveway of his latest acquisition, an eight unit apartment building which was falling apart right in front of him. He had paid sixty thousand dollars for the building three months before, and by charging seven hundred and fifty dollars per month he had already recouped eighteen thousand dollars of his investment in rent alone. The crack house he ran in the basement was the real moneymaker. His cut of that enterprise had raked in an additional thirty-five thousand dollars already, and with the cash he had earned, Ellum was ready to buy the building next to it.

The four workers were sweaty and dirty when Ellum pulled up. He got out of his car and quickly inspected the work. His mind was on the mysterious phone call he received, and so long as the mess behind the building was cleaned out, he was satisfied. Ellum pulled four, twenty-dollar bills, and four, five-dollar bills off a large roll of cash in his pocket and handed it to the lead worker who began to count it slowly. The man counted the money while looking Ellum in the face. Ellum didn't like the look he was getting. Somehow it looked as though this man was challenging him.

"Que es la problemo?" Ellum asked as he pulled the sunglasses off his face and looked squarely at the man counting the money. The man said nothing.

"You savvy?" Ellum wasn't sure if the man was ignoring him, or if he simply did not understand his poor attempt to do a tough guy [What's your problem] routine in Spanish.

The man smiled revealing brown and broken teeth that probably had never been brushed. "No problemo man, no problemo."

Two of the four men jumped into the bed of an old Chevy pickup that was parked in the driveway next to Ellum's T-Bird. A third man got behind the wheel. The lead worker stared at Ellum for a second longer before walking away toward the pickup and getting into the passenger seat. Ellum stood still trying to understand what the staring was all about as the pickup truck backed out of the driveway then pulled away with the passenger side facing him.

As the truck drove around the corner, Ellum saw the lead worker hold up four fingers. The lead worker said in perfect English as the truck pulled into traffic, "four o'clock don't be late."

Ellum's first thought was to jump in his car and follow the truck, then he realized how ridiculous the thought was. He was an unarmed white man running from the law in the middle of one of the most ethnic neighborhoods in Dallas. What did he think he was going to do once he caught up to them? Ellum got in his car and decided to grab a bite to eat before his meeting with the mysterious caller. He ordered off the menu at a local Tex Mex restaurant in Oak Cliff and waited for his food to arrive. He wasn't very hungry, but he needed to kill a little time and try to figure out what his next move would be. Making the meeting was not an option; it was a necessity for two reasons. First, someone knew more about him than he was comfortable with. And second, someone knew where he could find Ricardo Garcia, and Ricardo was on the top of Ellum's priority list.

*

Ellum had found himself in a difficult situation shortly after arriving in Dallas. Razor was certainly no genius. He was caught selling drugs right out of the First Avenue Bar. The good news was that he had gone back to Minneapolis the day they had arrived in Dallas just as Ellum had told him to. The bad news was that Razor could not keep his mouth shut in the joint. That was how the two of them met in the first place. Razor could not stop talking about the jobs he had done and the people he had done his dirty work with. Ellum couldn't afford to have Razor telling all their mutual acquaintances what they had been up to with complete details on how it had all been done. Ellum knew enough about the prison system to realize that some convict desperate for a break in his sentence would use that information with the authorities to buy his way out sooner. Ellum had no intention of going back inside.

In prison, a thousand dollars could buy a lot. The prison economy is usually measured in cigarettes and other little extras, but for cold cash in an inmate account, a person can buy so much more, even a homicide. Especially in Oak Park Heights Prison where most of the inmates were doing at least one life sentence and had very little to lose. During his stay at Oak Park Heights, Ellum had befriended many such individuals that thought his Wyatt Earp style shoot out in Deep Ellum was rather impressive. So, with the clout he had earned from his rap sheet and a thousand dollars cash, Ellum was able to arrange a convenient suicide for Razor within days of his return to the prison.

The problem was that word of Razor's untimely death reached Ricardo all the way back in Texas, and he was no dummy. Ricardo had spent just enough time with Ellum and Razor to know that Razor had not committed suicide, and that Ellum was somehow involved. With the remainder of his thirty-one thousand dollars and a good tail wind behind him, Ricardo headed for the border before Ellum could find him. In hindsight, Ellum realized it would have been smart to take out Ricardo first, but that was hindsight. Although he had kept an eye out for Ricardo as best he could for a couple years, in time Ellum had decided not to worry about him anymore. If he resurfaced, Ellum would hear about it and take the appropriate action. The phone call he received today was good news, but he was uncomfortable not being in control. He was also uncomfortable with someone else watching him. Ellum knew he might need to return to his violent ways very soon.

*

Four o'clock on any given weekday presented a carnival of activity at the West Transfer Station. Commuters traveling from surrounding suburbs into downtown Dallas transferred from rail cars to buses that brought them within walking distance of downtown office buildings. The cobblestone ground gave the station an historic feel among the West End area which was known for new age art, alternative fashions, and alternative life-styles. Dallas was famous for its pigeon population. The birds swarmed the West End by the thousands, often to the chagrin of local businesses who suffered the constant bombardment their droppings. Commuters read local newspapers while waiting for their next bus. Police officers patrolled the station on bicycles, and hustlers went from one person to another begging for spare change as hip hop music blared from boom boxes.

Ellum knew why the mysterious caller had picked this particular time and place. The place was so well populated at that time. He would be a fool to do anything rash. There were simply too many witnesses everywhere, and the police were just a whistle away. In addition, it was easy for someone to blend in among the crowd so long as they didn't do anything foolish to draw attention to themselves. If Ellum were going to pick a meeting spot with someone known for killing, this would be it.

The raspy voice came from behind him.

"I appreciate your punctuality; I'm a very busy man."

Ellum spun around to see a tall muscularly built black man wearing a tank top, shorts and sandals. His muscles literally bulged. It was immediately clear to Ellum that brute force and intimidation were not on his side. In the background, Ellum saw the lead worker from his apartment building, and another Mexican he had not seen before. The second Mexican was a short, chubby, unshaven man whose top front teeth were missing when he smiled.

"Okay," began Ellum, "you have my attention. Now what do you want."

"I want your keys, your purse, and I want you to die." The large black man began to laugh. "Just kidding ma man, but you gotta admit, that was a great line." He and the other two men began to laugh again loudly. Ellum didn't see the humor at all.

"Hey, look man. I'm a fan of your work. Don't get all serious on me okay?"

Ellum kept his cool as he spoke. "Okay, so you've spent some time talking with Ricardo. I'll give you that. What will it cost me to find out where he is?"

This time the chubby Mexican spoke. "More than one hundred dollars for sure, but I think you can manage it."

The black man moved closer to Ellum. "Look, I know all about your reputation and the only reason I looked you up is because I figure you've got some brains in your head or you wouldn't have stayed out so long and done as well as you have. So I'm selling my information to you at a bargain because the two of us have some mutual interests."

The man removed a locker key from his shorts pocket and handed it to Ellum.

"Put thirty thousand dollars cash in this locker at the Greyhound station tomorrow by four o'clock. After you lock the money up, stick the key in the sand in the ashtray next to the locker. If the money's all there when I check, you'll get a call from me on your cell phone tomorrow night."

Ellum cleared his throat, "thirty thousand is a bargain, but why should I give you anything if we have certain mutual interests as you put it?"

"Because I can afford to let him live, and you cannot."

Ellum allowed a slight smile to form on his lips as he spoke. "You never told me your name."

The black man snapped his fingers as though he had just remembered something he had previously forgotten, then he smiled himself. "You know, you're right. I didn't."

The three men turned and walked away. The lead worker turned and held up four fingers while saying again in perfect English, "four o'clock. Don't be late."

Ellum wondered if those five words were the extent of his English vocabulary.

*

Whether it was arrogance, a morbid sense of humor, or just his uncanny knack for pushing the envelop a little too far, no one will ever know, but Ellum had incorporated his business under the name of Daisy's Seville Inc in August 2001 with a thirty-two thousand dollar cash deposit in a small business account at Compass Bank in Ennis, Texas. The transaction only required a phony driver's license and Social Security card in the name of Sam Dawson. He rarely made an appearance at the bank in person, preferring electronic banking and mailing checks whenever necessary. One of the things Ellum liked most about living in the twenty-first century was that cash was so rarely needed, but so easily accessible. That is, small amounts of cash. He knew the $30,000 he needed to find out where Ricardo was hiding would require a rare personal appearance at the bank. He could have gone to one of the branches in Dallas, but he liked keeping some distance between his place of operations and his bank, that was the reason he had opened the account in Ennis rather than Dallas.

The day after meeting the mysterious man at West Transfer Station, Ellum took a late morning drive to Ennis. He didn't mind the forty-five minute drive. In fact, he welcomed it. Ellum realized he had little choice regarding the money. He was buying more than an opportunity to tie up a loose end. He was purchasing his anonymity from the strange man. But Ellum had no intention of letting this man live with the information he possessed.

By the time Ellum arrived in Ennis, the lunch rush was over and no one was in line ahead of him or behind him. He walked up to the teller line and presented a check from the corporate account in the amount of thirty thousand dollars along with the phony ID he so rarely used.

The teller accepted the check and the ID before she began to walk away from the line. "I'll have to get approval for an amount this large, sir. I'll be just a minute."

"No problem," responded Ellum. He had expected the teller to have to get approval; it was nothing to worry about. Every bank had policies on how much cash a teller was allowed to handle in a single transaction.

The teller returned to the line with a female banker who smiled a lot and thrust her hand toward Ellum.

"Welcome to Compass, Mr. Dawson. I just need to make sure you're aware that the federal government requires us to record and specially document all transactions that exceed ten thousand dollars, so we will make a copy of your ID, and we have a short form we need to fill out. We'll have your money to you in no time."

Ellum smiled back at the banker while shaking her hand. "I was expecting that. I don't usually transact business in cash, but I have an out of town vender who is new and not set up yet with a credit card system, so I've agreed to pay him in cash this time only. Thanks for your help, ma'am."

"That's quite alright. We'll be with you in just a moment sir."

There was something about this women's accent that was familiar to Ellum, and he couldn't put his finger on it. She walked behind the teller line and through a doorway which led to a back room. Ellum waited patiently for about five minutes before she returned with a handful of large bills.

"I hope one hundreds are okay, sir."

"That's fine. Your accent is familiar. Where are you from?"

The banker blushed as she set the heavy wad of cash on the counter. "After ten years of living here, I thought I'd picked up the native tongue. I'm originally from Minnesota I moved down here back in 1995. I'm Maggie, pleased to meet you, sir."

Suddenly, Ellum wished he hadn't asked the question. He tried to manage a smile while standing still and waiting for the banker to count out the cash. When she finished, Ellum scooped up the money, tucked it into his briefcase, and headed for the door. This was not the discrete way Ellum was accustomed to conducting business. For the moment he was glad he didn't live or do business in the community near the bank where this woman might see and recognize him again. Ellum wanted to put as much distance between himself and this woman as he could.

The drive back to Dallas went fast and Ellum headed straight for the Greyhound bus depot. He waited until four o'clock before going inside and making his way to the locker. Ellum opened the locker and placed the briefcase inside. He took a quarter from his pocket and slid it into the money slot before placing the key in the sand of the ashtray next to the locker as instructed. Ellum left the depot and walked back to his car, then drove to the car dealership and waited for his cell phone to ring.

At five thirty Ellum's cell phone chirped.

The raspy voice came on the line. "Check the pink envelope in the top drawer of your desk. I got there a little ahead of you, but couldn't stick around to chat." The line went dead.

Ellum opened the top drawer of his desk and removed a bright pink envelope. Inside the envelope was a brief computer generated message:

4:00 PM Saturday April 8th at the Ballpark in Arlington. He'll be on a work crew going through the front gate.
Happy hunting

Chapter 22

Falling

Minneapolis/Dallas
March 18, 2005

From outside the second story window and across the yard it mocked and sneered at him. A lifetime ago it represented hard work, persistence, patience, and thrifty living. In a word, success. Now it served to remind him of his most devastating failure of judgment and misplaced affinity. He had been so proud of it the day he brought the car home new. He should have given the old car he had been driving to his daughter. But he refused to do so, hanging on to worthless principles, none of which could bring her back from the dead. The pearl white, 2001 Cadillac STS stood in stark contrast next to the old, 1968 Mustang in Sam Dawson's driveway. Almost as though it were a providential sign from above, the Cadillac arrived from Texas the day after Sam and Benny had begun restoration on the Mustang for Alethea. The restoration project had gone smoothly, although they still had plenty of work left to do. Sam and Benny had found most of the parts they needed in the Bernard's garage. In addition to setting aside parts for the restoration, Nick had drawn up a detailed plan for putting the old car back together which made Sam and Benny's work a joy.

During the prior week while working on the Mustang, the Dawson's had reached a decision which had been four years in the making. They would sell their home of over two decades and move to a smaller home in one of the suburbs of Minneapolis. Seeing the Cadillac again brought feelings that had been dormant, to the surface. The once dormant feelings forced the family to seek closure by letting go of an old, unimportant, icon of their past. To everyone's surprise, the decision to sell became a source of hope and relief, rather than tension. Even the older boys who had moved out of the house were on board with the decision. With the twins now away at college and Benny the only sibling still at home, they all agreed the time had come to move on.

Within the hour, a tow truck would be there to take away the Cadillac. Sam had donated the car to the church. The church in turn had sold the car to a dealership in Rochester, Minnesota. For over a week, Sam had avoided contact with the Cadillac. He even managed not to look at it most of the time, but today, he and the old car stared each other down from a distance.

Diverting his attention from the car, Sam continued to pack a box full of memorabilia which was in a closet on the second floor of the house. There on the top shelf was a dusty, brown, vinyl photo album he had never seen. Sam took down the photo album and laid it on a table near the window. Inside he discovered a letter written like a journal entry. Daisy had written the letter on July 14, 1997. Sam figured the letter and photos must have been among some of Daisy's personal belongings they had missed after her death. Under the letter were dozens of pictures taken during a church outing to Minnehaha Falls with Nick Bernard and the True Vine youth group. Sam picked up the letter and read it.

*

It's hard to describe what happened today but I think I should try. Pastor Bernard took us on another "Youth Outing." This time we went to Minnehaha falls. A group of us were running back and forth across the stone bridge, throwing sticks at one another when I stopped to look over the edge. I found myself mesmerized by the sheer power of the water going over the falls. There I was, safely standing on a man made bridge, while hundreds of gallons of water per minute went rushing over a stony cliff. I wondered at that moment, who made that cliff, and who told the water to rush over it. I know, that's pretty lame, but that's what went through my mind. I kept thinking that the bridge had been made by humans about fifty years ago, but the water had been rushing over those rocks for centuries. I guess it all made me feel really small and unimportant.

The water rushing over the falls looked so pure and clean. I asked myself, where did it come from? The Mississippi river? And before that, the Atlantic Ocean? How many other girls just like me had stared at those same waters in other parts of the world? How many lives had these waters saved, and how many lives had they taken? If I had stood at the bottom of the water fall, it would have crushed me in an instant, yet standing there on that bridge I could see how wonderful the falls were in complete safety like young Indian girls must have done over two hundred years ago. I wanted to be a part of this great natural beauty, so I leaned forward to get closer. I kept leaning forward until I felt dizzy and couldn't tell where I left off, and the water began. All the sudden, the water seemed like an extension of myself and I couldn't stop reaching for it.

The next thing I felt was Pastor Bernard's strong grip on my ankles. I had leaned too far and had almost fallen in. Somehow, Pastor Bernard saw what I was doing and caught me just as I was about to go over. I know that if he hadn't caught me I would have fallen in the water and gone over the falls. He pulled me up and sat me down on the ground. At first he didn't say a word but the look on his face told me he thought I was behaving foolishly.

I have no idea what came over me or why I did what I did. But after I had calmed down a bit, Pastor Bernard used the incident as one of his, "Teachable moments." He said life is but a vapor and that we don't know how much time we have on earth. Pastor Bernard told me my life could have been over in an instant. He asked me what I had to show for thirteen years of living if that had been my last day. Sometimes I hate those questions. It seems like he puts everything into a Christian context like he wants to force me to be something I am not. I am grateful he was there, and I can tell he really cares, but I don't know how to respond to a question like that. What bothers me even more is that I felt that same question in my head as I was hanging over the falls. I wondered, what good is this life of mine? Everyone tries to tell me that I need to live for Christ, yet I want to live for myself. But today was somehow different. Today I dared to ask myself if life could be about something bigger than me. I asked myself what it might be like to live like the water running over the Minnehaha falls, touching others around the world for so much longer than just an instant. I feel as though when I was reaching for the water, I was reaching for God.

After Pastor Bernard finished talking to me I stood by myself for a moment thinking about what had happened and what he had said. As quickly as that deep feeling of reaching for God came, it left me. The feeling hung on for an instant until I knew I was back to myself, then it was gone. As good as that feeling was I cannot understand why I don't miss it? Why didn't I fight to keep that feeling, and why didn't I reach for God like I reached for that water. I had to write this down because I don't think I'll ever feel that way again. Its not that I love my life the way it is. I'm just afraid of giving up who I am.

July 14, 1997

*

Sam read the letter and examined the pictures several times. He knew there was little chance that Daisy had become a Christian before dying, and that knowledge was far more unbearable than the knowledge that she had died. For years Sam tormented himself with guilt, wondering if he had done enough to share the love of Christ with his only daughter. He tried to put it out of his mind as he gently placed the letter and photographs into an empty box. Looking back out the window Sam could see the old Mustang. Benny would be home soon, and they would resume their work on the car. For Sam, the Mustang represented new possibilities from old realities. The Mustang had been his mother's, and now it would be passed on to a young girl who needed to believe that God is still God, even in the face of tragedy and loss.

*

One of the wonderful mysteries about Minnesota winter is the extreme vacillations in temperature. Each day Sam and Benny worked on the Mustang it had been in the mid to upper forties, but the day after they installed the exhaust system the sun came out, and the temperature peaked at seventy degrees, melting all the remaining snow. Benny hopped into the driver's seat and slid the key into the ignition while Sam opened the garage doors. When Benny turned the key, like smooth jazz in the summertime, the engine filled the air with rhythmic soul.

"Wooooooooo Whooooooooo, Dad do you hear that! This thing is ready to roll!"

Sam smiled at his young son and clapped his hands triumphantly. The hard part was over, and all that remained was the interior work. Sam drove the car down from the ramp and back into the garage. They replaced all four wheels one by one with the wheels Nick had bought for the car. After all four wheels were replaced; they began to remove the seats and the carpet.

Once the interior had been gutted, Sam and Benny followed Nick's detailed directions for laying down the stereo wires. They decided it would be a good idea to install the amplifier, sub-woofer, and CD player before laying the carpet, just in case they got something wrong. Benny had seen his older brothers install car stereos and he thought he could probably handle that end if Sam could manage the amp and sub-woofer installation. Nick had purchased four speakers which went behind the rear seat in front of the rear window, and there was one speaker for each door. Sam and Benny installed each component exactly as the instructions indicated.

Benny ran to his room and grabbed a CD which he slid it into the CD Player. Sam turned on the ignition not knowing what to expect.

He had never done an installation like this before. After a few clicks, Fred Hammond's funky baseline boomed through the garage rattling everything that wasn't bolted down. It was late but they decided it would only take a couple more hours to lay the carpet and install the new seats.

The following day, an exhausted father and son surveyed their work. Sam couldn't help feeling pride in what had been accomplished, and a slight amount of sadness that the work was done.

"Do you think she'll like it Dad."

"No son, I can't say I do." Sam grimaced as if he were distressed. Then grinning a toothy grin he continued, "I think she'll love it."

"Are you glad we finished it, Dad?"

"Yes I am. Now that we know what we're doing, I'm looking forward to when you and I can put together a car for your 16th birthday." Benny Dawson beamed.

Chapter 23

Maggie

Ennis, Texas
January – March, 2005

"**G**od, I just want to thank you for calling me out of darkness and into your light. You took me from the sewage of death, cleaned me up, made me righteous and gave me life. You adopted me when I was as bad as I could be. You saw in me what I never saw in myself. I thank you just for being my God. Right now I can think of nothing more important to say than thank you. When I turned my back on You, thinking my way was better than Yours, You kept on loving me. I thought I had it all figured out, I thought I knew right from wrong, but I didn't know a thing. I am nothing. You are everything.

I thank You for filling my life with people who care about me, and who worship You. Lord protect us tonight, watch over us and keep us safe. I ask also that You watch over Stacy and Mitch, and I pray dear Lord that someday soon Mitch will become a part of Your family. In Jesus name I pray, AMEN."

-A tiny voice said in agreement, "Amen, Mama"-

*

Margarita Sarai remained on her knees contemplating her life for several long moments. So many things which she could neither understand nor articulate had happened in her short twenty-eight years on earth. There was a time when she believed, as Forrest Gump's mother had put it, "Life is like a box of chocolates." For Maggie, as most people referred to her, life had been full of surprises and was unpredictable to any degree. She had given up on trying to do the right thing years ago, reasoning that no matter what one did, life would have it's way with you whether you liked it or not. To Maggie, there had been a wide gulf between a person's actions and the consequences for those actions.

Michael lay on his bed fast asleep, curled into a fetal position. It seemed to Maggie that Michael was born to pray, and he was just waiting for his mother to figure how to minister to him. Before she had begun praying with him, Michael had a difficult time falling to sleep. Once he did fall asleep, it was rarely restful. Lately, he slept soundly and woke up refreshed. Michael would even pray on his own during the day. There were times when Maggie walked into his room only to hear him talking to someone that wasn't there. It was not the same as him having an imaginary friend, though he had one of those too. Michael would talk to God, praising Him, and asking Him questions on a regular basis.

*

Since the first part of the year when Maggie gave her heart to Jesus, everything in her life had changed. She had begun attending the First Baptist Church of Ennis a few months back. Maggie started attending the church after developing a friendship with a coworker of hers at Compass Bank named Tara. Always looking for a sympathetic ear, someone to whom she could complain about her lot in life, Maggie bent Tara's ear on many occasions, discussing her plight as a single mom, doing it all on her own.

Usually Tara, a battle weary mother of four including two teenagers, listened patiently and with genuine empathy to Maggie. On a cool January day in 2005, Maggie stepped into Tara's cubicle first thing in the morning and sat down. Tara could tell it was going to be another one of those days when Maggie would start complaining. And, it was not likely the complaining was going to stop before lunchtime.

"Girl, you will not believe what that man did this time." Maggie started in as soon as she sat down.

Tara hunched forward as though she was about to offer some prophetic insight as to what "That Man" must have done. With a look of true concern and interest, Tara began to speak slowly and with cool calculation.

"Maggie, why did your parents name you after a cocktail?"

For a split second Maggie looked confused by the question, then she answered.

"Well, they were the only two white folks at the Riverview Supper Club during happy hour the day they met, and they were both havin' some strawberry margaritas. Later, after havin' enough of those things, they got busy in my daddy's conversion van which was parked out back, and that's when and how I was conceived. So they figured they

271

should name me after the drink that got em' loose enough to create me. I never have used that name though; since I was a kid everyone just called me Maggie. Anyway Mitch actually had the nerve to send his new girlfriend to pick up Michael on Friday."

Tara looked intrigued, "So whose idea was it to name him Michael, yours or Mitch's?"

Maggie was confused again. She leaned back, crossed her legs, took a nail file from behind her ear, and began to punish her nails with the file as if one of them had done her some serious wrong.

"It was my idea. Mitch didn't want nothin' to do with that child 'til he was born. Anyway, Miss Thing walked up to the door, rang the doorbell, and started introducin' herself like it was no big deal."

Tara leaned back into her chair and began to reply.

"I always wondered why parents named their kids Brandy or Margarita. I even heard of one kid named Alaze. Can you believe that? Why didn't they just name the kid Remy Martin, or Cognac? But I like Michael. That's a sweet name."

Maggie stopped trying to erase all traces of the nails from her fingers and gave Tara a puzzled look before continuing. "As I was saying, she starts goin' on about how she wanted to save Mitch from havin' to drive all the way down here so he could have more time with Michael. And I'm like, 'Look heifer,' (scuse me, I know you don't use that kinda language, but she was really workin' my nerves.) But anyway, I was I like, 'Look, I know when Mitch has a long weekend, and I don't need you telling me about how much time they have together.' Can you believe this?"

Tara looked right into Maggie's face as though she was really engaged in what Maggie had to say, then she looked whimsically toward the ceiling before reaffixing her gaze back on Maggie.

"Well, I guess it's not that much different than a person naming their cat, "Nip" or something. I mean if you could name a cat Nip, why not name a person Brandy?"

Maggie set the file down, leaned forward, and got right in Tara's face. "Excuse me, earth to Tara. Are we having the same conversation here or are you communing with your inner self or something like that?"

Tara refocused her eyes and came out of her self-induced trance-like state, then began laughing at her friend.

"Maggie, I love you dearly, and there is very little I wouldn't do for you, so take this in the spirit of Christian love. You need to get a life and get your head out of your butt. And if you want to know how to do that, come see me after work. In the meantime, I have work to do. So please find your way out of my cubicle and back to your own."

Maggie sat stunned for several seconds with her mouth wide open. She began to mouth something but no words came out. Eventually, she collected her nail file, thrust it back behind her ear, and as Tara sat looking at Maggie with her hand extended outward toward the cubicle opening – Maggie got up and marched out mumbling something under he breath about how rudely she had been treated. As Maggie walked out, Tara could not hold back a laugh, which Maggie heard.

"You wrong girl, you know you wrong." Maggie marched down the hall toward her desk, then disappeared behind a row of file cabinets.

*

Maggie sat behind her desk fuming. She couldn't believe how she had been treated by her friend. And, she didn't understand what had caused Tara to act that way. Maggie usually got along well with everyone, but she had been particularly drawn to Tara. It seemed odd that Tara, who was usually willing to listen to whatever was on Maggie's mind, had suddenly turned so cold. After cooling off for a few minutes, Maggie figured Tara must be having a bad day and simply needed a moment to herself.

Maggie hadn't told Tara that Mitch's new girlfriend was black, and that although nothing could be further from the truth she probably thought Maggie reacted to Stacy the way she did because of her color. Most of Maggie's life she had dated black men, and as a child, most of her friends were black. In high school anyone would have predicted Maggie would marry someone outside her race, but Maggie had no real intentions of marrying anyone. It had been years since Maggie had loved anyone, and her last love was a huge disaster. For the most part, Maggie didn't date for love; she dated for validation. If a man was infatuated with her, and went overboard to be with her, she was happy for a while before breaking his heart. If a man rejected her, which rarely happened, she spent months believing she was worthless.

During her teen years Maggie had developed from a cute girl into a woman who knew how to accessorize. She learned how to wear makeup, and how to walk in heels at an early age. By the time she was seventeen, Maggie was a regular at most of the night clubs in her hometown, and she knew how to make herself look years older than she was. A few years after moving to Dallas, Maggie met John Mitchell. She was working at a Dallas branch of Compass bank where Mitch did his banking.

Mitch was gorgeous and had the full attention of every teller on the line when he walked in. Maggie was being groomed as a banker, but put in time on the teller line whenever they were short staffed. The other two tellers on the line that day noticed Mitch when he walked in and knew he was a regular. After a few discrete whispers back and forth, Maggie decided she was up to the challenge. Mitch made his way to the front of the line and found himself face to face with Maggie who did some of the best flirting she had done in years. It worked, and Mitch asked her out to dinner that weekend.

Mitch and Maggie dated only twice before becoming intimate. Although they were careful and used contraception, Maggie was soon pregnant. Mitch's initial response to the pregnancy was denial because they had used protection. He called Maggie some horrible names and accused her of trying to trap him just so she could get him to marry her. Maggie honestly had no desire to marry Mitch, although she did enjoy being with him. The two had terrible fights which went nowhere. Maggie ordered blood tests as soon as Michael was six-months-old which confirmed Mitch was the father. Mitch surprised Maggie by agreeing to pay the child support backdated from the time Michael was born. However, during the eighth month of her pregnancy, Maggie put in for a transfer to work in Ennis, a smaller community where she could get away from city life and raise her baby in a saner environment.

*

Intrigued by Tara's offer, Maggie stepped cautiously around the corner of Tara's cubicle at four thirty as though she fully expected Tara to snipe at her with a loaded pistol.

"Well, you said come back at quittin' time if I wanted to know how to get a life, so here I am."

Maggie knew Tara was a Christian and therefore doubted this "getting a life" would have anything to do with a fun party with lots of cute single men.

Tara was amused by Maggie's approach. She smiled warmly and leaned back in her chair before speaking.

"Do you have plans this evening?"

"Nope, just me and Jack Daniels hangin' out." Maggie was not much of a drinker, but when Michael was with Mitch, she sometimes ordered in and enjoyed a few drinks alone.

"Cool. Scott and I'll pick you up at about five-thirty. Just put on some jeans and whatever else you have lyin' around."

Maggie was confused, "What exactly did you have in mind? Where are we goin."

"Just be ready at five-thirty, okay?"

"Okay, long as we're not goin' to an Amway meeting, I'm game."

Tara laughed. She was really enjoying this.

"I'll see you at five-thirty."

*

Tara sat quietly in the passenger seat as Scott maneuvered the mini-van through the parking lot of Maggie's apartment complex stopping at her front door and honking the horn. Scott looked at his wife. "Are you sure this is a good idea?"

"Yes dear, I am absolutely sure. Its one thing to be a good friend and a good ear, but it's another thing to actually get involved in someone's life and try to help them find a better way. Maggie needs to stop talking about how bad things are and to take some steps to make a difference in her life and in the life of her son."

"Here she comes. Hey, you didn't tell me she was so cute." Scott felt a bony elbow in his ribs. "I mean – not that I noticed," he added.

Maggie walked out to the minivan wearing casual blue jeans, a soft pink button down blouse, Nike tennis shoes, and a black leather jacket. She bounced into the minivan and extended her hand into the front compartment toward Scott.

"Hi, I'm Maggie. It's nice to finally meet you. Tara is always saying sweet things about you."

"It's nice to meet you too, Maggie. My wife talks about you quite a bit also. All good stuff I might add."

Maggie stuck her head between the drivers and passenger seats, "So, where we goin'?"

Tara responded, "You'll see in a few minutes."

Four blocks from Maggie's apartment, the minivan pulled into the parking lot of the First Baptist Church of Ennis. The lot was beginning to fill up and there were several people walking about. Scott, Tara, and Maggie walked in the back door of the church where the aroma of delicious food hung in the air. "Oh, this is great. You guys are gonna feed me dinner at your church."

"No," said Tara, "you're gonna feed dinner to others. Then the evening will begin."

"I'm gonna feed others? You got a strange way of showin' a girl a good time Tara. It's a good thing I happen to love you so much."

Tara chuckled at her friend and handed her an apron which Maggie reluctantly tied around her waist. They served a meal of baked chicken, mashed potatoes, green beans, salad, and cookies for desert. Maggie chatted with the people who came through the line and seemed to be having a lot of fun. She had a gentle way with the people she served. Tara decided to lift the veil of secrecy as she; Scott, and Maggie sat down to eat.

"Maggie, this is an Alpha class. Scott and I volunteer here during the Alpha program serving meals to the people who come to the church. After we eat, there will be a short video, then we break into small groups to talk about God. You will be in the group with me and Scott. I know this seems a bit strange, but the people here have come because they are curious about God and they're seeking answers. I know you have never asked me directly about God, but I can tell by your frustration with life that you do have questions about what is going on and why. So, I thought this might be a good opportunity for you to get involved, and possibly find some answers to things that are going on in your life."

Maggie just nodded her head and remained silent throughout the meal. They took their seats in the room next to the dinning hall and a man talked for a few minutes about the Alpha Program. Then, the lights went off. Nicky Gumbal came on the screen and began to share information about Christianity with a distinct British accent during a thirty minute video presentation. After the video, Maggie had numerous questions which she asked one after another in the small group. Tara was delighted to see Maggie's interest in the program. She was also pleased that Maggie interacted so well with the rest of the group. Tara and Maggie continued with the program from that day forward attending all of the sessions without fail.

Chapter 24

The Minneapolis Delegation

Dallas
March 19, 2005

The Dallas-Fort Worth Airport was beyond chaotic; it was an absolute mad house. Mel Sanders had always been grateful he didn't have a job that required too much travel. He didn't like to fly, and driving took too long. The best thing for a guy like Mel was to stay at home where everything was familiar and predictable. Airports in distant cites were neither. Mel flew into Dallas on Sun Country Airlines, a charter service which also took him to Las Vegas whenever a few of the guys from the department could talk him onto an airplane for a weekend of gambling and drinking. Pastor Jenkins flew in on Northwest Airlines.

Mel dragged his one piece of carry on luggage through terminal E17 and began to look for the rental car area. He figured he had enough time to grab his rental and head for the Wyndham Anatole Hotel to check in and clean up before contacting Melissa. He didn't like conventions, but the IACP convention was usually worth attending. He wanted to see if he could check up on a few friends before heading into the city to meet with Melissa. After wandering aimlessly and talking to unhelpful airport employees, Mel found his rental car agency in the lower level of the airport. The lines were long but they moved quickly. Soon, Mel found himself driving out on West 635 toward Dallas and away from the dreaded airport.

The powerful V8 engine under the hood of his rented Mercury Marquise hummed as Mel picked up speed on the highway. He maneuvered in and out of traffic with ease and felt right at home in the sedan. The car was laid out exactly like the police cruisers he was so used to driving. Mel always rented either a Ford Crown Victoria or a Mercury Marquise when he traveled because they were familiar to him and he didn't have to put any thought into what he was doing as he drove the car. He also liked the size of the cars and felt he could bully his way around in traffic rather than being intimidated while driving an economy class car.

Mel looked down at the directions in his lap then looked up to see the signs directing him toward Irving, then west toward I35 in Dallas. After flipping through the channels on the car stereo, he found a smooth jazz station on 107.9 FM. He needed to think through what he would say and do if the person he was supposed to meet turned out to be Nick Bernard. Before leaving Minneapolis, Mel had consulted with the psychologist for the department's Employee Assistance Program. Her job was to counsel officers that suffered from various mental illnesses associated with their occupation.

After Ray Bernard was killed, Mel had spent time with the psychologist. Mel had left that shooting feeling like the world was against him and all cops. He felt that if a man like Ray Bernard, with all his experience could be killed in an instant, there was no chance of him surviving the job. Every time Mel went into a cafeteria, the entire incident came back to him like it had just happened. The smell of certain foods that were in the school cafeteria the day Ray was killed brought it all back to Mel with crystal clarity. Moira, the department psychologist, worked with Mel for months and diagnosed his condition as PTSD, Post Traumatic Stress Disorder. It was the same psychologist who suggested that if it was Nick Bernard in Texas, it would be a good idea to have his pastor near when he discovered his true identity.

*

Before leaving for Dallas, Gerry North from the prison called with a few important details.

"Hey Mel, it's Gerry North, you asked me to call you if I heard any news that might have something to do with that cold case of yours."

"Yeah, whatcha got Gerry?

"Well, I dunno how much help this is gonna be, but we had a training session here at the prison with a criminal psychologist who is helping us understand criminal logic. I told you all about Ellum, the guy Razor hooked up with when he was in here. Well, during this training, the psychologists used Ellum as a case study to talk about criminal pathology. According to this psychologists, one of the things guys with Ellum's personality type are prone to do is to leave subtle clues of their criminal behavior as if they're daring anyone to catch them."

"Okay, but what does that have to do with the case I'm investigating? We worked all the clues at the scene and came up empty handed."

"Yeah, you worked all the clues at the scene, but I took what the shrink was saying and got on the internet. See, Ellum fancies himself as some sort of smart entrepreneur, so I did a web search using as many combinations of names involved in your case as I could find to see if they matched any business in the DFW area, and I may have gotten lucky."

"What did you find, Gerry?"

"There's a used car dealership right in Dallas called, "Daisy's Seville." At first I didn't think anything of it, but then I realized that the car stolen from one of your victims was a Cadillac Seville. I figured it was probably nothing until I checked another website that pulls up all Texas-based small corporations and I found something else interesting. Apparently there's a corporate account registered in the name of a Sam Dawson opened at the Compass Bank in Ennis Texas just 45 minutes outta Dallas. That account is the main bank account used for all Daisy's Seville business transactions."

"Oh, Gerry, I owe you big time now."

"Look Mel, all I ask is that you let me know right away if you bring this guy in. He'll get to us eventually, but I have a special interest in this case. I just want to be the first to know when you get him."

"You got it, North. I'll keep in touch."

Mel made a few phone calls to the Dallas Police Department and started the process for checking out Daisy's Seville. He was assured that if their detectives came up with anything worthwhile they would give him a call.

*

The Anatole's recent thirty-nine million dollar renovation included one of the world's most complete art collections, which easily rivaled many of the finer museums around the world. Original works by Pablo Picasso, J. Seward Johnson Jr. and Josiah Wedgwood lined the massive lobbies and corridors. In the hotel courtyard a giant Jade Elephant sculpture was displayed in front of a 15-foot section of the Berlin Wall. Many of the works of art were once displayed in the royal palaces of kings, emperors and czars from Japan, China, India, Southeast Asia, and Europe, dating as far back as the fifth century BC.

A typical cop, the hotel's art work was completely wasted on Mel Sanders. He found it interesting only in that someone thought it worth while to spend millions of dollars on a bunch of junk that didn't even look all that good. What Mel did find fascinating was the Trammel Crow Suite built to house the president of the United States whenever he was in town. It cost three thousand, five hundred dollars per night to stay in the suite if you were not the president, and the room was designed by the secret service to meet all their security specifications. The high vaulted ceilings of the hotel were impressive and gave one the sense they were very small and insignificant. Mel liked the Anatole because it looked comfortable and clean, but beyond that and the Trammel Crow Suite, he was mostly unimpressed. He checked in quickly, took a shower, and sat on the edge of his bed ready to call Melissa McCree.

"Hello Lieutenant, how was your flight?"

"Okay, I guess. I hate flying but if I'm gonna fly I really need to stop flying charter airlines. They're pretty cramped, and there are no frills."

"I wouldn't know, haven't done much flyin', but I guess if I was gonna fly I'd want frills myself. I'd want a nice meal and lots of comfort. I don't drink anything hard but it would be nice to have a cool drink served to me, or at least some of those peanuts."

"Can we talk about your friend Rocky for a moment?"

"That sounds like a good idea, Lieutenant. I was thinkin' maybe we should meet at an open area like the downtown Galleria. There's a Westin Hotel in there with a large food court downstairs were we can sit and talk."

"Do you have a recent picture of Rocky that I can take a look at?"

"Sure I just took a picture with him and my husband last week. You can look at that one."

"Perfect, where can I meet you?"

"Well, I have to run some errands tonight. I could drop it off at the Anatole if that's alright with you."

"I'll meet you in the lobby."

"I'll be there around eight o'clock"

"I'll see you then, Mrs. McCree."

Mel ordered room service for dinner and finished in time to meet Melissa. He got in the elevator and started down the eleven floors to the ground level. The elevator opened up and people moved about in every direction. Cop's had such a distinctive look about them whether they were male or female and regardless of their ethnicity, a cop could always tell another cop, they just had that copish look about them.

Mel walked to the concierge desk and found that it, too, was packed with people trying not to look like cops. Off to the side standing on tip toe Mel found an unmistakable Melissa McCree. Her white sandals bent graciously as two dainty feet stood tip-toe, struggled to elevate her above the crowd of authoritarians hustling to and fro, barking out orders to intimidated bell hops who tried desperately to please their imposing clientele. Melissa was a rose planted in a garden of thorns, standing out among the throng of stoic, unyielding, commando's who took themselves too seriously – she was a fragrant breeze of fresh air.

Approaching her directly, Mel knew why she did not recognize him as easily as he did her. Dressed in a pair of navy blue pants and a button down shirt, his hair neatly trimmed and parted at the side, he had no moustache and no beard. Mel's gait was confident and resolved. He knew exactly where he was going and exactly what he was doing. Mel blended in with the crowd to the same degree that Melissa did not. Somehow he managed to soften his expression and his tone when he reached Melissa.

"It's good to finally meet you, Mrs. McCree. I'm Mel Sanders."

Melissa's expression went from bewilderment to elation. She actually looked happy to meet Mel, which Mel found fascinating. He was accustomed to the standard greeting, but unaccustomed to the sincerity with which this woman extended it to him. She smiled broadly and took his thick calloused hand in hers shaking it eagerly as she spoke with that southern drawl Mel found so amusingly irritating – yet somehow not so irritating in person.

"It's a pleasure to meet you too Lieutenant. I see you picked me right outta the crowd. Must be that cop sense of yours."

In an almost patronizing gesture that he immediately regretted, Mel jerked his head slightly to one side, clucked his tongue, and winked simultaneously.

"Yeah, I guess it must be that cop sixth sense."

Melissa smiled warmly, releasing Mel's hand and sliding her own hands into the pockets of her shorts.

"This must be a pretty important convention there having here. There's police cars all over this place."

"Well the convention is actually at the Dallas Convention Center, but a lot of the cops are staying in this hotel."

"I hear the president stays here when he's in town too."

"Yeah, I heard the same thing," said Mel. "The room he stays in was designed by the secret service. I was hoping to get a look at it before I leave."

"What do y'all do at this convention?" Melissa's drawl became more obvious as she spoke.

"Well, it's turned into a trade show for the most part lately, but there are also a lot of classes, or sessions taught on various law enforcement topics. It's a whole lot of cops that think pretty highly of themselves, and some police chiefs that think the world revolves around them."

"Do you do this every year?"

"No, I've only gone a couple times. When the convention was held in Minneapolis back in 2002, I was one of the people that helped put it together so we got to travel to San Diego and see how they did theirs in 2001. That was my first time going to one of these. It's a great way for us cops to learn what's going on in the world of law enforcement. We get to meet officers from around the world. We also get to see old friends that work in departments around this country that we've met in our professional lives."

"Do you know a lot of these officers?"

"No, but some of my friends are here this week, and if I don't get too bogged down, I would like to catch up with them."

Melissa was looking around the lobby with renewed interest. Her eyes wide open she fired questions at Mel.

"Do you like what you do? I mean, is it dangerous or exciting, or just a little of each?"

"Well, when I was a patrol officer, it was pretty exciting to work the streets during the night shift."

Mel and Melissa began to move toward a grouping of chairs where they could sit and talk out of the way of those still trying to get settled in.

"I think police work is exciting when you are able to catch a bad guy or help serve justice, but it's not what people see it on television. Sometimes working a case as a detective can be down right boring, and sometimes when you are working a patrol district you can go for hours with no action. You have to be proactive to keep yourself awake at night."

Mel was beginning to enjoy the conversation. It wasn't often he found someone who was interested in hearing about his work.

"My husband Robbie is a whiz at school. I thought I would be too but it didn't turn out that way. I wanna serve the Lord with my life, but more and more I wonder if that's ever gonna happen. I like learnin' about the Bible, but I don't get excited thinkin' bout doin' women's ministry or somethin' like that. But when I was calling around to those police departments and lookin' up old stories in the newspaper, I really did feel like I was doin' somethin' worth while. When I found that article on your friend, I felt really alive, like I was makin' a difference. It's like bein' right here where ya'll get together ta talk about crime and how to solve it makes me feel alive. Anyway, I know ya don't wanna hear me ramblin' on bout my issues."

Actually, Mel was enjoying this conversation far more than he thought he would. He remembered when he first got into police work. How it made him feel like he was making a difference, and that feeling of being really alive rather than just existing. He could relate to what Melissa said in a very personal way. He wondered if she didn't have the makings of a good police officer.

"Have you ever considered a career in law enforcement?"

"Heavens no, that's not a suitable career for a woman. I wanna finish Bible school and eventually find work in full time ministry 'til Robbie and I decide to start a family." Melissa appeared to be shocked by Mel's suggestion.

"Well, suit yourself. I just thought I heard an emerging cop there when you were talking, but I didn't intend to plant any dangerous ideas in your head."

Melissa looked lost in thought and for a moment, she didn't respond. Her gaze was distant. She wore a pleasant expression as though she were entertaining some satisfying fantasy.

"I know you didn't mean anything by it, it's just that until this moment, I never considered doin' anything other than full time ministry, but now I actually allowed myself to think about somethin' different. It wasn't your fault. It was just me bein' ungrounded."

Mel thought for a moment before responding.

"Don't become so grounded that you lose sight of what's really important to you. You just sound a lot like myself when I was getting started in this business. And when you've been doing this as long as I have, you learn how to spot someone else with all the makings of a good cop. Anyway, let's have a look at that picture you've got there."

Melissa had almost forgotten what she was there for. She reached into her right pocket and pulled out the picture of Rocky taken a short time ago.

"Oh, yeah, here it is." She held the picture out toward Mel.

Mel took the picture and slowly looked down at it. The picture was taken in someone's back yard against what appeared to be a wooden deck. A handsome, rosy cheeked white man in his middle twenties was in a headlock laughing while his friend gave him a rigorous noogie. Robbie McCree looked positively happy being muscled around by the very large, jolly, and obviously aged, Nick Bernard. There was no doubt who the man in the picture was. In an instant, the mystery was solved. Mel had found what he was looking for.

"I'm going to bring Rocky's old Pastor with me when we meet tomorrow. I'm pretty sure this is Nick Bernard. If you can get him there at about two-thirty in the afternoon it shouldn't be too busy at the food court. The crazy thing is that his wife and daughter are also here in town visiting his sister who lives right here in Dallas."

Melissa placed her hand over her heart and gasped, "Rocky has a sister that lives right here in Dallas? And he has a wife and daughter that are also here?"

"Yeah, and there's only so much truth he will be able to absorb at one time, so we have to take it easy with him."

"I understand. I won't let you or Rocky down. Just tell me what I need to do."

Chapter 25

Confessions

Dallas
March 19, 2005

Maggie laid her Bible down on the nightstand, and stared at it as though she expected it to jump up and bite her. Michael had been asleep for over an hour, and it was Maggie's nightly devotional time. The strange man who showed up at the bank got Maggie thinking about her past and the life she left behind. A true pragmatist, Maggie rarely lamented about life before Texas. She was where she was supposed to be, doing what she was supposed to be doing. Maggie didn't waste time regretting her past, but rather tried to live to the fullest in her current circumstance.

After picking up Michael from day care, Maggie drove home and started dinner. While dinner was cooking, she took the picture of her high school sweetheart from the mantle and stroked it with her thumb. She rarely thought of Alonzo Mason, who had been locked up in prison for years. Lately, it seemed Maggie was drawn to her past in a powerful way. When Stacy first shared her faith with Maggie,

Stacy's testimony struck Maggie like a bolt of lightning. She never would have guessed that not only was Stacy from Minneapolis, but that their lives were so incredibly intertwined. Maggie knew it was only a matter of time before she would have to let Stacy in on the mysterious connection between them.

Since kindergarten, Maggie had wanted to be a police officer. It was her plan to graduate from high school before attending a junior college to earn a two year degree in law enforcement. After junior college, she planned on applying with the Minneapolis police department. All of that changed during her sophomore year at Henry High School. She adored Ray Bernard, the school liaison officer at Henry, who had spent a lot of time telling her his "war" stories. He constantly encouraged Maggie to pursue her dreams in law enforcement, and even brought her information on various educational programs that were available.

The day Alonzo shot and killed Ray Bernard became a pivotal point in Maggie's life. Alonzo was not given to random acts of violence. It was completely unlike him to carry a gun. The entire time she and Alonzo dated, he had never expressed a desire to harm anyone. It was Alonzo who always spoke with disgust at the foolishness of gang warfare that had gained momentum in the city. It was Alonzo who took Maggie to church on Sunday mornings, trying hard to convince her that she needed Jesus in her life. It was Alonzo who talked to Maggie about the importance of learning to forgive her parents for their selfish, neglectful ways. All of this made Alonzo's actions even more difficult to comprehend.

Alonzo and Maggie were practically inseparable for over a year. They fantasized about marriage and what it would be like to have their own place. As much as they were alone, intimacy was not an option; Alonzo had a deep respect for Maggie and was committed to purity until marriage. Maggie and Alonzo often dreamt of marriage despite the fact that the odds were stacked against them due to their differences, racially, culturally, and religiously. Maggie's parents were indifferent to anything she did or did not do. They barely noticed she existed, and knew nothing about Alonzo.

Shortly after the two met, Alonzo began to insist on calling Maggie, "Sara." Alonzo said she had a biblical name she should be proud of. When Maggie asked Alonzo where her name could be found in the Bible, he told her she needed to study the Bible for herself and find out. Each Sunday, Alonzo picked Maggie up and the two made the fifteen minute drive to south Minneapolis, where Alonzo and his family attended True Vine Church. Alonzo's family had attended True Vine since he was in grade school.

During one of Pastor Jenkins' sermons based on Genesis 17, Alonzo got excited. With a broad smile on his face, Alonzo said to Maggie. "Maybe today you'll learn about your name." Maggie listened to the sermon and learned that her last name, Sarai, was the name of Abram's wife before God changed it to Sara. Although she didn't find any significance in the name at the time, it delighted Maggie to know that her name was special to Alonzo.

That Sunday after church, the problems that eventually led to Ray Bernard's death and Alonzo's imprisonment began. Maggie wanted true intimacy between she and Alonzo. She knew that meant being honest with him about her past and that she had not always been a lady. In fact, she had behaved downright shamefully at times. During her freshmen year in high school, Maggie had taken some horrible nude pictures with a boy she was sleeping with named Troy. Troy had shown the pictures to several students at the school already. Maggie felt certain Alonzo would find out about them soon. So she decided to reveal the truth herself. Their conversation that Sunday about the pictures exposed a dark rage in Alonzo Maggie never imagined. His response terrified her, and she knew nothing good would come from what she had done.

Over the next two weeks Alonzo refused to see Maggie, saying he had too much homework, or that he had no time to spend with her. Maggie knew he was becoming angrier about what she had told him, but she didn't know what to do, or how to reach him. The sweet young man she had fallen in love with vanished before her eyes, and in his place emerged an inconsolable emissary of wrath whom she did not recognize.

The morning of the shooting, Alonzo told Maggie he was going to make things right and that she was not to worry. He asked to meet her before school at the McDonalds located at 44th Street and Lyndale Avenue North where they had spent so much time during the first few weeks of their relationship. When Alonzo walked in Maggie barely recognized him. He had a rugged, disheveled appearance as though he had not slept in days. Skipping all pleasantries, Alonzo threw a handful of pictures on the table in front of Maggie.

"I plan to fix this, Sara. He never should have dishonored you like this."

Maggie looked at the pictures and began to cry. She didn't know how to respond.

"I'm gonna make this right, Sara, I promise you, I will make this right," said Alonzo through clinched teeth."

The couple sat together without saying a word, anguishing over an act that could not be undone. But in his heart, Alonzo was determined that justice would be done that day.

*

Maggie picked the Bible up again and held it to her chest. Remembering the past and her tragic childhood romance with Alonzo began to settle in and Maggie knew what she must do. There was a time when she wouldn't have given any thought to the strange man at the bank and the memories of Minnesota his visit brought back. She would have written the whole thing off as coincidence. However, she no longer believed in coincidence, but recognized the day's events as the work of the Holy Spirit. Maggie knew what she must do. She laid the Bible down again, picked up the phone, and dialed.

"Hey, Stacy, how ya' doin'?"

"I'm fine Maggie, is everything okay with Michael?"

"Yeah, everything's just fine. Mitch just left, and we had a little talk. I understand the two of you had quite a conversation tonight as well."

"That's putting it lightly"

"Listen, do you think you can drive down to Ennis and have lunch with me tomorrow? There's something important I need to talk to you about."

"Sure. Is it okay for me to grab Michael in the morning? I know you just got him back, but my sister-in-law and niece are in town, and I would really like for them to meet him."

"That's fine. He'd love that."

"Sounds like a plan. I'll see you tomorrow."

The line went dead. Maggie had an abiding sense of peace she could not explain. For the first time in many years, she felt she was about to close a terrible chapter in her past.

Chapter 26

Canal Park

Duluth Minnesota
March 19, 2005

An icy torrent blew off Lake Superior. Seagulls by the hundreds swooped across the shoreline before blanketing the lighthouse like a feathery winter coat. Tourists wrapped jackets tightly around shivering torso's and ducked their heads inside like tortoises as the winds kicked up. Locals, grateful for the end of winter, invited the temped breeze, offering dried bread and other snacks to the flocking birds they hadn't seen in months. Harsh waves pelted the rocks along the shoreline as small children ignored their parent's warnings and wandered too close to the water's edge. The sun shone brightly in the late evening sky with hues of blue, amber, and yellow, filtering through naked oak trees casting long shadows on the concrete ground. Benny, already an inch or two taller than his mother, kept up with his parents easily as they strolled casually along the tourists path of Canal Park in Duluth, Minnesota.

Kristen's dark brown hair tightly curled and layered short beneath her ears, frizzed in the cold moist air. Her bangs parted symmetrically in the middle of her forehead, blonde highlights caught the sun's rays – she looked much younger than her 46 years. The family needed a break, a short getaway from their routine. So, a weekend trip to Duluth was just the ticket. Sam and Benny had finished restoring the Mustang. The body shop did a phenomenal job on the paint, and the car looked truly fantastic. Exhausted physically and emotionally, Kristen had suggested the two hour trip north of the Twin Cities to clear heads and hearts, and to lift spirits that had become bogged down.

"Do you two remember when we used to all come up here as a family?" Kristen said as she tossed small pebbles toward the shoreline.

Sam shoved his hands deep into the pockets of his jacket and kicked at the ground as he walked. He puffed out his cheeks while exhaling and rolled his eyes. "Boy, do I ever. All eight of us would pile into that raggedy Plymouth station wagon in the summertime and drive up 35W with the windows down because the air conditioning didn't work. By the time we got here, all the kids wanted to do for the next several hours was run up and down this path like lunatics."

Benny smiled at the memory, "I remember Sam Jr., Ron, and Patrick used to tease me because I couldn't keep up with them."

"Yeah, but of course, your second mother always came to your rescue now didn't she?" Kristen interjected, while giving her son an elbow in the ribs. "She would have been so proud to see how you've grown."

Sam looked back down at his shoes, his hands still deep in his pockets as if he were pouting. "It seems like we can't go anywhere without something striking a memory of her, can we?"

"Is it hard, Dad?" asked Benny.

"Is what hard?" responded Sam.

"Is it hard for you to use Daisy's name when you talk about her?"

Sam stopped dead in his tracks and looked at Benny for a moment. "Wow, I guess I didn't realize until now that I don't use her name when I talk about her. I guess there's just something painful about saying… Daisy. Yes, son, it is hard"

A tiny pool formed in the corner of Kristen's sparkling eyes. With the sleeve of her jacket, she wiped her face. "I think," she said between sobs. "I think selling the house will be a good thing for all of us." Kristen stopped walking for a moment before continuing. "I miss my baby girl as much as anyone does, but the thing that's killing me now is the fact that we cannot seem to think about her, or talk about her, without beating ourselves up with guilt in the process." Kristen began to cry again, Sam took one of her arms, while Benny took the other. "We need to find a healthy way to let go of our guilt, while embracing her memory." She continued, "I'm so glad you two put that old car back together, that was a good thing. But now its time we put our lives back together. We need to find a safe place for Daisy in our lives." She brushed the hair from her eyes and stood silently for a moment before continuing. "Sam, will you please do something for me?"

"Of course, Dear."

"Sam, I want you to share with us a special Daisy memory using her name in the telling of it, without feeling guilt."

"Dad, I agree with Mom. I worry about you because it seems like you have it stuck in your head that somehow things would have been different with Daisy if you had given her your old car. The whole time we were putting together the Mustang, I could just feel you thinking you should have put that car together for Daisy. Dad, you have to believe that Daisy loved you with all her heart and she didn't die because of a car. Daisy died because some evil person didn't think she deserved to live." Benny fell silent again for a moment. "I guess I'm just tired of competing with my sister's memory for my father's love."

Sam turned to his son, "How long have you been carrying around that baggage Benny?"

They walked without speaking to one another. The sound of seagulls wings beating against the wind and noisy tourists filled the long empty minutes until Sam spoke again. "Rather than share one of my Daisy memories," Sam placed extra emphasis on the sounding out of Daisy's name, "I'd rather share one of Daisy's own memories with the two of you." He took a few more steps before continuing. "Last week while I was going through the closets on the second floor of the house, I came across one of Daisy's photo albums with a hand written journal entry in it. Perhaps you two would like me to share what I read there."

Benny and Kristen enthusiastically agreed to hear about the photo album Sam had discovered in the closet. Kristen's eyes were laughing once again; she looped her arm through Sam's as it remained buried in the pocket of his jacket. Benny skipped twice, then grabbed his father's other arm, boring his head into Sam's rib cage. The trio walked merrily through the park along the cobblestone trail. As the sun began to set, Sam told the story of Minnehaha Falls and the day that Daisy almost gave in to the call of God.

Chapter 27

The gathering storm

Dallas
Late Morning March 20, 2005

One of the things Rocky Jo-Bob liked most about Bible College was his internship with the St. Luke's Hospital Chaplaincy. On the one hand, it provided Rocky with valuable ministry experience, and on the other hand, it was an opportunity to give something back. Rocky knew what it was like to be laid up in the hospital in pain, feeling completely alone. He knew what great encouragement it was to have visitors when he was is in that predicament himself. Even if The Criswell College hadn't offered him college credit for his internship, Rocky was sure he would have volunteered anyway. The job was fairly simple. He made rounds throughout the hospital wards and asked if anyone needed prayer or just a little company.

Rocky was a natural at hospital work. He lumbered through the hospital corridors wearing that big smile of his and speaking to people in plain old English about the love of Jesus. Rocky found that one of the best places to minister was in the intensive care units because people there were in such desperate need of hope. And, hope was a great place to begin a conversation about Jesus.

By early morning, Rocky had made his way around to the fourth floor ICU surgery recovery area. He walked up to the nurse's station and plopped his large, black leather bound Bible on the counter. The nurses around the hospital had come to understand that loud thud as Rocky's way of asking, "Do you know of anyone around here that needs Jesus?" The charge nurse gave a cynical grin as she approached Rocky. She spoke in a loud voice.

"There's nobody here in need of Jesus today, Rocky. I think they got all the prayer they can handle."

Rocky leaned forward resting both elbows on the counter. He enjoyed the banter that ensued whenever he visited this particular floor. The charge nurse happened to be Rocky Jo-Bob's favorite.

"Now you know I don't believe non-a-dat, somebody round here needs the Lawd."

As Rocky and the charge nurse laughed and began to make pleasant conversation, Rocky felt something tug at his pant leg. He looked down to see the most angelic face on a little boy that couldn't have been more than four years old.

"We yike Jesus ova here, mister", said the little boy, "Come see, come see."

Rocky bent down and scooped the little boy into his arms.

"Alrighty Almighty, show me where the Jesus people's at, baby."

He put the little boy down, who scampered into a room not ten feet from where Rocky was standing. As he walked into the room, Rocky could hear several people talking. A smiling pregnant woman sat next to the hospital bed of a one-legged man. She cranked her neck around as Michael scurried into the room.

"Michael, who have you brought to visit us?"

"Someone who loves the Laaawwwd." Michael tried to imitate Rocky's drawl while everyone in the room, including the man in the bed, erupted in laughter.

"Well," started Tosha, "it's a good thing three people just left, or I'm afraid there wouldn't be room in here for anyone else. Come on in, mister. I'm Tosha, this is my husband Bart, and these two strappin' young men are our sons, Nathaniel, and Joseph. And this little guy is Michael. He's here with a dear friend of ours who stepped out of the room for a moment. And who are you?"

"M'name's Rocky Jo-Bob Eubanks, but ma friends calls me Rocky. An I'm jes' here spreadin' the good news of Jesus Christ for those that's lost and wants ta' find der' way."

Bart shifted his position and began to speak in a weak voice. "I know you. I saw you here a few weeks ago in the emergency room with a woman. You had that same Bible, and you were talking up a storm."

Rocky was surprised, "Yeah, dat was me and ma little girl-friend, Melissa. She ain't really ma girlfriend, jus a good friend. Her husband Robbie was sick dat night, so we had ta' bring em' into da' 'mergency room. Yeah, I member dat. What happen ta you sir, if I can ask?"

Bart's voice got a little stronger as he began. "That same night I saw you here with Melissa, I was walking back to my car at the end of my shift."

"You a doctor?" asked Rocky in a surprised tone.

"No, I was a police officer here. We watch the emergency room from behind the large glass window there. That's how I saw you but couldn't actually hear what you were saying. Anyway, as I was walking to my car I saw this little guy here about to run out into the street, and when I pushed him out of the way of a speeding Corvette…"

"The caw wan into mistew Bawt and chopped off his leg." Michael's head hung low as he finished Bart's sentence.

"My God, dat' musta' been awful, sir."

"Well, we're still sorting everything out, but we know God is going to use it in His plan for good," said Tosha.

"Yep, now he gets ta meet Eve," said Michael.

"Who's Eve?" asked Rocky.

Everyone shrugged their shoulders at once, but Tosha responded.

"We have no idea, but what we do know is this little guy is something special in the Lord. He has stolen all our hearts."

Rocky smiled and laid a thick heavy hand on the top of Michael's head. At that moment Rocky felt a sensation of peaceful familiarity he had never known. All at once, Rocky knew everything was going to be okay for everyone in that room.

"Well, its good ta' know da' Lawd is here. I spec I betta be getting' down da' the hall to someone who's lost, cause dere ain't no lost folk in here."

Tosha smiled and looked long and hard at Rocky. "What's your story, Rocky? Tell us about yourself and how you got into the ministry."

"Still trainin' fer ministry at da Criswell College down da street, but I hope ta' preach da' word someday. Don't know where I comes from, but I knows where I's goin' when I leave dis earth. Fact is, I cain't member nuttin' b'fore a few years ago. I gots amnesia."

Nathaniel looked at Rocky and spoke. "Praise the Lord, Rocky. Who knows what your first life was like, but it's such a blessing to see what you're doing with the one God gave you now."

Bart said amen, and the others in the room followed. Rocky sensed it was time to move on but felt the need to pray with the family first. Just as he was about to suggest a prayer, Joseph suggested that he pray for the entire group. Rocky was humbled and delighted. All agreed and the room fell silent for a brief moment with all heads bowed in prayer. After the prayer, Rocky shook hands with the Gelical family and made his way out of the ICU area with that abiding peaceful sense that all was well.

In a soft baritone voice Rocky sang the first verse of the Horatio Spafford hymn that Tosha had sung to Bart.

> When peace, like a river, attendeth my way
> When sorrows like sea billows roll
> Whatever my lot, Thou hast taught me to say
> It is well, it is well with my soul

The elevator opened in front of Rocky, and still feeling a bit melancholy, he paused for a moment. An impatient patient inside the elevator holding onto a mobile IV tree barked at Rocky.

"Hey mister, you comin' or not?"

Rocky jerked his head up, smiled, and stepped inside the elevator as the one next to him opened up. As Rocky stepped inside the elevator, Morgan, Stacy, and Alethea stepped out of the one next to him that opened. All three of the Bernard women turned toward the closed door of the elevator Rocky had just stepped into at the same time. Morgan shivered, then looked at her daughter and sister-in-law.

"I just got the strangest feeling right now."

"Me too," said Stacy and Alethea simultaneously. The three of them continued toward Bart's room to retrieve Michael.

Morgan looked at Stacy with concern. "You should have had something to eat, too. You work out all the time but you never eat anything. That's not good Stacy."

"I eat, but I told you I'm having lunch with Michael and his mother in a little while. Besides I'm not hungry." Stacy continued, "That was weird, us all getting a strange feeling at the same time wasn't it? I had the same kind of feeling a couple weeks ago after Bart's accident. Mitch and I were walking through the emergency room and all the sudden something just felt familiar to me. At the time I thought I recognized someone in the room, but the more I thought about it there was no one there I knew. Anyway, this was just strange, I don't know how else to describe it."

"Yeah, that was real strange," said Morgan. "Now let's go get your little friend."

*

Rocky finished his rounds a little early and stepped out of the hospital in front of the emergency room. He was still thinking about the encounter he had earlier in the ICU when Melissa's black 1986 Lebaron pulled up to the curb. Melissa was always on time. When she told Rocky she would pick him up for lunch at eleven-thirty, that is exactly what she meant. He squeezed his frame into the passenger side of the car and put on his seat belt before speaking to Melissa, who seemed to be all lit up inside.

"Well, miz Nancy Drew, what kinna capper you got us into today? I know dis ain't jus bout no lunch, so tell Rocky Jo-Bob what's goin' on."

"You always think I'm upta somethin' when I ain't, I jus' wanna take you out for a nice lunch."

"Ya' know God don't like liars an sinners, so ya' betta watch whatcha say, girlie."

Melissa giggled nervously before speaking.

"You're right, Rocky. This is more than just lunch. I need to talk to you about a few things. Do you remember when I told you I was gonna try to find out who you are?"

"Do you member when I told you I already knows who I am?"

"Yeah, I know, but listen for a minute before you close your mind. I been talkin' to this guy from up north in Minneapolis who's a detective. He thinks he knows who you are Rocky. I mean, who you were before you became Rocky."

Rocky sat still listening to every word Melissa said.

"Anyway, this detective thinks he knows you and your whole family. He said he's been a friend of your family for years and that you came from up north where he lives. Rocky, he says you're an educated man and was always a dedicated Christian. He says there's people back where you come from that love you and think yer dead. Are you listenin' to me, Rocky. He thinks he knows who you are."

Rocky turned his head toward Melissa for a moment then went back to looking out the window of the Lebaron. He spoke in a slow voice that didn't sound like Rocky at all.

"There's lots of snow in Minnesota. It's cold in the winter. Minneapolis has lakes and parks and it's beautiful in the summertime."

Rocky spoke as though he were talking in his sleep, and his drawl was completely gone. Even the tone of his voice changed, and it seemed to rise about an octave as he talked. Melissa stared at Rocky until she ran into the other lane and almost collided with an oncoming car. In a flurry of activity, Melissa steered the Lebaron back on course.

"Rocky, what happened to your voice? And what's that you're saying about lakes and parks?"

Rocky snapped out of it and looked at Melissa.

"I dunno, jes came ta me all a sudden." His drawl was back.

Melissa took a moment to compose herself before continuing.

"Rocky, this man wants to meet you today at lunch. He's bringing a man who he says used to be the pastor at your old church. Do you ever listen to 100.7?"

"Now you know I don't pay no tension ta those raydeo preachers."

"Well, this guy's name is Terrell Jenkins and he preaches on the radio from True Vine Church. Does any of that ring a bell, Rocky?"

Rocky's entire facial expression changed as he turned toward Melissa to speak.

"Hi, I'm Nick Bernard, youth pastor over at True Vine in South Minneapolis. I'm pleased to meet you ma'am."

Rocky extended his hand toward Melissa with a toothy smile plastered on his face that wasn't Rocky at all.

"Okay, I'm officially freaked. Maybe we should just save the rest of this til we get to the Galleria."

Rocky's drawl came back.

"Yeah, I spec you're right. I don't feel too good bout now. Think I need ta' jes' sit a spell ifin' it's alright wit you."

They drove the rest of the way to the Galleria in silence.

*

As he prayed for God's wisdom in dealing with the man who could be Nick Bernard, Pastor Jenkins could think of nothing he would like more than to bring good news to a wife and daughter who had suffered so much. A life of ministry exposed one to many heart breaking stories of suffering in the lives of God's people, but in his many years of service, he could think of no more tragic circumstance than that which had visited the Bernard family. There was a knock at the door.

"Brother Jenkins, the man you were expecting is here. Should I tell him you'll be right out?"

"Yes, Steve. Thank you very much," said Terrell from inside the door of the guest room. "I'm on my way right now."

Mel Sanders looked impatient when Pastor Jenkins walked into Steven Philo's living room. Steve was Pastor Jenkins old friend and host for the week. Steve had eagerly opened up his home to Pastor Jenkins.

"Lt. Sanders, this is Steven Philo, one of my oldest friends and a brother in the ministry."

"Yes, we've just met. I was just admiring his home when you walked in."

"Lieutenant, please, most people call me Brother Philo."

"Certainly," said Mel.

Pastor Jenkins gestured with his right palm up, panning the room.

"It's beautiful, isn't it? The architecture is so much different than the homes up north. Aside from having no basements, I think these homes have a certain warmth that you just don't see back home."

Brother Philo began to chuckle. "Perhaps the warmth comes from the fact that we don't have your sub-zero winters down here."

All three men laughed together.

Mel gestured toward the door, "Well, Pastor, shall we..."

"Yes, I suppose we better get going if we're gonna get there on time."

Brother Philo placed a hand on the shoulder of both men, "I'll be praying for you. I know how important this is and what's at stake."

"Thanks, Steve," said Mel, "I appreciate that."

*

On the way back to Ennis, Stacy listened to Michael's wild tale of the man who loved Jesus in Mr. Bart's hospital room. Stacy loved to hear Michael talk about Jesus even though half the time she had no idea what the child was saying. Stacy was more practical than most women, but she was certain some of the stuff Michael said was in some sort of heavenly language she was not privileged to comprehend.

Stacy parked in front of the bank and Maggie came out the front door as though she had been waiting and watching. They drove a few short blocks to Michael's day care and dropped him off. Stacy asked Maggie why Michael couldn't just join them, but Maggie was adamant they were to have a strictly adult conversation. In the back of her mind, Stacy wondered if her relationship with Mitch wasn't the cause of some friction between them that she had not been made aware of. They found a "Pot Belly's" sandwich shop nearby and were seated immediately. After ordering their food the two women enjoyed light conversation before Stacy began to ask Maggie the point of their meeting. At first, she asked Maggie if it had something to do with Mitch, but soon she realized it was about her father, Ray Bernard.

Chapter 28

Kujo

Dallas
Early afternoon March 20, 2005

He was a player, a street hustler his entire life. He wasn't stupid. In fact he was plenty smart. Many people thought he could have really done something with his life, but the streets were all he knew. The youngest of three boys born to Miriam Denise Jones, Marion was the sole survivor. His oldest brother Jessie died in Dessert Storm and middle brother Roger was brutally killed almost four years ago. He had Uncle Sam to thank for the loss of Jessie and there was nothing he could do about that. But, after years of doing his own street investigation, he now knew who to blame for Roger's death, and he vowed on his mother's grave to make it right.

Marion had always been the black sheep of the family, and often the bane of his mother's existence. He had a different approach to life that didn't include doing things the conventional way, but then in a sense, neither did his brothers. Jessie's route to an engineering career took him through the Marines, which in turn got him killed shortly after his thirtieth birthday. Roger's path was even more diffi-cult for Marion to understand. At the age of sixteen, he had joined the Jesus People movement out in Southern California where the three brothers were raised. Roger's zeal to preach the Word of God was unmatched among those of his age group. Although he never received any formal training, Roger committed his life to preaching the gospel to the homeless masses.

His strategy was simple. He would live as a homeless person and develop life changing relationships with those whom he encoun-tered. It was never Roger's intention to change the lifestyle of the people he ministered to; Roger simply wanted to turn their hearts toward Jesus regardless of whether or not they continued to be homeless. For nearly three decades, he swept the states from coast to coast living among the homeless and preaching the word of God until some two bit hustler put a bullet in the back of his head and burned his corpse beyond recognition. What the cops could not put together with their high tech investigative techniques, Marion "Kujo" Jones meticulously put together using his vast network of street informants. Today, he would spring the trap that had been in the making for some time now. It was coming together much better than he had expected.

Marion dialed the cell phone number he had acquired from a man who was a favorite snitch for several Minneapolis Police Detectives. The phone was picked up on the third ring.

"Lt. Sanders."

"Are you enjoying this wonderful Dallas springtime sun, Lieutenant?"

Mel had not planed to answer the call; he was in the first few minutes of his meeting with Pastor Jenkins, Melissa, and Nick

Bernard. The only reason he picked up the phone at all is because he was afraid he might miss a call from Dallas PD.

"Who is this? I'm in the middle of an important meeting, and I don't have time for games." The voice was muffled as though Sanders had his hand over the receiver.

"I respect your time more than you may know, Lieutenant. And, I realize your meeting with Rocky, or should I say Nick Bernard, must be an exquisite moment in your life and career. It brings a certain closure, doesn't it?"

Mel excused himself from the table the group was sitting at and stepped a few feet away before continuing.

"This is an official police cell phone, and I am on official police business. Now, get to your point."

"Good idea." The voice was calm and in control. Too much control for Mel's comfort. "I know your investigation here in Dallas has been fruitful, and I offer my congratulations and some free advice. You have your victim in front of you, and I will let you get back to your reunion momentarily. However, I bet you're having a little trouble motivating your colleagues on the DPD to get your back on this one. I mean, they haven't exactly been beating down Ellum's door, have they?"

Now he had Mel's complete attention.

"You've been following this case?"

"You have no idea how much I have done and will continue to do in an effort to help you close this case, Lt. Sanders."

"What do you have to offer to this investigation? Who are you? And why would you want to help me?"

"Let's just say we have mutual interests. As to what I have to offer you, I can give you the motivation you need to get the DPD and another local department off their butts, as well as the evidence you need to put this case to bed."

"I'm listening."

"There will be a murder today. I guess you could call it a murder, although I would call it more a matter of cleaning up the trash. Anyway, Ellum will be the trigger man in this cleansing. Now listen carefully, Lieutenant. He is wearing all denim today with snake skinned boots. You already have his physical description and a photograph of him. The shooting will take place in a public place and there will be an off-duty police officer there, but he won't know who the shooter is. When you hear about the shooting, you will know who did it. All you have to do is forward the information you have to the city police department where the crime will take place, and have Dallas PD check his place of business for the evidence."

"You will find plenty of evidence in his office at the car dealership. He'll use a silenced Berretta nine millimeter. You'll find that on him. The corpse will have a silver bullet in him, and you'll find that the rifling on the bullet will match Ellum's Italian imported weapon. In Ellum's office, you will find information on where the corpse is and the time of his death. Check Ellum's beige T-bird, and you will find a withdraw slip in the amount of thirty thousand dollars from the Compass Bank in Ennis. Thirty thousand dollars is what Ellum paid me for the information on the mark."

Mel had been writing feverishly trying to keep up with what was being said over the phone.

"Why don't you just tell me when and where this is going down now?"

"Because I want it to happen, and it will happen. I also want Ellum to spend the rest of his miserable life knowing that I brought him down."

"Okay, that leads to my other question." Mel did not like the idea of knowing someone was going to be killed somewhere in the metroplex and being powerless to do a thing about it. "Who should I tell Ellum brought him down?"

"Me? I was named after Mr. King's rabid, killer dog." The line went dead.

Mel walked back to the table where Rocky was slowly becoming acquainted with Nick Bernard.

*

On a typical weekday, the noon hour crowd at Pot Belly's required hungry business clientele to find a booth early or order a sandwich to go. However, the leisurely Saturday crowd allowed Maggie and Stacy to be seated easily. Maggie didn't like working Saturdays, but it gave her an extra day off during the week to spend with Michael, and because the bank closed early on Saturday, it was only a half day commitment. The two women decided to sit outside. The mild Dallas weather created an irresistible opportunity to soak in an absolutely gorgeous day. The noon day temperature rose to a comfortable seventy degrees. Shoppers rested decorative bags next to their chairs in the outdoor court where friends enjoyed one another's company over hot coffee or chilled Mimosa. Although Maggie and Stacy genuinely cared for one another, neither woman expected this would be a friendly encounter. The tension created by the unknown grew thick as they nervously ordered their food. After they had ordered, Stacy spoke first.

"Okay, this feels weird – so let's get things out on the table. Is this about me and Mitch? Because if it is, I have a feeling things are pretty much over between us."

"No, Stacy, this is not about you and Mitch." Maggie squirmed in her chair a bit. She would rather have faced ten hungry lions than face Stacy with what she had to say. She closed her eyes and asked God for strength to do what she had to do. "Stacy, I need to talk to you about your father, and how he died."

"Maggie, I already told you how my father died."

Maggie's eyes were bloodshot. "I know how your father died, Stacy. I was there."

"That doesn't make sense Maggie. My father died a long time ago and a long ways from here."

"I know it doesn't make sense, Stacy. It doesn't make much sense to me either, but I have a feeling it is all within the divine providence of God."

Maggie cleared her throat and took a sip of water from the glass on the table. "I used to live in Minneapolis, Stacy. I attended Henry High School where your father was murdered. Your father was a hero to many people, and I was just one of them. I left Minnesota to put that part of my life behind me, but it followed me here. Now, I have to tell you a very painful truth about the girl I was back then, and my connection to your father's death."

Maggie told Stacy all about her and Alonzo and about the day Ray Bernard was killed. She told Stacy about the kind of kid Alonzo had been prior to the shooting, and when she had finished, the silence between them was deafening, broken only by the clatter of dishes as the waitress brought their sandwiches.

After staring at their food for several long moments in silence, they both pecked at what was in front of them without saying a word. When they had folded their napkins in their laps with both plates still fairly full, Stacy began to break down. Maggie rushed around the table kneeling down at Stacy's feet to comfort her, but soon the sobs turned to a surreal laughter. In fact, both women embraced each other and laughed out loud seemingly about nothing, but the laughter was cathartic – cleansing – and somehow healing. Stacy spoke first.

"You know," Stacy said between laughs, with tears running down her face, "It would take Ray Bernard to bring two women like us together in a circumstance like this."

Both women laughed some more before Maggie spoke. "It takes the grace of God to bring the two of us together, Stacy."

The laughter turned solemnly back to tears as Maggie continued. "I am so sorry for the part I played in your father's death, Stacy. I spent the past ten years being sorry about it, but that was before I got to know and love his wonderful daughter. Now my grief is complete, and somehow I feel healing and closure. Obviously, I didn't know your dad as well as you did, but I have a feeling he would want to know that you and I found each other."

Stacy used her napkin to wipe her face. She leaned down to where Maggie was kneeling, smiled, and cupped her creamy delicate face in her soft, warm, brown hands.

"Maggie, you're right, you didn't know my dad as well as I did. But I can tell you for certain, this is exactly what he would have wanted."

The two women embraced, and in the middle of the outdoor seating area of the restaurant, they continued to mix laughter and tears – each exchanging favorite Ray Bernard stories as the healing set in.

*

Stacy's cell phone rang.

"Hello."

"Hello Stacy, this is Lt. Sanders from MPD."

Releasing Maggie's embrace, Stacy steadied the phone in her hand.

"This is an unexpected surprise. What's up, Mel?"

"Stacy, I'm in town here in Dallas, and I know Morgan and Alethea are also here. I need the three of you to meet me as soon as possible in Richardson at the home of a friend of Pastor Jenkins's."

"Is Pastor Jenkins in town too?"

"Yes, he's with me. And, we need to see the three of you right away. Can you come meet me, Stacy?"

"Sure, I guess. I'll give Morgan a call, Alethea and I were going to go shopping this afternoon but I suppose there's no reason we can't take a detour if you think it's important."

"Trust me Stacy, this is extremely important."

Maggie interrupted the conversation.

"Pastor Jenkins is in town? I haven't seen him in years. Are you going to meet with him?"

Stacy asked Mel to hang on a minute.

"Yeah, I guess I'm meeting him in Richardson this afternoon. Do you want to join me?"

"I'd love to. What time?"

Stacy turned back to her cell phone.

"What time, Mel, and where?"

Mel gave her the address and asked her to be there by three o'clock.

"Okay Mel, I'll be there. Look I'm having lunch with a friend of mine who manages a Compass Bank out here in Ennis. She knows the Pastor too. Is it alright if I bring her?"

"Did you say she manages the Compass Bank there in Ennis? Yes, by all means, bring your friend."

The line went dead. Stacy turned to Maggie again.

"Looks like we're on. Do you want to just ride with me?"

"Yeah, that will be great. Michael's day care is gonna think I've lost my mind, but can we go pick him up on the way?"

"Sure, no problem."

Chapter 29

The Hit

Dallas
Late Afternoon March 20, 2005

"Look Hubble, I don't wanna tell you how to do your job, but I think this guy is about to kill again. And this time, it will be in your back yard." Mel was growing more impatient by the minute.

"Mel, I'd love to help, but there just ain't a thing I can do without somethin' more than a phone call from someone that won't even identify himself."

"Roy, I got my own problem's here, but here's something you can do for yourself. At least run a DMV check on any vehicles registered to a Sam Dawson here in Texas. If you find a new beige T-Bird you have nothing to lose by sharing Havelock's name, description, and this vehicle info to as many off duty officers in Dallas and the surrounding area as possible. If this was a prank call, you're outta nothing, but if he does strike here in Dallas, you've got something to go on, and you become our hero."

"I don't know what kinda operation you guys run up north, but do you have any idea how many off duty cops are working on a Saturday night between Dallas, Richardson, Arlington, Garland, Plano, Mesquite, just to name a few? Not only that, we've got the hospital cops at St. Luke's and Presbyterian, not to mention all the college cops around town."

"Okay, I get the picture, but you can at least get it on the wire and let the other departments pass the information out at shift changes."

"Well, I'll send a teletype to the other departments. We have shift change here at three o'clock and some of the cops working off-duty jobs stop by the station and pick up the info sheets. Maybe that'll help some."

Mel was relieved. At least something was being done.

"Thanks Roy, I got a feeling this guy is dirty, and he's gonna strike today." Mel collapsed his cell phone and replaced it in his pocket. This could be very useful if the mysterious caller was really willing to help out.

Mel sat back down at the table with Pastor Jenkins and Nick Bernard. He had been interrupted from taking care of this dear man who had been through so much. Even though he was frustrated by the lack of full cooperation from the Dallas PD, he was truly excited about the fact that Nick Bernard was alive and well, and that soon he would be reunited with his family.

*

Ellum rarely had business in Arlington. He didn't care too much for baseball, and as far as he could tell there really was no other reason to go visit this city. He pulled his T-Bird into a slot in the employee parking lot at three-thirty and grabbed the Berretta from his glove compartment. Thirty thousand dollars and death by silver bullet was a small price to pay for peace of mind. He didn't understand the symbolic importance of the silver bullet to the "mystery man" at the West End Station, but if it meant tying up loose ends, it was well worth it to Ellum to just go along with it. The silver nine millimeter bullet would fit his Beretta. The Berretta had been modified with a silencer and high powered scope. Ricardo would be with a group of other workers, and because this would be a daylight hit, Ellum needed to give himself every possible edge. The modified Beretta was exactly what he needed.

As employees began to fill up the parking lot, Ellum did not see Ricardo among them. It was three fifty-five and still no sign of Ricardo. Ellum began to think he had bought bad information until he remembered the exact instructions. Nobody had said Ricardo would be driving to work or that he would arrive in a car at all. He was supposed to be going through the front gate at exactly four o'clock with the cleaning crew.

Ellum grabbed the Berretta, scrambled from the front seat of the T-Bird, and rushed toward the front gate of the ballpark. As he came around the north corner of the massive building, he could see several workers in green jump suits walking through the front gate past a uniformed Arlington police officer. He wasn't terribly concerned about the cop but he did want to get in position before the place got too crowded. Ideally, he would make his strike in such a way that would not draw too much attention. Then he would make a fast break for the T-Bird and get outta town before being noticed. That would mean catching Ricardo before he got through the gate.

Ellum slowed down and eased around the high brick walls that surrounded the ballpark. From the outside, the Arlington Field resembled a modern fortress far more than a recreational building. The high walls looked as though they were made for garrisons and high powered weapons rather than to keep the cheering fans inside and entertained. As he came within twenty feet of the front gate the hunter found his prey.

Ricardo was with a group of about five Hispanic-looking men in green jumpsuits lined up to go through the front gate. The off-duty police officer had moved inside so there was nothing between Ellum and Ricardo except the other four Hispanics. Ellum perched behind a large, yet barren elm tree in front of the north wall of the ball park and drew his weapon. Ricardo was the last in the line of workers. His squat profile was in cross hairs of the scope mounted on the Beretta. He took in a deep breath and held it in while steadying the weapon. Ellum pointed the gun at the back of Ricardo's head and squeezed the trigger. Ricardo was dead before he hit the ground. Ellum turned and walked back toward the T-Bird, quickly rounding the northeast corner of the ballpark a split second before the off duty officer sauntered out to see why the worker had laid down in the grass. Nobody noticed as the beige T-Bird slipped out of the lot and into the abyss of game-day traffic.

*

At two o'clock, Mitch sat down in the briefing room ready for another overtime shift. A lot of overtime had become available since Bart's accident. Today, he was assigned to the middle shift which would allow him to keep working right through his normal night time hours.

Earlier, Mitch had gone to the fourth floor ICU to say hello to Bart and Tosha. He was pleased to learn that Michael had been there with Stacy. The Gelical's had all taken fondly to Michael, especially Bart. It was a strange thing to Mitch that Bart held no ill feelings toward either he or Michael for what had happened to him. The more time he spent with his Christian friends, the more perplexed he was at their capacity for forgiveness. As Mitch considered these things, the officer sitting next to him handed him a copy of a BOLO, (Be On The Look Out). The BOLO had the face of a man Mitch had never seen before named Derrick Havelock, and a vehicle description of a brand new, beige, Ford T-Bird convertible. Mitch folded up his copy of the BOLO and put it in the black portfolio he kept in the squad car with him. After roll call, Mitch got in his cruiser and set out for a routine day of patrol.

Chapter 30

Rocky Meets Nick

Dallas
Late Afternoon March 20, 2005

As could be expected, Nick had about a million questions for Mel and Pastor Jenkins. He recognized both men almost immediately upon seeing them for the first time in the Galleria. For Nick it was like seeing someone he knew, but he couldn't quite put a name with the face. Melissa had her back to the two men as they approached. Nick sat facing Melissa. She spoke unemotionally about the lousy grade she earned on a final in Eschatology, when Nick began to look over her shoulders as though he recognized someone. Melissa, knowing Mel and the Pastor would approach her if they were convinced the man she was talking to was Nick Bernard, tried not to pay too much attention to his expression. Rocky raised his finger and began to slowly shake it up and down as if he were searching for a name in his internal database. He had a semi-grin on his face but his lower lip kind of dragged downward in a curious expression. Nick looked completely away from Melissa and past her, clicking his fingers as if catching the beat of a soulful melody.

"Mark – no Mickey – no that's not it – Marvin, right? Wait, I know, man what is it."

Nick began to rise out of his chair and extend his hand toward Mel.

"I'm sorry, sir, but I know you from somewhere, what is your name?"

Mel clasped Nick's fleshy hand with both his hands. He smiled warmly and held both his gaze and his hand for an uncomfortable moment.

"Yes, we do know each other, Nick. My name is Mel Sanders."

The smile vanished from Nick's face and was rapidly replaced by a look of complete bewilderment. His head was swarming. Something was happening and he wasn't sure he liked it. He knew this man. This was someone from the past.

"Excuse me, but what was that name you called me?"

Mel hesitated for a brief second.

"Your name is Nick Bernard; I've been looking forward to seeing you again for some time now. It's good to finally be here with you, Nick. It's really good to see you again."

Nick stood frozen, gazing at Mel without a sound. Mel continued.

"Nick, I came down here from Minneapolis. That's where you came from, Minneapolis, Minnesota. Does any of this seem familiar to you, Nick?"

"Yes, it does, it really does. I remember Minneapolis, its cold in the winter time there. It snows a lot. In the summertime there are lots of parks and lakes to visit. There's a church, True Vine Church, and I'm the youth pastor. You are Sgt. Sanders, an old friend of my father's, I think."

Melissa, who had been silent during the encounter found her voice.

"Lt. Sanders, listen to his voice. That really freaks me out. I mean, Rocky speaks with a distinct southern drawl that even I notice."

"Yes, I know."

He motioned for Pastor Jenkins to come forward. Pastor Jenkins walked slowly toward the threesome.

As Jenkins approached, Nick smiled broadly.

"Pastor Jenkins. Oh my God, Pastor, where have you been?"

*

Stacy and Maggie made excellent time getting back to Dallas. Saturday traffic was light. Stacy's Magnum wagon provided a comfortable and speedy ride down the highway. When they pulled up in front of the Radisson Hotel on I-35, Morgan and Alethea were waiting. They piled into the back next to Michael's car seat, and were more than happy to see him.

"Hey, Michael. I didn't think I'd get to see you so soon," said Alethea.

"This is my good friend, Maggie. She's Michael's mother." Stacy made the introductions.

Both Morgan and Alethea looked at Maggie at the same time with the same quizzical expression. Stacy answered the question on both their minds.

"Maggie and I have a wonderful relationship which just got better over lunch. I know it sounds strange but we are both friends and most important, we are sisters in Christ."

Morgan and Alethea nodded and said hello to Maggie.

"Pleased to meet the both of you," Maggie's greeting was warm and sincere.

Michael giggled as Alethea tickled his rosy cheeks. She continued to entertain Michael while they made the short fifteen minute drive to the northern suburb of Richardson."

"Stacy, what's this all about? I got a call from Pastor Jenkins telling me it was "absolutely imperative" that we get to this place in Richardson."

"You got a call from Pastor Jenkins? I got a call from Mel Sanders telling me he was in town and asking if I could pick the two of you up."

"I had almost forgotten that Pastor Jenkins was going to be in town with Lt. Sanders. He said the Lieutenant was going to be out here for some sort of conference. I still think it's a little strange," said Morgan.

Stacy got off Highway 75 at Spring Valley Road and headed east according to the directions provided by Mel Sanders. In a few moments, they pulled in front of a two story stucco home on a cul-de-sac behind Mel's rented, dark grey Mercury Marquis.

*

"Praise the Lord, good to see you all, what a blessed day this is. Please come, in come in. Welcome little guy, hello and welcome to my home. Folks, call me Brother Philo."

They walked into the foyer and Brother Philo escorted them into a small dining room with a table, six chairs, and settings for coffee and hot chocolate where Pastor Jenkins was already seated. "Hello ladies. I'm glad you could make it. You must be Stacy's friend." Pastor Jenkins looked toward Maggie.

"Hello, I'm Maggie Sarai. I used to attend True Vine years ago, and I've been wanting to meet you."

"It's nice to meet you Maggie and I'm sure we will have an opportunity to talk later, right now Lt. Sanders would like to speak to you in the next room."

Pastor Jenkins motioned to a small den to the right of the dining room where Mel Sanders was waiting.

Morgan, who had just sat down stood up immediately when she heard Maggie introduce herself to Pastor Jenkins. "Excuse me, it's nice seeing the two of you, but could someone please explain what's going on. And did I just hear Maggie say her last name is Sarai, as in Margarita Sarai, the little girl whose boyfriend killed Nick's father?"

Stacy understood Maggie's secret, but nothing else made sense at all.

Pastor Jenkins spoke up. "Why don't we all step into the den with Lt. Sanders and I'll explain everything." Melissa walked into the room followed by Morgan as Pastor Jenkins introduced the two women. "Melissa, this is Morgan Bernard. Morgan, this is Melissa McCree. Melissa has played a substantial role in bringing us together today."

*

The den had the smell of old leather furniture and pipe tobacco. The walls were lined with bookshelves on all four sides containing a well organized selection of Bibles, concordances, commentaries, and reference books. The cherry wood desk had a high gloss finish and a flat screen computer monitor on top. The floors were exposed hard wood with several area rugs placed under practical and sturdy wooden office furniture. On the north wall of the room was an unlit gas fireplace adorned with a mantle supporting pictures of Brother Philo and several Christian dignitaries. Behind the desk seated in a high back plush leather chair was Lt. Sanders, who stood and offered his hand as Maggie walked in.

"Hello, my name is Lt. Sanders. I'm with the Minneapolis Police Department, how are you?"

"I'm fine, my name is Maggie, how are you?"

"Just fine ma'am, but you look familiar to me, have we met?"

"I dunno, you look familiar to me too."

Mel gestured toward a chair in front of the desk and asked Maggie to have a seat.

"I suppose you're wondering what this is all about, Maggie."

Maggie said nothing, but nodded her head. Mel continued.

"I'm not sure how well you know Stacy or her family, but they've been through quite a lot over the years. Stacy's father was a police officer. He died in the line of duty fifteen years ago."

"I know about that," said Maggie.

"Okay, well in addition to losing her father, almost five years ago, she lost her brother in another violent crime."

"That I didn't know."

"I was assigned to work the homicide case when Stacy's brother Nick was attacked. Stacy's father, Ray, trained me when I first came on the department. So this family is very special to me."

"Excuse me, Lieutenant, but you said you worked the homicide case when Nick was attacked, you didn't say killed."

Mel grinned at Maggie. "You don't miss much do you, Maggie?"

Maggie blushed. Mel continued.

"For almost five years, we thought Nick was dead, and then recently things just started falling into place. I got one lead after another, and to be honest, I owe it all to a woman out there named Melissa. But as it turns out, Nick is alive. He's right here in this house being reintroduced to his family."

"You mean all these years they thought he was dead and at this moment they are finding out he's alive? They are seeing him for the first time right now?"

"That's right Maggie."

"Where was he attacked, and where has he been all this time?"

"He was attacked at home in Minneapolis. Alethea was the last person to see him alive. Outside a bar in downtown Minneapolis called the First Avenue, we found the charred body of his next door neighbor, and another body we thought was Nick's"

"I know that place. That's Prince's old hang out."

"Right. Anyway, we closed the case because we found DNA from both victims at the scene, but we never found the killer. Somehow, Nick turned up here in Dallas under the name Rocky Jo-Bob Eubanks. He had complete retro-grade amnesia and no idea who he was. But now we think we have a lead on the killer, the one who tried to kill Nick."

Mel's phone chirped. "Mel Sanders."

"Mel, this is Roy Hubble, your boy just made his move outside of the Arlington Ball Park. Do you have anything else Mel, this is a homicide and they're asking me a lot of tough questions I can't answer. All I did was put out that BOLO info like you asked me to. Now everyone thinks I have all the answers."

"Sorry, Roy, I told you all I know. Did you run the name Sam Dawson to see if he's got a car registered here in Texas?"

"Yeah, I put that info out with the BOLO. It's a beige T-Bird just like you said. Look Mel, if you hear from this Kujo again, you've gotta call me right away."

"I will. Look, I'm working on something else here. I might have a little more info for you in a while. Do you know anyone at Ennis PD who can get a search warrant for bank records?"

"I'll see what I can do. Stay by your phone."

Mel turned back to Maggie, who looked like a third grader with her hand up anxious to give the teacher the answer.

"Lieutenant, did you just say Sam Dawson?"

"Yeah, that's what I called you in here for, I wanted to ask you if you knew a customer at Compass Bank with that name. So do you?"

"I sure do, I just met him a few days ago. I think he's from up north too. He came in and made a big withdraw from his business account."

"How much did he withdraw?"

"Thirty thousand in cash. The only reason I remember him is because he noticed my accent. When he asked where I was from, I told him I was from Minnesota. As soon as I said that, he got nervous and left the bank as quickly as he could."

"Maggie, I'll probably need you to sign an affidavit so we can get a search warrant for that bank record. In the meantime, it looks like the same guy that hurt Nick back in Minneapolis has just committed a murder in Arlington."

*

Morgan shook her head from side to side and held Alethea's hand too tight. "No, no, no. You can't tell me my husband's alive, how can this be? Where has he been? What happened to him? Why didn't he come home all this time?"

Stacy was finding it hard to speak. Philo handed her a glass of water which she swallowed in a single gulp.

"Does he know that we're here?"

Pastor Jenkins smiled reassuringly, "Yes, he's anxious to see you all. Things are a bit messy in his head right now, but he remembers each of you and he loves you very much. He was badly beaten that night when you saw him last Alethea. We don't have all the details and we may never have them. We know he was driven from Minneapolis to a small town just south of here called Groesbeck, where he was left for dead in a dumpster. Doctors there worked on him and he was in a coma for several months before regaining consciousness. When he did wake up, he didn't remember who he was or where he came from. He developed an entire life and a new identity. He even started college over again at The Criswell College in Dallas. He made lots of friends here, including Melissa. They all knew him by the name Rocky Jo-Bob Eubanks. Right now, he's anxious to see his family."

Melissa and Pastor Jenkins took Morgan by the arms as they all walked into the large living room. Nearly one hundred pounds heavier, bearded, and with a touch more grey, Nick Bernard held his breath as they walked single file into the room. Morgan buckled and nearly dropped to the floor while Pastor Jenkins caught her. Alethea placed her hands over her face and cried, while Stacy screamed with delight and threw her arms around her brother.

"I did see you in the emergency room, it was you." Stacy cried out as she smothered Nick with kisses.

Morgan steadied herself and threw her arms around Nick's neck and heaved tears of joy. "Oh, baby, it's you, it really is you. Oh thank You Lord, thank You thank You Lord for bringing back my husband."

In the corner of the room, Alethea stood smiling with tears running down her face. Speechless, she watched her hero resurrected from death. She ran into his waiting arms. "Daddy, I knew you would come back. I knew you would."

Later, in the cool, clear, evening sky, Cassiopeia made a glorious appearance as father and daughter once again looked to the stars and found hope in the heavens of a good and merciful God.

Chapter 31

The Chase

Dallas
Early evening of March 20, 2005

Texas State Trooper Brad Winther stepped out of Dickey's Barbecue on east I-30 and sat behind the wheel of his newly issued 2005 Crown Victoria, punching a few buttons on the Mobile Data Terminal (MDT) installed between the cruiser's two front bucket seats. The terminal allowed officers to pass information between themselves quickly and efficiently. The terminal also allowed officers to receive crime bulletins and other important information.

The MDT screen blinked to life as Brad punched several buttons on the keyboard. There was a property damage accident pending in Oak Cliff, and a motorist assist pending in Dallas off I-30 and Carroll. The motorist assist was not nearby but he was planning to head through Dallas anyway. The call was right on the entrance ramp, meaning Dallas PD would probably not take it. Brad picked up the radio microphone.

"Dispatch, this is 1 Adam 1033. Send me the motorist assist on east I-30 and show me en route."

"Copy that 1 Adam 1033. Please acknowledge the roll call advisory on an Arlington BOLO. Copy?"

"10-4."

The BOLO on Brad's MDT indicated there had been a shooting in Arlington at the ballpark earlier and the suspect was driving a newer, beige, Ford T-Bird. The shooter was a white male, thirty-five years of age. Brad figured he would be in perfect position to intercept if the suspect should decide to cruise his way. He grabbed the microphone again.

"1 Adam 1033 to dispatch."

"Go ahead 1033."

"Yeah, 10-4 on that BOLO info. Looks like our shooter might be comin' near my motorist assist call. Does DPD have all this info?"

"They're the ones who sent out the BOLO in the first place, you want me to send you the text image?"

"Yep, send it"

The MDT beeped twice and Brad punched the display button. Derrick Havelock's image developed on the screen. Brad looked down at the screen and winked, "Well, Mr. Havelock. I'd be happy to make your acquaintance today. After all, this shift has been kinda slow so far."

Brad pulled back onto the highway and headed east toward the Carroll Avenue exit just as dispatch contacted him on the two-way radio again.

"1 Adam 1033"

"This is 1033, go ahead."

"Yeah, you can disregard on that motorist assist. Somehow a St. Luke's squad is on the scene. They've radioed for medics. Apparently the driver went into labor while she was waiting for police to respond."

"Was that supposed to be some kind of joke or something?"

The dispatcher allowed a slight chuckle before responding.

"No, 1033. She actually went into labor, but I wouldn't take it too personally. I know you were trying your best to get that call."

"As a matter of fact, St. Luke's can have this one. I've never delivered a baby and to tell you the truth, I don't really want to start today."

The dispatcher began to laugh again.

"Should I put you on that fender bender in Oak Cliff?"

"Sure, I can be there in a few minutes."

Brad found a turn-around, drove down into the small ditch, and waited for traffic to pass by before re-entering I-30 westbound. As people drove from Arlington toward Dallas, Brad noticed a momentary increase in the amount of cars on the road. Knowing that an emerging trooper often confused and frightened motorists, Brad decided to wait patiently for the cars to go by. Out of the rear view mirror Brad saw something that caught his attention. A brand new beige T-Bird drove eastbound with the top down.

*

Tosha remembered that Mitch had stopped in to see Bart earlier. He was on duty working the middle shift. She dialed Mitch's cell phone number.

"Hello, this is Mitch."

Relieved that she had reached Mitch and not his voice mail, Tosha felt better already. "Hello, Mitch this is Tosha. I really hate to bother you..."

"Nonsense," interrupted Mitch. "What can I do for you, Tosha? Is Bart Okay?"

Tosha explained her predicament to Mitch and told him where she was.

"Say no more," said Mitch in a firm voice. "I'm not far. I'll be there in just a few minutes."

"Thanks, Mitch. I called the troopers, and they're sending a unit."

"Call and cancel them, Tosha. They're pretty busy. They don't have many squads in the area. Just let em know you got it taken care of."

"Okay, Mitch. I'll see you when you get here."

While Tosha was on the phone for the second time with the state troopers, she realized she was in trouble. If there was one feeling Tosha knew well it was labor pains. They started as her water broke right on the front seat of the family minivan. She ended her call with the state patrol and redialed Mitch.

*

Brad snatched the microphone for his radio and keyed it. "1 Adam 1033 emergency traffic."

Dispatch snapped back an immediate response. "1033 go ahead with your traffic."

"I've got the suspect vehicle from that shooting in Arlington headed eastbound on I-30 at mile marker seventy-eight. I need immediate back up. I'll be attempting a felony stop. Advise Dallas PD and any other trooper units in the area."

"Copy 1 Adam 1033."

Brad's cruiser kicked up gravel as he spun around and merged with eastbound traffic in an attempt to catch up to the T-Bird. As expected, Brad's hasty merge caused the vehicles around him to proceed somewhat erratically. Some were clearly confused. They didn't know whether to slow down or pull over. Still others made wild sway's to the left or to the right. Brad knew he would simply have to let them figure this out for themselves. He needed to move quickly or risk having the suspect exit the highway without him seeing it. He knew it would be a mistake to activate his red lights and siren too soon; doing so would alert the suspect before he actually had visual contact.

The cruiser picked up speed quickly, and within a few hundred feet, Brad was up to eighty-five miles per hour and gaining fast. Brad spotted the rear bumper of the T-Bird as they passed Camp Wisdom Road. By the time Brad was within four car lengths of the T-Bird, he knew he could no longer wait for backup. His hasty acceleration coupled with the erratic driving of the other motorist on the road had surely tipped off the suspect that he was in pursuit. Brad activated his lights and siren. The brilliant display of flashing lights and the blaring of his siren caused the cars in front of him to slow down and pulled to the side. That is, all of them except the beige T-Bird which sped up. Brad grabbed the radio microphone again.

"This is 1 Adam 1033. All units I am in pursuit. The suspect vehicle is refusing to yield. I repeat I am in pursuit of the Beige T-Bird suspected in today's shooting at Arlington Ballpark."

*

Mitch pulled his cruiser behind the minivan. Tosha explained to him that her water had broken. He used the radio to summon an ambulance, and was advised the Dallas Fire Department would send a medic unit as soon as one was available. In the meantime Mitch would have to do his best to make the patient comfortable. Tosha slumped over the wheel in obvious pain.

"Mitch these contractions are one on top of the other. Is the ambulance on the way?"

"They're sending one, but they said it may take a while to arrive. How're you doin?"

"I'm just fine, Mitch, but this baby is coming now."

Mitch began to break out in a cold sweat. It was one thing to deliver a baby; it was an entirely different thing to deliver this baby. Bart had sacrificed his life so that Michael could live. Mitch did not want to mess things up while trying to help Tosha. This woman and this baby suddenly became extremely important to Mitch.

"It's gonna be okay, Tosha. The baby is going to be fine, I promise you. Do you have any blankets in the back?"

"Yeah, if you look in the very back, there's a box with some stuff Bart keeps for emergencies. There should be some blankets, water, booster cables, and a few other things. Ohhhhhhh." Tosha let out a loud scream of pain and doubled over the wheel again.

Mitch hastily folded down the rear seat and found the cardboard box Tosha had mentioned. Just then dispatch came over the radio. "1304 are you still out on I-30 off Carroll?"

Mitch pulled the radio from his belt and keyed the microphone. "Ten four and it looks like she's about to have this baby right here and now. Any update on the ETA of that medic unit?"

"Sorry, no update, but you may have bigger problems to worry about. We've got a state trooper involved in a high speed pursuit headed right at you. With any luck, he'll stay on the highway and pass right by, but I thought you should be advised. Mitch, you know that so long as that chase is in the area the medic unit isn't coming near you?"

Mitch knew, and that wasn't exactly what he wanted to hear at the moment.

"Ten four that dispatch. I'll keep you advised."

Mitch spread the blanket out over the rear of the minivan and helped Tosha lay supine with her feet hanging out over the edge of the tailgate. He knew he couldn't take the chance of moving the minivan with Tosha ready to give birth, so he ran to the cruiser and parked it diagonally across the ramp, prohibiting any other traffic from entering the highway. Unfortunately, time didn't allow him to position the squad at the mouth of the ramp, so any cars attempting to enter I-30 from Carroll would have to drive onto the ramp, then back up once they saw the cruiser. He wished there was time to park the cruiser farther up but he desperately needed to get back to Tosha. Mitch knew that if the medic unit started up the ramp, they would park facing his cruiser and maneuver the stretcher through the grass toward the minivan to pick up Tosha. By the time Mitch got back to the minivan, the situation was very serious.

"Oh Lord, Mitch. This baby is coming right now. I never have short labor, but I tell you this child is coming right now ready or ohhhhhhhh!"

Mitch positioned another blanket from just below her breast line down over Tosha's feet, and without looking down he helped her out of her under clothes.

"Mitch, this is not a good time for you to be a gentleman. You need to see if the baby's crowning, and the only way that's gonna happen is for you to look down there."

He swallowed hard and bent down to take a look. Just then they both heard the sound of sirens coming in the distance. Every police officer knew how to discern the difference between a police siren and a medic unit; this was the unmistakable sound of a police cruiser. The siren sounded like it was about a quarter mile away, but the screeching of tires made it clear the chase was much closer. Mitch knew through his training that sound of the tires indicated the chase was moving at extreme speeds and the cruiser was out running the siren.

Mitch could see the patch of curly black hair begin to protrude from the birth canal as Tosha pushed and screamed simultaneously. The pink torso of a new born baby began to emerge quickly – the miracle of life was remarkable but Mitch feared in a near panic that neither he, Tosha, nor this new born child would survive the next several seconds. The cars were so close. Mitch knew they would never be able to stop in time. The unfairness of the situation was unbearable. Mitch cried out a prayer as Tosha bore down again.

"God, if you are real, show me a miracle today and save this precious woman and child. I do not deserve your mercy, but please don't allow these two to die – I'm trusting You with our lives, God. Please let them live – please let me live."

*

The chase was now reaching dangerous speeds in excess of one hundred miles per hour. Brad had learned in the police academy that after about sixty miles per hour, by the time a person heard the siren, the source of the siren was already upon them. Therefore, the siren served little purpose at high speeds because it became incapable of warning drivers of the impending danger.

The T-Bird was moving fast, but Brad knew he could overtake it at any time. The problem was that the only thing he could accomplish by overtaking the suspect vehicle was to do a pit maneuver. Brad had been trained in the pit maneuver, which was a process of tapping the rear bumper of the vehicle under pursuit with the front bumper of the cruiser from either the right or left side. The contact would cause the vehicle being struck to career out of control and eventually have to stop. However, this was an extremely dangerous thing to do on a busy highway because there was always the potential for the vehicle being struck to run into other cars and force them off the road.

As the chase flew past downtown, Brad knew he would have to do something soon. As dangerous as the pit maneuver was, it was also dangerous to continue a pursuit at one hundred miles per hour. A clearing in traffic presented Brad with the opportunity he was looking for. There were no vehicles in sight other than Brad's high powered Crown Vic and the T-Bird, so Brad pressed the accelerator hard and easily caught up. The suspect vehicle was all over the road trying desperately to keep Brad from overtaking him. Brad refused to back down. As the T-Bird telegraphed a move to the right, Brad countered with an exaggerated move to the left, which caused the suspect to overcorrect and move right into his trap. As Brad swung to the right, he tapped the accelerator and struck the rear bumper of the T-Bird with pin point precision.

The T-Bird swung around in an out-of-control three hundred sixty degree turn sliding into the left shoulder before correcting itself and heading back east. The maneuver did not have the intended results, and the T-Bird began to pick up speed again as they approached the Carroll Street exit. Brad's heart sank as the T-Bird began to exit where he knew a pregnant woman and a St. Luke's officer prepared for emergency childbirth.

*

Ellum was mad. He was angrier than he had ever been in his life. There must have been a double cross – mystery man had set him up. There was no other way to explain what had happened. He had slipped out of the parking lot in Arlington with no problem and made his way onto the highway. He had driven that car for months since purchasing it, and never attracted the attention of the police. There was no reason for police to take notice of him now except that someone had betrayed him. Everything had been going just fine until he had passed that trooper near Oak Cliff. Now he found himself running for his life. Ellum had no intention of going back to prison. Someone was going to die before this chase was over, and it was not going to be him.

He had no idea what that trooper had done to cause him to go into a tail spin but Ellum wasn't taking any chances on letting it happen again. The T-Bird was designed to look sporty, but in truth, it was no match for the powerful Crown Vic on his tail. Ellum corrected his spin after nearly rolling the T-Bird and punched the accelerator as soon as the car set right on the highway. There had to be an exit soon, and he was going to take this chase onto his turf. He would take advantage of the city streets where he knew he could lose the trooper. If he could make it to Carroll, he would fake an exit and continue on toward Garland where there were several good spots to ditch the T-Bird and regroup himself. Ellum knew he would have to take a chance and barrel through the intersection at Carroll without stopping. It was Saturday. Traffic shouldn't be too heavy in that part of town. Carroll Avenue at I-30 was a rundown part of town and the trooper would no doubt think Ellum was making his way toward some home or business in that area.

The T-Bird eased toward the Carroll exit with the Trooper still on his tail and gaining. *"There should be enough time to pull it off,* thought Ellum. He gripped the steering wheel of the T-Bird and picked up speed as he eased to the right and off the highway. The ramp dipped at a slight grade and he could see the intersection at Carroll clearly in both directions. There was no traffic at all. Anticipating the possibility of a foot chase, Ellum removed his seat belt before he gunned the engine and ran through the intersection, making his way toward the entrance ramp. The entrance ramp went up a slight grade before dipping downward toward another downward grade. Ellum could see flashing lights but assumed it must be a work crew fixing a patch of the ramp shoulder. As he cleared the first grade, to his horror, Ellum realized he couldn't have been more wrong about what lay on the other side.

At the last second, he pulled hard to the left. The front wheels of the T-Bird hit the curb and Ellum felt the car's front end leave the road as it soared straight up and rolled once in mid air. On the first rotation, the unbuckled Ellum was ejected from the T-Bird and pitched like a shot put in the Olympic games toward the grassy knoll just beside the hard paved highway. The T-Bird burst into a million pieces as it made contact with the bridge abutment, narrowly missing the parked minivan by inches.

*

Brad Winther silenced the siren before stepping out of his cruiser. He ran toward the suspect who lay motionless on the now burning grass. Another dozen Dallas police officers screeched to a halt along side Brad's cruiser. All the officers ran toward Ellum like a swarm of locust just as he began to stir. Mitch took the newborn baby girl in his shaking arms, wrapped her in a small blanket, and placed her in the trembling arms of her mother, just seconds after the T-Bird exploded into a bridge thirty feet from the minivan. With three broken ribs and a broken collar bone, a screaming, cussing, Derrick Havelock found himself in handcuffs, dragged toward the make shift birthing room. Ellum paused briefly as he approached Mitch and Tosha looking hatefully at the newborn baby. Brad's radio repeatedly barked out an unanswered question, "1 Adam 1033, your status?" Ellum winced in pain and sneered at mother and child. He spat out cynically, "One Adam, so who's that, Eve?"

Brad shoved Ellum forward and he howled in pain. Tosha Ann Gelical held her baby girl close and smiled. "Eve." She said, "Why not? Eve Ann Gelical. I like the sound of that." The medic unit and several news crews arrived as Ellum was seated in the rear of Brad Winther's cruiser. A team of paramedics gently lifted Tosha from the rear of her minivan and onto a stretcher. Another St. Luke's squad arrived with two officers, one of whom agreed to drive Mitch's cruiser back to the station. Mitch hopped in back of the ambulance with Tosha and sat by her side as the medics checked her and the baby. Soon they were under way back to St. Luke where Eve would meet the rest of her new family. Tosha held Mitch's hand tightly on the way back to the hospital, and Mitch remembered Michael's words when he asked for a sign from God, *"He will show you, Daddy. Eve will show you."* With his free arm, Mitch held Eve closely to his chest whispering to her between gentle sobs of joy.

Chapter 32

St. Luke's

Dallas
Late evening March 20, 2005

The mood at Brother Philo's home had taken several turns during the day. For the most part, everyone needed to sort out their feelings and determine what all the changes would mean for them. Piece by piece, memories began to flood Nick's conscious and parts of his being he had paid little attention to began to stir. During the time he was Rocky Jo-Bob, he rarely thought about marriage, intimacy, or family. There were times when his interactions with Melissa, Robbie, and others half his age had made him feel fatherly, but he had dismissed those feelings as a natural considering his age relative to his friends.

Now, Nick felt completely aware of what it meant to love Alethea and to be concerned about her almost as though he had never taken that fateful trip in the trunk of Sam Dawson's Cadillac so many years before. Unfortunately, this awareness brought a sense of guilt that he missed seeing her grow up. Instantly, awareness of his love for

Morgan brought more confusion than comfort. The gap left in their love by years of absence left despair that seemed insurmountable. Nick wanted desperately to embrace her, but felt sharply estranged, and uncomfortable with tactile contact.

*

Alethea knew she would never have a better birthday than this one. She had never told her mother or anyone else, but over the past four years she had continued to pray that God would bring back her father. Her mother and Pastor Jenkins had told her over and again during the first year after Nick disappeared to let go of him and find peace in the knowledge that he was with God, but Alethea could not let go. She sat out under the stars on endless summer nights praying that someday she and her father would sit there together and make new memories. She never gave up on her father coming home, even when year after year he didn't show up. What doctors called depression and an inability to let go was, for Alethea, manifest faith. At that moment, Alethea knew things were as good as they could be. She would never be happier than she was right then with Mom and Dad standing on either side of her, crying, laughing, rediscovering their love for one another.

*

Melissa tried her best to stay out of everyone's way. She knew the family gathering was far more important than her new found concerns about loosing Rocky Jo-Bob for good. But as happy as she was for him, it hurt all the same. She wished Robbie or Karen were there. They would know how to comfort her and share her pain. Melissa slipped into the kitchen where Maggie was also trying to stay out of the way. Maggie and Melissa had not been formally introduced. Before Melissa could introduce herself Maggie decided to take the lead.

"Hi, it looks like us blondes are kind of the odd balls around here. My name's Maggie, and who might you be?"

Melissa flashed one of her famous enchanting smiles while grasping Maggie's outstretched hand in both of hers. The handshakes and feelings were warm and sincere.

"I'm Melissa McCree, I brought my friend Rocky here, and now he's Nick Bernard." Melissa shrugged her shoulders and looked down at her feet. "Go figure. Crazy world, huh?"

"That it is, but God is good."

Melissa looked up and smiled again, though a tear escaped her pastel blue eyes and ran the length of her delicate face. She used her hand as a handkerchief, smudging her rouge a bit, then she let out a nervous laugh. Maggie grabbed a napkin from the kitchen table and began to dab at Melissa's face.

"You look like someone worth getting to know, Melissa. Don't worry about your face, I gotta feeling nothing can keep you from looking beautiful. It's both inside and outside you, girl. You are stuck with it."

Melissa began to lighten up a little in the awkward way she did when someone paid her a compliment.

"I think I would enjoy getting to know you too, Maggie. Do you know the Bernards?"

"Kind of. Let's just say we go back a long way, but didn't really connect until recently."

A small television mounted in an upper corner of the kitchen was turned to the newscast. Both women turned toward the television as the reporter stood outside at the Carroll street ramp to I-30. Brother Philo walked in as the newscast began.

A picture of Mitch was placed in the upper right hand corner of the screen across from Brad Winther's photograph on the left side of the screen. The camera panned around and showed Tosha's minivan up close. A female journalist gave a detailed account of the murder that had occurred earlier in the day, and the high-speed pursuit which resulted in Derrick Havelock's arrest. She also explained how Tosha Gelical gave birth on the side of the highway as the suspect vehicle crashed just a few yards from the birth site. A small picture of Ellum appeared in the lower center of the screen.

Maggie ran into the living room after seeing Ellum's picture. "Lt. Sanders, I think you better come in here and see this."

Everyone in the living room rushed into the small kitchen to see the rest of the newscast. When the reporter repeated Tosha's name as the woman who gave birth at the scene, Stacy placed a hand over her mouth and eased into one of the chairs surrounding the kitchen table.

"Stacy, isn't that…" Morgan didn't have to finish her question.

"Yeah, that's Tosha. I gotta get to the hospital right away."

"That's the man who came into the bank. That's Sam Dawson," said Maggie, speaking directly to Mel.

Alethea looked at Maggie as though she had lost her mind. "That ain't Mr. Dawson. I don't know who that is, but it ain't Mr. Dawson. At least not the one from Minnesota."

"You're right about that, Alethea," said Mel. "That is Mr. Derrick Havelock, the man who tried to kill your dad, and the one who did kill Daisy Dawson."

The house was in complete pandemonium as everyone piled into cars and left for St. Luke's hospital. On the way to the hospital Maggie and Melissa struck up a conversation. Melissa sat in the back of Mel's rented car with Michael. Maggie sat in the front seat next to Mel.

"Maggie, what's your little boy's name?"

"Oh, I'm sorry. I didn't introduce you to my son. This little guy is Michael." Maggie turned around and spoke over her shoulder.

Melissa gave Michael a discerning look. "So, Michael, what are you smiling about?"

Michael let out a mischievous giggle and turned toward Maggie.

"Go see Eve. Go see Eve."

Melissa didn't understand what Michael was going on about, but decided to smile back at Michael all the same. She looked at Maggie.

"Who's Eve, Maggie?"

"Beats me. He just talks about her sometimes, I think it's an imaginary friend or something."

"He sure is cute, and he seems really smart too," said Melissa.

*

En route to the hospital, Mel grabbed the cell phone out of his pocket and dialed.

"Hey Roy, it's Mel Sanders, I know you're busy, but could I have a moment of your time?"

Roy Hubble sounded a bit irritated, but kept it under control.

"Sure, Mel, what can I do for you? I assume you've been listening to the news."

"Yeah, look, I might have an important witness for your case here, but before I hand her over to you, I need a favor."

"What'dya have in mind Mel?"

"I told you that the shooter had made a withdrawal from Compass bank, but as it turns out, I have the teller with me who handled the transaction. I know you would've found her anyway, but I can save you some steps if you can get me a few minutes with the shooter."

"It's not my case, Mel. I expect Arlington detectives here any minute, but I think we can arrange a few moments for Minneapolis' finest."

"Thanks, Roy. I'll be there in about an hour. I gotta stop by St. Luke's first."

As soon as Mel arrived at the hospital, he explained to Maggie that she would need to give a statement concerning Ellum's withdrawal from the bank. "It won't take long, Maggie. In a case like this, they're gonna want to get all their ducks in a row. That means paying attention to every detail and speaking to as many witnesses as they can. I have a feeling the guy who was killed in Arlington tonight helped with the murders back in Minneapolis. I think the killer was trying to tie up some loose ends and was set up by a third party. But I have no idea who the mysterious third party is, and I may never find out."

The caravan of vehicles pulled into the St. Luke's parking lot outside the maternity building at the same time.

Chapter 33

Eve Ann

Dallas
The night of March 20, 2005

As Mitch opened the doors to the ambulance, bright lights from news cameras flooded the inside compartment. Little Eve shut her tiny eyes tight. Mitch waved an impatient hand at the cameras while a middle-aged fire plug of a nurse wearing a multi-colored smock with cartoon characters on it, barked at the reporters before taking Eve from Mitch's arms.

"Ladies and gentlemen, if you get in the way of me taking care of this patient, I will have you removed. Now move your lights and cameras back so these folks can get the care they need. Don't worry; you'll get your story."

The nurse sounded like she had done this hundreds of times before. Another nurse assisted the medics with lifting Tosha down from the rig while Nathaniel and Joseph rushed toward their mother. Tosha continued to hold Mitch's hand as though she had some important unfinished business with him, but she addressed her sons first.

"I'm okay, boys. This isn't the first time I've had a baby, you know. I'm okay."

Nathaniel bent down and kissed his mother and gave a broad toothy smile. "We know, Mama. We're just glad to see you. Now where's my new little sister?"

The maternity nurse was still wrapping Eve in a blanket. "You'll get to spend some time with her as soon as I've had a chance to check her out. Okay? Now let's get these folks inside."

The assembled medical crew whisked Mitch and the rest of the family inside the hospital as reporters tried in vain to get a statement from anyone. Once inside the hospital, Tosha tugged on Mitch's sleeve. Mitch told the medic to stop rolling the stretcher for a moment as he bent down to hear what Tosha had to say.

"I heard your prayer, Mitch. You know what that means don't you?"

Mitch was all lit up inside and could barely contain his excitement. He bit his bottom lip to keep from laughing out loud. "Oh yeah, I know exactly what this means."

Joseph picked up on what happened immediately, but Nathaniel looked a little puzzled. Joseph smiled and slapped Mitch on the back. The medic continued pushing the gurney. "Welcome to the family, brother."

Mitch laughed with joy, and although he didn't know Nathaniel or Joseph well, he placed an arm around each of their necks and hugged them tightly. Tosha smiled as tears of joy rolled down her face. She longed for her husband and her new baby, so aptly named Eve Ann Gelical, Evangelical.

*

In a distant corridor of the hospital, Bart felt the wobbly wheel of his wheelchair rapidly wiggle and gyrate as a teenage girl from patient transportation rushed him across the shiny linoleum floor that had just been polished. Thousands of times, Bart had patrolled these very hallways with a watchful eye out for vagrants and thieves taking advantage of the public access. They often stole cell phones, purses, or whatever was left out in the open. Sometimes they would just curl up on an unattended sofa in an empty waiting room to sleep for the night. Over the years, he had become familiar with every nook and cranny of the aged hospital, and although the legitimate guests were transient, Bart had developed a sense of who did and who did not belong there. As Bart passed radiology, he recalled an incident five or ten years before when one desperate soul tried to make off with a portable x-ray machine not knowing what it was, but believing he could pawn it for a few dollars. The memory caused Bart to smile even though he was concerned about his wife.

Bart tried not to worry; he knew worrying would do him no good. He was glad to hear that Mitch had been with Tosha when the baby was born. He hadn't always liked Mitch, but he knew Mitch was a competent and trustworthy professional. Bart had always trusted Mitch with his life. And now, he trusted Mitch with the lives of his wife and new child. Something had been stirring in Mitch that had made him a better man, and the craziness of it all sometimes mystified Bart. Even the irony involved in Mitch being there to bring his daughter into the world, when Bart had sacrificed his own life for Mitch's son, was somehow curious to him. Bart couldn't help thinking at that moment, *"God does indeed move in mysterious ways."*

The police department had picked up the tab for Bart's hospitalization, reasoning that he was still acting within the scope of his duties when he was hit by the car, even though he was technically off-duty at the time. They had also agreed to find some other occupation for him within the St. Luke's system. Bart knew things would be alright, but he had to admit this was a challenging way to bring a new child into the world. So much had happened in such a short period of time. It seemed to Bart that his life was passing by at the speed of the tile patterns in the linoleum as he looked downward.

Chapter 34

Equally Yoked

St. Luke's Hospital
March 20, 2005

The delegation from Brother Philo's house walked from the parking lot to the maternity ward en masse. Alethea and Morgan stuck to Nick as though they fully expected him to take off for another four years if they let him out of their sight. Melissa seemed to have formed a bond with Michael, while Maggie and Mel were hitting it off like old friends. Alethea insisted on carrying Michael into the hospital. He spoke directly into her ear the entire way. Pastor Jenkins and Brother Philo carried on a conversation with Stacy and tried to keep her calm as she raced ahead of the group.

When they reached the glass doors leading into the maternity ward, an officer, who recognized Stacy as Mitch's girlfriend, parted the crowd of reporters and escorted the group inside. Once inside, Nathaniel and Joseph greeted them enthusiastically.

"I had no idea Mom and Dad had so many close friends," said Joseph.

Stacy began to make introductions.

"Nathaniel, Joseph, this is Lt. Mel Sanders from the Minneapolis Police Department, Pastor Terrell Jenkins from True Vine Community Church, and this is his friend…."

"Call me Brother Philo."

"Hello, I'm Maggie, Stacy's friend, and I think you know my little boy, Michael." She shook both the boy's hands, "and this is my new friend, Melissa."

Melissa extended her hand then turned toward Nick. "Do ya'll know my friend, Nick here?"

Joseph spoke up, "Oh yeah, this is Rocky Jo-Bob the Bible man."

Nick wasn't sure what to say, and decided to just nod his head, tipping a hat that was not there.

After all the introductions had been made, Nathaniel led the group into a small outer room which had a large picture window with open blinds into which they could see the private inner room where Bart, Tosha, Mitch, and Eve were waiting. Tosha lay on the bed holding Eve while Bart and Mitch were talking in excited tones gesturing merrily as they spoke. Stacy was the first of the group to walk in and her gaze immediately focused on Tosha and Eve. Realizing instantly that mother and child were fine, she looked to the side of the bed at the conversation taking place between Bart and Mitch.

Stacy remembered the first time she had seen the two men at the health club and how much they seemed to dislike one another. Mitch would often talk about how insufferable Bart was with his "goody two-shoes" attitude. After getting to know Bart in the hospital months later, it became clear he had little affection for Mitch either.

Initially, Stacy wondered if Bart would have been so quick to save Michael's life had he known it was Mitch's son he was losing his leg for. However, it wasn't long before Stacy realized Bart would have done the same for anyone. His general dislike for Mitch was nothing akin to loathing. He simply did not approve of Mitch and the way Mitch lived his life.

Just then, it occurred to Stacy that while she was concerned about Tosha and the baby, she had also been concerned about Mitch. Something strange had transpired between Mitch and Bart. They carried on as though they were best friends. Whatever they were talking about, Bart was really excited, and so was Mitch. Stacy figured they must be talking about the baby and the exciting police drama into which she was born. There was something definitely different about Mitch. Stacy could not put her finger on it. It certainly seemed that their last conversation marked the end of their relationship and there was nowhere for them to go as a couple. She didn't want the negative feelings between her and Mitch to detract from the Gelical's happiness, so Stacy decided to say hello to Tosha and Bart, and make a quick exit.

"Well hello, gorgeous. How're you feeling?" Stacy tried to sound positive as she greeted Tosha.

"I'm absolutely blessed. Come give me a hug, young lady."

Stacy bent down and wrapped her arms around Tosha, kissing her on the cheek before sitting at the side of the bed next to Bart's wheel chair. She turned toward Bart and kissed him on the cheek, then turned toward Mitch.

"Hello, Mitch. It sounds like you've had a harrowing day. Are you okay?"

She was not prepared for the intensity of Mitch's gaze. His normally cloudy hazel eyes were somehow sharply focused as though they saw through her. There was an evident joy in his expression she had never seen in him before. When Mitch turned and placed one hand on each of her shoulders, Stacy was swept away by the gentleness of his touch.

"I've never been better, Stacy. I have a lot to tell you."

Tosha looked up and pointed at the picture window in front of the room. A nurse squeezed in the door and began to speak.

"As you can see, there is no way I can let all those people in here at once. If you'd like, I can hold little Eve up to the glass so they can all see her. Then, I'll let in the ones that want to see you, two at a time."

"That should be fine, ma'am." Tosha was tickled to see so many people lined up outside her room waiting to see the new baby.

*

On the other side of the glass, Alethea took a turn holding up little Michael who clapped his hands and shrieked, "We came to see Eve, we came to see Eve!"

Alethea looked at Michael and remembered sitting in her back yard hearing that same voice in her head just weeks before when she and Benny Dawson talked about lines for the children's play at church. But how could she have heard little Michael's voice then? She had only met Michael a few days before.

"Michael, why do you call her Eve?"

Michael gave Alethea a look as though she was the only one who didn't understand who the child behind the glass was.

"Becaws dats her name. Eve."

Alethea looked at the chart hanging outside the room door. In red ink under the section marked, "Name of Infant," someone had written, "*Baby Girl Gelical, Eve Ann.*"

*

Stacy got up to leave.

"I think I'll let someone else come in and visit Tosha. I'm so glad you and the baby are okay. When I saw you on the news, I didn't know what to think."

She bent over and kissed Tosha on her forehead. Before Stacy got up, Tosha pulled Stacy close to her.

"Listen to what he has to tell you, Stacy. It's good news."

Stacy stood and began to walk toward the door just as Mitch stood up to leave. He and Bart shook hands, then Mitch bent down to Bart's wheelchair and gave him a manly hug. Stacy wondered what had gotten into Mitch. He was still wearing his uniform, yet he looked very different to Stacy. Once Stacy and Mitch were outside of the room, Morgan and Nick slid in.

"Hello, Morgan. I see you met my good friend Rocky Jo-Bob."

Morgan took Tosha's hands in her own, "I see you've met my husband Nick."

Tosha looked at Morgan quizzically, then turned to Nick.

"I thought you told me your name was Rocky Jo-Bob."

Morgan interrupted, "It's a very long story. Right now, we need to know how you're doing."

"I'm fine, but I think I want to hear that story."

Bart's curiosity was also piqued, "Yes, I would love to hear your story too."

Nick told his story to those gathered in the tiny room.

"So you just found out who you really are today? You even sound different." Bart had never heard such an incredible story.

Nick wasn't sure what to say, he was still sorting out everything that had happened in the past few hours. "Like I said, it's all pretty new to us too."

"Well, bless your heart, Nick. It's good to meet you again," said Tosha.

The four of them sat and talked while Nick held Eve in his arms. In a world that suddenly made no sense at all, Nick held on to Eve like somehow she would help turn the world right side up again. Morgan and Tosha didn't know each other well, but they made small talk about the baby and the amazing circumstances surrounding her birth. Morgan hung on every word as Tosha told of the convertible soaring through the air over her as she gave birth to Eve, and how it was Ellum who gave her the idea for the name.

*

Mitch took Stacy by the arm and led her down an empty corridor. They walked several feet before Mitch stopped and faced her. Stacy wondered what could be so important and so exciting. She decided to keep an open mind. Mitch placed a hand on each shoulder as he had inside the hospital room. He slid his hands down the length of her arms and grasped her hands, one in each of his. Mitch held her hands and looked into her big brown eyes with a tenderness Stacy had never known. There was a peace there that passed all understanding, and suddenly she knew, and the knowing began to light her up inside – filling her with an inner joy that spilled out – covering her – spreading into her being like a warm garment on a cold winter day.

"Stacy, I have wonderful news."

"I know, Mitch."

She laid her head into his chest and threw her arms around his neck, feeling released by God to love him as one loves themselves. She cried tears of joy – he cried too, and they both knew at once that God had brought them together.

In a timed, humble voice he asked, "Stacy will you…."

With firm confidence she answered, "In a heart beat."

Chapter 35

Finding Home

Oak Park Heights Minnesota
April, 2005

Denny Hagel leaned back far on his chair releasing a long sigh as he surveyed the books that lined his bookshelves. From the top of the bookshelf adjacent to the door, Denny's gaze fell upon the book that, to a large degree, brought him to faith. Someone had once told Denny that coming to faith required a person to reconcile themselves with the truth that they are not the righteous man or woman they might think they are. Denny had been a relativist most of his life. As such, for him, no objective truth existed; all truth was dependent upon one's point of view. Believing he had no need for a savior, Denny rejected Christianity. Then, a dear friend gave him a copy of C.S. Lewis', *The Screwtape Letters*. Reading the *Screwtape Letters* opened Denny's eyes to Satan's schemes to keep him blind. This realization cleared the way for the Holy Spirit to bring him to salvation.

Denny's road to salvation gave him a passion for evangelism, but more specifically it gave him a passion to reach adults that had already done extensive damage to their lives, as he had. This passion led Denny to a prison ministry, where he knew there were men hungry for a way to change their lives. Denny learned over the years that it took a profound realization of one's sin to bring them to Christ for salvation. With this in mind, he searched the bookshelves for just the right thing. He saw an opportunity to share the gospel, but he knew the person he would be sharing it with needed to be softened, loved, and affirmed. The shelves were organized into various categories. Denny found what he was looking for, not on the shelves but in a small drawer in his desk. As if they had fallen from heaven, Denny opened the draw and found two books he had only recently read himself. He wrapped them and sent them in over night mail to the Dallas County Jail.

After returning to his office, Denny sat back at his desk and reflected on the phone call he received earlier that day.

*

"Hello, is this Mr. Denny Hagel?"

"Yes, it is. How may I help you?"

"Hi, this is Deputy Conklin from the Dallas County Jail in Dallas, Texas. I have a prisoner here who has asked to contact you by telephone. We usually just let the prisoners make their own calls, but on the rare occasion when they wanna call another correctional facility, we screen em and make sure every things okay."

Denny was confused. He didn't know anyone in Dallas, let alone an inmate in a county jail.

"Who is this prisoner, Deputy? I don't think I know anyone down there."

The deputy's response was terse. "Derrick Havelock. You know em?"

Denny was a bit stunned. It had been years since he'd spoken with Ellum. He couldn't imagine what Ellum could possibly want with him now.

"Sure Deputy, I know the man. I'll talk to him if you want to put him on the line."

"Hang tight a moment."

There were several clicks on the line while the call was being transferred. Soon Denny heard the unmistakable voice of Derrick Havelock, distressed, but obviously still arrogant, and still Ellum.

"Hey, Denny, it's Ellum. Do you remember me?"

"Yeah, Ellum, I remember you. What's goin' on? What are you doin' in Texas, and back in lockup."

Denny had spoken with Gerry North and a few other prison officials over the past several weeks and knew that Ellum may have been involved in some criminal activity, but he had not paid much attention to exactly what Ellum was supposed to have done. Ellum began to respond.

"I'm being charged with several crimes, a few of the charges are from Minnesota. I guess the authorities are trying to decide who gets first dibs on me. Listen Denny, years ago you told me that this God of yours loves sinners and that no sin was beyond God's ability to forgive. Do you really believe that stuff?"

"I believe what the Bible teaches, and the Bible says the Lord is able to remove our sins as far away as the east is from the west. Yes, I believe God forgives all sins."

Ellum was silent for a long moment before speaking again. It seemed to Denny as though he was thinking deeply about something.

"I did some pretty bad stuff, Denny, I mean really bad. I also saw something that I think was pretty good, but when you traffic in evil your whole life, sometimes it's hard to know what's good. Do you know what I mean?"

"I think so, Ellum." Denny didn't want to go into what Ellum had done. He was willing to believe whatever it was, it was probably very bad. "Why don't you tell me what you saw that you thought was good?"

Ellum began to speak.

"I saw a newborn baby, Denny. I mean, I saw a baby that was only a few minutes old in the arms of her mother. I looked down at that little baby, and I hated it. I hated the fact that my life was surely about to end, but this baby has its whole life ahead of it. I think the baby was a little girl, I don't know why I think that, but I do. Maybe I just want to believe it's a girl. I mean, this kid just made me think of beginnings, kinda like Eve from your Bible. This kid has the chance to decide how she will live. But I've already made my choices and I know God couldn't possibly love me like he surely loves that little baby. Denny; if Texas has their way, they're gonna kill me, and I know I deserve it. So here's my question. If a man forgives me for what I have done to him, how can God forgive me if He is a God of justice?"

"Ellum, you may have to pay for your crimes with your physical life, but God will forgive your sins and give you life after death. Forgiveness is not the same as a pardon. Even if God forgives you, there are consequences for the crimes you have committed. If you are going to lose your life soon, you have all the more reason to live what is left of it for God and receive eternal life in heaven. Do you remember when I shared the story of the two men on the cross with Jesus? I told you all that because the one thief believed in Jesus and asked for forgiveness, he went to heaven with Jesus. Do you remember that story Ellum?"

Ellum didn't respond. Denny wondered if Ellum remembered the time he'd gathered about thirty inmates in the chapel for a Bible study and shared the story of Christ's passion. Ellum, who was usually disruptive and sometimes disrespectful during the sessions, listened with rapt fascination as Denny told the story. Denny had never quite understood why Ellum bothered to attend the Bible studies, but he remembered this particular one seemed to land on Ellum rather hard.

"Denny, do you still have all those books in your office?"

Denny was caught off guard by Ellum's question. "Yes, Ellum, why do you ask?"

"Do you think you could send me something to read that would help me understand what you're tryin' to tell me?"

"I'll put something in the mail today, put the deputy back on the line, and I'll get the address there."

"Thanks, Denny."

Ellum folded the letter from Nick Bernard and stuck it back inside his pocket as if it were a treasure map.

*

The battle of jurisdiction over Ellum became a complicated matter that took several months and a host of attorneys to settle.

Eight months after his arrest, an agreement was reached wherein Ellum would be sent to Minnesota for his violation of supervised release and then answer charges for the murder of Razor, Daisy, Roger "Digger" Jones, and the attempted murder of Nick Bernard. Ellum's attorney devised a brilliant plan and advised him to plead guilty to the three murder charges which would carry three maximum penalties of ninety-nine years each. This way he would not be able to answer to the murder charge hanging in Texas, which was a capital crime. Ellum was to be transferred to the Maximum Security Correctional Facility at Oak Park Heights. During the eight months before he was transferred, Ellum read *A Grace Awakening* by Charles R. Swindoll, and *Letters From a Skeptic* by Gregory A. Boyd, which Denny Hagel had mailed to him.

The first day back at Oak Park Heights, Denny Hagel sent for Ellum to meet him in the chapel office. Ellum walked into the office without his usual cocky swagger. He had the appearance and the gait of a broken man.

"I can never figure out how to greet a man who comes back here after being re-incarcerated. I mean, what should I say, 'It's good to have you back?' Or perhaps, 'nice seeing you again?' Somehow that just doesn't seem right."

"You're right, Denny, that ain't right." Derrick sat with a serious expression on his face as though he had some deep thoughts he needed to share.

"I was told that you wanted to see me, Derrick. What can I do for you?"

Derrick gathered his thoughts for a moment. "You been preachin' to me and the other guys from that Bible of yours for years. The last time I heard you talk, you said God was a God of forgiveness."

Derrick moved about uncomfortably in his seat, lifting each leg and straightening out each pant leg. "Well, I just copped a plea to three murders, and if I hadn't, Texas would probably be prosecuting me on a couple of capital murder charges. I've done some pretty nasty stuff Denny, stuff I can't even forgive myself for, and the worst part about it is that I'm not sure I even care about forgiveness. Are you gonna tell me that your God can forgive all that?"

Denny Hagle dropped his head and said a silent prayer. He knew the next few moments could have eternal consequences. He was not about to trust his own ability to speak articulately and accurately about the love of God. He needed the power of the Almighty God to speak through him, and he needed it badly.

"God please, let my words be your words. Let the utterances of my mouth come from your Holy Spirit working through me to speak Your divine Truth. Lord, I greatly fear this opportunity to lead a lost soul to your loving embrace. Give me boldness, give me strength, that not my will, but Your will be done.

Denny raised his head and began to speak. "Did you get the books I sent you Derrick?"

"Yeah, I got both of 'em. I read 'em cover to cover several times because at first I didn't get what they were saying. Then after reading them a few times, I started to understand, but I'm not sure I believe what they're saying. My grandma used to talk to me about God's love and God's grace, but after my Mom died, I didn't have much time for that stuff."

"What do you know about me? I mean, what do you know about the real me, Derrick?"

"I know you believe in the Bible, and that you are a Chaplain for the Department of Corrections."

Denny cupped his face with both hands. "The details of my life are not important at this point, but I need to tell you that my past is no more notorious than yours."

Derrick leaned closer.

Denny continued, "I didn't do the things you have done, but in the eyes of God, that is not the issue. Sin is anything, no matter how small it might seem, that is apart from the perfect and Divine nature of God. Adam was a sinless man until he disobeyed God. But since then, all humans have been born with a will, a desire to live outside the perfection of God, and perfection is the standard for satisfying God. You see, a man can sin as a liar, a drunk, an adulterer, a thief, which describes only a fraction of my sins." Denny looked directly at Derrick. "Or a man can sin as a murderer. But in the eyes of God, it's all the same, it's all sin. Your sins are not any worse to God because you killed several people. You are a filthy sinner and outside of a relationship with God because you have not trusted Christ as Lord and Savior. You see, Derrick, the difference between you and I in the eyes of God is not what you have done, it is who you are. Unable to atone for my own filthy sinful existence, I have believed in God's own Son, Jesus of Nazareth, who saved me from sin, and you have not. Does that make sense, Derrick?"

Derrick slowly nodded his head, "Yeah it does. But what about that little girl I killed? She barely even had a chance to live. What if she never trusted Christ? What about those two kids I killed back in Texas? What if they never knew Christ?"

Denny exhaled a breath of exasperation. He was not prepared for this question. "Derrick, each of us, including you, lives each day of our lives on earth never knowing when we will die. A car may hit us, we may have an aneurysm, a heart attack, or we could be murdered when we are only seventeen years old. Each day we say no to Christ, we take a chance that we will die and go straight to hell. When we trust in Christ we have assurance that when we die, we will meet Christ on the other side, and spend eternity with Him in Heaven. Either way, it is for eternity, and the choice is ours."

"Part of what I do is a cursory background on the victims of the men incarcerated here. I have no information about the two teens in Texas at all. Their families did not want to talk to me, but the girl, Daisy Dawson, came from a strong Christian family, and only Jesus knows the state of her heart when she died. The question is, where will you spend eternity, Derrick?"

Derrick began to break down in front of Denny. Denny had seen this many times in his years as prison Chaplain and it never ceased to amaze him. The Holy Spirit would get hold of a big tough felon who had never shown any signs of remorse, and then without notice, there would be a complete visible change right in front of his face. Derrick sobbed, then mumbled in a soft tone, "I just want to go home, Denny. I just want to go home."

Denny leaned forward and spoke directly into Derrick's face, "Derrick, you have three consecutive life sentences hanging at Oak Park Heights Prison. Unless I've misread something here, you are home."

Denny let the words sink in for a moment, "But there is still a choice. Jesus said that in His Father's house there are many dwelling places, and that He has prepared a place for us. Until you leave this world, your home is right here, and of that you have no choice. But you can choose right now where you will spend eternity, Derrick. Believe in Jesus and accept Him as Lord and Savior of your life.

Give your life to Jesus and be saved Derrick. Are you willing to do that?"

There was a pause that lasted no more than a few seconds, but to Denny it seemed like several hours. Derrick convulsed with tears, his entire body shook, and he cried out loud, heavy, deep-voiced sobs that echoed off the walls of Denny's office. He lifted his head, face wet from tears and said, "I just did Denny, I just did. He's here right now. I don't know how I know, but I know it."

The two men, caged in an iron trap, surrounded by the sounds of loud cursing, and talk of drugs, vice, and murder, sat locked in an embrace and cried out loud as brothers celebrating a long awaited homecoming.

"Do you hear that, Derrick?"

Derrick got quiet for a moment and listened intensely.

"I don't hear a thing, Denny. What're you talking about?"

"There's a party going on in heaven right now. Scripture says that whenever a single soul comes to Christ, the angels rejoice. Listen, Derrick, it's your party. Welcome home."

Chapter 36

Letting go, and letting God

Minneapolis
Late November 2005

B lasts of hot steam burst forth from large flared nostrils – the clipity clop of hooves beat out syncopated rhythms accompanied by the brilliant sound of jingling bells which dangled from the mane of a powerful draft horse. The handsome cab was cozy inside as a happy threesome ate warm chestnuts from a brown paper bag and sipped hot cider from a tin thermos. The fresh snow decorated barren trees with dazzling whitecaps atop branches – long icicles on the branch bottoms created a prism, reflecting the seasonal colors of red and green launched at the speed of light from quaint shops and upper rooms luminously decked out in ornamental bulbs, wreaths, and tall Christmas trees. This time of year, downtown Minneapolis was always a Norman Rockwell in waiting – longing to grace the canvas of genius strokes that would inspire nostalgia for waiting generations.

Wearing thick down parkas, fur lined boots, warm mittens, and hoods that covered all but the smiling faces inside; the Bernards took in the moment and watched as shoppers with rosy cheeks and runny noses ducked into warm retail stores to grab the perfect gift for a loved one. Others sat behind the wheel of frozen cars, waiting for a windshield to thaw out before driving to one of the suburban malls. Carolers walked en masse. Bell ringers shouted Merry Christmas. The mood was festive and life was good once again.

Nick Bernard spoke to his wife and daughter in a cold, cracked, voice. "It's hard to believe I forgot all this. All those years I could feel that something was missing, but I just couldn't remember the details. Now, I remember how good it feels to be home at this time of year."

"What did you think about at Christmas time when you were Rocky Jo-Bob, Dad?" Alethea had a confused look on her face, as though she couldn't believe he had forgotten either.

"Alethea, your daddy's been through some stuff we will never fully understand. That's why he still sees a counselor twice a week," said Morgan.

Nick managed a smile and swung an arm around his daughter.

"Its okay honey, she wants to know, and to tell you the truth, talking about it helps me put things in perspective myself."

"Okay, Nick." Morgan smiled at her husband and snuggled closer to him. "I just want to make sure you don't over do it. You know what the doctor said about that."

"I don't think this is gonna hurt anything." He turned toward his daughter. "Alethea, most of what I thought about were the things I had been told. It's like taking everyone else's memories and building your own out of whatever they have. I would listen to what Robbie,

Melissa, Karen, and other friends said about how Christmas was when they grew up, then I would create memories for myself that had a little of everything each of them had told me about theirs. Of course, some of it I would make up. I think that may be the little bit I got from my real past."

"You mean like having memories of snow in South Texas?" Alethea was glad to contribute to her father's explanation.

"Yes, exactly. See, Karen would talk about growing up in Houston and how they would go out in the back yard on Christmas Eve and look up into the sky for Santa Claus. Well, in my made up memory, I would go out in the yard on Christmas Eve, but we would all be wearing mittens and snow boots, and there would be snow on the trees."

Morgan suddenly felt sad for her husband. "It must have been so frustrating for you, Nick, when you told others about your thoughts."

Nick looked ahead without expression for a moment before turning to Morgan and Alethea with a warm smile.

"It wasn't so bad. God blessed me with some wonderful friends who loved me and understood what I was going through. They never judged me. They never made me feel foolish for giving my rendition of a Christmas memory. They just loved on me and tried to understand."

Now Morgan was curious. "What about in Personville? Were they understanding too?"

Nick shook his head and showed a toothy, sly, grin. "It's funny, but when Derrick Havelock did this to me he was only trying to find a way to dump me somewhere I would never be found, or where no one would connect him with my dead body. But God put me in the best place I could have been. The people in Personville took me in like I was their own. They never made me feel like I was a burden. Now whenever I think about the holidays, there will be memories of you two, and many rich memories of the town that adopted me. Someday, maybe next spring, we'll all visit Personville and you can both meet Jo-Bob and Willie, the sisters from the church, and Doc Evans. But I can tell you right now, when the good Lord put me in Personville, he placed me in good hands."

Morgan loved the sound of her husband's voice. It made her feel good to know that while he was away, presumed dead, he was loved by God's children. She snuggled close to him again. "Nick, do you miss any of them?"

"Yeah, there are times when I miss them all. Mostly I just get a feeling sometimes that God sent me on a short mission trip to Texas. While I was there, I was doing the work of the Lord. Now, he has called me back here. I praise Him that I have my wife, my daughter, and my old ministry to come home to. I guess I have nothing to complain about."

Alethea looked up at her father for a moment. He had lost most of the weight he had put on during the time he was Rocky Jo-Bob. Morgan had him back on a diet. He admitted he felt much better than he had felt in years. His once fleshy face looked almost gaunt, his shoulders were still muscular but had narrowed. Gone was the round belly he had become known for.

"Dad, do you ever miss Rocky?"

Nick smiled and hung his head for a moment before responding.

"Yes, I speck I do miss ole Rocky a bit," he said with a thick Texas drawl.

They all began to laugh at once. Then Morgan got quiet for a moment before speaking.

"Baby, have you forgiven him? Have you forgiven Ellum?

Nick didn't answer for a long time. His face seemed somehow distant, then cold and emotionless. Slowly a dark expression began to form on his face and he almost seemed malevolent. Alethea moved away from her father as though she didn't know for certain whom he was. Then as suddenly as the dark look appeared, the warmth of Nick Bernard and Rocky Jo-Bob combined into one joyful expression before he began to speak again.

"I have found that forgiving Derrick Ellum Havelock is something I have to do every day – sometimes several times a day. When I think about what he did to Daisy, that homeless preacher fellow, and all the others he hurt, I get angry and it's hard for me to understand why God allows such hatefulness in the world. Then I think about Jesus hanging on the cross, never having done a thing wrong in his life. Dying for sinners like me, while the ones He died for beat him, spit on Him, and nailed Him to a cross. I think about how he forgave us for all we do to break the heart of God. Then, I realize that forgiving Derrick for what he did to me is nothing. I sent him a letter telling him I forgive him and that I hope he gets right with the Lord. I pray that he does."

The downtown noises began to fade away leaving the clipity clop of the horse's footfalls and jingling bells to serenade a family brought back together in joy and heartache. They snuggled together as the handsome cab made its way along Hennepin Avenue. They didn't speak another word. The Bernards thought about how blessed they were to have one another again, how very blessed, indeed.

Epilogue

Oak Park Heights Prison

Spring 2010

errick Havelock sat in a large overstuffed leather chair in the chaplain's office. On the desk in front of him was a large stack of mail he had not yet responded to. He wanted to finish early then get back to his cell for some personal time with God, but he was distracted. Derrick's ministry, Clay Pigeons, had grown like wild fire over the past five years. With correspondence to inmates throughout the world, the ministry had outgrown his ability to manage by himself some time ago. Nowadays, Derrick had a small staff of inmates at Oak Park Heights that helped put together brochures and tracts. There were also hundreds of volunteers on the outside. Some of the volunteers were former inmates who came to Christ as a result of the ministry. Others had never been to prison but found themselves drawn to the ministry for their own reasons.

In the five years since arriving back at Oak Park Heights, so much had happened. With a great deal of direction from Denny Hagel, Derrick created Clay Pigeons as an outreach to inmates at Oak Park

Heights. Derrick learned how to write interesting Bible tracts that he passed out to other inmates. When the demand for tracts began to overwhelm Derrick, Denny convinced the warden to give Derrick access to one of the prison's large printers. Recently, Derrick had begun to write letters to schools warning parents how to look out for predatory inmates who meant to do their children harm. Between the tracts, the school outreach, and helping to arrange weekly convocations held at prisons around the country, Derrick was the busiest inmate at Oak Park Heights.

Clay Pigeons was a huge success and was gaining attention from local and national media. What Derrick found most exciting was that God had used his entrepreneurial skills to reach inmates throughout the world that were looking for a way out of their dead-end existence. Many times Derrick found himself in awe that God could use someone like himself to accomplish so much for His glory. On the office wall hung a framed picture of Denny and Derrick taken the day after Derrick gave his life to Christ five years ago. Written in gold letters below the picture was the Clay Pigeons mantra. *We are Clay Pigeons, shaped by the Master Potter, soaring the heavenly heights to spread God's good news of redemption!*

Derrick took a piece of paper and a pen from the desk drawer in front of him and began to write.

Dear Grandma B, it seems like forever since I've actually said, "Grandma." For so long, I didn't want to say or think about anything that reminded me of you or Mom. But lately, I'm drawn to memories of both of you, taking me to the neighborhood park, and buying me an ice cream. You taught me right from wrong, and I chose wrong. I think often now of Mama's soft kisses and warm hugs. I can still remember her perfume like she's right here in the room with me. It's so sad to think of how I pushed away everything good in my life, just to keep from feeling anything at all. It's horrible what a man can do when he no longer feels.

Today, I was thinking about a passage Denny Hagel used to share with me before he went to be with the Lord. In John 14:2 Jesus said, "In my Father's house there are many dwelling places." After the past five years I have begun to realize there are gonna be a lot of surprises when we finally get to heaven. I used to joke with Denny that when I move into my heavenly house the property values in the neighborhood will probably go down. I guess when you think about it, our job here is to just spread the good news so that everyone has a chance to get there. And that's what I plan to do with the rest of my life, spread the good news.

It's really kind of funny but when you think about it, there's gonna be a whole lot of us misfits up there in heaven. I imagine there'll be robbers, rapists, arsonists, even murders. If I understand this thing right, it's also gonna be kinda strange to see who goes to the other place too. Right there in hell there'll be church folks, philanthropists, healers, even preachers. I was reading this book by an eighteenth century preacher named Jonathan Edwards. He said we are all souls mercifully held in the hand of God, suspended over a fiery pit. Edwards said that if it weren't for the grace of God, we'd all fall into an eternity of endless torment, breathing the sulfuric fumes of hell day and night. I hate the fact that I've sent so many people there myself. That's something I'll have to live with until I meet Jesus. It's the cross I bear. I guess the only thing that stands between me and the stuff Edwards talks about is the grace of God.

Listen Grandma, I'll write to you again as soon as I can but right now there's something I need to tell you. A reporter from the New York Times came to see me today. He got interested in Clay Pigeons and decided to do a story on our ministry here. He asked me a bunch of questions about how I grew up, and what changed me from the man I was to the man I am. I tried to tell him that I had a praying Grandma and a loving God, but I don't think he ever got it. I guess he's already talked to Eve Ann's parents, Nick Bernard, the Dawson's, and all the other folks I told you about in my first letter. He said he was flying back out to Dallas to talk to you next so I thought I should let you know he was coming. I hope this letter reaches you before he does, but he seems like a nice enough fellow, so if you feel like it, give him some of your time. Anyway, I love you, and thanks for always praying for me. I don't know how you kept it up, but thanks, Grandma.

With all my Love,
Derrick

Look for the next book in this series of Christian Fiction by D.W. Belton called, *Tamar's Redemption.*

A serial killer is loose in a section of Dallas known as Deep Ellum. The killer has eluded top detectives from State and local law enforcement agencies for months. Now the community is demanding answers and an arrest. As things heat up a young police recruit from Dallas PD is brought on the case because of her in-depth knowledge of the killer's patterns. An alliance is forged between lead investigators and a man doing time in a Minnesota prison. Only the providence of God could create this story's resolve of redemption for a forgotten lady of the evening in a tale of justice, grace, and salvation.

Breinigsville, PA USA
15 September 2009
224101BV00002B/1/P